No River Too Wide

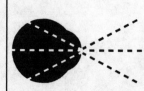

No River Too Wide

Emilie Richards

WHEELER PUBLISHING

A part of Gale, Cengage Learning

GALE
CENGAGE Learning®

Farmington Hills, Mich • San Francisco • New York • Waterville, Maine
Meriden, Conn • Mason, Ohio • Chicago

GALE
CENGAGE Learning®

LIBRARY OF CONGRESS CATALOGING-IN-PUBLICATION DATA

Richards, Emilie, 1948–
    No river too wide / by Emilie Richards. — Large print edition.
        pages ; cm. — (Goddesses anonymous) (Wheeler publishing large print
    hardcover)
    ISBN 978-1-4104-7463-6 (hardcover) — ISBN 1-4104-7463-1 (hardcover)
    1. Abused wives—Fiction. 2. Mothers and daughters—Fiction. 3. Large
type books. 4. Domestic fiction. I. Title.
PS3568.I31526N6 2014
813'.54—dc23   2014031981

Published in 2014 by arrangement with Harlequin Books S. A.

Printed in the United States of America
1 2 3 4 5 6 7 18 17 16 15 14

Dear Reader,

How does the author of a series, like God-desses Anonymous, choose which characters to feature next? If you read *One Mountain Away* or *Somewhere Between Luck and Trust*, then you know half a dozen women are introduced who loosely band together to reach out to other women in turmoil. So how did I decide which ones in this ever-widening circle to feature in *No River Too Wide*?

Have you ever been in a conversation with a friend who tells you the gripping tale of another woman's life, then stops before the end? On the edge of your seat you ask her to continue, and she tells you sadly that she can't, because she doesn't know the ending. You're riddled with frustration, right? Because you need to know!

If you've had that experience, then you understand why I couldn't introduce Har-mony's mother, Janine, in passing — as I did in *One Mountain Away* — and not learn more about her. We know Janine's trapped in a nightmarish marriage. We know that despite this, she did everything she could to give Harmony the start she needed to grow up and finally move far away.

But that smidgen of a story wasn't enough. Domestic abuse is a difficult subject, but sadly it's all too real. Over a million women are assaulted by their partners every year, and yes, 85% of domestic violence victims *are* women. The statistics are grim and worth your exploration, but this book isn't about statistics. *No River Too Wide* is a story of triumph, of a woman moving beyond her terrifying circumstances and regaining control of her life.

Women can, especially if they have help.

As I thought about Janine and Harmony, about bad marriages and good ones, I found I needed to explore the way we women choose the men in our lives, and how we learn to make good choices and avoid bad ones.

My story was born.

The River Arts District of Asheville, North Carolina, where Taylor's fictional health and wellness studio, Evolution, sits above the French Broad River, is real. The week I was in Asheville for research, the river overflowed its banks and seeped into far too many artists' studios. Despite that rare occurrence, the District is definitely worth a visit. The studios are fascinating, and the personable artists are willing to stop and chat about their work. I hope you'll find the time to visit someday.

Good reading,
Emilie

To women everywhere who work
tirelessly and creatively
to help other women who need them

CHAPTER 1

In an Oscar-worthy performance, Harmony Stoddard put all the enthusiasm she could muster into her voice. "I just *know* you're going to love spending time with your grandma, Lottie."

In reality she wasn't sure that her nine-month-old daughter, happily exercising her chubby little legs in her bouncy chair, was going to love the upcoming visit one bit, but she continued the charade.

"And your daddy will be there. You remember Davis, right? You've seen him twice. He even held you once."

Of course, not with any enthusiasm, but Harmony's job was to ready Lottie to be carried off by strangers and to make her baby girl think this was going to be a terrific afternoon. By her own critical standards, she was doing an admirable job, even if she was developing a roaring headache from the effort.

She wasn't surprised at the good face she was able to put on upcoming events. After all, she had been raised by a mother able to turn a day rimmed with fear and foreboding into an adventure. So many afternoons she and Janine had baked cakes and cookies, or set the dinner table with their best china and carefully folded napkins, pretending they were a normal mother and daughter brightening their happy little home.

In reality, of course, their preparations had only been a pantomime. Pretending all was normal had helped them get through the hours until Rex Stoddard walked through the door to lavishly compliment them or — more memorably — knock Janine to the floor.

Sadly, Janine Stoddard wasn't the grandmother on her way to see Lottie. That grandmother, Grace Austin, was Davis's mother. Lottie's father had only recently gotten around to telling his family about his nine-month-old blessed event. Harmony didn't know if her ex-boyfriend had been too embarrassed, or if the baby's arrival had simply slipped his mind.

Whatever the reason, Davis's father had no interest in meeting Lottie, but his mother was curious and expected Davis to produce her new granddaughter. So producing

Lottie was the activity of the day.

"Let's make sure we have everything you need," Harmony continued in her own mother's chirpy counterfeit voice. "Diapers, just in case one of them is willing to change you. Your sippy cup. Spring water. Snacks you can feed yourself."

She paused a moment, wondering how that would work. Would Davis and Grace let messy little Lottie experiment with the lightly steamed vegetables Harmony had prepared, the little squares of whole wheat toast? Or would they lose patience and feed her French fries or crumbled-up hamburger from whatever restaurant they took her to?

The mystery was about to be solved. The bell at the bottom of the stairs pealed, and Velvet, Harmony's golden retriever, who had been sleeping on the sofa, gave one sleepy bark before closing her eyes to finish her nap.

Harmony took a deep breath. For better or worse, Lottie was Davis's daughter. Harmony had no right to dictate everything he did with her. After all, he did send regular support checks. Of course, if he didn't, he would have to explain his reasons to his stodgy employer when the state of North Carolina garnished his paycheck.

"Okay, off we go." She lifted the baby into

her arms and settled her into the car seat to carry her downstairs. Harmony had insisted that Davis check the manuals for his car and the car seat to be sure he could use it safely. Luckily his Acura was new enough that she didn't really have to worry, which was a good thing, since she doubted he had bothered with his homework.

The doorbell rang again, longer this time, followed by a third blast. She smoothed the wisps of pale brown hair off Lottie's forehead, then hoisted the car seat and the diaper bag and carried both to the door, nudged it open with her hip and peered down at him.

"It takes a minute to get her into the seat, so next time you can ring once, Davis. If you'd like to take the diaper bag, that would help."

Davis, good-looking in a brooding sort of way, deepened his perpetual frown, but he came up the steps, stopped just below her and held out a hand. She swung the diaper bag in his direction, and he caught it. She followed him down, taking her time so she could grasp the rail. The stairway up to her garage apartment was wide and as safe as any outside stairway could be, but she always took her time, even when she wasn't carrying precious cargo.

The woman waiting at the bottom of the stairs was obviously Grace. She had the same vaguely dissatisfied expression as her son, the same dark hair, the same impatient, almost jerky, movements. Although she smiled politely, her eyes didn't change. She was examining Lottie, and not with grand-motherly affection.

"She seems small for nine months," Grace said. She didn't bother to smile at the baby, who was playing with a ring of plastic keys Harmony had given her. She continued her assessment. "Davis had more hair."

"I probably had less," Harmony said, struggling not to dislike Lottie's grand-mother on sight. "She *is* small, but well within the normal range."

"Davis was walking by the time he was that age."

"You must have had your hands full."

Grace gave a humorless laugh. "We had a nanny until he was five, so my hands were full with better things. His father and I both traveled frequently for business."

"I'm sure she took excellent care of him."

"Of course she did," Grace said with obvi-ous irritation. "We made sure of it."

Harmony thought one response was as pointless as another, so she gave none at all.

"We'll bring her back in a couple of

hours," Davis said quickly, as if even he had picked up on his mother's animosity. "Mother's flying out early this evening. This is just a brief visit."

Harmony managed a tight smile. "I'll be waiting, and I'll have my cell phone with me if you have any questions."

"Oh, I think we can manage," Grace said. "Davis's sister has two children, and we see them frequently. Of course, that situation is very different. They live in a two-parent family."

"There's no point in bringing that up." Davis sounded annoyed.

"Why not? It's the truth. Your father and I are happy to be seen with *them*. We can show *them* off to our friends."

The rest of the sentence was unspoken but clear. *Not like this one.*

"Your son proposed, and I declined," Harmony said, "so don't blame him. I hope you won't punish Lottie. Times have changed, and there are plenty of unmarried parents raising children."

"I doubt you have any idea what I consider appropriate."

Enough was enough. Harmony lifted her chin. "I doubt that I want to."

"Let's go," Davis told his mother. "As usual you've thrown a damper over the afternoon. Let's see what we can salvage."

Grace just smiled, as if his words had been a compliment.

Harmony watched them head toward Davis's car, and for the first time she felt a twinge of sympathy for Lottie's father. She'd just gotten a peek into Davis's childhood, and while the scenery surrounding him had probably been lovely, the actors and script had been B-movie grade, at best.

As Harmony watched, Grace got into the passenger's seat, leaving her son to set the car seat on the ground, open the rear door and finally juggle it inside to begin the process of trying to fasten it in place.

Like her own mother, Harmony yearned for the best in bad situations, so she had foolishly hoped Grace would welcome Lottie and shower the baby with unconditional love. Instead, it was clear Grace and Davis would take Lottie to a restaurant closer to Asheville, do their familial duty and return her well ahead of schedule. Their visits — if Grace visited again — would always be short and stressful. Eventually Lottie would refuse to go with them.

Harmony had chosen a real winner when she'd moved in with Davis almost two years ago.

"Men . . ."

Not for the first time she wished her own mother could be here with her. Without a doubt Janine Stoddard would fold her baby granddaughter into her arms and smother her with all the love she had to give–and was so rarely allowed to.

But that, too, was a bad situation with no "best" to hope for. Right now, in a secluded house in Topeka, Kansas, her mother was probably preparing dinner for Harmony's father, hoping as she struggled for perfection that tonight Rex Stoddard would praise what she cooked and otherwise leave her in peace.

Sadly Harmony could only guess, because she hadn't talked to her mother in over a year. The last time she'd tried, Janine had told her never to call home again.

CHAPTER 2

From the audio journal of a
forty-five-year-old woman, taped for the
files of Moving On, an underground
highway for abused women.

I was a happy child. My father worked in a
factory, and my mother was a dressmaker
who sewed and made alterations in a corner
of the bedroom she shared with my father.
She was always home when I returned from
school. There were homemade cookies waiting and open arms for my friends.

Most of the money Mama made was
turned over to my father, who decided how
to spend it, but her wishes were always
taken into account. Daddy was a kind man,
generous in every way, who found joy in
providing for his family and keeping us safe
from harm. When our front door was closed
at night, love, not fear, was locked inside
with us.

Every Sunday we attended a church where God's mercy was preached from the pulpit. Every Monday I walked through a neighborhood of small, tidy houses to a school where I was expected to do my best. While neither of my parents had gone to college, they saved what money they could to guarantee I did. They wanted to give me the best.

Had they lived, my life would have been different, but in my third year of college, as they were on their way to visit me, a car traveling in the other direction crossed the interstate median directly in their path. The cars exploded on contact, ending a midday drinking binge for the driver and the lives of both my parents.

The accident left me without a compass. My sheltered background left me with little insight into people who were not decent and well-meaning. My parents left me with a yearning for what I had lost, but sadly they left me when I was too young to understand the difference between a marriage based on respect and one based on fear.

By the time nine months had passed, I had learned.

One month after their deaths, the Abuser came into my life.

Rex had done this before.

At two a.m., as she tossed underwear and socks into a canvas backpack, Janine Stoddard reminded herself this was not the first time her husband had stayed away all night without warning her ahead of time. Keeping her off guard was part of a strategy to keep her from leaving him. Sometimes, by piecing together hints in later conversations, she'd even concluded that Rex had stayed close to the house the whole time to see what she would do in his absence.

It wasn't enough that she obeyed every whim when he was at home. He wanted to be sure she followed his orders when he wasn't, too.

While their son, Buddy, was still alive, Rex had never needed to worry. At the first sign of his mother's defection, Buddy would have called his father. Of course, Rex's faith in Buddy had never been put to the test. Janine had loved her son too much to put that kind of pressure on him.

She couldn't think about Buddy. Not now.

It was possible Rex was observing her right this minute. He might be in his car in a vacationing neighbor's driveway, eyes trained on the road to see if Janine tried to slip away. He might even be camping in the woods behind their house, with binoculars and night-vision goggles. Rex considered himself something of a survivalist, and while he was too much of a loner to drill on weekends or join a militia, he collected survival gear the way some men collected fishing lures or model airplanes. He kept all his equipment under lock and key in the same room where he kept an arsenal that included an AK-47 and an assortment of Rugers and Remingtons.

He liked to tell her exactly what each gun could do. Sometimes he gave his lectures with the gun pointed directly at her.

For a moment she was frozen in place, one hand raised toward the dresser, as she thought about those guns. Was she insane? Did she really believe that after all these years she might be able to pull this off? That Rex had really been fooled by her eager attempts to please him, by her waning interest in anything that wasn't centered on his needs, by her reluctance to go out in public without him?

For months now she had carefully waged a campaign to make her husband think his efforts to turn her into one of the walking dead had succeeded at last, that there was nothing left inside her except a desire to please him. The masquerade had given her hope and a reason to live. Having a plan, even a sliver of one, had slowly reinfused her with energy and purpose. As she had pretended to sink lower and lower, she had watched his reaction and gauged his state of mind.

Rex had believed her. She was almost certain. After all, not to believe would have been an admission that twenty-five years of his best efforts to subdue her hadn't borne fruit. He had set out to change his wife to suit his every need, and Rex Stoddard succeeded at everything he set his mind to. He was so superior to those around him that even the possibility he might fail never really entered his mind.

She had known that. She had used that.

But had she really convinced him? If she had, where was he tonight?

One more time, just one more, Janine forced herself to consider other possibilities. Rex wasn't a drinker. Had he been hurt, the police or the hospital would have called her. If his car had broken down on the way home from work, he would have driven home in a rental car, angry at the world and anxious to take his frustrations out on her.

She squeezed her eyes shut and forced herself to picture the best scenario. Rex had probably gone off on an overnight business trip, as he was sometimes forced to. Truckers and trucking firms in the Midwest were the primary clients of Rex's insurance agency, and occasionally it was necessary to visit in person to settle claims or sell policies. He hadn't told Janine he was leaving, because he wanted her to think he was still in town, eyes trained on her from some hidden location.

Janine reminded herself that she had carefully practiced her escape. Her husband's most powerful weapon was fear. Most likely he would saunter in for dinner in about sixteen hours as if nothing had happened. With luck Rex was sure by now that there was no longer a reason to watch her. As long as she *thought* she was being watched, she would never leave.

No, even though her escape plan hadn't been fully activated, even though she still had weeks before every tiny detail was put in place, now was the time to go. She had been given a chance, something she had prayed for back in the days when she believed in prayer. If she let this moment slip by, there was no telling when she might be given another.

Fumbling in the dark with the assistance of a penlight, she continued packing. She didn't have time to bring much. For months she had made a mental inventory of essentials, knowing it was too dangerous to pack before it was time to go. Instead, she had rearranged her drawers so the important things would be easy to find quickly.

Now she mentally reviewed the list as she stuffed items inside a canvas backpack Buddy had once used for scouting. Her watch. A nightgown that was the last gift her daughter, Harmony, had given her before leaving home. Two T-shirts, one pair of pants thin enough to roll. She finished with two letters her parents had written her when she was still in college. For years she had safely kept them in a county fair cookbook that Rex never opened, only daring to move them recently in preparation for this moment. Rex had "encouraged" her to forget her past. Had he found the letters, he would have destroyed them.

Once she was in the bathroom, packing toiletries was easy. She had moved the items she needed into one drawer in the vanity, and now she removed the drawer and dumped everything into her backpack. Then she knelt, reached through the opening where the drawer had been and peeled away an envelope of cash that had been taped to the wall along with a checkbook linked to a secret savings account.

The cash would help her get out of Kansas. The savings account would help her start a new life in New Hampshire, where she had never been and never wanted to go. New Hampshire, which had one of the lowest number of truck and tractor registrations in the nation.

New Hampshire, where she might be safe.

She rested the backpack against the wall and stepped into the closet to dress. The night air was cool, not cold, but she chose corduroy pants, a black turtleneck that she topped with a heavy black sweater and ankle boots. Nothing fit. As part of her plan, she had lost almost twenty pounds. Now when she looked in the mirror she saw a hollow-eyed woman with lank graying hair and cheekbones so sharp they looked as if they might do damage to the skin stretched over them. She looked beaten and defeated.

It was only steps from the truth and would be completely true if she didn't leave this house immediately.

She cinched the pants with a belt and pushed the sweater sleeves high. Her coat was downstairs, so for now she slung the backpack over one shoulder.

She was almost ready.

Without a backward glance at the knock-off Louis XV–style bedroom she had always despised, she went into the upstairs hallway and stood quietly to listen. Outside she

26

heard an owl in the woods at the border of their property. While technically the Stoddard house was in a suburb with the unlikely name of Pawnee Parkland, the neighborhood was rural, with houses set acres apart and separated by woods and fields. Rex had chosen the location because of its isolation. Contact with neighbors was limited here, and social events nonexistent. Any friendly overtures had been pleasantly rejected by Rex years ago, and after Buddy's death, sympathy had been rejected, too. The only communication she had these days was the occasional perfunctory wave as a neighbor's car sped toward town.

She descended the stairs as quietly as she could, but each footfall sounded like an explosion because there was no longer a runner to muffle her footsteps. Two weeks ago Rex had stripped the carpeting and refinished the pine stairs himself, ever the helpful family man who took great pride in his prison. She was sure he had removed the runner to better hear her as she came and went.

Downstairs in the front hallway she slipped into her coat and settled the backpack into place. The disposable cell phone that Moving On had given her was zipped into an inside pocket. She slipped it out and hit Redial.

"I'm on my way out," she said softly when a woman answered.

"The meeting place we discussed?"

Janine calculated how long it would take to cross the neighbor's field, take the back way behind his pond and over to a dirt road that ran about a mile west to meet her contact at a deserted barn she had discovered on one of her rare trips to the grocery store without Rex. After much uncertainty she had decided that sneaking away from the house alone, unseen by anybody, was the safest course. Her contact could have picked her up at the front door, but even if Rex wasn't watching, someone else might notice a car on the quiet road, someone getting up for a glass of water or a cigarette. Someone who could give Rex a description and a place to start his search.

"Give me forty-five minutes," Janine said, factoring in the cloudy skies, the absence of stars and the narrow beam of the penlight.

She slipped the phone back into her pocket and buttoned her coat.

She was ready.

Leaving by the front door was too obvious. Instead, she hurried through the expansive country kitchen, took the stairs to the basement and followed a narrow corridor into the storm cellar. The door opened onto what was little more than a hole. She found the steps up after carefully closing the door behind her.

Outside now, she slipped behind the row of trees that separated this section of their yard from a field and the woods beyond. The night was as thickly black as any she could remember. This was the most dangerous moment of her escape, the one she had been dreading. She had to be careful not to make noise or draw attention in any way. Even if Rex *was* nearby, he couldn't look everywhere, be everywhere. If she could get to their neighbor's property without being noticed, she had a fighting chance.

She had almost made her goal when she realized she had forgotten her son's scrapbook.

"Buddy." The sound was more of a sigh than a whisper. She had tried so hard to remember everything, but this golden opportunity to leave had presented itself too soon.

Tears filled her eyes. She had carefully, lovingly, assembled scrapbooks for both her children, old-fashioned scrapbooks crammed with photos and report cards and faded ribbons. Harmony had taken hers when she left Topeka for good after high school graduation, but Buddy's was still packed away in his bedroom. Janine had planned to retrieve the album and take it with her, the last link to the son who hadn't been able to find his way out of the morass of his childhood.

If she left the album behind, how long would it be before she could no longer remember his face or his sweet little-boy victories?

She had to go back. If she did, she could still make it to the meeting place in time.

Ignoring the sensible voice that told her to keep moving, she retraced her steps, fear expanding with every one. At the house she slipped back through the cellar, the basement and up the steps to the first floor. She was trembling by the time she reached the downstairs hallway.

She paused in the entryway, which was adorned with a dozen or more family photographs in gold leaf frames. Rex had arranged the little shrine himself. He had chosen an Oriental carpet made of the finest silk and placed it under a massive mahogany table that displayed the photos. Each photo had its own special place, and he always checked carefully after she dusted to be sure she hadn't rearranged them.

Harmony wasn't in any of the photos, of

course, since she had left home without Rex's permission, and Buddy was only in a few, because this was supposed to be the Rex and Janine Happy Show, visual proof that she had been under her husband's control for more than two decades. The photos were taunts meant to humiliate and shame, horrifying reminders of the years she had spent in the prison of this house with a man she despised.

Rex was at fault for everything. *Rex* was the reason she was sneaking back into her own house, trying to recover memories of the child he had destroyed, trying to save something, anything, meaningful from the twenty-five years of hell her husband had put her through.

She was not so beaten down that she couldn't feel anger. Now the attempted escape set it free. She grabbed the most hateful photograph of all, the one taken by the justice of the peace on the day of their wedding. There in the hallway of the Shawnee County Courthouse she was smiling up at Rex as if he had all the answers to life's mysteries.

"What a fool."

Before she realized what she was doing, she stripped away the cardboard at the back of the frame and pulled out the photo. She tore it into four pieces, then eight, and threw the pieces to the table. In moments she'd dispensed with another frame and mutilated another photo, then another.

Elation filled her as she shredded each photograph and each frame landed on the floor. But once she was finished, the pile of scraps didn't make the statement she wanted. She needed something more, something bigger, something for Rex to find when he returned.

Something that announced Janine was gone forever.

She strode across the room and grabbed his favorite ashtray and lighter; then she took both to the table and piled the fragments inside the ashtray.

The surge of joy she felt as she lit the first corner was like blood returning to an unused limb.

"So goes our life together, Rex." She watched the photos catch fire, and then she started up the stairs to Buddy's room.

The scrapbook was in a box in the closet. She had been the one to pack away all their son's things, since Rex had wanted nothing to do with that final parting. To her knowledge he had never come into Buddy's room since his death, so she was hopeful nothing had been disturbed.

She thought she remembered which box the book was in, but when she began to dig through it, she realized she was mistaken. Minutes passed and her elation vanished, replaced again by fear. She needed to leave now. This time for good. Forever and ever, world without end.

She was just about to give up when she saw the shiny blue cover at the bottom of the last box. She unearthed the scrapbook, but she knew better than to take the necessary time to make room for it in the backpack. On her way out she stripped a pillowcase off the bed and slipped the scrapbook inside so nothing would fall out. Clutching the pillowcase to her chest, she was ready.

In the hallway outside Buddy's bedroom she noted a strange smell, then a noise downstairs. She froze, but from here both the smell and the sound were unfamiliar, not the footsteps of a man returning home, but a crackling that seemed to be gaining steadily in volume.

She edged along the wall toward the stairs and paused, afraid of what she might see, but she had already recognized the smell. Her eyes began to burn, and smoke tickled her lungs.

Below her, flames were shooting from the

flammable silk carpet under the entry table. A wall of fire separated the two floors.

As she watched, the flames leaped to the stairs and began to lick their way toward her, feeding on the pine boards that had been recently stained and varnished.

She was trapped.

She had done this. For twenty-five years Rex had told her she was worth nothing without him, that her judgment was poor, her abilities second-rate, that every mistake her children had ever made could be lain directly at her feet.

And now, with this blatant act of defiance, she had proved him right.

For twenty-five years she had believed she was going to die in this house. Now she knew it was true. But not by her husband's hands. Not by Rex's.

By her own.

CHAPTER 3

Harmony knew how lucky she was. Life hadn't been easy, but at almost every turn good people had stepped forward to help her. Right now she was sitting in the home office of one of them, Marilla Reynolds, who had given her a job when Harmony was pregnant with Lottie. Marilla, known as Rilla to her friends, had hired Harmony to be the official Reynolds family "Jill-of-all-trades," and that was a good description for the way the job had played out.

Rilla, Brad and their two little boys, Cooper and Landon, lived outside Asheville in a lovely old farmhouse they had painstakingly restored and expanded. They had the usual farm animals, including horses and goats, and a kennel where they bred service dogs to be trained, most often to assist people with epilepsy. The organic vegetable garden and orchard totaled nearly an acre, and food was canned, frozen and dried for the winter. In fact, that was how Harmony had spent most of the past week since Davis's visit. Now that it was early September, harvest was well under way.

Before bringing Harmony on board, Rilla had managed most of the work on her own, until a car accident changed everything. These days she only needed to use a cane if she was on her feet more than an hour or two, but Rilla would never be able to work as many hours as she had before.

During Rilla's recovery Harmony had proved herself to be invaluable. She loved the Reynolds family, and she was pretty sure they loved her back. The variety of work never failed to delight her, and she was looking forward to a new project. She and Rilla were planning an herb garden for spring, a large one to produce organic herbs for some of Asheville's finer restaurants.

In preparation the new plot had been spread and tilled with compost and manure, followed by a planting of winter rye that would be mowed and plowed under to further enrich the ground in early spring. They had surveyed the market, and half a dozen chefs had given them wish lists.

Now, late in the afternoon, Harmony was finishing up an internet search to get wholesale prices for plants, so she and Rilla could gauge start-up costs. In a little while she had plans to go to dinner and a movie with her friend Taylor Martin and Taylor's daughter, Maddie. They were probably on their way to pick her up.

Lottie was napping in her Pack 'n Play in the corner, and Rilla was still down at the kennel with her sons. The internet connection in the farmhouse was better than the one in Harmony's garage apartment, and as Lottie slept on, Harmony completed her research. The house was unusually quiet, as if taking a quick nap itself before the hectic predinner rush.

Harmony knew what she had to do.

In the months since she had last spoken to her mother, she had fallen into something of a ritual. Every three or four weeks she checked the *Topeka Capital-Journal* online to see if there was any mention of her parents. She didn't expect to find them in descriptions of Topeka's most coveted social events or as participants in a 5K for charity. This was not casual surfing. She was fairly certain that if she discovered anything it would be in the obituaries or the headlines.

"Murdered Wife Wasn't Missed for Months."

With those expectations it was always difficult to make herself go to the website.

Harmony had considered closing the door to her past and locking it tight. But she still loved her mother, and despite Janine's plea that Harmony never call again, she believed that her mother still loved her, at least whatever part of Janine Stoddard's heart and soul were still alive and functioning. Trying to forget her was a betrayal, and Harmony's mother had already been betrayed much too often.

She wished Lottie would wake up to stop her, or the front door would slam and Rilla and her sons would entice her into the kitchen to chat while Rilla made dinner. But the house remained silent, and with a sigh she typed in the URL and once the right page was on the screen in front of her, she typed "Stoddard" into the search box and waited.

No matter how pessimistic or realistic she was about her mother's future, the headline that came up in response stole the breath from her lungs.

"House Fire Still Smoldering After Devastating Propane Tank Explosion."

For a moment she simply stared at the screen as the words she had read out loud blurred. Was this a mistake? Was the name "Stoddard" mentioned elsewhere on the page and that was why she had been led here? Surely that had to be the explanation. There were other stories in the sidebar, advertisements at the top and at the bottom a site menu.

But even while she tried to avoid reading the article, she knew.

Time passed until she realized she was only making things worse by waiting. She steeled herself and read the article out loud, as if pronouncing the words would somehow make sense of them.

"Topeka Fire Department crews were called to the site of a fire in Pawnee Parkland after an underground propane tank exploded on Saturday, about three a.m., rocking the rural neighborhood and triggering more than a dozen phone calls, said fire investigator Randy Blankenship.

"The first crew to arrive at the scene established a safety perimeter that prevented immediate investigation, and only after three hours was the department able to control the blaze. A long-standing drought coupled with the powerful explosion of the tank contributed to the difficulty. By nine a.m., the worst of the fire was extinguished, but by then the house had been destroyed.

"The cause of the blaze is under investigation, and there is no information about the fate of the owners, Rex and Janine Stoddard, who have lived at the address for more than two decades."

The house Harmony had grown up in. Gone? Just like that? And her parents?

She stared at the screen, and only then did she notice that the article was a week old. A week had passed, a week in which she had spread manure, rocked Lottie to sleep and canned two dozen quarts of apple butter.

A week in which her mother hadn't been alive in faraway Kansas.

Only then, as tears flooded her eyes, did she realize the article was linked to another more recent one.

She forced herself to click, but she couldn't look at the screen, not yet. Not when she felt sure she knew what it would say.

The front door slammed, and she heard the shrill voices of little boys heading through the front hall. She had only moments before she was interrupted. She forced her eyes open and stared, scanning the synopsis of information she already knew at the beginning of the article. Then she focused on silently reading the update.

Investigators are still trying to determine if anyone died in the blaze. Cadaver dogs have been brought in and continue to search, but

the home's residents, Rex and Janine Stod-
dard, remain unaccounted for at this time.

"You doing okay, Harmony?" a voice asked from the doorway. "Taylor's not here yet?"

Harmony wiped her eyes with the back of her hand before she turned in the desk chair. "Rilla, I think my mother's dead."

If someday Hollywood scouted the Asheville countryside for the perfect farm wife, Rilla Reynolds, clothed today in overalls, would easily be chosen. She was stocky but not overweight, easy to look at without being either plain or pretty. Her face was rectangular, her nose snubbed, and her brown eyes searched for answers even when she was engaging in small talk.

This wasn't small talk.

"Did you get a phone call?" she asked, coming to stand beside Harmony and placing her hand on her younger friend's shoulder for comfort. Then, before Harmony could answer, she shook her head. "Of course not. Nobody in Topeka knows you're here."

"I found this on the internet." Harmony got up, as much to put distance between herself and the computer screen as to give Rilla a chance to read it.

Rilla took the chair, slowly bending her

41

knees until she was finally sitting. From some distant point in her mind, Harmony realized that Rilla had already been on her feet too long today and would pay the price when she tried to sleep tonight.

Rilla silently read the article. Then she swiveled to face Harmony. "That's the house you grew up in?"

Harmony nodded, thankful that Rilla hadn't called it a home.

"They haven't found a body yet. You saw that part?"

Harmony nodded again.

Rilla never danced around anything. "I guess it's possible the fire was so extreme they never will, but it's also possible nobody was home."

"My parents don't go anywhere except a cabin up north where my father can fish, and my mother can wait on him. They always do that during the first week in June, not September. If my father has to be away for work, it's usually only for a night, and he never takes my mother. She's always in that house unless she's making a quick trip to the grocery store."

"You haven't been home in how long?"

Harmony shrugged, because doing math right now was impossible. "I'm twenty-

three. I left right after high school graduation."

"That's years, Harmony. And you don't
talk to your parents. Maybe things have
changed."

"Sure, maybe my father found Jesus."
Harmony paused. "Or a different Jesus than
the one he claimed he found years ago. You
know, the Jesus who insisted that he beat
my mother into submission if she planted
petunias when he preferred marigolds."

"People can change."

Harmony considered that, but not for
long. "He likes himself too much to think
there might be a reason to."

"No family they might be visiting?"

"My mother has no family, and my father
only has distant cousins. They stay far away
from him, which shows there might be good
sensible people on the Stoddard side and
my genes aren't complete poison." She
heard the bitterness in her voice, but she
didn't care. She would deal with her father's
death if she had to, but right now her only
concern was for her mother.

Rilla was assessing the situation, looking
past Harmony's shoulder as her mind
whirled. Harmony could see it in her eyes.
Rilla was compassionate and empathetic,

but right now Rilla-the-problem-solver was in play.

"I think we ought to call Brad at the office and get him to make inquiries. You don't want to give yourself away, and Brad will know how to go about doing it so the call isn't traced back to you."

Harmony wasn't sure what to say. Brad Reynolds was a lawyer, and a good one. She needed answers. She just didn't feel ready for them.

"It will take him some time," Rilla said, reading her expression. "You'll have time to prepare."

"He could have killed her. Finally. He could have set the fire and locked her inside to die, or killed her first and set the fire to cover what he'd done."

Rilla grimaced. "Don't jump to conclusions. It's not going to help if you make up scenarios."

Harmony knew Rilla was right. And could her father do something that horrible? Abuse was one thing, but murder? Yet wasn't that the path abusive men took? Especially if they believed their wife or lover was trying to leave them?

Marilla got up a little faster than she'd sat down, and she stepped forward to put her arms around Harmony, although she was the shorter of the two. "Let me call Brad, okay? Not knowing is going to be worse than knowing. If nothing else, the truth will pare down the fantasies."

But Harmony was already thinking of another. "She could have killed him, Rilla, to protect herself. Finally and forever. Maybe she set the fire and escaped. Or died with him."

Marilla held her at arm's length. "You can see this isn't helpful?"

Harmony realized she had tears running down her cheeks. She reached around Rilla for a tissue from a box on the desk and blew her nose.

"Brad?" Marilla asked.

Harmony nodded. "You'll ask him to be careful? Not to give me away?"

"I'll remind him, but he thinks like a lawyer, remember? That's the first thing he'll figure out."

One of Rilla's sons — they sounded so much alike it was never easy to tell who was calling — began to shout from the family room at the back of the house. Harmony registered something about the television and promises, but her mind was whirling in other directions.

"I'll get the boys settled. Then I'll call Brad. He's got trial tomorrow, so I know he's still at the office. Why don't I get you some iced tea while I'm at it?"

Harmony shook her head. Her stomach was roiling. "Taylor and Maddie are probably on their way."

"Taylor will understand if you don't want to go out tonight. Try her cell phone."

"She won't answer if she's driving."

"Good for her. Why don't I make enough dinner for all of us, then? The boys adore Maddie. She won't be bored."

"You're exhausted. I can see it."

"Then come help me."

Harmony knew what Rilla was doing. There were better distractions at the farm than dinner out and a movie would provide. "What do I tell Taylor?"

Rilla looked surprised. "The truth."

"But it's not her problem."

"This is when people rally around you. She'll consider it her problem, too. We're here for support."

Harmony hadn't experienced much of that as a child. No Stoddard talked about anything that went on at home for fear of retaliation from the master of the house. "Support" was a word best used in conjunction with a mattress or a bra and never for friends. How could anybody support her if they didn't know she needed it?

Of course, things had changed since she left home. Taylor's own mother, Charlotte, had been responsible for the difference. She had supported Harmony, a complete stranger, when she most needed it, and before her death she had gathered a group of women around her who continued to support each other.

Sometimes, though, Harmony forgot everything she had learned from Charlotte. The lessons of her childhood were powerful.

"I'll talk to Taylor if you like," Rilla said. "But right now I have to talk to Cooper."

"You don't mind calling Brad?"

"I never mind calling Brad. He never minds helping."

Cooper screeched again and Rilla left, closing the door behind her to give Harmony some privacy.

Before Harmony could get back to the computer, Lottie began to stir, jiggling the soft sides of the Pack 'n Play until it was clear that in moments she would sit up and start making demands.

Harmony hurried over to scoop her up and hold her close. She breathed in the sweet fragrance of her daughter's hair until she realized Lottie was beginning to fuss. While these days she got a healthy portion of her calories from other sources, Lottie still liked the closeness of breast-feeding as she woke up, and Harmony liked providing it.

She took the baby to a chair across the room and settled her, tossing a shawl over her shoulder to wrap around the baby for a little privacy.

What would her mother have thought of Lottie? Would she have seen traces of Harmony as a little girl? Lottie's hair was going to be dark, like her father's, but her face was shaped like her mother's, and everybody said the resemblance between them was unmistakable.

Would Janine have seen that? Would it have pleased her? Although she had her father's paler coloring, Harmony resembled her mother. Dark-haired Lottie might well look like her grandmother had as a baby. There were no photos, of course, and now Harmony would never be able to ask her.

For years, more than anything, she had wanted to help her mother escape. Janine could have come to Asheville with her and started a new life. But she had been too frightened. Harmony knew that at least part of her mother's refusal had been a desire to protect her beloved daughter. Had Janine disappeared, Rex Stoddard would have turned the world on end searching for his wife. Janine belonged to him, and he would have done anything to find her. Janine had not wanted to lead him in Harmony's direction.

But what else had played a part? Harmony really didn't know. Was her mother afraid to be on her own? Had she lost the ability to make decisions for herself because she had been allowed to make so few? Had she begun to believe Rex's degrading lectures about her incompetence, her lack of skills and talents, her inability to take care of herself? How could those things not play into Janine's reluctance to abandon everything she knew, even as terrible as her life had become? Could a woman suffer brainwashing all those years and not carry the scars?

Getting away had been hard enough for Harmony, but through the years her hours at school had helped her develop strength and inner resources, fueled at least partly by the contempt she felt for her father. Her mother had encouraged her, too, building up her confidence whenever she could, making it clear that the problems at home had nothing to do with Harmony. At the first opportunity Janine had helped her daughter escape, despite knowing she would pay a heavy price when her husband found out.

Harmony had been so lucky to have Janine to help her, but who had stood up for Janine?

Nobody.

"I wanted to save her," she told Lottie, brushing her daughter's silky hair over one ear. "I wanted us to be a family, a real family. . . ." Tears filled her eyes again. She was sure there were more in her future, floods of tears.

"You would have loved her," she whispered.

Someone knocked on the door, and before she could answer, it opened. Rilla stood on the threshold, a strange expression on her face. "Harmony . . ."

"You couldn't have found out anything yet." Harmony hoped it was true. She wasn't ready.

"I haven't even called Brad. No, it's something else." She paused, as if she was trying to figure out how best to say what was on her mind.

"Just tell me." Lottie pushed away and struggled to sit up, and Harmony adjusted her blouse and bra. Then she looked up, as ready as she was going to be.

"There's a woman at the door. She says she's here to talk to you about your mother.

She wanted to know if she had the right house."

Harmony could hear a buzzing in her ears. She closed her eyes and took several deep breaths before she opened them again. "Who is she, did she say?"

"Do you have an aunt?"

The question seemed so strange that for a moment Harmony thought she'd heard wrong. "Aunt?"

"Does your mother have a sister?"

"No. Like I said, she has — had — no family."

"She's in the living room waiting."

"She didn't give you her name?"

"She refused. She doesn't seem . . . comfortable? I think you ought to get out there right now."

Harmony stood, moving Lottie to her hip. She was probably wet, possibly worse, after her nap, but changing her was the last thing on Harmony's mind.

Rilla strode over and took the baby. "I'll change her. You go. I'll bring her to you when I'm finished."

"Who do you think the woman is, Rilla? I can tell you have an idea. Is she a cop? Somebody from a newspaper who traced me here?"

Rilla shook her head, but Harmony

wouldn't let it go. She raised her voice. "Who?"

"I don't want you to be disappointed if I'm wrong." Rilla paused; then she turned her eyes to the baby for a moment, only looking up when Harmony refused to move.

"I'm not sure she's planning to stay, so you need to get out there quickly." Concern and something else shone in her eyes. "Harmony, I think she might be your mother."

CHAPTER 4

From the audio journal of a
forty-five-year-old woman, taped for the
files of Moving On, an underground
highway for abused women.

My parents shielded me from life's darker
side, and whatever their reasoning, they
never encouraged me to be independent. I
was their only child, and their role as
parents meant everything to them. Looking
back on my life, I see how ripened I was by
grief to replace their love and guidance with
more of the same. I was also primed to trust
strong men who seemed to know what was
best for me.

Had the Abuser been anything but kind
and charming before we married, I think I
would have been smart enough to back
away. When we met I still believed I was
worthy of a good man, a man like my father
who would treasure and protect me. This

man was knowledgeable and able to help me settle my parents' estate, and he seemed to be all the things I wanted. Best of all, he stepped forward to help make the decisions that faced me. He helped me sell the house I had grown up in, helped me drop out of school without penalty so I had an opportunity to heal.

Now, of course, I know this was the beginning of a campaign to strip me of all my connections. My family was gone. Then my home. Finally my college friends. The investments he recommended were long-term, and while sound enough, yielded nothing for my immediate use. By then, of course, that hardly mattered. The Abuser adored me. He wanted me to be his wife. He would support me whenever I decided to finish my degree in early childhood education. We would have the kind of marriage I had witnessed up close.

We would be happy.

Janine hurried down the farmhouse path toward the road. She hoped leaving the house without waiting to see Harmony wouldn't scare her. She had promised to tell Bea whatever occurred here, but she hadn't factored in a lack of cell coverage inside the house. The disposable phone

Moving On had given her wasn't state-of-the-art, and she had nearly used up the minutes that had come with it.

The sun was going down behind mountains, something she wasn't used to after a lifetime in Kansas. When she was a young teen, her parents had taken her on a camping trip to Colorado, and they had spent two blessed weeks cooking out, hiking and swimming in crystal-clear lakes. She had thought of that trip so many times over the years, sinking back into the memories when her reality was particularly bleak, lulling herself to sleep at night with dreams of a happier time.

The Blue Ridge Mountains were nothing like the Rockies. She wasn't sure why her daughter had stayed in Asheville when the family who had invited Harmony to live with them had moved to California. Perhaps Harmony hadn't been able to afford another move, or perhaps she had made so many connections she'd felt secure on her own. But Janine guessed that the natural beauty had affected her decision. The majesty of it, a more approachable majesty than the Rockies, would have appealed to a young woman from the plains almost as much as settling somewhere far from Topeka, a city that would be blighted forever by her childhood memories.

The air under a canopy of hardwoods was turning chilly, and Janine shivered inside somebody else's jacket. Her body temperature dropped too easily now, probably as a result of the weight she had lost. Losing so much had been easy. She had always been thin, but in the past year her appetite had simply vanished. Her secret would never be marketed in diet books. During meals with Rex she had silently replayed her decision to find a way out of the prison he'd created. Fear of what lay ahead, as well as the consequences if he found her, had made it nearly impossible to eat.

Rex had noticed, of course, but he had seemed pleased. The shadow she had become was the wife he had wanted all along.

As she rounded a curve she wasn't surprised to find Bea lounging against a tree casually observing the driveway. Tall, wiry, threatening enough that her male colleagues called her Grandma Grouchy, Bea was older than Janine, but even in her sixties she exuded a raw power that Janine found a bit intimidating. Bea *was* a grandmother, but she was more likely to teach hunting and fishing to her grandsons than to play dress-up with her granddaughters.

"You okay?" she asked when Janine got

closer. "This the right house?"

Janine eased Buddy's backpack into a more comfortable position. "I haven't seen her yet, but Harmony's here."

"You okay, Jan?"

Janine gave a short nod. "The phone didn't work inside, and I didn't want you to worry."

"You want me to wait?"

"You go on and settle in for the night. If this doesn't go well . . ." Janine swallowed, because the rest of the sentence stuck in her throat.

"It's going to be fine."

"I'll find a way into town, and I'll call the hotline from there."

"Just call me direct. I'm going to stay nearby and wait while you have that re-union. Things don't go well tonight, you just give me a buzz, and I'll come back. I don't hear, though, we'll need to be on our way in the morning early. So you have to let me know where to pick you up then."

Janine realized she was crying. Bea didn't seem surprised, and her voice softened a little.

"It's always like this, honey. I've seen it too many times before. You been through too much. You been scared practically every minute for years now. You'll still be scared some, but at least that part will feel familiar. And it will ease."

Janine wiped her cheeks with her palms.

"We did a good job for you," Bea said, retrieving a tissue from a pocket and handing it over. "It's not likely he's gonna find you. And the house burning down, that was a stroke of good fortune."

"No, I shouldn't have burned those photos."

"Might have been divine intervention. You just being able to squeeze through the first flames without damage to anything but that old coat of yours. That tank going up like some kind of atom bomb." Bea smiled as Janine finished wiping her eyes. "And now nobody knows if you burned up or ran away or anything else. Including old Rex."

"They're looking through those ashes for no good reason. I know he wasn't in the house."

"Think of it as good practice for the fire department, forensical training."

"But where *is* Rex? Why hasn't he come forward?"

"This point in your life? You need to stop thinking about Rex, and start thinking about yourself and that girl of yours."

Janine couldn't imagine a life in which Rex was not the central figure. "I'll always

58

be looking behind me."

"We'll be keeping an eye out on your behalf, and we'll get in touch right away if we hear anything you need to know. I'm as sure as I can be that the trail we left won't lead him in your direction."

Janine didn't know what to do next, but as if she sensed that, Bea stepped forward and put her arms around her for a brief hug. "Now you get on back there and have that reunion. Call me if you need me tonight, but be ready to go at first light."

A whole night with Harmony. If Harmony would have her.

Janine shivered, and not from the cold this time.

Bea started back toward the road, and Janine knew she had to return to the house. She was sorry she had left, because walking up the driveway the first time had been hard enough.

"Hello? Are you still here?"

Janine whirled at the sound of her daughter's voice somewhere behind her. She started toward the sound, picking up speed as Harmony called again. "Hello!"

"I'm right here," Janine managed. "I'm coming."

She rounded the corner and saw her daughter's familiar figure half loping toward her, the tall, slender body, the long blond hair flying out behind her. She forgot she had ever been frightened that Harmony would reject her. She forgot she'd had serious qualms about coming to Asheville, because now Rex might find their daughter. She could only think that this was her beloved child, whom she had feared she would never see again. And somehow they had been given this moment.

"Mom!" Harmony paused a moment as if making sure she was right. Then her face lit up. "Mom! It really *is* you!"

They were in each other's arms in a moment. Janine was laughing, but she felt tears running down her cheeks, too. "Harmony. I thought . . . I thought —"

"I didn't think I would ever see you again." Harmony held her away but gripped Janine by the shoulders. "I thought you were dead!"

Janine had hoped Harmony wouldn't learn about the fire, but the fear that she *might* hear of it had brought her to Asheville. In the end she had realized she had to prove, in person, she was still alive.

"I'm okay. I —" There was so much. Where did she start? Janine realized she was floundering.

"But the house burned to the ground,"

Harmony said. "I just found the story on the internet. You weren't there when it exploded?"

"I was . . . I mean I wasn't. I was there when the fire started, but I got out."

"Was Dad there?"

Janine couldn't tell from Harmony's tone what she hoped the answer might be. "No, he was . . . I don't know where your father was. *Is.* I don't know a thing except that I used . . . Well, he didn't come home that night. I — I'd already made plans to leave him, but not quite this soon. Things weren't quite in —" She stopped.

"You'd made plans?"

"Is there somewhere we can talk? I can't stay more than the night, but there's so much —" Janine couldn't seem to finish a sentence. She was drinking in her daughter's lovely face.

"What do you mean, you're not staying?" Harmony tightened her grip on her mother. "Of course you're staying. Please don't tell me you're going back to Kansas."

"No. No! It's just —" Janine shivered.

"I'm sorry. You're cold. We can go up to the house." She shook her head. "No, we'll go to my apartment because it'll be quieter, but I have to get Lottie first."

"Lottie? Is she . . . ?" Janine's voice trailed

off. The question she'd been about to ask seemed inconceivable, but she knew so little about Harmony's life. She knew there must be a baby, but not whether the child was a boy or a girl.

"Lottie's my daughter," Harmony said, rescuing her. "Charlotte Louise, but she's Lottie Lou or mostly just Lottie."

"Who's taking care of her?"

"Rilla has her. Rilla's my employer. I live and work here as her assistant."

"It's so beautiful. The land. The house."

"You look tired, Mom. Let me take that." Harmony hooked a hand under the strap of the backpack and tested the weight. "It's heavy."

"Because I have Buddy's scrapbook inside, but it's, it's . . ." She didn't want to explain all the details of how she'd gotten away.

"Buddy's scrapbook?" Harmony seemed surprised.

"It's all I had left of him."

Harmony slipped the backpack down Janine's arm, and Janine gratefully relinquished it. With the loss of twenty pounds had come a significant loss of strength. And the last week had exhausted her.

"Lottie." Janine managed a smile. "It's beautiful. I bet *she's* beautiful."

Harmony slung the pack over one shoulder and began walking back the way she'd come. "How did you find me?"

What little energy Janine had was flagging dangerously. She touched her daughter's hair and catalogued the obvious changes. Harmony had a gold stud in her nose and several piercings in each ear. Her hair was longer. "I need to sit. Can we talk when we're settled?"

"I'm sorry. Of course. I'll show you where my place is, and you can wait there. It's no farther than the house. I'll get Lottie and join you." She hesitated. "You won't leave? You'll be there waiting?"

"I promise."

They had reached the farmyard, and Harmony pointed to a building that looked like a garage, tucked not far from the house. "My apartment's at the top, and the door is never locked. We'll be right there to join you. I'll make you hot tea."

"With lots of milk and sugar?" Janine tried to smile, because whenever she and Harmony had been given the gift of time alone together, that was one of the ways they had celebrated.

"All you want."

Janine started toward the apartment. Beyond it in a fenced pasture two horses grazed, one lifting a dark head to watch her.

In the distance she saw what looked like a garden, although she couldn't tell for sure because the sky had grown darker in the brief time she'd been here. The garage was painted the same dark spruce as the house, but the stairwell and the garage doors were painted a red so dark it was slowly turning black as twilight descended. Someone, maybe even her daughter, had planted a wide bed of black-eyed Susans and cone-flowers along the side of the stairs.

She was so grateful Harmony had landed in this healing place, but she knew so little, not what had brought Harmony here, or how she had coped until she had a job and a place to live. Until now she hadn't even known her grandchild's name.

Instead of going upstairs, she sat on the bottom step and listened to the music of crickets as the sky quickly darkened. From the house she thought she heard the voices of children. How old was Lottie? Certainly not old enough to be one of them. Did Harmony help care for the others, too? So many questions, and even if they stayed up talking all night, so little time for answers.

The front door opened, and Harmony came out carrying a child with a blanket thrown around her against the chill of the descending night. As she watched, Harmony turned and spoke to a woman who was now standing in the doorway. Then she started toward her apartment.

Janine stood and waited for them to join her. When Harmony got close enough she pulled back the blanket, and Janine glimpsed her granddaughter for the first time. She immediately saw the resemblance.

"She looks like my baby pictures," Janine said, reaching out to pull the blanket back a little more. "And she looks so much like you, although her hair's darker."

"Rilla warned me the woman waiting for me might be my mother. She said we looked so much alike. All of us. That's how she knew."

Janine didn't ask to hold Lottie, but Lottie held out her arms to her grandmother, and without a word Harmony boosted her closer so Janine could see her better.

"Oh, you are such a beautiful baby," Janine said, tears filling her eyes again. "And I guess after what I just said about her, that's bragging, right?"

"She wants you to hold her."

"May I?"

"Who better?"

Janine took the soft little bundle and placed her on one hip, tucking the blanket securely around her. "How old is she?"

"Nine months. Just."

"I've wondered every single day since you told me you were pregnant."

"I could have told you myself if I had been allowed to call."

Janine heard the note of disapproval, but she understood. "Right after you left, your father did everything but hire a detective to find you, Harmony. If you had called while he was there? He would have started searching all over again, beginning with the number you called from. That's how I found you. The people who helped me get away also helped me trace the last number you used, and eventually they traced you here."

"I was careful never to call when he was there."

"You couldn't know for certain. After you left he took to dropping in on me unannounced during the day, sometimes two or three times, to make sure I was doing what he told me to. I memorized that number, and I was able to delete it from our caller ID that last night we talked. But I might not always have been able to do that before he got to it."

"Why didn't you leave him right then? If things were getting worse? If it was possible for things to have *gotten* worse?"

Too much was at stake. Janine couldn't

hedge the truth. She saw the moon peeking over a stand of trees, between two mountaintops, and she watched it for a moment before she looked back at her daughter.

"Because if I had just walked out the door without a good plan, a foolproof plan, he would have killed me. He still might if he finds me, and that's why I can't stay longer than a night. Because if your father traces me here — and he still could, no matter how careful I've been — then he might hurt you and the baby, too."

CHAPTER 5

Her hands were trembling. Harmony looked down at the spoon grasped in her right hand and watched it wave gently side to side. If she had needed proof she was shaken to the bone by her mother's arrival, there it was. Of course, Janine's surprise appearance was especially dramatic, considering that just moments before Harmony had believed she was dead.

In the living room Lottie was laughing as she and Janine played peekaboo. The sound was silvery and unfettered. Harmony loved to make her daughter laugh. She was never sure which of them was the most delighted afterward.

Gripping the spoon tighter, she stirred the milk and sugar she'd managed to get into each mug; then, better safe than sorry, she decided to carry them one at a time.

Despite good intentions, she didn't move. Her mother was here, but only for the night.

And once she left? While she hadn't said so exactly, Janine had made it clear that once she moved on, she would have little or no contact with her daughter.

All because of the devil who had fathered her.

Harmony caught a glimpse of herself in the glass cabinet front, and for a moment she stared. Did she look anything like Rex Stoddard? She had never seen any outward resemblance, except her coloring. Buddy had looked more like him, a rounder face, one eye that drifted subtly despite two costly surgeries, a high forehead that, at least for Rex, had climbed slowly higher as he began to go bald.

Of course, her brother had died well before he had the chance to lose his hair.

She didn't want to think about Buddy.

Looks were one thing, but more frightening, did she have any of her father inside her? She had been angry enough at the way he treated his wife and children that she had, as a girl, lain awake at night fantasizing ways to rid the world of Rex Stoddard. They had been childish thoughts, and she had never acted on them, but was that the way her father's sickness had begun? Had he, too, lain awake at night plotting revenge and destruction?

Rex had never been able to forgive even the smallest slight. A gesture, an offhand remark, an opinion he didn't share. Rex held on to those things forever and waited. When he finally had the opportunity to get even, he took full advantage of it.

Harmony knew that most of the time she wasn't that way. She knew from living with her father just how damaging revenge was to the soul. She had witnessed demonstrations again and again, and each time she'd vowed never to be like him.

Sadly, though, in one way they *were* alike, because there was one person she would never be able to forgive and didn't even want to try. She was grateful beyond measure that her mother had not died in the explosion that had leveled her childhood house, but a part of her was sorry her father hadn't been locked inside and unable to escape.

Had he been, she and her mother could finally stop living in fear.

More laughter erupted from the living room, and she knew she had to stiffen her backbone and start a discussion about the future. She gripped the mug handle. Then she turned the corner of her tiny kitchenette and stood in the wide doorway as her mother whisked a blanket from her face and cried "Peekaboo!"

Janine was so thin. That was the first thing Harmony had noticed, followed by shock at how old she looked. She was only forty-five, but she looked at least ten years older, her skin sallow, her hair salted with gray and pulled back in an unflattering low ponytail. She walked like someone in pain, each foot placed carefully in front of the other, as if she wasn't sure the ground wouldn't rise to swallow it. Now she was smiling at her granddaughter, but even that smile seemed tentative, as if admitting she was happy might bring down disaster on all of them.

Janine looked up and saw her. "Need help?"

"No, you take this one. I'll get mine."

"Lottie's okay in the bouncer while we drink it?"

"She'll let us know if she's not." Harmony went back for the second cup, then joined her mother on the sofa. Before she sat back, she sprinkled Cheerios on the bouncer tray so Lottie could practice feeding herself.

"Just the way I like it," Janine said, joining her against the cushions and turning so she could eye her daughter. "You didn't forget."

"I haven't forgotten anything, Mom. I missed you so much."

"I thought about you every day, but I . . ."

71

Janine sipped a little tea before she finished. "The only thing I could be proud of was helping you get away."

"Please tell me what happened. You said you were planning to leave yourself, only not so soon?"

Janine sipped and didn't answer. Harmony hoped she was figuring out how to tell her story.

Finally she put the mug down on a side table. "I wanted to leave for years. Now it seems like forever, only that's not true. There was a time . . ."

"When you . . . loved him?" Harmony had trouble getting the words out.

"I did. Even despite, well, everything."

Harmony waited for her to go on, but Janine changed tack. "Then a time came when I knew if I stayed, he . . ." She shrugged.

"He would kill you." It wasn't a question.

Janine gave a short nod. "But it wasn't just that. I realized I was shrinking. Literally. Because I was always hunched over, trying to protect myself. In other ways, too. Nobody knew me anymore. After you left, for a while your father got more and more possessive and paranoid."

"I didn't know he could get more of either."

"It seemed to multiply every week. I couldn't go anywhere or do anything without him, not pick up a library book or a quart of milk. My set of car keys went missing one day, and I never saw them again. And even leaving the house *with* him was rare. Strangers looked right through me when I did, like I wasn't there."

Harmony's throat was raspy from unshed tears. "Nobody who ever really knew you would have looked through you."

"I'm afraid your father made sure nobody had that chance."

"You said you had to have a plan?"

"Women like me are most likely to die *after* they try to leave the men who abuse them."

"I know it's not perfect, but wouldn't the police have protected you?"

Janine gave one emphatic shake of her head.

Harmony didn't know why she'd asked. She'd seen too many stories herself about abused women who had been killed on the way to the courthouse to get restraining orders, or even inside the courthouse itself.

Janine said the rest in a rush, with more energy than she'd shown to this point. "One day I realized I could barely get out of bed in the mornings, that even being afraid of what he might do if the house wasn't clean enough or the dinner perfect enough didn't motivate me anymore. I knew I had to do something or else. The agency was having its New Year's open house, and it was one of the few things your father still expected me to attend. It would have looked bad for him if I didn't go. I met a woman there. She . . . she suspected. She told me to call her the first moment I could."

"And she helped?"

"She knew how." Janine didn't go on.

"She'd done this before?"

"It took a while . . . to trust her. You can understand. I was putting my life in her hands. We decided on steps to follow. I was supposed to obey your father's orders and act like whatever he told me was just meant to protect me from a cold, cruel world. To pretend I didn't want to go out, that I was afraid of my own shadow, that I needed his guidance. Little by little."

Harmony tried to remember how her mother had behaved when she was still living at home. Janine had made a point of not arguing with Rex, true, but sometimes she had found clever ways around his edicts. And despite everything she had still smiled, still laughed, still shown a certain joy in living that he hadn't been able to extinguish.

There had been moments, days, even

74

weeks, when their lives hadn't seemed that much different from those of other families. Janine had known how to diffuse her father's anger. Or make herself the brunt of it. But she had been actively involved in life. The spark inside her had never been extinguished.

"Did he go for it?" Harmony asked.

"It seemed to be working. He was still violent, erratic, but after a while he . . . well, *he* was different. I made mistakes and he didn't always notice. At first I thought he believed I'd changed, that I had finally become the wife he wanted, and he was cutting me some slack. Then I realized he just didn't seem to care that much. I wondered if he had figured out my acceptance of our life together was a lie, and he was just waiting for me to prove it."

"Do you still think he knew?"

"No, I don't." Janine bit her lip. "Because if he had figured out I was going to leave him . . ." She didn't have to finish.

"Then what? Frustrations at work, maybe? Something else going on?"

Janine turned both palms up, as if to say *Who knows?*

Harmony thought this replay of the past had gone as far as it could. What her father felt about anything, or what had gone on in his life outside the home, was of no interest to her. Rex Stoddard might think he was the center of the universe, but that wasn't a universe she wanted to inhabit again. She changed direction. "Before, when we were outside, you said he didn't come home the night of the fire. But you don't know where he was?"

"It had happened before, some kind of game he played for years, leaving town without notice. He had all kinds of ways of checking on me while he was gone. Sometimes he would line up repair men to conduct roof inspections or clean out our septic tank. Then they were required to report what they found by phone immediately. The first question Rex always asked was 'And my wife was there to show you around?' I heard their answers, so I knew."

"I never realized."

"Sometimes he was watching the house, testing me. Sometimes he was really out of town, but he didn't tell me ahead of time in case I used the opportunity to leave. This time I don't know what happened. But I knew I might not get a chance like it again. And even if I wasn't prepared completely?" She swallowed hard, audibly, as if the fear was still there waiting to choke her. "I was ready enough," she finished.

"What about the fire? Did you set it to make escaping easier?"

Janine looked shocked. "Oh, no."

"Then what happened?"

"It was stupid. Impulsive. As I was leaving, I burned all the photos on the downstairs table. I took them out of their frames, and I burned them. Whenever he finally came home, I wanted him to know how I really felt about our life together."

Harmony stared at her. "Wow, he loved those photos."

"You called that table the zoo, remember? You said we were like caged animals on display."

Harmony *did* remember. She had despised every attempt to portray them as the all-American family. The photos in the entry-way. The four of them sharing hymnals in the same pew every Sunday. Cheering together from the bleachers the year Buddy had been a linebacker on the high school football team.

Then going home together after the team lost and listening to her father criticize every play her brother had made.

"How did the fire start if you didn't start it on purpose?"

"I can only guess. I'd left earlier and was already at the edge of the woods when I remembered Buddy's scrapbook. I went back, and on the way to the stairs I saw those photos and . . . I just snapped. I burned them in your father's favorite ashtray."

Harmony remembered talking to friends at school whose parents smoked. She had been the only one who'd wished her father would smoke more and suffer the consequences.

"I went upstairs," Janine continued, "but it took me some time to find the scrapbook. When I came out of Buddy's room, the stairs were on fire. Your father took up the runner just a few weeks ago and refinished the steps by himself. The house still smelled like varnish. Maybe whatever he used?" She shrugged.

"But how did you get past the fire?"

"I was wearing my heavy coat because I knew I might need it later. I took it off and used it to beat back the flames so I could make it outside before the whole place went up. Then I didn't look back. I was gone, really gone, well before the tank exploded."

"Nobody saw the fire? Nobody reported it?"

"It was the middle of the night, and you know how far away the neighbors are. I don't think anyone realized the house was on fire until the explosion. Then probably everyone within twenty miles knew."

Lottie, tired of bouncing and ready for dinner, finally began to whimper. Harmony went into the kitchen to retrieve cereal and organic pears she had prepared that morning — which now seemed like years ago. By the time she returned, Janine had lifted the baby out of her chair and was walking the length of the small living room, murmuring softly.

"She likes you," Harmony said. "She's going to love having you here."

"I can't stay. I wouldn't have come at all, but I was afraid you might hear about the fire and be absolutely beside yourself."

"You could have called."

"No, I thought you needed to see me, to be sure it wasn't some sort of hoax."

"I think *you* needed to see *us.*"

Janine fell silent.

"Dad hasn't traced me here yet," Harmony said. "And I've been gone for years."

"Your dad never had as much motivation as he does now. Now he's going to be looking for both of us, and looking hard."

"That's part of why you didn't leave before, isn't it? Because you were afraid he would double his efforts to search for *me* as a way to find *you.*"

Janine didn't deny it. "He will. Which is why I have to leave in the morning." She seemed to hesitate; then, as she handed Lottie to Harmony, her voice grew softer.

"He'll think I've traveled west."

"West? Why?"

"That was part of the plan. Things were in place."

"You mean that's what you planned? To go west?"

"No, but he'll think that's what I did."

Harmony settled Lottie in her high chair and pulled a chair up beside her. She gave the baby a plastic spoon to play with as she fed her because she was in no mood to let Lottie fling food all over the living room.

The details of Janine's escape niggled at her, but compared to her mother's future, the past seemed unimportant.

"If he has good reason to think you've gone west, then you can stay here. Has he ever said anything to make you think he knows I'm in North Carolina?"

"It's no good, honey. I can't risk it. If he does find you, God forbid, I don't think he'll hurt you if I'm not with you. You're settled here. He knows you have friends who could come forward to protect you. If he shows up you can even tell him the truth, that I was here but I wouldn't tell you where

80

I was headed. I hope it doesn't come to that, but if it —"

"It's not going to come to that, because you're going to stay with me in Asheville. Or if you absolutely refuse, then I'm going with you. Wherever you go."

"You can't. The only good thing about you leaving home was that I didn't have to be afraid for both of us anymore. I can't live that way again, being afraid all the time that he'll show up one day and harm us both, and maybe the baby, too."

"Does he know about the baby?"

"He's never said anything."

Harmony thought that answer was as good as a no, because when her father was angry, everything came out. If he'd learned about Lottie, he would have flung the baby's birth at her mother and blamed her for not raising Harmony to be chaste.

"This is North Carolina. Rex Stoddard has no friends here, no link to the community. We'll talk to the sheriff and ask how we can best protect ourselves."

"We might as well call your dad and give him our address. We can't involve the authorities. They keep records. Records can be located." Janine came to stand beside her daughter. "That's what I mean, honey. Those kinds of slipups are too common when more than one person is involved."

Harmony fed Lottie another spoonful of cereal, then swiveled to face her mother. "Hasn't he run your life long enough? Are we going to spend the rest of our days letting Rex Stoddard make all our decisions? I'm kind of out of the habit, and frankly, I'm a lot happier. Even if I know he's still a threat, I'm willing to take my chances."

Janine's exhaustion was showing, her mouth drooping, her eyes puffy. "I would give almost anything to change things, but not your safety."

Harmony could feel her mother slipping away again, and she wasn't willing to let her. "Then you and Lottie and I will take new names, get new documents. Somebody will help with that. We'll move to a big city where everybody's anonymous. You can take care of her while I work."

"No, you aren't going to give this up." Janine lifted a hand to indicate everything around them. "I won't allow that. There are ways we can stay in touch. Then, after time passes, maybe if things have improved or changed significantly, we can see each other again. Find a place to meet and plan carefully."

"You're just going to disappear, aren't you? Like that." Harmony snapped her fingers. "And you think that will make things okay? That now I won't be worried every minute? That I won't lose sleep at night picturing you just a step ahead of him? Or dead by his hand and me not knowing?"

"Honey, I —"

"No! You didn't think this through. You're back in my life, and no matter what you do or where you go, you can't change what you've already done." She handed a piece of whole wheat toast to Lottie and stood. "I knew what you were facing before. Do you think I ever forgot for one moment what you were going through every day back in Topeka? But I thought it was your choice, that you just didn't have the strength to get out or maybe even the desire. Now I know you do."

"I can't stay here. You don't have enough room. I know you don't make enough money to support us both, and what hope do I have of finding a job way out here? You don't need me for child care. I think you've managed that just fine. I have no place here, and it's dangerous."

"We'll find a way." Harmony nodded as she spoke. "Just tell me you're willing to stop running. That we can stand together now, the way we used to. Tell me the mother I love, the one who raised me to be strong

83

despite everything going on around me, is still in there. The mother who accidentally set our house on fire and still managed to escape. The one who traced me here and came to make sure I knew she was okay."

"Honey —"

Harmony wouldn't let her finish. She rested her arms on her mother's shoulders. "Tell me *that* mother's going to stay here and start a whole new life. You can change your name and the color of your hair, but please don't let that mother escape again. Promise me you won't."

CHAPTER 6

Taylor Martin braked in the driveway of the Reynolds Farm and wished she could turn the car around and take Maddie home, where her daughter could pout and complain out of earshot. She was fairly certain that not having an audience wouldn't actually stop Maddie — there was always a girlfriend at the end of the phone line to sympathize — but better a prepubescent peer than Taylor herself.

Instead, because Harmony was waiting for them, she came to a stop and waited for the girl to fall silent. She reminded herself that for most of Maddie's existence, Taylor had only hoped for a normal life for her child, a life in which every move, every decision, wasn't factored through the reality of epileptic seizures.

Now, following surgery that had transformed Maddie's future, she had her wish. These days every move, every decision was instead factored through the normal reality of approaching adolescence. And at eleven, this was just the beginning.

"Are we finished?" she asked when the only remaining sound was the twilight serenade of crickets in the woods nearby and, from closer to the house, the grouchy bleating of a goat.

"*We* weren't talking. *I* was talking, and *you* weren't listening."

"You're wrong. I heard every word you said. I am not going to leave you at home alone in the evenings when your grandfather can't stay with you. You are only eleven, and now that we've moved, we don't know our neighbors well enough to ask them to intervene in an emergency. For now, you're going to have to buck up and go to meetings and classes with me."

"You don't trust me."

Taylor turned to face her daughter's profile. "Are you going to spoil our fun tonight? Harmony doesn't get many chances to get away without Lottie. I think she's looking forward to having dinner together and watching a movie. I hope she won't regret going with us."

Maddie said something that wasn't audible, which was probably a good thing. Then she muttered louder, "Can I have a hamburger? I eat them in Tennessee."

Taylor tried not to smile. She had raised her daughter to be a vegetarian. Harmony was a vegetarian. Of course eating meat in front of them would be Maddie's revenge.

"You can have anything you want. You know that. As long as you have vegetables with it."

"French fries are a vegetable."

"Healthy vegetables," Taylor amended. "I know you eat meat when you're at your father's house, but he tells me he's also big on salads and cooked veggies, and he limits fried foods to special treats."

"I liked it better when the two of you weren't speaking."

Actually Maddie hadn't liked that at all, since the discord between Jeremy Larsen and Taylor had been tough on everybody. But now that her parents were on better terms, it was easier for them to present a united front, along with Jeremy's wife, Willow, who was an excellent stepmother and followed their lead.

"You could probably stay here and help Rilla with Lottie and the boys," Taylor said. "I could pick you up again when I drop off Harmony tonight."

"It's kind of weird that you two are friends now."

"Why? We're both goddesses. We see each other a lot."

Taylor and Harmony were both trustees of a house in the mountains near Asheville that had been left to a small group of women by Charlotte Hale, Taylor's mother. Because Charlotte had particularly loved the story of Kuan Yin, a Buddhist goddess who had remained on earth anonymously after death to continue helping those who suffered, they had taken the name Goddesses Anonymous for their little group. Together they tried in whatever ways they could to follow the example of Kuan Yin and help other women who might need them.

Not that any of them really thought they lived up to Kuan Yin's standard.

"Well, *I* think it's weird because Harmony was friends with Grandma when you weren't even speaking to her. You're like . . . rivals."

Taylor wondered why this had never come up before. She wondered if Maddie and her close friend Edna, daughter of Samantha, another of the goddesses, had been discussing it.

"Life is complicated," Taylor said, and without looking she could imagine Maddie's eyes rolling. "Here's what you need to

88

learn from everything that happened with Mom and me. We loved each other, but we let our differences get in the way. I held a grudge for years, almost to the end of her life, and I was wrong to do that. Very wrong. Your grandmother wanted badly for us to be close again, and when she couldn't make that happen she kind of adopted Harmony, who needed her."

"And you don't feel jealous?"

Taylor did look at Maddie now and saw that she was actually engaged in the conversation, interested. Her brown hair fell around her earnest little face. "I don't. I feel humbled."

"What does that mean?"

"It means I wish I could do something for Harmony to pay her back for what she did for Mom, Maddie. Because she really helped your grandmother feel like she had a reason to live and a place in the world, something I didn't do until it was almost too late."

"But she died, anyway."

"Yeah, she did. But she died knowing she'd made a difference. And thanks to Harmony, who helped me see what a mistake I was making, your grandmother died knowing how much I loved her, despite everything. And she got to spend time with *you,* which meant everything to her."

"That *is* complicated."

"Tell me about it." Taylor started the car again and shifted into drive. "So no, I'm not jealous. Harmony was like a bridge where your grandmother and I could meet after too many years apart. She probably doesn't realize how much she did for us both."

"Why did Harmony need Grandma? Doesn't she have family?"

Taylor knew that was Harmony's story to tell and not hers. "She couldn't be with them. I think there are problems there."

"The kind you had with Grandma?"

"I don't know the whole story."

"And now that Grandma's gone, Harmony's all alone?" Maddie paused and thought that through. "No, I guess she has lots of people. All the goddesses, for sure."

"So let's go feed her and take her to a movie. What do you say?"

"That's pretty lame after all she did for us." Now Maddie sounded bored.

Taylor knew their moment of communication had ended. These days her daughter was as difficult to predict as the autumn weather, and often as stormy.

"It's a start," she said as she drove toward the house.

Taylor had expected to meet Harmony at

the Reynoldses' house, since that was where Lottie was supposed to spend the evening, but when they pulled into the farmyard she saw that all the lights were on in the garage apartment where Harmony lived.

"I guess she's at her own place," she said, and parked near the base of the stairs. "She's probably getting Lottie's things for Rilla."

Outside the car Taylor took a moment to stretch. She was physically active, too active sometimes, and late this afternoon before enticing Maddie into the car she had taught a ninety-minute hot yoga class in a 105-degree studio. While she had carefully hydrated before and after, she realized she was still thirsty. On top of a full morning of consulting with the contractors who were turning an old building in the River Arts District into Evolution, a brand-new health and wellness studio, she was dragging.

"I would like living in the country," Maddie said. "Daddy and Willow do. It's so peaceful there, and nobody bothers you."

Taylor lifted her hair off the back of her neck and wondered if she ought to cut it boy-short again if she was going to work this hard. "Nobody bothers us at home in Asheville, either."

"But you could leave me alone in the

country and not worry."

"Get over it, kiddo. I wouldn't leave you alone anywhere. Let's go get Harmony." Taylor started toward the steps, but the grumbling Maddie didn't follow. Velvet, Harmony's golden retriever and the mother of their own dog, Vanilla, came around the corner, and Maddie squatted to pet her.

"We'll be down in a few minutes," Taylor told her, and escaped.

Upstairs on the tiny porch she heard women's voices from inside the apartment. Assuming that Rilla was helping Harmony get Lottie ready, she waited, but when Harmony opened the door and Taylor saw an older woman who strongly resembled her friend, she wondered if she had been wrong about their plans for the night.

"Taylor . . ." Harmony looked surprised, too; then she shook her head. "It's later than I thought. I lost track of the time." She hesitated, then stepped aside and let Taylor in.

"If something came up we can go another evening." Taylor smiled at Harmony's visitor, who was holding Lottie. Then before she could stop herself she asked, "You look familiar. Have we met?"

"I'm Jan," the woman said, and returned

Taylor's smile with a strained one of her own.

Harmony was looking back and forth between the two women, as if she was trying to decide what to say. Finally she shrugged. "Mom, Taylor isn't going to tell anybody you were here. You don't have to worry."

Jan looked troubled, but she gave a short nod.

Harmony turned back to Taylor. "This is my mother, Janine Stoddard. She just arrived."

"Jan," the woman said. "I always preferred it."

"I never heard anybody call you Jan," Harmony said.

"Because your father preferred Janine."

Taylor was trying to remember everything she knew about Harmony's family life, but none of this was making sense. "Are you visiting?" she asked. "It's nice to meet you at last."

"I'm just here for the night," Jan said.

Taylor realized now that Harmony had been crying and still looked upset. "Look, this is obviously a bad time for me to be here."

But Harmony was already addressing her mother. "Mom, we can be honest about why you're here. Taylor knows about Dad."

Jan looked unhappy at Harmony's words, and Taylor grew even more uncomfortable.

"I ought to leave," Taylor said.

"Mom left my father. She finally managed to get away. And I'm trying to get her to stay here with me."

Now Taylor was at a complete loss. "I shouldn't be involved."

"It's complicated," Jan said, as if she hoped that would put an end to the discussion.

"My father's a scary man," Harmony went on, ignoring Taylor's protests and her mother's obvious discomfort. "She's been afraid to leave him for years, because she knew if he found her he would retaliate, and now that she's done it, she's afraid if she stays he'll trace her here and take it out on me, or even on Lottie."

Taylor wasn't sure now whether she was feeling light-headed from the hot yoga or the conversation. Whatever it was, she suddenly felt weak-kneed. "I think I need a glass of water and a place to sit."

Without a word Harmony motioned to the sofa and left for the kitchenette. Taylor gratefully took a seat while Jan walked back and forth with the baby.

"I know this sounds crazy," Harmony said

94

when she returned with a glass. "I'm sorry you walked into the middle of it."

Taylor drank half the water before she finally rested the glass on her jean-clad knee. "He's that bad?" She addressed the question to Jan.

Jan looked torn. She didn't answer.

"You left him, but you can't admit how frightening he is?" Harmony asked her mother. "Can't you tell her how many times he hit you or how many bones he's broken?"

"He's possessive and . . ." Jan hesitated, then lifted her eyes to Taylor's. "I'm afraid he's capable of almost anything where I'm concerned."

"Has he ever hurt anybody else?"

"He's a successful businessman," Harmony said. "He's also a deacon in our church, and he used to be on the boards of two charities, maybe still is. I don't think anybody really likes him, but they respect him well enough. Unless he changed after I left home, he was careful to save his fury for his family, mostly Mom. When he was angry at other people, his revenge was always more subtle or aimed at us." She looked at her mother. "Is that still accurate?"

Jan looked distressed, but she nodded.

"He sounds like a monster," Taylor said, and waited for Jan to deny it. When she didn't, Taylor began to get the full picture.

She wished one of the other goddesses, Analiese or Georgia, had walked into this instead of her. They were both older and more experienced. Analiese was a minister, used to dealing with family problems, and Georgia was a school administrator who worked with difficult kids and their difficult home lives every day. Her own degree was in health and wellness promotion, and it had never prepared her for this.

But she was here, and they were not.

"What can I do?" she asked, when nothing more profound occurred to her.

Jan was a slight woman, rail thin and haggard, but now that she was inside, Taylor could see even more clearly the resemblance to Harmony. "There's nothing *to* do. I have to leave. I can't stay here."

Her conviction was absolute. Taylor could hear it. "But where will you go?"

"I've laid plans. I've been . . . working on getting away for a long time, and I have help."

"Mom says Dad will think she's gone west."

"But you're not going west?" Taylor asked.

"She's not going *anywhere,*" Harmony said. "She's going to stay here, with her daughter and granddaughter. Dad's not going to find us. I've been in Asheville since high school graduation, and he never traced me here."

Taylor thought Harmony was being a bit naive. Motivation was a powerful factor. If Harmony's father viewed his wife as property he'd been robbed of, he would undoubtedly do anything to find her.

"Do you have another place you really want to go?" Taylor asked Jan. She watched as Jan looked down at her granddaughter, and before she looked up again the longing on her face was clear and strong.

"It's not about wanting to go anywhere. I just know I can't stay here. And Harmony and Lottie can't come with me. We shouldn't be in the same place at the same time . . . Not until I know Rex isn't looking anymore."

"How will you know that?"

"People are watching him."

Taylor liked the sound of that. "Then they'll be able to keep track of where he is and when?"

"Not every moment."

"But generally."

Jan shrugged.

"Can you be nearby?" Taylor asked. "Where you and Harmony can see each other sometimes if you're careful? At least until you know it's safe?"

"It would be safer to be far away."

"Okay, safer, maybe, but would it be safe enough to be, say, on the other side of Asheville, with somebody who knows you both?"

"I . . ."

"You?" Harmony asked.

"I'm twenty miles away, and you and I don't see each other very often. We're both too busy and it's too far to be easy." Taylor realized she and Harmony were making plans for Jan without consulting her.

She turned to Harmony's mother. "Jan, I just moved into my father's house in a quiet neighborhood. He's living in a condo, and Maddie, my daughter, and I needed more room, so we bought his place, although he still uses the workshop out back, so he's around a lot. Maddie's eleven. We have an extra bedroom where you can stay."

"I couldn't —"

Taylor suddenly realized how ideal this could be. "Look, it's not charity. Please don't think of it that way. Maddie and I fought all the way over here because she hates the way I drag her to classes and meetings. I'm renovating an old warehouse, and turning it into a health and wellness center, and I can't leave Maddie alone at night if I have to go over to the site or teach a class. Sometimes my dad or her father's parents can stay with her, and sometimes she can go to a friend's house. But on school nights that's not a great idea. She thinks she's too old for a babysitter. But if you were staying with us, anyway . . ." She let her voice trail off.

"Mom, that would work, wouldn't it?" Harmony was pleading. "Taylor's a good half hour away from here. If we were really careful we could still see each other sometimes. And I would know where you were and how you were doing. It's perfect."

"And if Rex finds me at your house?" Jan asked Taylor.

The silence was heavy for a moment, until Taylor sat forward. "We live in a neighborhood with people all around us. And you said yourself he's only violent with his own family."

"That's not a guarantee."

"He was never violent in public," Harmony said. "I think —" She stopped.

"What?" Taylor asked.

Harmony looked at her mother. "If he located you and wanted to hurt you, Mom, he would make sure to get you off by yourself. He wouldn't do it in front of anybody else or anywhere he might get

99

caught. I don't think there's a chance he would want anybody to see or know what he'd done unless there was no other choice. He's too smart to risk hurting strangers."

"It's taking too big a risk."

Taylor's mind was whirling. "Isn't any-where a risk? Are you going to live by yourself for the rest of your life because he might find you and hurt somebody in your house, or on your block, or in your city? You'll always be near somebody. This is as good a situation as there is. We'll be alert, and we'll be careful, plus he's got to realize that by now all kinds of people must know the story behind your escape, so he would be the first suspect if anything happened to any of us. I'll get a security system. And if people are watching him in . . ." She looked at Harmony for help.

"Topeka."

"Topeka," Taylor said, "then with luck we'll have warning if he leaves town, so we can be extra vigilant."

Jan was shaking her head. "You have a child? You want to expose her to this?"

"I'll tell you what. I'll run this by a friend who knows more about this kind of thing than I do. But I think she'll agree that Maddie and I aren't taking much of a risk. If she doesn't agree, we'll figure out something else."

Jan still looked torn, but she didn't say no.

"How careful have you been?" Taylor asked. "How good is the trail that's supposed to lead him out West if he looks for you?"

Jan looked away. "It's not complete yet. I . . . I left before we had everything in place."

"But?" Taylor heard that word in Jan's voice.

"The people who are helping me are very good," she said at last.

"They've done this before?"

Jan nodded.

"With success?"

She nodded again.

"Jan, I think you have to take another chance." Taylor got to her feet and held out her arms for Lottie, who held out her own and went right into them. "You left this man and you arranged for help to do it. You made it all the way here to be with Harmony and see your granddaughter. You're resourceful and obviously careful, and you're being helped by people who are both, as well. We can be both, too. Don't sell yourself short, and don't sell us short. We can make

101

this safe for everybody and help you get a new start."

"It's asking too much."

Taylor looked at Harmony, whose eyes were welling with tears. Then she looked back at Jan, whose eyes were beginning to brim, too.

She settled Lottie on her hip, and lightly rested her free hand on Jan's shoulder and squeezed. "I owe your daughter so much, Jan. I'll tell you the whole story once you're settled in your room at my house. But let me do this for Harmony. Let me do this for you, okay? Let me do this for *me.*"

CHAPTER 7

From the audio journal of a
forty-five-year-old woman, taped for the
files of Moving On, an underground
highway for abused women.

Before I married, were there signs that all
wasn't what it seemed? Were there moments
when my confidence in our happy future
was shaken?

Had I been educated enough, wary
enough, perhaps, I might have wondered
why the Abuser was in such a hurry to put
a ring on my finger. Or why he often
planned surprises on the nights I intended
to spend with my friends. Or why he suggested we begin a family immediately after
we married instead of waiting until I completed my degree. I might have wondered
why the house he bought had no immediate
neighbors, or why he worried so frequently
and loudly about our city's dangerous traf-

fic that I began to question my own ability to drive through it.

But the Abuser and his kind are masters of subtlety and excuses. He was in a hurry to marry because he loved me so much. He always seemed genuinely sorry that I'd made other plans when he arrived for a surprise date. Why not have children while we were young, so we could still travel and enjoy ourselves after they left home? Didn't I love the countryside, where I could have a larger house? Not only was the country lovely, but I was safer there, outside the city, with all its hazards.

In those early months, before we said our vows, he never lifted a hand to me. He rarely even lifted his voice, although he did talk over my comments frequently enough that alarm bells should have sounded. Nor was he aggressive or belligerent when we were in the company of others. Not that we often were. The Abuser wanted me all to himself, and like the romantic girl I was, I thought that showed how much he loved me.

He was often critical of others, but less often of me. When he did criticize, his words were framed as suggestions, patiently issued, lovingly meant. He wanted the best for me. A friend I'd chosen, an activity I loved?

Perhaps there were better options.

I can't place all the blame on the man I chose to marry. I wanted to be loved and taken care of. I wanted to believe that someone could turn my sadness to joy, and I could be happy again. I had never learned one of life's most important lessons. I am responsible for my own happiness. Letting somebody else take on that responsibility was like diving into murky waters without checking for rocks or sharks.

Jan stared out the side window of her new bedroom at a narrow pergola adorned with hanging flower baskets.

"Like I said, this was my father's house," Taylor said from the doorway. "He's an architect and of course, he can't leave anything alone. This used to be a pretty standard little ranch house, but when he finished, it was sort of modern Asian, sleek, stark. . . ."

"It's anything but stark now. It's lovely." Jan turned and saw that Taylor's arms were filled with fresh linens. She made a pretty picture, chin-length dark hair falling forward, sheets and blankets piled in front of a willowy body. Before Jan could take them, Taylor set them on the white bedspread.

"Oh, it was lovely when he finished it, too,

but Maddie and I wanted something a little warmer. It was pretty masculine. So we painted the siding cream, added shutters to match the porch pillars and planted flowers everywhere. A lot of the furniture was Dad's, but we added pillows and slipcovers, rugs on the floors and lots of things on the walls. We tried not to go overboard, though. We wanted simplicity. Not too girly."

"It's beautiful."

"I'm glad you like it. Will the room be okay? It's not huge, but having your own bath is a plus. I'm guessing before too long Maddie's going to be camping out in hers. I did when I was a teenager."

Harmony had never been allowed to camp out in their bathroom. She and Buddy had shared the one in the upstairs hallway, and he had often lingered until it was almost time to drive to school, just to point out that a man's needs always took priority.

"Jan?"

Jan realized Taylor had asked a question. "I'm sorry. I was woolgathering. It will be more than okay. It's perfect."

"Good, then. Would you like to share a glass of wine before dinner?"

"I'm sorry I ruined your plans to go out with Harmony tonight."

"I don't think she's a bit sorry you showed

up, do you? And Maddie's thrilled because her friend Edna just called, and she and Vanilla are heading over there to spend the night. I never would have heard the end of it if she'd missed that chance."

Jan had already been introduced to Vanilla, the grown puppy of Velvet, Harmony's dog, and the smallish golden doodle had won her heart by offering a paw on introduction. "I can't remember the last time I had a glass of wine."

Taylor nodded. "Okay, you don't drink. I'll remember that."

"No. I *didn't* drink because my husband . . ." She managed a smile. "I would love a glass of wine."

"Great. Once you're settled, come in the kitchen and talk to me while I cook. Harmony warned you I'm a vegetarian, right?"

"Harmony says she's a vegetarian, too."

Taylor turned to go. "I hope you didn't mind not spending the night with her tonight, but it just seemed to make sense to bring you here right away and let you settle in. It gives you a chance to see how you like it, just in case."

Jan knew that "just in case" meant that if she didn't like it, she could still leave town in the morning, as planned. That was the compromise they had all come up with. Taylor would have time to consider the safety issues, and Jan would have time to get used to the idea of staying in Asheville.

Of course, it was also clear that if she did decide to leave, she would break her daughter's heart.

She had brought so little with her that it only took a minute to empty her clothes into a drawer and store her few toiletries on the bathroom counter. Once she'd had time to squeeze Buddy's scrapbook into the old Scout backpack, it had taken up most of the room. The few other things she had brought were a testament to her desire to leave the past behind. She'd brought no jewelry except her watch, and that only because she'd worried she might need to know the time during her escape. Rex had given her the pretty jewel-encrusted Bulova on her last birthday, and the moment she was sure she no longer needed it, she would donate it to the Salvation Army.

Rex had given her lots of jewelry over the years, and now most likely every bit of it had melted in the fire. Most of the necklaces and bracelets had come with sincere apologies instead of wrapping paper. He hadn't meant to hit her last night, but she should have known he wouldn't like A, B or C. He hadn't meant to take out his bad day on her, but didn't she know by now that she needed to stay clear of him when things weren't going well at the office?

She had dutifully worn every bit, faithfully keeping track of each item. Had she not worn a particular piece, he would have been angry all over again, and the cycle would have been eternally perpetuated.

All gone now.

She felt herself smiling a little. "Good riddance," she said softly.

She combed her hair and wrinkled her nose at her reflection in the mirror. In the past year she hadn't bothered to visit a salon, a process she hated, anyway. Inevitably Rex would go along, and then he would sit nearby and instruct the stylist on what he wanted her to do. No layers, no bangs, not too short. Plain and simple, like the woman he had married.

"Simpleminded, more likely." She realized she was talking to herself.

"Which is what happens when you're the only decent person in the house to talk to," she said, then clamped her lips shut to cut off the conversational flow and went back into the bedroom.

The room *was* small, but it was comfortable and comforting. There was room for a double bed, a nightstand and a dresser, plus a television stand in the corner with a small flat-screen and DVD player. The walls were a pale sea-green, dotted with impressionistic seascapes and a trio of embroidered samplers from a time when they were a requirement for learning needlework skills. She leaned forward and read the motto on the closest. " 'To thine own self be true,' " she read out loud.

Had she paid attention to that saying earlier, she would be either happily divorced or dead. She wasn't taking bets on which way things would have gone.

She headed toward the kitchen.

She liked the open-floor plan, which made the smallish house seem larger. Only a granite counter separated the kitchen and living area, although an Oriental carpet in muted tones, and plush sofas and chairs, broke up the long expanse of cherry flooring. Taylor was setting two wine bottles on the counter when Jan approached. Jan saw she had changed into leggings and a long green T-shirt that said "Namaste" on the front under what might be a lotus blossom, but thankfully, since she had nothing clean to change into herself, the theme was casual.

"White or red?" Taylor asked. "I'll warn you, I'm no connoisseur. I buy good wine on sale, but then you have to ask yourself why the store is trying to get rid of it."

"I'm less of one than you are." Rex had been against drinking, holidays, dancing. She had often wondered if he was afraid alcohol or just plain fun might dull the pain of her life with him.

"I'm having red," Taylor said.

Jan realized that again she hadn't answered a question. "Perfect."

Taylor poured two glasses and motioned for Jan to take her pick. "I'm a vegetarian, not a vegan, so I've got cheese and crackers. Are you hungry?"

"I'm not sure I'll ever be hungry again," Jan said, before she realized how that sounded. "I mean . . ." She couldn't find a way to explain.

"You mean you've been through hell and that puts a dent in your appetite," Taylor said. "At the worst times in my life I've stopped eating, too. I'm not sure which is worse for us, stuffing ourselves over every trauma or forgetting that skipping meals makes us susceptible to worse depression and every little germ in the hemisphere."

"Put like that, cheese and crackers sounds like a plan."

Taylor smiled, and the room seemed to glow. She was an attractive young woman, but her brown eyes were luminous, and when she smiled, she approached beauty. "As Maddie moves toward puberty I get better and better at instilling guilt in those around me," she said.

Jan heard herself laugh and hardly recognized the sound. "It's called developing parenting skills."

"Did you have to do that with Harmony?"

"It was more my job to make her outlook on life as guilt free as possible. I wanted her to look beyond what was going on at home and believe in herself."

"I'm sorry you've had such a rough time." Taylor returned from the refrigerator with a block of cheese and set it on a cutting board. "Will you slice this for us?"

Jan sawed away, and as she did she realized she was growing hungry, which might have been Taylor's plan. "I promise I'm not going to bore you with stories from our past. I owe you more than that for offering your house to me for a while."

"That's fair enough, but —"

Jan's cell phone rang. She looked up. "I'm sorry, I need to get this."

"Go ahead. I'll start dinner."

Jan answered and took the phone into the living area, where she hoped she wouldn't disturb Taylor.

"Bea?" she asked.

"You okay?"

"I'm fine, but, well, there's been a change of plans." Briefly Jan outlined what she, Harmony and Taylor had come up with. Then she waited, expecting Bea to protest.

"That's as good as any idea the rest of us had," Bea said instead. "I like it."

"Really?"

"Nothing sacred about New Hampshire, woman. That was just one place to store you for a while. I might be worried if you were staying right there with your girl, but it sounds like you'll be far enough away to make a difference. Nothing beats being with friends who'll watch out for you, either."

"I'm worried if Rex finds me, he might hurt my hostess or her daughter."

"You need to remember something. We've done this more than fifty times. We never had nobody traced. So he's not going to find you, and if he does, Rex won't hurt nobody but you. He's not on drugs. He don't even drink, so he keeps his head more than some and calculates. He thinks he's a big man in the community, so he's not going to risk that. Your friends will be safe, and I think you will be, too. You just be careful, and if you get too worried, we'll move you again. Get yourself a better phone for everyday use, only use cash, no credit, and don't give them any info. Keep this phone just to call me, add minutes here and there and I'll know who's calling when I see the number."

"Do you know if anybody's seen him yet?"

"Nobody's sighted the man, so they're still sifting the ashes, and far as I know the authorities aren't looking anyplace else for him. Not yet."

"Where could he be?"

"The minute we know, we'll be watching him. You just go on and start your new life. Be careful, but not so careful you're not happy."

"You've been so wonderful. How can I repay you?"

"Just help somebody else when you can."

Jan said goodbye and put the phone back in her pocket before she turned.

Taylor, at the counter, didn't pretend she hadn't heard the conversation. "Just so you know, while you were unpacking I called the friend I mentioned and asked her opinion on whether it's too much of a risk to have you here. She's a nurse with some experience with domestic violence. She said the first two years after you leave a situation like yours are the most dangerous, and you'll have to be careful, but putting distance between you was important and positive, the best thing you could have done."

"That's what I've been told."

"There aren't any guarantees, Jan, but after I told her how careful you were getting away, she said if we observe security precautions here, if you're careful to vary your routine, get your mail somewhere else, use a different name, then we'll most likely be safe. If he does show up, then we go to the police. They take stalking seriously, and under some circumstances it's a felony. Harmony witnessed your husband's abuse. The police won't be able to blow this off."

"I didn't think . . ." Jan's voice trailed off.

"What?"

"*Everyone* seems to think it's okay to stay here, even the people who brought me this far."

"That's who you were talking to." It was more of a statement than a question.

"She wished me well, and she told me to call her directly if I need help."

Taylor motioned to a stool in front of the counter. "Come have your wine and something to munch on."

Jan did as she was told, something she was particularly good at. She ate a cracker with a slice of cheese and waited for her stomach to reject it. But instead the food made her hungrier. She took a second, then a sip of the wine.

"I only poured you a little," Taylor said. "On an empty stomach it's twice as powerful. But let me know if you'd like more."

"Less is better, I think."

"If I were you right now, I would need to relax, and maybe a little wine will help."

"It's hard. For months I've been gearing up to go one place, and now I'm in another. I never intended to come to Asheville at all. It seemed too dangerous. But after the fire? I just knew Harmony would find out somehow, and she would be sure I was dead. I couldn't let that happen."

"I'm so glad you came."

Jan still wasn't sure. All this well-meant reassurance didn't take into account the will or the whims of the man she had been married to.

"Did you have a place to go?" Taylor asked. "I mean a house, a job, a life somewhere else?"

"We were working on it. Then Rex didn't come home from work, and I knew I had to leave right away while I had that chance."

"But you were able to get things in place quickly."

Jan wanted to tell Taylor more, but sharing her life, even a little piece of it, was a luxury she hadn't experienced in years.

"Not quickly," she said. "Last New Year's I met a woman at a party. I didn't go to many parties, but this one was, well, it was required for my husband's job, so I had to go along and look happy."

"I'm guessing over the years you've learned to be a good actress." Taylor set a salad on the counter and turned to do something at the stove.

"I like to cook," Jan said, while she decided how to respond to that. "I could cook for you while I'm here, take some of that off your shoulders, anyway."

"Great. We'll work that out."

Jan took another sip to steady herself. "At that party? There was a woman who knew my husband. I'd met her a couple of times over the years. She got me off to one side when he was talking business with some men. And she said she worried about the way he treated me. She told me to call her if I needed help, that she was part of a group of women who helped other women who had trouble at home."

"How did she know that just from seeing you at a party?"

"Later she told me her first husband nearly killed her before she got out of the marriage. She recognized a fellow sufferer from the fear in my eyes. And she knew Rex well enough to suspect he could be mean."

Taylor whistled softly. "It was that obvious?"

"I had bruises on my wrist. She paid attention. And she said I needed to get out while I still could."

"You said she was part of a group of women who do this?"

"More like a network all over the country." Jan hesitated, but there was no reason to do so. Taylor wasn't going to turn anybody in. "Lady truckers. They call themselves Moving On. My husband sells insurance for trucks, and that's why we were all at that party together."

"That's rich. Who better?"

"I called her two weeks later. One morning she waited until Rex left for the office. Then she came into our place the back way. We talked for an hour. She told me what they did and how successful they were. It's been going on for years. Sometimes women go back to the men who beat them, because they can't adjust, but nobody who stayed away has ever been found. I've wanted to get away for years, but . . ." It was too difficult to explain. She shrugged. "Anyway, I wanted to leave sooner, but Rex was watching me."

"I'm not a counselor, just a friend, and a

new one. I think it's going to be difficult to put all that behind you. It's going to take years. But you said something earlier that I want to put out on the table. You said you weren't going to bore me with stories of your past?"

Jan realized she had done just that again. She didn't know what to say, but Taylor went on.

"If we're going to be friends, and I want to be, we're going to have to bore each other with stories of the past. Because that's what friends do. Only neither of us will be bored, Jan, because friends are interested in each other. I know you've been through hell, and whenever it's helpful to talk about it, I'll be happy to listen. I probably won't have any answers, but that's okay, too."

"Do *you* have stories you'll share?"

"I could spend hours just telling you about my mom and me, and all the years I kept her away. And about getting pregnant at seventeen and holding a grudge against Maddie's father most of her life. I'm light-years from perfect, so with that out on the table, we can just find our way together, okay?"

Jan felt tears glaze her eyes, but she smiled. "Friends," she said.

"Good. Now let's talk about something

that's also important." Taylor smiled, too. "What we're going to put on our pasta tonight."

CHAPTER 8

Harmony's mother had been living at Taylor's house for three days. Harmony still couldn't quite believe it. Using Rilla's cell phone, she had spoken to her mother twice. In the unlikely event the Reynolds' landline was being monitored, they had all agreed that Harmony would use Rilla's cell and Jan would use Taylor's for extra security.

Jan.

She still couldn't get used to her mother's new name. Janine Stoddard was Jan Seaton now, and while the Jan made sense and might even be risky, Seaton had been picked out of thin air. Moving On had found it was easier for women to remember their new names if their initials stayed the same. That might be risky, too, but not as risky as a woman forgetting what she called herself these days.

The name change wasn't official, of course. Jan had no ID that said Seaton, but she also had no intention of needing ID.

Harmony had tried to fill her days with work and Lottie, but her mind was focused on the extraordinary turn of events that had brought her mother to Asheville. The Topeka paper had moved on to other stories, so news was difficult to come by, but she knew from the last conversation she'd had with her mother that her father still hadn't been sighted. His disappearance was perplexing, even worrisome, since no one could monitor his movements. Was he searching for both of them, following the trail Moving On had so carefully laid to the West? Was he following the *real* trail to North Carolina, so that one day soon he could show up on Harmony's doorstep?

Neither seemed particularly likely, and that was the worst of it. After years away from home, trying to think like her father brought back a childhood in which she'd tried to anticipate his every move and mood. She had hoped those days were gone forever. She never wanted to give him that much thought again.

Right now, though, she was thinking about the evening to come. "Lottie Lou, you're going off with your daddy again," she said, bending over the car seat where her sleepy daughter was fidgeting.

Lottie flailed her fists and screwed up her face in protest. Harmony wondered if Davis would give her back the moment Lottie started to fuss. The baby was normally good-natured, but her afternoon nap hadn't gone on nearly long enough.

Harmony was still surprised Davis had asked to take Lottie for the evening. She had assumed his mother was back in town, but when she asked he'd said no. Maybe he had been vague, but Harmony had been pleased at the opportunity to have a baby-sitter.

Because she had a date.

With everything else going on, she had forgotten all about it until that morning — too late to back out politely — when Taylor called to remind her. She was having dinner with a friend of Taylor's, and she hadn't been to Cuppa — where she used to be a server — for months, but it was a comfort-able, casual kind of place to meet a guy, so she'd agreed. The plans had been made, of course, before her mother arrived.

Since she believed in signs — at least when they were good ones — the fact that Davis had called right afterward to say he wanted to take Lottie for the evening had convinced her she had to go.

The doorbell rang, and she wondered if

Davis would remember it took time to lug the baby downstairs. She was almost at the door when he tapped and opened it. "I thought you might like some help getting her down."

This wasn't a sign; it was a *miracle*. She swung the car seat in his direction and he took it. "I'll bring the diaper bag," she said, gathering it from the sofa, along with her purse. "I'm going out, but I'll have my cell phone with me."

"I'll call before I bring her back." He bent over the car seat and smiled at his daughter, who still didn't look happy. "Are you ready, Peaches?"

"Peaches?"

"She has cheeks like little peaches. You never noticed?"

She was thunderstruck. Was this the same Davis whose main thought when he found he was going to be a father was whether a baby might help him secure a promotion at work?

"I might as well tell you I have a woman with me," he continued. "Her name's Amy, and she wants to meet Lottie."

That sounded more like the old Davis, and Harmony sniffed. At least he'd told this Amy person he had a daughter.

She followed him down the stairs to his

car, and as Davis struggled with the baby's car seat, the woman on the passenger's side opened the door and swung her legs around to sit sideways. Shining red hair was arranged over one shoulder, and her makeup was so carefully applied that Harmony figured it had taken as long to do it as she had spent on her own in all the months since Lottie's birth.

"You must be Amy. I'm Harmony," she said when Amy didn't speak.

Amy nodded. "Does she cry a lot?"

"Just when she's unhappy."

As if on cue, Lottie began to whimper. Amy's lovely face tightened into something approaching a grimace.

Harmony really didn't want to help, but she knew it was the right thing to do. "She didn't have a very long nap this afternoon, so she's tired. She'll probably fall asleep quickly. She'll be in a better mood by the time she gets out of the car."

"Maybe you should have given her a longer nap."

"Short of drugging her or hitting her over the head, I'm not sure what I could have done."

"I believe in schedules."

"Most people who don't have children do." Harmony stepped back and addressed

Lottie's father. "Davis, make sure you call if you need advice. *Me,* not your mother."

He grunted something profane about seat belts and infant car seats, and she left him to figure out the mysteries of parenthood by himself.

Upstairs she took a moment to peer at her face in the mirror. Freckled, with sandy lashes. Wide mouth, slightly crooked teeth that should have worn braces — which her father had frowned upon as vanity — long, pale brown hair that was only streaked with blond because she was out in the sun so often, not because she had the time to do anything about her hair except let it grow.

She was going to be late if she did anything much to improve what she saw. She scraped a little mascara on her lashes and brushed some mineral powder over her freckles; then she grabbed her purse, which felt as light as air after hauling a diaper bag, and peeked through her window to make sure Davis was gone. Since the coast was clear, she headed downstairs and away.

Fifteen minutes later she was walking into Cuppa after scoring an amazing parking place right in front, another sign. On the drive she had tried to remember what Taylor had told her about Nate Winchester. They had been friends in high school, and then he had gone off to college, followed by the army. He had only recently returned to run the family custom cabinetry business, which did a lot of work for Ethan, Taylor's architect father. Taylor said Nate was one of the good guys, a sweetheart. They had been friends so long they would never see each other as anything else, but she'd thought maybe he and Harmony might strike a spark or two. Taylor thought they had a lot in common.

Harmony and Nate had shared one rushed phone call. They'd nailed down the time, but now she couldn't remember how she was supposed to recognize him. In a minute she realized it didn't matter, because all her old friends on staff came over to greet her and find out how she was doing. When the crowd cleared away, Nate was the only one left.

"Hi," he said, holding out his hand. "I'm Nate."

She smiled because his smile was infectious, and she took his hand for a firm shake. "You've guessed who I am."

"Taylor told me to look for a tall blonde with lots of friends."

Harmony hadn't been on a date since she and Davis were a couple. She tried to remember how she was supposed to examine a guy without looking as if she had a checklist. Her initial impression was that once she had a list in hand, she would need a good pen, because this time she would be making lots of check marks.

Nate was taller than she was, lean and muscular, with friendly brown eyes and auburn hair cut short, but not too short. His clothes were casual, but not sloppy. His trousers looked freshly pressed, which almost made her smile, since she wasn't sure she owned an iron.

"I have a table," he said. "I bet the service is going to be great. They'll be fighting over you."

She followed him to a corner. Cuppa had been little more than a coffee shop when she began working there, but later it had morphed into a bistro. Now it sported topiaries on the sidewalk and hanging ferns in the windows, along with an expanded menu, although the coffee bar jutting along one side was definitely casual. Tonight the room was crowded, but Nate had a good eye, and he had chosen the one corner table where they might have a little privacy.

"I hope you're hungry." Nate waited for Harmony to choose a seat; then he pulled out her chair.

She thought this was, quite possibly, a

first. When had anyone seated her, except possibly the waiter at the country club dinner she had once attended with Davis? She put a mark next to "polite" on her mental checklist and smiled her thanks.

She thought it was wise to immediately bring up the subject of Lottie. If Nate wasn't interested in a single parent, he ought to know right now that she was one. She made sure she sounded matter-of-fact.

"The closest I've gotten to eating since breakfast was finishing the Cheerios on my daughter's high-chair tray."

"Is she old enough to feed herself?" he asked without missing a beat.

"She thinks she is. I shovel in whatever I've prepared between her finger food."

"I'm the oldest of six. I was the only kid who went to Covenant Academy with rice cereal and mashed bananas on his shirt."

"Your job was feeding the babies?"

"Until I got my driver's license. Then I was in charge of pickup and delivery. My sister still talks about the time I took her to ballet class with a crate of chickens and a goat in the back of our minivan. My mother was trading livestock with another farmer across town."

"You come from a farm family?"

"We have two acres, and Mom used every

inch while we were growing up, but now a lot of the garden area is devoted to wildflowers. She got rid of the goats last month. I think the bees will go next."

"Six kids?" She tried to imagine it.

"Devoted Catholics, although they sent us to Covenant Academy instead of Catholic schools because they liked the curriculum better."

"I think I'm more a Buddhist than anything, although I don't really go to church," she said, waiting for him to scrunch up his face and remember a prior commitment.

"I'm just trying to live a good life," Nate said with a grin. "I leave all the theology to people who are more worried than I am."

He hadn't flinched over her single-parent status. He hadn't flinched over her religion or lack of one. "The veggie pizza here is a standout," she said. "Did Taylor mention I'm a vegetarian?"

"I don't remember. I'm one of those guys who'll eat anything. Buffalo burgers? Brussels sprouts?" He shrugged, as if to say he didn't care which.

She put down the menu, which hadn't changed since her days on staff. "It's possible you're too good to be true."

"I hitchhiked to San Francisco when I was sixteen to attend a *Star Trek* convention. I

130

have an autographed poster of Captain Jean
Luc Piccard in a safe-deposit box."

"That's the worst you've got?"

"Geekier than that? I played tuba in the
academy band, mostly because I was the
only one who could lift it out of the case. I
went into the army because they promised
me the Mideast. Then they sent me to
Honolulu. I spent the whole time upgrad-
ing cabinets in officers' housing at Schofield
Barracks." He grinned, an infectious,
friendly grin. "Bad enough for you?"

She smiled, too. How could she not like
Nate Winchester? Still, she had to counter.

She leaned forward. "I'm the product of a
family who gives the word *dysfunctional* new
meaning. I got pregnant despite using birth
control and refused to marry the father
when I realized he wanted to use our baby
to impress the partners in his accounting
firm. Now I work on a farm. Digging in the
dirt and cleaning out the barn makes me
happy in a way nothing else ever did. I want
to be a lawyer, but I haven't even started
college and won't until Lottie's a little
older."

"Just so I know?"

She nodded. "Just so you know."

"How about a glass of wine? And I'm
good with the veggie pizza if you want to

split one."

"White wine for me, and you won't have much choice on the brand — they're probably still working on their wine cellar. Oh, and I don't like Brussels sprouts."

"Duly noted."

She didn't like Brussels sprouts, but she did like Nate. How could she not? As he gave their order, though, she was also aware that while she liked him just fine, sitting here with him was like sitting with a new girlfriend she'd met at the gym or the produce section of Fresh Market. He was good-looking, funny, intelligent and kind.

And she didn't feel even one faint spark igniting between them.

CHAPTER 9

From the audio journal of a
forty-five-year-old woman, taped for the
files of Moving On, an underground
highway for abused women.

The first time the Abuser slapped me I was
stunned. Three weeks after we were married
in a simple ceremony, he came home to find
that I had rearranged the kitchen of our new
house to better suit my needs. Since I did
all the cooking, I never considered that
when he unpacked our new utensils and
dishes he had meant for them to stay in the
cabinets he had chosen. Foolishly I had even
expected him to be pleased I was settling in
and making our house a home.

He was sorry afterward, of course, tired
from a long day at work in a job he despised
because he hated taking orders from people
who weren't as smart as he was. Sorry
enough that as he moved the kitchen con-

tents back where he had first put them, he said he would have to remember to be more patient, that he knew I was learning to be a wife. But since he lived in the house, too, I should remember that all our decisions were to be made together.

Of course, as time passed I realized that there was no "together." The Abuser decided everything, and when he did consult me, often his intention was to find out what I wanted so he could do the opposite.

Not always, though. Sometimes he surprised me with things he knew I yearned for — frequently enough, in fact, that I continued to believe he loved me and there was hope for our marriage. Sometimes, too, if I asked sweetly enough he would let me have my way, as long as I understood it was a privilege he had granted because he was a model husband.

Some things, of course, were permanently off-limits. He claimed we couldn't afford a second car so I could do errands on my own, and on the rare occasions I had the family car to myself, I was suspicious that he checked the mileage to be sure I hadn't gone places I hadn't told him about. He preferred that my old friends not visit when he wasn't at home. Wasn't daytime set aside to clean and cook? He had his job; I had mine.

Of course, evenings and weekends were our time together and not to be shared.

The second time he hit me I had just returned from a spontaneous shopping trip with a college friend. When he demanded to know why I had ignored his wishes, I reassured him, pointing out that the night's pot roast was simmering in the slow cooker and freshly ironed shirts were hanging in his closet.

So much time has passed I wonder now if I realized that afternoon that the trap was closing. That apologies were meant to keep me in line just as much as striking me was. That I could still find a way to be free of him with a little cunning and the help of the friends who hadn't yet forgotten me.

I really don't know. I do know I was determined to make our marriage a success. And wasn't the violence rare and the Abuser sorry? Didn't that make all the difference?

Jan had known she would have to shop for clothes since she was washing the few things she'd brought every other day. When she was making plans to escape and gathering necessities, she had even told herself shopping once she "moved on" would be fun.

She could choose colors Rex had discouraged and styles that might actually look good instead of her usual drab, loose clothing that guaranteed she would fade into the background.

Of course, fading into the background might be a good thing until she knew for sure where her husband had gone. But in an odd sort of way, brightening her wardrobe might actually help her hide, since if anyone besides Rex was searching for her, they would be looking for a frumpy woman with no fashion sense and no courage.

Which, she was afraid, was sadly accurate.

"I can drop you off in town, but we'll need to leave shortly," Taylor said, glancing at the kitchen clock as she put away their lunch things. "My dad's going to meet me over at the studio to see how the upstairs renovations are going. But he has another appointment at four, so I can pick you up just a little after. Will you be okay in town that long?"

Jan couldn't imagine that much free time. And in a strange town? Where nothing was familiar, and she had no idea where to go?

Taylor seemed to sense her discomfort. "We can wait and go to the mall next time I have a few hours off. I'm just afraid if I try to drop you off there today, I'll be late."

"Oh, absolutely not. I'll enjoy prowling around Asheville." Jan put on her brightest smile. "And if I get lost, you can guide me in once you come back to pick me up."

"The city's small enough I think you'll be fine."

"Although what about Maddie?" Jan hoped she didn't sound as if she was grasping at straws. "Shouldn't I stay home so she's not alone when she gets back from school?"

"She's going over to her friend Edna's house. You'll meet Edna before too long. Her mom, Samantha, is one of the goddesses."

Jan had heard all about the goddesses, an idea that hadn't seemed too far-fetched, since her own goddesses, the truckers of Moving On, only did what they did because they wanted to help and for no other reason.

"Just let me grab my wallet," Jan said.

Ten minutes later Taylor pulled into a space beside the curb of a hilly downtown filled — at least from what Jan could see — with restaurants and small shops with colorful, quirky merchandise displayed in their windows.

Taylor must have seen the look on her face, because she laughed. "You're not in Kansas anymore, Toto."

Jan's gaze wandered across the street, and her eyebrows shot up. "Well, if I can't find anything to wear, I can get a tattoo."

"Just wander a little." Taylor pointed. "Go up that way and you'll run into a few stores with clothes you might like. And if you don't, we'll hit the mall later this week."

For Jan this meant she had to find new things to wear today, because Taylor was already doing too much for her and didn't need to hold her hand.

"I'll meet you back here about four-fifteen," Taylor said. "If you get tired, there are plenty of places to have coffee, and there's a park just up that way with benches." She hesitated. "I hate to ask this, but if you need cash —"

"No, no, I'm really fine. I have enough money to see me through until I can find work. It's a long story. But I intend to pay rent, too, until I find a place."

"Don't you dare. Pay rent *or* find a place. I need you, and I'm not kidding. Maddie's so much happier now that I'm not dragging her all over the place."

Jan knew she had to get out of the car, but her arms and legs felt as inflexible as steel girders. She forced herself to open the door, swing her legs to the curb and stand.

"See you back here," she said, forcing a

smile that Taylor returned.

When Jan closed the door, Taylor pulled out into traffic.

And Jan was alone.

She would have been alone in New Hampshire, of course. More alone than this. Here she had Harmony just a phone call away, although she certainly couldn't call or visit her daughter without advance preparation. Still, just knowing she was nearby helped, and Taylor had told her if anything came up, all she had to do was call her cell phone.

Getting a new phone was on her list of things to do, a phone registered to the stranger Jan Seaton, but she would have to check into what questions might be asked and how she could answer them. The very basic disposable that Moving On had provided had limited minutes remaining, and she needed to save them in case she had to contact her benefactors.

The sidewalks seemed to undulate like ocean waves. It was unlikely there was any place in the Asheville area where she wouldn't be walking either up or downhill, and for a while her legs were going to feel it. The terrain, like everything else here, would seem strange for some time to come.

She assessed her surroundings. To her right was a shop that sold chocolates. Across the street, beside the tattoo studio, was a café that looked to be closed, either already done for the day or not yet open for the evening. She trudged in the direction Taylor had suggested, to what looked like as major a street as she would find here. Some of the buildings were painted bright colors, and while she didn't stop to investigate, the shops seemed filled with things she didn't need. Jewelry, crafts, photographs and exotic statues.

By the time she got to the corner, she could feel unease turning into panic. The feeling was familiar, even if nothing else was. She had felt just this way on the evenings Rex was late coming home, not because she'd worried about his safety, but because trying to keep dinner warm had been nearly impossible. After an hour had passed, she had then been faced with trying to make something new, something quick that would still be fresh when he arrived. Nothing had made him angrier than walking through the door to find his dinner was dried out or just being prepared.

She told herself the kind of panic she had felt back then was finished. She told herself there was no reason to transfer those feelings to a simple shopping excursion. Unfortunately nobody knew better than she that telling herself something helped very little. Because for too many years at the beginning of her marriage she had told herself if she just learned to be a better wife, she would have a happy life.

She needed to sit down. Taylor had said something about a park. She saw a green space to her right and started in that direction.

The little triangular wedge was picturesque, with rocks that mimicked the surrounding mountains and a waterfall running over them. Cantilevered steps, or possibly seats, led to a flat area near the center. People were playing chess at one end, and not far from her a disheveled old man on one of the benches strummed a banjo. In between bursts of discordant music he fed a pointy-eared boxer bites of a sub sandwich.

Had she been snatched by aliens and deposited on Mars, she couldn't have felt more like a stranger in a strange land.

She headed for a bench without an occupant and gratefully sat before her knees gave way. She closed her eyes. She knew fear. She understood fear. What she didn't understand was why, now that the person she feared most was hundreds of miles away, she was still trembling.

"Got room here?"

The voice startled her, and her eyes flew open. A young man with dark hair covered by a colorful baseball cap didn't wait for her reply. He sat on the other end of the bench and stuck his legs out in front of him.

"This is my favorite bench because of the sun," he said.

She hadn't chosen the bench for any reason except proximity, but now Jan noticed that she was sitting in a puddle of sunshine.

She wanted to move away. Her stomach was rebelling, and talking to a stranger seemed impossible. She had enough problems thinking of things to say to Taylor and Maddie. So many years had passed when simple conversation had been denied her that sometimes in Topeka, in the hours when she was home alone, she had pretended to be two people.

Nice to meet you, Janine. Tell me about yourself.

Well, thanks for asking. There's not much to tell except that I hate my life and I can't figure out how to have a better one and live to tell the story.

"Do you come here often?" the young man asked.

She ventured another glance. He was still

142

sitting exactly where he'd flopped down, his face turned toward the sun and his eyes hidden by sunglasses. He had a strong profile with a nose like a hawk's beak. Even seated he seemed tall and muscular.

"No," she said.

"Been to the drum circle?"

"No."

"You ought to give it a try. Crowd-watching's a big part of the fun. Lots of different kinds of people come. Tourists . . . Are you just visiting?"

"I don't know."

"It's a good place to live if you're looking for one."

"Why?"

He opened his eyes and lifted an eyebrow. "Why is it a good place to live?"

"Uh-huh."

"Not too many places where so many different kinds of people get along. Nobody stands out much here. You can be whoever you want to be, and nobody thinks you're strange. At least most people don't think so."

"How do you figure out who you want to be?" she asked before she thought better of it.

He looked surprised. "Isn't that the easy part?"

"No."

"I guess you figure out who you admire, and you try to be like that."

She admired people with courage, people who'd had dreams they'd pursued despite obstacles. People who had been able to protect their children.

She blinked back tears. "And if you fail?"

"Aren't you too young to write off life that way?"

She wondered.

He stretched and stood, long arms reaching out as if to embrace the world. "I say go for whatever it is you haven't done yet. You've got time right up until you draw your last breath." He gave a quick, final wave, almost a salute, and strolled off.

She asked herself what she hadn't done yet, and the answer was so overwhelming she could hardly breathe. If she took his advice, where would she start?

She gazed around the park, searching for a clue. Minutes passed and finally her heart rate began to slow. Then she saw the answer was simple.

"Blue jeans."

It didn't matter if she was frightened by everyday things that others took for granted. It didn't matter if she felt alone in the world, something Rex had repeatedly warned her would happen if she ever tried to leave him. It didn't matter that she no longer knew what a woman like her could actually achieve. Perhaps it didn't even matter that she had failed at the things she had most hoped to accomplish and was still seeking forgiveness.

What mattered now were jeans. From what she could tell, she was the only person in Asheville who didn't own a pair. If she didn't want to stand out in the crowd, now was the time to remedy that.

She got to her feet, and her knees still trembled, but life was going to be like this. A pair of blue jeans. An afternoon alone in a strange — in more ways than one — city. Participating in a short conversation with someone she'd never met and wasn't likely to see again.

Life. One step at a time with nobody blocking the way.

And if, for one moment after Taylor had dropped her off, she had yearned for Rex — who had all the answers as well as all the questions — then she supposed she could seek forgiveness for that, as well.

But first, one small thing. A pair of jeans.

This she could do.

CHAPTER 10

From the audio journal of a
forty-five-year-old woman, taped for the
files of Moving On, an underground
highway for abused women.

Some people believe violence comes directly
from the traditional family, when one person
is awarded all the power as well as the right,
even obligation, to enforce his values or lack
of them. Others believe domestic violence is
caused by the *disintegration* of the traditional
family. Neither view is true. Domestic
violence is the result of one family member
with sickness in his soul, and the desire to
infect those who are weakest and most
vulnerable. Sometimes fatally.

And yes, I've used the word *he.* The vast
majority of batterers are men. Mine certainly was.

And yes, I've also used the word *was.*
Now that I've left the Abuser, I have no

doubt that if given the opportunity he'll cause more and greater pain, perhaps ending our struggle once and for all, as happens too frequently. I've been warned that 70 percent of all women who die from domestic abuse die after they leave their abusers, as I left mine.

For now I'm free of him. I have dreams in which he finds me and exacts his final vengeance, but I believe that someday I may have just as many dreams in which I find him first.

Adam Pryor hadn't known he could fly. He had spent most of his life on the ground, never realizing that if he flapped his wings he could soar with the eagles and vultures. Today he felt kinship with both, the eagles with their hooked beaks and lethal talons that tore the flesh from their prey, and the vultures, who fed on carrion, destroying evidence so the world could pretend death wasn't an ugly business. Right now, though, he only wanted to get away, to rise above the clouds, up, up, just high enough that he didn't lose consciousness and plunge back to earth.

He was especially careful about that. He never wanted to touch the ground again, particularly not the ground just below him.

If he could gaze through the clouds, he knew exactly what he would see. A rural bazaar, a brief spot of color against a desolate landscape, with crude wooden sheds lining an unadorned village roadway. Sides of meat hanging from hooks. Yellow plastic jugs with labels in Arabic script. Shelves of cans, some which would have been perfectly at home in an army commissary and probably had been before they mysteriously disappeared.

Children. Boys in their long shirts over baggy white pants, colorful wool *pakol* covering heads. Girls in an array of colors, pants, overdresses, scarves over dark hair, walking or skipping beside their mothers.

He knew better than to watch the children's progress. He had wings; he could fly away and should. Yet, somehow, he was powerless to do so.

Suddenly, despite struggling to lift himself higher, he realized he was floating downward. He wasn't above the clouds at all. Now he saw that the clouds were really plumes of smoke. It tickled his lungs, then filled them until he began to cough. His eyes burned as he drifted. Then he picked up speed until he was falling like a meteor streaking toward the earth.

Through the veil of smoke he saw flames

below, and then, as the air rushed past him, he could hear screams.

The wailing began.

"No . . ."

Adam tried to sit up but was only partially successful. For a moment he didn't know where he was. The answer that left him momentarily paralyzed was this: he was inside a coffin or a crypt.

"No!" He struggled to lift his arms so he could feel something, anything, around him, but his arms were pinned to his sides. A scream gathered inside him, even as he saw light seeping through an unfamiliar doorway, and heard clinking and shuffling just beyond it.

Just in time, he remembered.

The ice machine near the elevator. A cheap motel on the highway. The only room still vacant when he had arrived after midnight two nights ago. The clerk had given him a discount — but not much — because of a bathroom sink that dripped without remorse and a shower nobody seemed able to fix.

He clamped his lips shut and forced himself to lie flat again until he could untangle the top sheet that bound him. Once he was free, he sat up and rested his head in his hands. In the hallway, whoever had needed ice at 2:00 a.m. rattled a bucket one more time, then slammed the lid on the machine. In a moment Adam could hear footsteps die away, then silence, except for a hum as the machine set out to replenish its supply.

Even the dripping no longer kept him company. He had fixed both the sink and the shower on his first morning, although he hadn't told the guy at the front desk, who probably would have raised the price of the room.

Now that he was awake he wasn't surprised that the dream had visited again. In the past year he had fought to get away from the same familiar scene a hundred times or more, although he hadn't had the full-blown nightmare, this Technicolor, stereo version, for weeks. He had known he wouldn't be lucky enough to evade it forever, but in the secret recesses of his psyche, that was what he had prayed for.

The one good thing about repetition? From past experience he knew that now he wouldn't be able to sleep for hours. He could toss and turn and pretend all he wanted to, but deep inside lurked a realistic fear that the dream would return. He could try to sleep, but that stronger part of him would win.

He moved to the edge of the bed and turned on the nightstand lamp. These days he was never without a book. The motels he frequented didn't always have working televisions, and it was too late to prowl . . . he tried to remember the name of the city . . . Asheville. North Carolina.

That was right. That's where he was.

He rose and rummaged through an overnight duffel to find the paperback he had picked up at the grocery store. From experience he'd learned what he could safely read. Cookbooks. Certain biographies. Philosophy. He'd tried a romance novel one night, but that had kept him awake for different reasons.

He opened his selection and began to read about Abraham Lincoln. Like everybody else who'd been to elementary school, he already knew how the story ended, so he would encounter no unwelcome surprises.

His own story was much more a mystery.

Jan hadn't slept well in weeks. Her final nights in Kansas had been filled with dread. She had known she would be leaving in the coming weeks, so in the middle of the night she had gone over plans, looking for a flaw or even a reason to forget them.

The devil you know . . .

Rex always slept soundly, so night was a time when she didn't have to worry he might turn on her. Small infractions or imagined slights dissolved into dreams. She could lie next to him and let her mind roam. And roam it had — to all the worst outcomes.

What would happen if he found her as she tried to leave? What would happen if he tracked her to New Hampshire and tried to force her to return? What would happen if she refused? Would he make sure she simply disappeared? Even if her body was found, who would suspect that a church deacon and respected business owner had succumbed to his dark side and traveled that far to kill his wife?

After the escape she hadn't slept well, either, because she still expected to pay a price down the road. All the years she had spent with him had made such deep wounds she would never be completely free of them.

For a change, tonight she had fallen asleep quickly, a deep, dreamless sleep that her exhausted body had insisted on. The shopping trip had been the final straw. Between the panic attack and the struggle to decide which jeans to buy, she had been so tired she had barely stayed awake during dinner.

Now, though, she *was* awake. Wide-awake

152

and terrified.

The house was dark. No light showed under her door. By now Jan knew Taylor's ritual. The younger woman usually went to bed about eleven, and she turned off the lights, everything except a night-light in the kitchen and another in the hallway bathroom. There were few street lamps in the neighborhood, and the one closest to Taylor's house was shielded by a maple that hadn't yet dropped its leaves. Only glimmers of light seeped in through the windows.

Clearly Taylor was asleep. If she was up, she would have turned on a light to make her way through the house. But someone else was creeping slowly down the hallway, or at least making his way through the kitchen. Jan heard someone bumping into furniture, not normal footsteps made by somebody comfortable with the layout, but intermittent thumps, a chair knocked into a table, perhaps, a small collision with a counter stool.

She forced herself to sit up and focus. The noise had been loud enough to wake her, but her head was still fogged from sleep. She could think of no other explanation for the noise. A stranger had to be in the house, and she was terrified she knew who it was.

Rex had traced her to Taylor's. No matter how careful they had been, he'd traced her. He was methodically searching for her room.

And when he found her . . .

Maddie wasn't home, and she had Vanilla with her. Taylor was home, though, and if Rex found her room first . . .

She had to get up. She had forgotten to charge the Moving On cell, and there was no regular telephone in her room to call 911, although there was one in the hall. Taylor had decided that Maddie didn't need a phone in her room, but the girl could take the one in the hallway if she asked for permission. If Jan could just get to it, punch in those three numbers . . .

Her body was stiff with dread, but she couldn't lie still and wait for the worst to happen. She swung her legs to the floor and forced herself to stand. She listened. For now, the house was silent, but she wasn't reassured. The intruder was probably getting his bearings after the last misstep.

She crept soundlessly to her door. The moment she opened it she might be spotted, depending on where the intruder was standing in the kitchen. Her best bet would be to crack the door just wide enough to slip out, then press her body against the wall. She might be harder to spot that way. It might buy her time to make the call.

The house remained quiet. For a moment she reconsidered. Had she dreamed the noise? If she got to the telephone and made the call successfully, would the police arrive to find Taylor embarrassed and she herself ashamed she'd made a fuss for nothing?

Then another subdued crash echoed from the kitchen, and she knew this was not her imagination. The knob felt slick under her perspiring hand, but she turned it somehow and pushed the door just wide enough to slide carefully through the crack. The nightlight in the bathroom warmed the polished cherry floors but didn't really light the hall. Jan thought if she could quickly slide past that thin puddle of light she wouldn't even cast a shadow.

Another crash, and she knew she couldn't wait for even one more breath. Blindly she slid along the wall, judging the distance to the telephone, judging it incorrectly, as it turned out. She nudged the table with her hip well before she thought she would get there. The phone fell out of the cradle to the table, then to the floor.

She might as well have set off a bomb.

With a soft cry Jan fell to her knees and searched for the phone in the darkness. But it wasn't dark for long.

"Jan? Is that you?"

Jan jumped up. "Get in your room and lock your door!"

Taylor, whose room was on the other side of the kitchen, came out instead and turned on the kitchen light, nearly blinding Jan. Taylor sounded sleepy. "What's going on?"

Jan searched wildly for the intruder. Taylor walked right past the spot where Jan had imagined him, her sleepy face screwed up in question.

"Are you okay?"

"There's somebody in the house!"

Taylor looked around, then walked to the wall and flipped a switch, and the hallway, too, was suddenly bright with light.

"Were you dreaming?" she asked.

"No!" Jan took her arm. "I heard —"

Another crash from the kitchen. She stepped forward to shield Taylor, but nobody was there.

"Is that what you heard?" Taylor put her hand gently over Jan's and left it there. "Listen, that's our ice maker. It scared me at first, too, until I figured out what it was. Sometimes it's perfectly quiet, and sometimes like tonight the darned thing sounds like Godzilla trampling Manhattan, but honestly, it's harmless. I even had the repair

156

guy out to look at it, but he said it's this particular model and they're all like that. There's nothing we can do about it except replace it with something more expensive."

"Ice maker?"

"It's awful, I know. I'm sorry. I would have warned you, but I just didn't think about it. Maybe I ought to disconnect it." Taylor paused. "What were you going to do out here?"

"Call 911."

"Glad you didn't, although it would have made their night, I'm sure."

Jan felt tears filling her eyes, then, despite her best efforts, slipping down her cheeks.

"Hey." Taylor put her arm around her. "I'm so sorry. You must have been terrified. Did you think your ex had found you?"

Jan had never thought of Rex that way. Her ex. Not officially, of course. How did you divorce a man without revealing your whereabouts? But in every other way . . . ?

She nodded, as much to her own question as to Taylor's. "I was afraid." She sniffed. "He might hurt you."

"If you believed that, you were beyond brave to come out into the hall and try to make the call."

"Please, I'm sorry I woke you. But can we check around a little, just to be sure?"

157

"We'll check. Then I'm making us some herbal tea." When Jan began to protest, Taylor stopped her. "We both need it. Humor me, okay? Grab the phone and get ready to dial if we need to."

Ten minutes later Jan was sitting on the sofa beside Taylor sipping a steaming cup of chamomile and mint tea. She wasn't sure what made her feel worse. Believing that an ice maker was an intruder? Waking Taylor from a sound sleep? The knowledge that for the rest of her life every unexpected noise would make her tremble this way?

"My parents were complete opposites," Taylor said. "My father's unbelievably tactful and understanding. My mother was blunt to a fault. If she thought something needed to be said, she said it."

Jan wondered where she herself fit on that spectrum. Her job as a parent had been to soften everything her husband did or said. But if she hadn't married Rex, who would she be?

"I'm more like Mom," Taylor continued. "I've tried to be more like my dad, but so far I haven't been too successful. Tonight, though, I'm going to be Mom. You've been through so much, Jan. More than most people could handle. I know it's marked you. You don't have to tell me. How could it not? I just wonder if you need to talk to somebody who could help you make this transition. Somebody who could listen and guide you through the worst."

"A shrink?" Jan managed a laugh. "He would think I was so crazy for staying with Rex all those years, he would probably lock me away."

"Domestic abuse is never simple. He or she would know that, and it's not a shrink's job to judge you, anyway. But actually I was thinking of a friend of Harmony's and mine, one of the goddesses. Her name is Analiese, and she's a minister."

"I went to my own minister once, and I told him what was going on at home. I thought he would help me work out what to do. He told me it was my job to stay with Rex and make him happy, that like Daniel, a good wife would find a way to tame the lion in her den, so I just needed to be a good wife."

"What kind of church was that?" Taylor sounded horrified.

"One Rex carefully chose for us."

"Oh . . ."

"I don't trust ministers. I'm sorry."

"You need to tell your story to somebody, don't you? To get it out in the open and look at it?"

"I *am* telling it." Jan took a sip and considered how much to say. But in the end, what difference did this make? Taylor wouldn't tell anybody, and she had nothing to be ashamed of.

"Moving On gave me a little minirecorder a couple of months ago. They told me to record what had been happening over the years so there would be evidence in case . . ." She didn't want to think about "in case."

Taylor figured it out. "In case something happened to you before they could get you away."

Jan nodded. "Tiny little cassettes. I was able to pass them on without a problem. I just dropped them in the mail or slipped them to somebody the few times we were able to meet and go over plans. Bea gave them back to me when she left me here. She made copies for their records, but she wanted me to have the originals. So, you see, I'm telling my story, even though nobody's ever going to hear it but me."

"Has it helped?"

"It has."

Taylor was silent so long that Jan thought the topic had ended. Then she said, "Have you thought about making them available to other women?"

"Making what available?"

"The tapes. Have you ever heard of pod-casts?"

When Jan shook her head, Taylor went on. "Podcasts are audio files played over the internet. People can listen on their computers. They have all different kinds. Travel advice, how to fix your car or make a soufflé, philosophical ramblings, anything. There are directories divided by subjects, region, et cetera. People who need advice or just encouragement can find a subject that's important to them and listen."

"But those must be professionals making them."

"Not everybody. Not by a long shot. I was just thinking that you have the tapes, and with some editing you could make them into podcasts. We could put them online for you. You could change enough of the details that nobody would know who was speaking. We could even change the sound of your voice. Maddie's father has his own recording studio. He would be happy to help."

"I don't have anything to say. I lived this. Who wants to hear the details?"

"Are you kidding? Other women going through it. Women who need to know that even after years of abuse, you got away. And how about the women who don't understand how something like this ever happens, who believe no reasonable, intelligent woman could ever get herself into your situation? Maybe it would help them, too. Maybe they would be more careful themselves, or reach out to somebody they're afraid might be a victim."

Jan wanted to say no. What did she have to offer except a life in which she had failed on every front?

"We all have something to give," Taylor said, when she didn't answer. "Maybe your *story* is the gift you need to share. You were a victim for so many years, but now you've taken back your life."

Jan couldn't manage a smile. "I wouldn't go that far."

"You can't see it, but you've made big steps. Maybe putting your story out there for other people to hear is the next one. Or a future step, at least?"

"Do I tell the story of the night I almost reported an ice maker to 911?"

"A little humor might be appreciated."

"I can't imagine what I could have to say."

Taylor drained the last of her cup and stood. She reached out and laid a hand on Jan's shoulder. "But don't you see? You've already said it. Now you just have to decide whether you want anybody to hear it."

CHAPTER 11

From the audio journal of a
forty-five-year-old woman, taped for the
files of Moving On, an underground
highway for abused women.

Surely one of the worst things a woman can
do is have a baby to strengthen her marriage. Abuse often escalates after the pregnancy test is positive, and one in every six
women is abused during pregnancy. Even in
a happy family, preparing for a new family
member is a stressful time, both emotionally and financially. In an abusive marriage?
A man who wants the world to center on
his needs may not want to put up with a
wife who no longer has the energy to meet
them. He probably won't like sharing the
limelight with a squalling infant.

The Abuser wanted children, most notably
a son. His own father had deserted him
when he was a toddler. He had been raised

by a flighty mother who, in between hope-less love affairs with unsavory men, spoiled him to make up for his father's abandon-ment. Even though he hadn't known a father's love or a mother's discipline, he was certain he would be the perfect parent.

I was less enthusiastic. In some ways I was still a child myself. I also found the Abuser's demands tiring, and I wondered if adding a child would completely exhaust me. By then I knew child care would be entirely my domain. The Abuser would return home in the evening and expect a clean house and warm meal. I would need to schedule the baby's needs around his and pretend I was happy to do so.

The Abuser convinced me not to take my birth control pills by hiding them. They were dangerous, he claimed, a heavy dose of hormones draining into my delicate feminine system. I used a diaphragm in-stead, but not always. There were times his sexual demands made it impossible to use it in time. He always assured me that the tim-ing was wrong to get pregnant, but it was no surprise to either of us when we learned his calculations had failed and I was going to have a baby.

I can't pretend a part of me wasn't happy. I've always loved children, and before my marriage I had hoped to teach them. I told myself if we were a real family, the Abuser would finally be content. He would dote on our child as I foolishly believed he doted on me. And once he saw I was still devoted to him, his fears would ebb. He would have the happy, secure family he hadn't experienced as a child and become the husband I knew he could be.

When he learned the child inside me was the son he had yearned for, he said he wanted nothing more from his life than to mold his little boy into a man just like him.

I didn't sleep that night, fearing what life would be like for the helpless creature growing inside me.

Adam checked out three apartments before he settled on one in an old house so close to Asheville's downtown he could jog to Pack Square if he ever felt so inclined. In its twentieth-century heyday the house had probably been attractive enough, but now it sagged sadly on its foundation. If houses had feelings, this one was probably disheartened by the way it had been divided into four lackluster apartments with no attempt to preserve architectural integrity. The do-it-yourselfer who'd made the changes had used cheap paneling and cheaper vinyl flooring, all now showing decades of wear.

Adam lucked out with the smallest of the four units and, happily, the most isolated. He only had to climb two flights to a converted attic with a window air-conditioning unit that hummed loudly enough to drown out the other residents' stereos or televisions.

On his first morning of occupancy, as he finished putting away the contents of his duffel bag, he debated removing the dusty plastic flower arrangement on the dresser and the 2003 calendar with photos of the Pioneer 10 spacecraft on the wall. In the end he left both. He didn't really care how the place looked. He had a fridge, a two-burner stove, a bed and a shower. He could buy anything he needed for the kitchen right in town. This wasn't his dream home, and he wasn't going to stay in Asheville longer than he had to. The apartment was better than the rent-by-the-hour motel on the highway, and the air conditioner was more acceptable than the hallway ice machine.

"Home, sweet home." He punctuated this by stowing the empty duffel under the bed.

These days he never wore a watch, and since the room had no wall clock he pulled out his smart phone to check the time. He had taken exactly half an hour to move in, and that long only because he had been forced to chase down the landlord to get his key. The well-beyond-senior, who owned three houses on the street, had forgotten to meet him downstairs as planned, which wasn't so bad. If the old guy forgot things that easily, when Adam pulled up stakes he might forget he had ever lived here, too. Adam had paid three months' rent up front, along with a hefty security deposit in lieu of a credit check. Once Adam left, his landlord would have a nice little nest egg and an empty apartment he could rent all over again.

Time to get busy.

Pocketing keys, phone and wallet, he reconsidered his decision not to add a wireless alarm to the inside of the door. He had a good one in his car, and installation was quick and simple. But what did he have here that anybody might want? He was traveling light, the way he always did, and even if somebody pulled out a credit card and made swift work of his flimsy lock, there was nothing in the room to steal, nothing that indicated anything that was true or important about him. He carried everything that mattered on his person.

It was better not to make a fuss.

He locked the door, since that was expected behavior, and made short work of both flights of stairs. As he clumped past the other apartment doors, he noted a dog whining inside one and the odor of incense from another. He hoped the person burning incense wasn't also a candle freak who fell asleep with flames flickering in substandard candleholders. The old house would go up quickly.

Of course, the first thing he'd checked before he told the landlord he would take the apartment was the safety of the outside metal stairway leading from his apartment to the ground.

While the house had no yard to speak of, it did have a muddy parking spot for each unit. His was the closest to the street, which suited him perfectly. He unlocked his SUV and climbed in.

He didn't like or dislike Asheville. His job could be done anywhere, and there was no point in getting attached to a location, because he would move on once he finished. He did like the mountains, lusher and greener than the most recent mountains in his past. He liked the diversity, too. The only thing predictable about this town was its unpredictability. That made his job more interesting, his life more interesting. And considering how boring most of his days were, that was a bonus.

He didn't have to drive far. Ten minutes later he was parked on a street lined with trees that were just beginning to change color. He was sandwiched between a pickup and a Honda CRV, and while his view wasn't blocked, the trees and his heavily tinted windows acted as a disguise.

The houses he could see were simple enough, not identical cardboard cutouts, but built some years ago from an array of styles. A few were two story; more were not. Many had been renovated. Some showed impish charm, with statues in yards, and bright paint on porches and shutters. Others were staid and traditional, with the requisite petunias fading in flower beds and new chrysanthemums in concrete planters.

The house he turned his eyes to was neither impish nor traditional, but sleek and clever, with landscaping that was deceptively simple, almost Asian in style. He knew a little about the owner and wondered if she was the one who'd done the work or the design.

He hoped to learn a lot more very soon.

Adam slid down into his seat and made himself comfortable. Then he reached over to open his glove box and take out a granola bar to go with the coffee he'd stopped for on the way.

"Breakfast." He unwrapped the bar and took a bite, screwing up his face in distaste. "But not lunch."

A man could learn a lot in a short time. That was exactly what he was hoping for today. That was what the man he was working for was hoping for, too.

"Will I need my key this afternoon?" Maddie, about to depart for school, looked hopeful, as if the possibility existed that she might be in her house alone, at least for a little while, when she returned that afternoon.

Jan hated to disappoint the girl, but she and Taylor had carefully tweaked schedules so Jan would be here when Maddie arrived. She tried to think of a way to let her down easily.

"I think you should bring it. You never know what's going to come up, and I might be a few minutes late."

That seemed to satisfy her. "You don't have to rush."

"Thank you, I'll remember that."

"My mom's afraid I'll have a seizure, but I haven't had one in a long time. Not since they operated on my brain."

Jan lowered her voice, as if she were trying to keep a secret from Taylor. "Moms are that way."

Maddie rolled her eyes. "Tell me about it."

"I'm going to buy a new cell phone today, and then you'll be able to call me if you need anything."

"My mom thinks I need a babysitter, but I don't."

"I think your mom is babysitting *me,* so that just makes me a friend with a phone."

Maddie laughed, her feelings obviously soothed. "Bye, friend." She left for school in a flurry of flopping brown hair and flapping pink baby-doll top. Vanilla, all fluffy fur and big brown eyes, stood at the door and whined. Then, job finished, she trotted off to make herself comfortable on the sofa.

"You two are getting along." Taylor spoke from the kitchen. "I'm delighted."

"Maddie's great. You're doing a wonderful job with her."

"She likes having you here. She won't admit it, but she's so much happier now that I don't drag her everywhere."

"She's a good student. I can't believe what they're learning in school these days. I barely knew what she was talking about when she showed me her math homework last night."

"My dad's the math wizard. He'll be the go-to math tutor when we need one."

Ethan Martin, Taylor's dad, was on his way to the house right now, and Jan would be meeting him for the first time. She couldn't remember when she'd had a conversation with a man other than Rex, who'd made sure she was never alone with anyone of the opposite sex. She'd had that brief encounter in the park with the young man with the brightly colored cap, but he had been a stranger who would remain one. She had no idea what to say to Ethan, who would be visiting often, and she wasn't looking forward to the encounter.

The day's schedule was complex. Maddie's school had started two hours later, because of special testing for some of the older students. Taylor and her father were heading over to the new studio to check on renovations, so Taylor had offered her car so that Jan could have lunch with Harmony. Jan would meet Taylor at the studio after lunch and take her home.

The lunch plans had been all too cloak-and-dagger. Harmony was borrowing Rilla's car to get to the restaurant, and Rilla would use hers. It was a simple precaution, similar to making calls using Taylor and Rilla's cell phones. The restaurant itself was in

Black Mountain, a longer drive for Harmony than for Jan, but she had promised she didn't mind. She planned to take a few back roads just to be sure she wasn't followed, although there was no reason to think she might be. No strangers had been seen prowling around the Reynolds Farm or parked on the road. They hadn't received strange phone calls. So far all was as usual.

They were meeting early enough to avoid the lunch rush and because Jan wanted to buy a cell phone before she picked up Taylor. With a little internet research Taylor had confirmed the information that Moving On had given her. She could buy the phone, along with activation and refill cards, at a discount or electronics store using cash. When she activated the account, she wouldn't be required to give information about herself that anybody could trace. From that point on, when she needed more minutes she could buy them at a participating store, again with cash.

Life under the radar wasn't going to be easy. She still had to find a job without using her Social Security number, because that number was the quickest way for Rex to find her, but luckily a job wasn't yet an emergency. A car was also essential, but Taylor had suggested that Jan find one she liked, then give Harmony the money to buy and register it in her name. There were ways to accomplish what Jan needed to. It was even possible that the government might give her a new Social Security number if she could prove she had been abused and was in danger. But right now her life and those kinds of decisions were on hold.

Because Rex still hadn't surfaced.

"So here are my keys," Taylor said, coming to stand beside her. "I had a problem with the engine stalling last week, but my mechanic did some adjustments and it's fine now. There's nothing unique about driving it. It's just an ordinary sedan."

Jan knew that wasn't quite true. The young Buddy had been an enthusiastic *Star Trek* fan, and the dashboard of Taylor's car looked like something from the starship *Enterprise.* But Jan was used to nice cars. Rex had traded his every two years, an expense he had justified, although he had never justified any make or model for his wife.

Whatever else Taylor planned to say was interrupted when the front door swung open again and a man with grayish-brown hair and Taylor's golden-brown eyes came through it.

"I'm late. I'm sorry," he told his daughter, who was right in front of him. Then his eyes turned to Jan. He smiled warmly and immediately held out his hand. "You must be Harmony's mom. I'm Ethan."

She could not make herself touch him. She couldn't have done it even if everyone's life had depended on it, if the roof had threatened to collapse on the three of them if she didn't.

Clearing her throat, she nodded, carefully not looking at the outstretched hand, as if by not seeing it, she wasn't being rude not to take it. "I'm Jan."

He realized immediately he had made her uncomfortable. She saw a flash of recognition and regret in his eyes, but he nodded as if nothing had happened and slipped both hands in his jeans pockets. "How do you like Asheville?"

The question was simple enough, basic and easy to answer. She wet her lips. "It's lovely," she said through gritted teeth, feeling as if she'd given a two-hour lecture on a subject she knew nothing about.

"I'm glad you think so. I know Harmony loves it here. And for that matter we love having her here, too."

"I'm glad." She realized that was the third two-word sentence she had uttered, but there was no hope for better. She just wanted to get away from Ethan Martin. He looked nothing like her husband. She was sure he *was* nothing like her husband. But he was male, like Rex, vibrantly so, and she felt as frightened as a rabbit being run to ground.

Taylor smoothly took over. "Enough small talk. We've got to get over to the studio before the flooring guy gives up on us, Dad. Let's walk out together."

"Did I hear you and Harmony are going out for lunch?" Ethan asked on the front porch.

"They're heading over to Black Mountain," Taylor said, as if she had been asked instead. "Jan, make sure you try the fried green tomatoes, if you like them. I had them the last time I was there, and they were amazing."

"For such a skinny lady seriously into health and fitness, you are way too fond of fried food," Ethan told his daughter.

"Jan's promised to make beer-battered eggplant for us one night this week. She serves it with cocktail sauce as an appetizer. Like oysters."

"I'll bet Jan's eggplant's a keeper."

Jan could not let this go on. She was an adult who had once thrived in social situations, and now something better was called for. She cleared her throat. "I'll have to make it. When you're coming to dinner. So you can see, I mean."

"That's an invitation I'll accept with pleasure."

They were in the driveway now, and Jan noticed Ethan had parked just behind Taylor's car. She had quickly learned never to go outside without investigating her surroundings. Now, as Taylor and her father said goodbye and pulled away, she took a long look up and down the street before she went around to the driver's side. Satisfied that nothing seemed out of the ordinary, she opened the door.

She wondered when things would get easier. Right now everything was a challenge. She no sooner got over one hurdle than the next one appeared.

In a minute she would take a stranger's car for a twenty-minute drive through one town she hardly knew to another she didn't know at all. For a moment she wasn't sure she could do it, just as she wasn't sure she would ever again be able to have a normal conversation with a man.

But what kind of life would she have unless she tried?

And if she didn't try, then no matter where Rex Stoddard was, no matter what

he was up to, wouldn't he have succeeded
in his plan to destroy her?

CHAPTER 12

Lottie looked like a little princess in the dress Davis had bought for her at an expensive children's boutique. Harmony knew where it had come from and what he had paid, because he'd forgotten to remove the price tag.

Davis had bought his daughter a dress. Furthermore he hadn't taken the price of the dress out of his monthly support payment.

She was still waiting for the end of the world as she knew it.

"You look so beautiful," she told the baby as she lifted her out of the car seat and pulled the dress back down over her diaper. And Lottie did. The emerald-colored dress with white smocking and pink embroidery brought out the green in the baby's eyes, which, after months of uncertainty, seemed to have settled on hazel as the color of record. Clearly Davis had noticed.

Lottie squirmed restlessly in her arms, and Harmony turned her so she could see the world go by. The baby's fine brown hair was clipped back from her face with gold barrettes that, with luck, might last until Harmony got her inside the restaurant.

She wanted her mother to at least glimpse her only granddaughter at her very best. Janine had missed so much. The birth, the first smile, learning to crawl. In a way it was like meeting a stranger for lunch. There was so much to catch up on, it was really like starting all over again.

Too much to catch up on, and too much to bury.

Rilla had recommended the bistro, and as Harmony climbed the stairs and went inside, she was sorry the weather wasn't just a little warmer so she and her mother could sit at a table on the wide front porch. On the rare occasions when her father and brother had been away in the evenings, she and her mother had taken dinner out to their front stoop to sit on the steps to eat. Impromptu picnics had been one way of trying to make their time together special.

Janine would love this expansive, breezy porch, but maybe that reminder wasn't the best.

Inside, Harmony scanned the room. She

liked the light wooden floor, the jewel-toned walls. She didn't like the fact that even though she was a few minutes late, her mother wasn't already sitting at a table.

She asked to be seated in a corner, and the hostess brought a high chair for Lottie, but Harmony decided to hold the baby as she waited so she wouldn't be in the chair too long.

One glass of iced tea later — as well as two gold barrettes now in the diaper bag — she saw her mother come in.

For years she had wished for this moment. She had wanted Janine to be free of their past. Now here she was.

"I'm sorry I'm late." Janine approached the table tentatively, as if she was afraid Harmony might ask her to leave.

Harmony's joy at seeing her mother was dampened by annoyance. What did Janine — Jan — expect? That Harmony, like her father, would attack her for this small infraction, these minutes spent waiting?

"You don't need to be sorry." She heard the edge in her voice, and she toned it down immediately. "I'm just glad you got here. Did you have problems finding the restaurant? Or Black Mountain?"

"No. Taylor has a GPS unit, but I stalled at a stop sign. I'm not used to her car." Jan sounded anxious, although Harmony could tell she was trying to hide it.

"What did you do?"

Instead of answering, Jan held out her arms for Lottie, and Harmony lifted the baby off her lap so her mother could take her.

"She's so beautiful," Jan said with a catch in her voice, as Lottie went to her without a fuss. "I see you in her, but she's not a dead ringer."

"Her father's not bad to look at. If Lottie takes after him a little, it won't be a tragedy."

"There's so much I don't know." Jan sat and settled Lottie on her lap. The baby immediately began to play with her watch, utterly absorbed in turning it around and around.

"First tell me how you handled stalling," Harmony said.

Jan looked up. "Other than a few words I told you never to use?" She gave a short, nervous laugh. "I wasn't sure what to do. The last thing I wanted was to call for assistance and show the police my driver's license. Luckily nobody was behind me, and when somebody finally did come up, I just waved them around. After the car sat awhile I tried it again, and it started right up."

The words had all come out in a rush.

Harmony realized her mother must have been really frightened. "I hadn't thought about that, about your license, I mean. Could somebody trace you here if the police made a report?"

"Anybody can be found, no matter how carefully they hide. It depends on how much money is spent looking for them, and how willing they are to live under the radar. When you left . . ." Jan shook her head.

"What?"

"Your father was sure he could find you without anybody's help."

"That sounds like good old Dad."

"If he had hired somebody with qualifications, they probably would have found you pretty fast."

"I guess I'm lucky he's such an egomaniac."

"It's hard to hear you talk that way, Harmony," Jan said gently.

Harmony felt a flash of anger. "You think he deserves my respect? No chance of that. Please don't tell me he did the best he could and loved me in his own way, okay?"

Jan didn't answer.

Harmony knew she had to stop snapping at her mother. "I'm glad you restarted the car," she said in a softer voice.

"I need to buy my own. I can't continue

to inconvenience Taylor. But I think I'll need your help. The smartest thing will be for me to find one I like and let you put it in your name."

"Mom, how are you going to afford a car?"

"That's a story. Let's order first."

A few minutes later, order made and Lottie in the high chair working on chopped fruit and dry cereal Harmony had brought along, Jan sat back in her chair. She looked exhausted, her skin an unhealthy gray, her hands unsteady, as if the simple act of having lunch with her daughter and granddaughter had completely drained her.

"You were going to tell me about your financial situation," Harmony said.

"You were going to tell me about Lottie's father." Jan managed a smile.

"You first."

"It's not complicated, although keeping it secret was. I met your father after your grandparents died. He was already working in insurance — this was before he started his own agency. Anyway, he was knowledgeable about finances, and he helped me settle the estate. Of course, everything went into our joint account after we married, and because of . . . well, who he is, I lost any real access to the money."

Harmony took a deep breath. "Oh, yeah, I

remember."

"When he cataloged my parents' assets, he missed two policies. They were small ones my father bought through his lodge, just meant to pay funeral expenses and help bridge any financial gaps. He got one for my mother, too, since she was eligible. I'm guessing mail from the insurance company was returned after their house was sold, and there was nothing in any legal papers that I found about the policies."

"That's pretty ironic. Dad, the great insurance agent."

"A few years after we got married I saw one of my father's lodge brothers at the grocery store. One of those rare times your father wasn't with me. He mentioned the policies, said how glad he was that Daddy had taken them out, that he had been the one who talked him into it. So I called the company the next morning when your father was at work and learned there *were* two policies, and I was the beneficiary. They hadn't tried very hard to find me."

"And you didn't tell Dad?"

"By then . . ." Janine took a long sip of tea, as if her throat was dry from this rare opportunity to talk about herself. "By then I knew having money Rex knew nothing about was a good idea. Just in case."

Harmony knew how important this decision had been, and how courageous, because her own stomach was in turmoil when she considered what would have happened if Rex Stoddard had learned his wife was deceiving him. "What if he'd found out?"

"I decided I had to live with that. I established a post office box on my own and had the money delivered there. Since they'd died in a car accident, the company paid double. Two policies, double payments. It wasn't a fortune, but it was a lifeline. I started a checking account at a bank your father didn't use, and I put the money in there. I couldn't put it in savings because I would have been forced to report the interest on taxes. Even so, the money's enough to help me make a new start."

Harmony realized this was the answer to a question she had asked herself since leaving Topeka. "That's where you got the money to help me move here, isn't it? You used some of that?"

Jan nodded.

"I thought that, well, after I left you'd had to explain to Dad why you used money from your joint checking account to help me leave. I worried."

"I would have done that if I'd been forced to, Harmony. I knew you had to get away."

186

"But all that time you had *money. You* could have left, too. Anytime. Why didn't you leave a long time ago?"

Jan hesitated, and then she shrugged. "I wasn't ready."

Harmony considered how crazy that sounded. But how could she argue with the facts? She said the only thing she could. "I'm glad you have savings."

"I want you to take half of it. I want you to go to college. You were always such a good student. It won't send you to a private school, but North Carolina has good universities."

Harmony held up her hand. "I'll go back to school when the timing's better. Taylor's mother left me some money when she died, so I can start whenever I'm ready. But Lottie's too young right now, and I'm happy doing what I'm doing. I *will* go, though, and I'll probably go to law school, too."

"Law school?"

"I want to —" Harmony decided not to be specific. Her goal was to help battered women, but that seemed an unkind announcement. "I want to help people who need it."

"My daughter. A lawyer."

"Too bad I haven't graduated yet. You could use a good one right now."

"The law can't be much help to me. I just have to lie low until I know what's —" Jan stopped herself, as Harmony had done. "You were going to tell me about Lottie's dad."

Harmony hadn't missed where her mother had been going before the turnaround. "Dad hasn't shown up yet? In Kansas, I mean."

Jan gave a slight shake of her head.

"What do you think's going on with him?" Harmony asked.

"I wish I knew."

"Want to guess?"

Jan shook her head again.

"You think he's looking for you, don't you?"

"It's the only thing that makes sense, but it doesn't make much."

"The fire department doesn't think anybody was inside when our house burned down. I saw that on the internet. And if I know it, so does he. But he never came forward to say he was all right when they were still sifting through the ashes, at least not that the local news is reporting."

"He's still the central figure in our lives, isn't he? Rex would like that."

Harmony was glad to hear a hint of anger in her mother's voice. "Then I say we stop putting him there. I'll tell you about Lottie's father instead, although I can sum up everything you need to know in a sentence. Too much like Dad, minus the violence."

"Good for you for not making the same mistake I did."

"Growing up in our house? I got daily lessons."

Jan's eyes filled with tears. "I can't tell you how much I wish things had been different."

Harmony felt awful. Her mother had cried enough tears in her lifetime, and now Harmony was responsible for more. She wasn't sure why she couldn't seem to leave their past alone. She really was so happy to have her mother here.

"Look," she said, "we've circled right back to Dad again. Let's bury him and talk about how you like Asheville."

Jan pulled a tissue out of her purse. "The mountains make me dizzy to look at them. Did that ever happen to you?"

Harmony reached across the table and rested her hand on her mother's. "I just pretended the mountains were a wall between me and everything that happened before. But I made sure there was a pass through them for you, Mom. I always hoped you would find it. And now you have."

CHAPTER 13

Even though it hadn't yet opened, Taylor was already unreasonably proud of Evolution, the health and fitness studio she was creating in a former warehouse in Asheville's River Arts District. She was also terrified she would fail.

The River Arts District housed a variety of artists and eclectic studios in vintage factories and other historic buildings. The studios were often open, and tourists and locals prowled the area to enjoy the intimate and innovative restaurants, as well as opportunities to speak with the artists themselves. The hilly landscape, the distant mountains and the French Broad River added to a unique ambience, and from the beginning Taylor had pinned her hopes on finding the perfect building right in the midst of it.

Evolution sat above the French Broad River — and above the floodplain — with its own vintage brick patio to enjoy the view. Originally the building had been used to store agricultural supplies, and then it had housed transients, until a fire gutted the first floor. Decades of abandonment and neglect had followed, until only a renaissance of the area and Ethan Martin's keen eye had brought it back to life.

Taylor knew that without her father's help she would never have visualized the possibilities. And without her mother's help she wouldn't have been able to afford it. Even though Charlotte had died months before her daughter first saw the building, Taylor still thought of the studio as a family affair. Her mother's legacy had financed it; her father had designed the renovations and overseen the work. And she? By trusting her own good instincts, which insisted a studio like the one she envisioned would flourish here, well, she was making the commitment of a lifetime.

If she failed, of course, she would have used up a significant part of her inheritance, and Maddie would no longer have as many choices for her future.

As they stood gazing at the sign over the studio front door, Ethan must have seen the mix of expressions on his daughter's face, because now he rested a hand on her shoulder. "You've come this far. You'll go the distance. Don't worry."

Taylor rarely admitted doubt. Not about anything. But today her heart was too full for evasion. "I can't believe I did this. What was I thinking?"

"That you're an intelligent lady with a keen eye and excellent judgment? That all the research you did pointed to buying the building and going for broke?"

"That last part? Broke? That's the part that worries me."

"You have enough money to see you through the first couple of years."

"Not as much as I did before we discovered *all* the floors had to be replaced."

"I'm sorry. I was hopeful we could salvage more upstairs."

"In the long run it's probably better. The new floors are stronger, resilient." She turned to smile at him. "And it's unlikely anybody's going to slip on them and sue me."

For the yoga classes they had chosen a special environmentally friendly flooring with superior traction, shock absorption and waterproofing, which was being installed this afternoon. For the rest of the building — the workout rooms, the café, the classroom — Taylor had gone with strand-woven bamboo, which was already in place. Once ancient layers of linoleum had all been removed, the original fir floors were so warped and damaged that even Ethan, who lived to salvage and reuse, hadn't been able to save them.

Ethan slung his arm over his daughter's shoulders. "You're going to be okay. With all the interest in this area, even if you decide you don't like owning a business you'll be able to sell the building for everything you put into it and more."

"I think Mom would like what we're doing here. I hope Evolution will change lives in a good way. That would make her happy."

"Everybody who walks through these doors will be healthier after your classes and the food at the café."

"Maybe we'll even make a vegetarian out of *you.*"

He laughed, and she playfully punched his arm. In reality she had given up on changing her father's eating habits and settled for knowing that the nights he ate dinner at her house, he consumed at least some of the vegetables he needed for the week.

From the second floor she heard a loud crash, followed by a curse. She winced. "I hope this new wave of workers will actually be finished with the floor when they say they will. The painters come in to finish up on Thursday and Friday."

"They're competent. You don't have enough experience to be amazed at how quickly this all came together. It's small stuff now. I'm sure your classes will start on time." Ethan checked his watch, squeezed her shoulder and stepped away. "I'm going to be late for my appointment if I don't head out. Jan's coming to pick you up in time to get you home to meet Maddie?"

"We have it all worked out." Taylor hesitated, then added, "I know she didn't make much of an impression today, but I think men frighten her, which makes sense after what she's been through. You'll give her the benefit of the doubt?"

"It doesn't matter what I think, but I'll be using the workshop from time to time, and she'll have to get used to seeing me around your house."

Ethan's workshop was in Taylor's backyard, and the plan had always been for him to continue using it for woodworking projects. He had built all the cabinetry for the Evolution office there, as well as shelving for the studios.

"She needs time to adjust," Taylor said.

"I think it's great you've opened your

194

house to her."

She heard the doubt in his voice and spoke to it. "But you would be happier if she didn't treat you like a stalker."

"I just hope with help she'll be able to live normally someday. Only I don't know how possible that is, do you? Especially when she's still worried every minute that her husband will find her."

"Analiese came up with a great motto for the goddesses. Ways for us to think about helping. Have you heard it?"

"I don't remember."

"Abandon perfection. Welcome reflection. Nurture connection." Taylor paused. "And to that I think we need to add 'offer protection.' "

He still looked skeptical. "You're certainly nurturing connection by having Jan in your house. Does she talk to you?"

"She doesn't bare her soul, but she *has* shared a little of what she's feeling. It's a good start. And Maddie likes having her there."

"I worry about the protection part. All of you alone in the house. If her husband really is looking for her . . ."

"The group that helped her escape was very careful, and she's more than cautious. No cell phone records. No credit cards. I'm guessing she'll be looking for a job where she can be paid under the table."

"You be careful, too."

"I promise. I'm installing a security system next week."

"My meeting's going to last a couple of hours, but if something comes up . . ."

"Nothing will. Stop worrying."

Ethan gave her a hug and a peck on the cheek before he left for his car.

Taylor stayed where she was and continued to stare at the building. She planned to start slowly, but classes were set to begin the following Monday, hopefully indoors, not outside on the patio, and she already had sign-ups. Unless she couldn't find experienced and reliable staff, the café would open next month. Luckily, in a town where half the population had worked in food service, she wasn't expecting a problem. In fact, a candidate for chef was supposed to be on his way here for an interview, which was why she hadn't asked her father to drop her off at home before his meeting.

From the street the building was attractive. The scarred brick facade had been painted a blue that wasn't quite navy, not quite royal, and the narrow window trim was forest-green with burgundy ledges. The sign, which she had agonized over, would go up tomorrow: "Evolution" painted in white over a sun rising between mountain peaks. She'd had T-shirts made with the logo for staff, and dozens more to sell at cost in the café. If people wore them around town, that was free publicity for her new venture. In fact, she was wearing one herself.

She had asked Cristy Haviland, the Goddess House caretaker, and Cristy's friend Dawson Nedley, to do the landscaping. She was pleased with their ideas, and while the flowering shrubs would take a year or two to settle in, bloom and look thoroughly at home, the chrysanthemums, lamb's ears and ornamental grasses in front of them already looked as if they belonged there. While fall wasn't the right season for tender herbs in the long planters that walled the patio in on three sides, Cristy and Dawson had tucked hardier oregano, thyme and chives between ornamental cabbages and kale.

She was nearly ready for business.

Behind her somewhere on the street she heard a car door slam, then footsteps heading in her direction. She only turned as they drew closer.

"Taylor Martin?" a deep voice asked.

"You're a little early. Always a good selling point."

"Am I?" He sounded surprised.

Taylor was surprised, too, not by how prompt the man was but by her immediate almost visceral reaction. He was tall and broad-shouldered, not heavy but muscular, substantial. She wasn't sure what she had expected, but not somebody who looked more apt to butcher a cow and roast it over a campfire than to create wheatgrass-pomegranate smoothies and tofu wraps. He was carrying a notebook and nothing else.

She pulled herself together and managed a polite smile. "Would you like to see the space first? Then we can talk about your ideas for using it."

He hesitated before he gave a quick nod. Tanned skin and a prominent nose set off dark blue eyes. His hair was dark and cropped short, and there was no sign of tattoos, although who knew what lay under his white polo shirt?

A thought she wished she had avoided.

She started inside. "They're laying flooring upstairs, so it's pretty noisy inside. But the downstairs is nearly ready. And the café and kitchen are all finished, although we're still waiting for some of the equipment. We need a menu and supplies. I'll pay my chef for time organizing both before we open."

He fell in step beside her. "What are you planning to serve?"

She thought that had been clear enough in the emails they had exchanged, but as she opened the front door and ushered him inside she humored him. "Smoothies, of course. Hopefully some originals so they aren't like everybody else's. You can't throw a stone in Asheville without it landing in a smoothie."

He grunted, as if he agreed that was marginally funny.

She went on, speaking louder over the din above them. "Fresh juice, herbal tea. I think we have to offer coffee, but fair trade and organic, of course."

"Of course."

She didn't look, but if she'd had to guess, she would guess he was smiling.

"Sandwiches, with at least half appropriate for our gluten-free menu. Salads. Healthy desserts and breads. We'll contract for those. There are plenty of people who can bake for us. Everything doesn't have to be vegan, but at least half of what we offer should be. Soup when the weather's cool, which means as soon as we open the café."

"It sounds like a lunch menu."

She took the narrow hallway that divided

the downstairs studio from the reception area that also held her office. The café with room for six small tables and a counter with stools was in the back. "Well, like I told you, we won't be open for dinner. But I do like the idea of packaging some of what we serve and offering takeout if we find there's interest. That way our students can pick up something to take home after classes."

"You could waste a lot of food that way."

"Maybe not. I'd like to partner with a homeless shelter or maybe a women's shelter and take our leftovers to them." She glanced at him. "Have you ever been part of anything like that?"

"A time or two I helped make sure MREs got to relief workers who needed them."

"MREs?"

"Meals ready to eat. Military-style."

"You were in the military? I didn't notice that on your résumé."

They were in the café now, with its soothing sage-green walls, shining bamboo floors and Baltic-brown granite counter opening to the kitchen beyond.

"Miss Martin, I never sent you a résumé, although I did bring one today." He opened his notebook to show her a neatly typed sheet. "I think there's some confusion about who I am."

She had no choice but to face him. "You're not Dante Gilberto?"

"No, my name's Adam Pryor. Somebody in town told me you'll be offering an array of classes here, and I'm looking for a place to teach self-defense. I'm a third-degree black belt with a load of experience, and I think I would be an asset."

At lightning speed Taylor ran over their few minutes together and realized that at no time had she asked him for his name. She had just assumed he was Dante, arriving a few minutes earlier than planned.

Why? Because he'd known her name and used it? Because with the olive-toned skin and strong nose she had assumed Italian heritage? She thought of Jan, who had to think about her own security with every move she made. Clearly Taylor could learn a thing or two about being cautious.

She tried not to sound as embarrassed as she felt. "This has been really careless of me. I jumped to conclusions. Dante's supposed to be here in a few minutes for an interview. I guess if I'd been paying enough attention I would have noticed you seemed kind of foggy about our so-called emails."

"I liked the tour, anyway. And your plans for the café, but I can't cook, unless you count pouring milk on a bowl of cereal."

"Good cereal? Whole grain? Nuts, fruit?"

He smiled, and she felt the same buzz of electrical energy she'd felt earlier when she turned to see him standing there. He had a slightly sardonic smile, as if he thought the world was a pretty silly place. Adam . . . what? Pryor? Adam Pryor might not be every woman's cup of tea, but as rusty as she was in the matters of men and women, he seemed to be hers.

"I don't have any plans to offer self-defense classes," she said. "Regular yoga. We want to build a hot yoga studio."

"What's hot about yoga?"

"We heat the studio to 105 degrees."

"So you sweat a lot?"

"That, but we also get better, deeper stretches. Some people really get into it, and I love teaching the class, but the equipment I need is beyond reach just now. We'll have Pilates, Zumba, tai chi."

"Tai chi is a martial art. You're on the right track there."

"I have a tai chi instructor already." She was sorry she did, too, if not having one had meant she could hire Adam, even though the teacher was an old friend.

When he didn't add anything she continued. "I'd like to offer cooking classes, maybe some stress reduction or coaching, even support groups. We'll start slowly and build up. I don't want to poach customers from other places. I'm hoping to fill a different need for people who want a community, not just an occasional class, but a place where they'll make friends and hang out in their free time at our café or patio, and drop into classes to try them on for size."

"Classes like self-defense."

She thought of Jan, who hadn't been able to defend herself against her husband. Wasn't self-defense appropriate here?

"Who's your target student?" she asked.

"Whoever you might want it to be."

"What's *your* ideal, then?"

He studied her. She thought he might like what he saw, because his gaze seemed to warm. "Women who feel helpless in their daily lives and need confidence. Women who don't know what danger signs to look for, so they fall into situations they can't fight their way out of." He paused. "Women who aren't afraid to run and run fast if that's their best option."

"So we aren't going to pretend that women can beat men at their own game with just a little training?"

"Some women actually can. I've met a few I'd never want to go up against myself. But there are lots of things all women can do to stay safe and increase their chances of survival in a dangerous situation. The other things you're planning here are important. Strength, agility, stamina. Those things matter, but using them to stay safe is a different skill set. And in the long run, what good is anything if a woman's life is in jeopardy because she doesn't know what to do in a confrontation?"

"You've done this before?"

"Like I said, I brought my résumé."

"Why didn't you tell me you weren't a cook right at the start?"

"Because I was enjoying myself, and you let me in here so easily I thought it would be a nice chance to look around."

"Maybe *I* could use a few tips on avoiding dangerous situations."

"You're not in any danger from me."

As if on cue there was an explosive bang above their heads and, startled, Taylor jumped back and snapped her head toward the ceiling.

Adam's reaction was more marked. He grabbed her before she could even see if plaster was about to rain down on their heads, and together they hit the floor, his powerful body half covering her before she could protest or even gasp for air.

Above them muffled curses replaced the

banging, and Taylor registered the harsh sound of Adam's breathing, the heat from his body, a whiff of spicy aftershave or cologne, before she put her hands on his chest and shoved. "Hey!"

In an instant he had rolled to the floor beside her and pushed himself upright. He hesitated; then he held out his hand. She just stared at him a moment, trying to order her thoughts, then pushed herself to a sitting position and finally up to her feet again — without his help.

"One too many tours of duty," he said without looking right at her. "I'm sorry. Are you okay?"

He *looked* sorry, but she wasn't sure for what. For knocking a stranger to the floor to protect her? Or for demonstrating that he hadn't yet recovered from life in a war zone?

As she straightened her T-shirt she questioned him. "How long have you been out of the service?"

He shook his head, as if he couldn't believe what he'd just done. "Apparently not long enough."

"Afghanistan? Iraq?"

"Yeah."

She was so far removed from the reality of war she couldn't imagine anyone who had served in *both* places. "And now you're teaching self-defense to earn a living?"

"I don't expect to earn a living from teaching. I have other income."

She noticed he didn't say from what. "Do you have family in Asheville? Are you from here?"

"I'm not from anywhere. I'm an air force brat. Now my mother lives in a retirement community in California, and I don't have siblings. My father died a few years ago. I like these mountains, and I thought I'd give them a chance."

"So you're looking for a place to settle?"

He seemed to shake off whatever had sent them sprawling to the floor. Anything he'd felt was now tucked away, and his expression had become carefully neutral.

"I'm not sure what I'm looking for. But I'll be around here at least as long as I need to be. Teaching's a good way to meet people and take the pulse of a community." He smiled his sardonic smile. "If you're interested."

"I don't know if I have the money to pay you."

"We could split the tuition this first time and call it done. If I stay around and you like the feedback, then we can figure out how to handle the future."

"You have an answer for everything." Despite the events of the past minute, she softened her words with a facsimile of a smile. "I might want to take your class myself. I might be able to use some defense tips if somebody tosses me to the ground for real next time."

He relaxed a little. "Do you have time to show me where the classes would be held if you decide to give this a try?"

Her cell phone rang, and she checked to see who was calling. She held up her hand to let him know she needed to take it, and he wandered toward the kitchen to look around.

In a minute she joined him there. "My chef candidate witnessed a fender bender, and he's waiting for the police to show up. I have to leave in a little while, so he's not coming today. While I'm waiting for my ride home I can show you what's here, but no promises. I'll have to think about your offer."

"Of course."

Half an hour later she couldn't help being impressed by Adam Pryor. His questions were perceptive but not intrusive. She'd been particularly interested in the way he questioned the workers laying floor in the two yoga studios. Without even a hint of criticism he'd quickly gotten to the bottom of the boom they had heard — one of the workers had gotten distracted and crashed a heavy floor sander into a stack of cement board — then he had stepped back while Taylor found out how long the mistake would set back their schedule.

He'd been complimentary, but not effusive, about the design and the renovation, and he had admired the breezy upstairs classroom as a potential site for his class. He had particularly liked the view of the river from new windows that took full advantage of it.

"I've been told the French Broad is the third oldest river in the world, behind the Nile and North Carolina's own New River," Taylor said, as they went back downstairs. "I don't know how they decide those things, but I like having the studio so near it, like we're part of something flowing this way for millennia. It's perfect in so many ways, and the local community's only getting more interesting and active."

"I appreciate the tour." He stopped at the bottom of the stairs as her phone rang again, and she took another call.

Maddie was on the other end, home from school already. Surprised, Taylor glanced at her watch in distress. "I didn't realize it was so late," she said. "And Jan's not here to pick me up yet."

She listened to her daughter, shaking her head and glad Maddie couldn't see her when she realized what she was doing. "Of course, you'll be fine. But if Jan doesn't show up in a few minutes, I'll call Sam and see if she can pick me up and take me home." Even as she said those reassuring words, she realized Edna's mom, Sam, would still be at her job at a maternal health clinic, where Taylor would never dare to bother her.

Silently, as her daughter tallied all the reasons she would be fine alone, Taylor ran through a list of people she could ask for a ride and discarded them one by one. Everyone, including her father, was doing his or her job. Stopping to fetch and take her home would be an imposition. And a taxi might take a long time to arrive. She could probably walk faster.

"So glad you're comfortable there. I'll be home soon," she said cheerfully when Maddie finished her list. "Make yourself a snack." She listened. "Yes, you can watch television."

"Trouble?" Adam asked after she put the phone back in her pocket.

"My ride's late, and my daughter's home

alone. She's eleven, but . . ." She stopped. She didn't know why she was telling him this.

"But maybe not mature enough for an emergency?" he guessed.

"She has epilepsy. She had surgery almost a year ago, and she's been seizure free ever since, but I still —" She shook her head. "I still don't think she should be alone. Because surgery isn't foolproof, and not enough time's gone by to —"

"Her dad can't pick you up?"

"Her dad lives in Tennessee."

"Let me take you home, then."

"I couldn't."

"I know. I'm a stranger. A little while ago I knocked you over and pinned you to the floor — although in all fairness, I did offer to help you up. But I'm big and you're not. You have no way of knowing where that ride home will end up, which is good thinking."

She didn't reply.

He reached in his pocket and pulled out keys. "So here's an idea. You can drive. In fact, you can drive by yourself, and tell me where I can pick up my car once you're home. I'll figure out a way to get myself over there with a minimum of fuss, but you should get to your daughter as soon as you can."

She debated silently.

"I can't say another word to persuade you," he said. "Not if I'm going to teach self-defense here. Because we both know you shouldn't take a ride from a stranger."

She decided to take him at his word. She held out her hand, and he deposited the keys in her palm. "The white Cherokee with the Arizona license plate."

"You're from Arizona?"

"The car is. It's a rental. My plans are too temporary to buy one."

"You'd really let me do this?"

"I insist. As thanks for not kneeing me in the groin after I tackled you."

She closed her fingers around the keys and started for the door. "I'll need a lesson on how to do that. I'll give you my address."

"Just a tip here. You would be safer to meet me at a gas station, not your home."

"I definitely need to take that class."

"Do the guys upstairs have a key?"

She nodded.

"And you'll change the locks as the very last renovation detail, right, because lots of workmen probably have copies?"

"Darn, you're good."

"Anything here I can steal?"

"Not yet, and even after we open, not much."

"Then I'll hang around awhile. I'll go up and talk one of those guys into taking me to get my car once they've finished. They said they were about to wrap up for the day."

At the door she took a card out of the case that held her phone and handed it to him. "Call my cell once you're ready, and I'll give you the address. *My* address, because I'm listed everywhere and you could find me anyway, if you wanted to. I'm not even fifteen minutes away."

"I'll see you then."

"Oh, if a woman shows up looking for me, will you tell her to meet me at home?"

"What's her name?"

"Jan. Jan . . . Seaton."

"Will do."

"Thank you. This really is very generous."

"I was an Eagle Scout. Read my résumé."

"I guess I'll need a copy."

He opened the notebook and handed one to her. She left him at the top of the steps and walked down to the road, where she saw his car. She unlocked the door, then nodded. He was still standing there when she drove away.

CHAPTER 14

Adam arrived at Taylor's doorstep just minutes after she called to tell him where to pick up his car. In the interim she had satisfied herself that Maddie was not only fine but basking in the joys of being home alone for a full half hour. She had also combed her hair and shed her clunky sneakers for sandals, telling herself as she did that she would have done both even if Adam Pryor wasn't on his way.

Okay, sandals, maybe, hair, most likely not. But she could pretend.

When he knocked she called for him to come in. She was putting the finishing touches on iced tea when he opened the door.

He filled the doorway but didn't enter. "How did you know that was me? For that matter, how do you really know that 'me' is a safe person to let inside?"

"I read your résumé. Even if I didn't think

you were safe, you could batter down my door in a matter of moments."

"If that's true we need to work on your locks."

"As it turns out, you don't need to worry. I already have a security guy coming to turn my house into a fortress."

He didn't even take a breath. "And a résumé is just a piece of paper until you've checked to be sure it's legit."

"Duly noted. A glass of tea is just a waste of ice and tea bags until it's been drunk. Will you join me?" Taylor held up the two glasses. "A thank-you for helping."

"Sure. I'll pillage and vandalize later."

"I like a man with priorities." Taylor inclined her head toward the sofa and carried the tea in that direction to place it on the coffee table. "I have cookies, too, or I can rustle up something else if you're hungry."

"Thanks. I ate before I came over to the studio."

Taylor thought a guy Adam's size probably ate more than three meals a day, but how would she know? She was seriously uneducated about men and their nutritional needs.

All their needs, actually.

Adam took more than his share of the

sofa, and she took the rest. She handed him his glass and a napkin. "Sweet tea's a fixture here, but I make it with honey. Then I tell myself the lemon I add makes it healthy."

"I'm getting used to it. But I'll never get used to eating shrimp on grits. Never get used to grits, as a matter of fact."

"As long as you get used to tofu and tempeh, you'll still feel at home anywhere in Asheville. Oh, and kale. Lots and lots of kale."

He settled back against the batiked cushions adorning the sofa. "How long have you lived here?"

"All my life. That must seem odd since you grew up all over the place."

"A little, yeah."

"My dad's here, my friends, and now my studio. I don't see myself leaving any time soon. Probably never."

Maddie took that moment to wander in from her bedroom. Her gaze flicked over Adam as she spoke. "I've got this stupid math homework. I'm supposed to reflect drawings, you know, like draw a figure, then flip it over or something, on the other half of the square, and I need somebody to check to make sure I did it right. If we get all our math homework pretty much perfect this week, we get to watch a video on Monday."

Taylor did a perfunctory introduction of Adam. He nodded after it was complete. "What kind of video, Maddie?"

"I don't know, something about fractals. Mrs. Peck says it's really beautiful, but she's probably trying to sneak in stuff we need to know and make us think we've earned some kind of reward while she does."

"This sounds like something your grandfather should check," Taylor said. "Architects are better with shapes than yoga teachers."

"But we're going out to dinner, and he might not even stop by this afternoon."

"I can check it," Adam said. "I'm not too bad at shapes. I like jigsaw puzzles."

"Me, too," Maddie said. "Do you like the big ones with a thousand pieces?"

"The bigger the better. Do you like the 3-D ones?"

"Those are my favorites! I got the Eiffel Tower for Christmas."

"That's one I haven't seen."

"It took a while."

"I bet."

Taylor wasn't sure exactly why, but Adam seemed much less intimidating now that he was talking to her daughter. He was relaxed and smiling, and Maddie was clearly charmed.

Which made perfect sense to Taylor. "You go finish everything else," she said. "Then when you're done, and if Adam really doesn't mind, we'll let him go over your math homework."

"I just have a page of reading. I'll be back." Maddie headed out the way she'd come.

"She doesn't seem any worse for wear for having stayed alone for a while this afternoon," he said. "Seems like a great kid. Levelheaded?"

"It's just been the two of us most of the time since she was born. It's possible I'm overprotective."

"You're talking to the wrong guy if you think I'm going to agree with that."

"Her father says he's polishing his shotgun to scare away the boys."

"It'll be needed soon enough." Adam shifted his weight to see her better. "You and her father haven't been together in a long time?"

She had brought the subject up, so it didn't feel intrusive. "We were in high school together. I thought my mother was too strict, so I rebelled. For his part Jeremy was just doing what boys his age like to do best. As a reward for trying to see how far he could get, we both got Maddie. By the time I figured out I was pregnant, he already had another girlfriend, and I didn't care."

"If he's polishing his shotgun . . ."

"He's a good dad. We're more or less friends these days. It makes being Maddie's parents a lot easier."

"Not the usual happy ending."

"Jeremy calls it a good-enough ending. Considering everything, we're lucky to have it." She realized she wanted to ask Adam about his marital status, yet wouldn't that be too obvious? Not a job interview, but something much more personal?

As if he had read her mind he filled in the blanks. "You're lucky to have her. I always wanted kids, but I never found the right woman or the right time. And after everything I've seen —" He stopped abruptly. Then he shrugged.

"I can understand that."

He took another swallow of his tea before he set down the glass. "Are you going to offer classes for kids or teens?"

"I might after a while. Thinking about self-defense for the younger set?"

"The martial arts are great for confidence, dexterity and strength when they're taught correctly. Not to mention self-control. Self-defense is more about getting away and getting help, which isn't a bad skill to have at that age."

"You don't want to open your own martial arts studio?"

"First I would have to settle down for good. A studio is a long-term commitment."

"And self-defense is a shorter prospect." It wasn't a question.

"You can teach enough techniques in a brief period to make a difference."

Taylor thought about Jan and wondered how much self-defense might have helped her. She spoke out loud before she thought better of it. "Could a class like the one you want to offer help a woman dealing with domestic violence?"

Adam didn't answer right away. When he did she could tell the question had bothered him.

"That should be easy to answer, but I've learned through the years that it's not. A victim has to believe that she — or he — deserves to get away. Depending on how long the abuse has gone on, that might not be the case. I work on that, too, or I have in other classes I've taught. I figured out that I had to. But it's harder. Destroying confidence is the first thing a chronic abuser does. And usually pretty thoroughly."

"How do you teach self-worth?"

"First you have to be sure victims have information and support on other levels. A team approach is optimal, so every helper is reinforcing the good work of the others. Victims have to know that getting away and staying away isn't just good, it's right."

"You're a big strong guy. Let's say a woman is or has been abused by a man. Won't she be scared to death of you?"

"She might be. But once she gets over that initial reaction and sees that a strong man never uses his strength to intimidate or injure a woman, then she can begin to compare what's happening at home, or what happened at home, with what's happening in class and draw her own conclusions. Having a man as her advocate and mentor, a man who tells her she can protect herself and deserves to, has an added benefit."

"You mean she thinks, my husband says I deserve to be hit and hits me, but Adam says he's wrong, that a good husband never raises his hand to a woman. And everybody in the class trusts Adam."

"Something like that, yeah."

"Does it work?"

"Sometimes. It works better if the violence isn't long-standing."

Jan had been married to Harmony's father

for more than two decades. Her struggle to get away and restart her life seemed even more admirable, even if submitting to his abuse for so long still seemed inconceivable to Taylor.

"You seem to have a really good grasp of this," she said. "I'll make a few phone calls, but I think we need to find a spot for you on our schedule. Will you be ready to start next week when we open? I can get the class on the website immediately if you write it up for me. We'll figure out what to charge together. And I can add it to our next round of ads in the local papers."

The front door opened and Jan walked in. She looked like the last leaf clinging to a maple tree in the midst of an autumn squall. One more gust of wind, and all would be over.

"Jan." Taylor got up and crossed the room to her. "You look awful. Are you okay? Did something happen? What can I do?"

"I'm so . . . so sorry." Tears filled her eyes. "I just . . ." She turned her hands palms up, as if words had completely deserted her.

"Come in and sit down. I'm getting you some tea. No ifs, ands or buts, okay? Pull yourself together, then tell me what happened."

Jan didn't move. Her gaze had flicked to Adam.

"This is Adam Pryor," Taylor said, understanding her hesitation. After all, this was a strange man and a physically intimidating one. "He's going to be teaching a class for me. He loaned me his car so I could get home to be with Maddie when you were late. He's here to pick it up. Adam, this is Jan."

Jan gave the most perfunctory of nods. "Is Maddie . . . okay?"

"Happy as a clam that she got to spend a little time alone. But you don't look okay. Come in and sit down."

Jan's gaze flicked back to Adam; then she frowned. "I've seen you."

Adam was standing now. He moved closer, but not close, as if he knew there were boundaries. "I think we met at the park the other day."

Jan stared at him.

"You've met?" Taylor asked. "That's a coincidence."

"You told me I was too young to write off my life," Jan said to Adam.

"If I did, I apologize for being obnoxious."

"It wasn't obnoxious. It was helpful."

He smiled. Taylor just glimpsed it, but she thought how kind a smile it was, as if Adam

222

understood he was dealing with the walking wounded.

Taylor's doubts about the self-defense class ended. If she had any doubts that spending more time with Adam Pryor was a good idea, well, they slunk back into her unconscious just a little further.

"Your car . . ." Jan had turned back to Taylor. "I'm sorry. It just died on me. Nothing I did to restart it worked."

"Damn." Taylor saw Jan wince. "Not damn — darn — *you,* Jan. Of course not. Darn the car. Darn me for believing my repair guy when he said he'd fixed the problem. It's not your fault. It's the car's fault. I'm just so sorry you had to deal with it."

"I thought —" Jan stopped.

Taylor could only imagine what she had thought. That Taylor would blame her, because wasn't Jan always wrong? That Taylor would be furious, because, well, that one was obvious. That Taylor might even ask her to leave since she had failed to live up to her part of their bargain. Taylor wanted to hug the other woman, but something told her not to.

"You probably thought you did something to make it stall," Taylor said instead, "but trust me, you didn't. So what did you do with it? I wouldn't blame you if you just left it on the side of the road." She saw by Jan's expression that she had hit that nail squarely on the head. In a flash she understood why. What else could Jan have done? After all, giving her license to a police officer who would jot it down for his records would set up a whole new round of problems.

"That was the perfect solution," Taylor said. "Now I can call my mechanic and tell him to get himself to wherever you left it and haul it into the shop so he can find out what's really wrong with it. At least he knows what's *not* wrong with it. That's a start."

"While I was out I bought a new cell phone, but I couldn't use it to call you. It's not activated yet. And there were no phone booths along the way. What happened to phone booths, anyway?"

Taylor thought that was a perfect example of how isolated Jan had been. She had missed so much. "How far did you have to walk?" she asked.

"I stalled on the other side of town. I wrote down the name of the intersection. I managed to roll the car to something like a parking spot on the roadside."

"Good grief, you've been walking and walking. Miles and miles. You must be exhausted. Go sit. Please."

Maddie came scooting in from the hallway. "I'm ready for Adam to look at my homework!"

"Why don't you two do that at the table?" Taylor said. "Jan's going to commandeer the sofa while I get her tea."

"You don't have to —"

Taylor put her hand on Jan's arm. "Of course I do. Let me, okay? Go sit."

Adam and Maddie were already on their way to the table when Jan hobbled over to the sofa. Taylor was struck by how cozy it was somehow. Adam helping Maddie. Taylor making tea for Jan. All of them here, in her house, acting as if they were important in each other's lives instead of nearly strangers.

She and Maddie had lived alone for so long. For the most part she had shouldered the burdens of Maddie's physical problems by herself. But now those problems were fading into the past, and her life was filling up with people, as if, for the first time, it was a perfectly ordinary life.

She wanted to hold on to the moment, to savor it. There was nothing special here. What could be more normal? So why did she feel so happy, so suddenly and completely blessed?

"I'll take you to find your car once your mechanic's on his way," Adam said, turning to look over his shoulder, as if this had been an afterthought.

Taylor started to say no; then she wondered why. Adam wanted to help. She needed help. Wasn't that the way the world worked?

"Great," she said instead.

He smiled, not the kind, almost-gentle smile with which he'd favored Jan, but something warmer and more personal.

She smiled back.

Maddie had said the women were going out to dinner that night, and on the way to make sure her car was picked up, Taylor had mentioned going out with friends. Adam hadn't been in the mood for surveillance, but he knew better than to let that stop him.

He also knew better than to use the SUV with Arizona tags. After he'd dropped her off at home, he rented another for a day and parked it on her street where he was least likely to be noticed. Somebody at the end of the block was having a party, and he took a spot between their house and Taylor's. Then he waited.

About six-thirty a dark red Subaru Forester pulled into Taylor's driveway, and the driver honked. When Taylor, Maddie and Jan emerged, the driver slid out, along with a girl who seemed older than Maddie, certainly taller. The women walked around the car, and the driver, a willowy young woman with masses of curly dark hair, was gesturing, as if she was pointing out features. He suspected she was giving a tour of what was probably a brand-new car, at least to her.

Tour over, the women piled in, and in a moment they pulled into the street and started in the opposite direction. He waited, then discreetly followed them.

He didn't have far to go. They parked in front of an Italian restaurant on Merrimon Avenue and got out. He made note of the name and watched them go inside. Then when there was nothing else to see, he pulled up the restaurant website on his phone and clicked on the menu. The prices were moderate in a city where many restaurants catered to tourists and wealthy retirees.

The woman calling herself Jan Seaton certainly wasn't tossing money around. She was sharing a house with a young family, wearing well-worn clothing, driving Taylor's car, then walking a long distance home after it stalled. And now she was eating in a restaurant almost anyone could afford.

They would probably be here for most of an hour. That meant that if he wanted to, he could drive back to the house and let himself in through the back door. Taylor had told him she was beefing up security. Now would be the time to search. While he could.

Of course, breaking into her house was illegal and ill-advised. He might find the information he sought, but what could he do with it? At best he would know he was on the right track — something he was fairly certain of, anyway. At worst he might end up in jail.

Did he want easy answers? They might cut his stay in Asheville short, but probably not. He would still need to watch what happened next, where Jan Seaton went if she did, and what excuse she gave for leaving. Breaking in and going through her things wasn't worth the risk.

It probably wasn't worth the guilt he would feel as he did it, either. He was beginning to develop a theory about Ms. Seaton. It was time to explore the possibilities and see if he was right. In the meantime, he needed to be cautious. He wasn't there to cause anybody harm.

Hoping he could meet that standard, Adam backed out of the parking lot and went to look for his own dinner. He wasn't surprised he suddenly had a yearning for eggplant Parmesan.

CHAPTER 15

From the audio journal of a
forty-five-year-old woman, taped for the
files of Moving On, an underground
highway for abused women.

The Abuser was kind during my pregnancy.
I carried precious cargo and could do no
wrong. These were the best days of our marriage. While he still managed my life, I was
so tired and depleted from constant nausea
that having a strong husband seemed like a
blessing.

For once he was happy to eat simple
meals, to ignore cushions out of place on
the sofa and soap scum in the shower stall.
At night he rubbed my aching back, and in
the morning he brought me crackers and
warm tea to help with morning sickness.

I began to believe the abuse had ended,
until the day I told him I wanted to name
our son after my father. Foolishly I didn't

back down the moment he refused.

That night I learned that the son growing inside me belonged to the Abuser, not to me.

I should have heeded the lesson and made my escape plan. I will go to my grave regretting that I didn't.

Had she been forced to predict the immediate future, Harmony would not have envisioned sending Lottie to spend a whole afternoon with one of her grandmothers. Yet here she was, handing over the baby, along with all Lottie's snacks, drinks, diapers and multiple changes of clothing, for just that event. This was normal family life, something she had never expected to experience, but Jan had asked, and Rilla had volunteered to do the transportation because she was going into Asheville anyway to visit a friend.

Since Nate had invited Harmony on a picnic in the afternoon, and because she hadn't felt that introducing Lottie at this point in their dating life was wise, she'd accepted her mother's offer. Afterward she would pick up Lottie at Taylor's. By then she would have been away from home most of the day, with almost no chance that anyone would have tailed her on every step of her date. They had all agreed the scenario seemed safe. After all, Taylor was her friend, and friends visited.

"I've packed half of everything she owns," Harmony told Rilla as she settled her daughter into the car seat newly installed in Rilla's car. "She'll be fine if there's a blizzard or a heat wave, and I put in enough diapers that my mother can change her every five minutes and still have diapers to spare."

She straightened and saw that Rilla was trying not to laugh. "Okay, so I'm overcompensating. This may be the most normal thing in the world to you, but to me it seems completely abnormal. I just never thought . . ." She shook her head.

"You said she's good with Lottie?"

"Lottie loves her."

"And Taylor and Maddie will be there to help?"

"She loves them, too."

"And you also packed the stroller, the Pack 'n Play, about a zillion toys?"

Harmony hadn't known what to pack, so she had packed almost everything. "And her bouncy chair. It's kind of a long time, that's all. A whole afternoon. Not like when Davis takes her. He's usually back in an hour, two tops."

"He does seem to be coming more often, though."

As a matter of fact, almost once a week. The last two times Davis hadn't brought anybody else along, either. No snooty girlfriend. No judgmental mother. Just him, along with silly gifts for his baby daughter.

So what if the stuffed giraffe took up an entire corner of Harmony's tiny apartment? Lottie loved it.

"We'd better get." Rilla closed the side door and made shooing motions. "You get ready for your picnic. When do you think you'll pick up Lottie, so I can tell your mother?"

Harmony settled details, then thanked her friend. Finally as the car pulled away she started up to her apartment to shower and change.

Twenty minutes later she was on the road. The picnic was at a farm outside the city belonging to friends of Nate's, and by the time she arrived, the driveway leading up to the house was crowded with cars.

Farm, she decided as she parked toward the road, was wishful thinking. This was a farmette maybe, or more accurately suburbia on steroids, with neighboring houses within spitting distance and a vaguely barnlike shed set against a narrow strip of woods

233

in the back. She found the description sort of touching. A starter farm, a practice farm, and she could tell at a glance that the owners were struggling to make good use of every inch. The house was small, but someone had built an expansive deck at the side, which was now crowded with people. Since everything was close together, she noted a substantial vegetable garden, a small orchard and a fenced-in area with a chicken coop.

She was almost to the house when Nate came around the side and waved. She was glad to see him, as much because she had dreaded asking strangers to help her find him as because she liked the guy. His khakis and sport shirt were spotless, and his smile was warm. He hugged her briefly and chastely, like the gentleman he was, before he took her hand and led her to meet their hosts, Karen and Jeff, who were maybe a decade older with two adorable towheaded daughters in matching polka-dot dresses. Karen's dress was a grown-up version, with a sweater that looked hand knit. Jeff, just recently out of the army, held himself stiffly but smiled easily.

Duty done, they started toward the tables set up behind the house. Nate had already commandeered a spot for them with bottles of lemonade, bright blue plastic plates and tableware. On the way he introduced her to half a dozen people. Everybody seemed to know him; everybody seemed to like him. *She* liked him, but despite being outdoors, she was beginning to feel claustrophobic.

Everything was picture-perfect. The tables had matching cloths with hand-stenciled flags and *e pluribus unum* embroidered around the edges. The potted flowers were red, white and blue, although only the colors tied them together. Each pot was carefully unique, red geraniums in one with blue-and-white lobelia, cherry-red impatiens in another accented with blue ageratum and white petunias. The pots themselves had been decoupaged with black-and-white photos of presidents and men in uniform. Each was ringed with patriotic slogans in shiny gold script.

"Umm . . ." Harmony wasn't quite sure what to say. "It looks like somebody spent a fortune decorating the place, Nate. It's so . . . so . . ." She shrugged and turned up her palms, as if she couldn't think of a phrase with enough superlatives.

"Knowing Karen, she got everything on clearance or rescued it from the side of the road. She's known for that."

"Known?"

"She has a blog for military wives, or that's how it started, anyway. You know, how to make healthy meals on a budget, how to turn military housing into a real home. Now that Jeff's been discharged, it's mostly arts-and-crafts stuff for people who don't have much money. Gardening with nursery throwaways, making tablecloths out of old sheets. Probably everything you see today has already been featured online. Her girls are getting to be as famous as cover models because of the patterns Karen designs and sews for them."

Harmony worked hard every day. If Brad and Rilla Reynolds could be accused of any mistake, it would be overreaching. They had more plans for their farm than they had hands and hours, and everybody, including her, worked hard to achieve success. But she couldn't imagine a life in which everything she did had to be perfect, so innovative and yet so traditional, that she could use it to generate business or publicity.

"That just seems so . . . hard." She couldn't think of a better way to phrase her feelings.

"Oh, Karen loves it. She really does. She and all her blogger friends. It's like a great big club of happy homemakers. You read their blogs and you really believe that rais-

236

ing thriving kids and having a good marriage are goals anybody can achieve with a little work."

"It's a crock."

Nate had been looking around, as if to see if he knew anybody else to introduce her to. His head snapped back to the front and his eyes widened. "Are you kidding?"

Harmony could feel her temper igniting, but she couldn't seem to control her tongue. "I am *not* kidding. If these people are happy, it's because they made lucky choices, or because they won some kind of heavenly lottery. I'm delighted for them, and glad they feel inclined to pep up the rest of us and share the wealth. But people make lots of unlucky choices, too, and they get stuck with the results, sometimes forever. Not all marriages are good. In fact, a lot of them are awful. And you can't decoupage over a bad life and turn it into a good one."

"You don't think Karen and Jeff deserve what they have? That maybe they worked hard to get it?"

"Nate, look around. Look how hard Karen has worked to make *this* happen, and she'll probably keep working until the last guest is gone and the last dish washed. I'm tired just thinking about it. Is she allowed to make mistakes? Is she allowed to try

237

anything that has a high risk of failure? Can she be late for a teacher-parent conference, or forget to take one of those carefully groomed little girls to a piano lesson, or even let them wear raggedy jeans and play in mud puddles? She has a reputation at stake. She probably puts sequins on their raggedy jeans and turns them into fancy shopping bags. The closest those girls get to mud puddles is to show off brand-new rain slickers Karen's created from heavy duty garbage bags or something."

"Wow. What brought this on?"

Harmony knew what had brought it on. Surrounding her she saw the same struggle for perfection she had witnessed her entire childhood. She didn't know if Jeff abused Karen, and abuse was the reason Karen tried so hard. For all she knew, Karen was abusing Jeff, instead, insisting he be part of her maniacal march to the top of the home-maker blogs and never track in mud or ask for something for supper other than one of the two hundred variations of Crock-Pot chicken she was turning into a cookbook.

Of course, maybe they were truly happy doing everything they did, and perfectly happy when they made mistakes because they could laugh and try again. But Harmony's mother had never been perfectly happy.

And even when she had been perfect in every other way, she had still borne the brunt of her husband's abuse.

"I'm sorry," she said. "It's just that I look around and I worry. That's all. Because you know what? I bet even now Karen's looking around, and instead of feeling pleased and proud, she just noticed a weed in the flower bed or a wrinkle in her husband's pants, or a flea on the family dog."

"Family *cat*. Not a dog. Foo-Foo. She has her own blog."

"You have got to be kidding!"

He grinned, and she realized he was.

"Harmony . . ." He took her hand and leaned over the table so she could hear him. "Jeff was injured in Iraq, so he can't hold down a job, because he's spending too much time in the hospital while they finish putting him back together. Instead, he takes care of this property when he's not in an operating room, and Karen supports the family doing whatever she can to stay at home to keep her eye on him. They aren't perfect. Sometimes they yell at each other, and they both cry a lot, and when nobody's taking photos they eat McDonald's and watch dumb movies on television and forget to make the bed. They're getting by the best way they can, but they'll make it."

She felt awful. "Oh, I'm so sorry."

He squeezed her hand. "Apology accepted. Now what about you? Are *you* going to make it?"

Jan hadn't really forgotten how adorable babies were; she had pushed that memory into a dark closet and locked it away where it would stay safe from her husband's scorn. Rex had never approved of the way she "spoiled" their children, how she had gone out of her way to fix them whatever they wanted for breakfast or hand-washed a special T-shirt to wear to school the next morning. He had often belittled her parenting skills, but she and the children had learned to save the special moments to enjoy when he wasn't at home.

Then, when there were no more children in the house, she'd had no one to share those moments with and remembering them had been too painful.

Now the memories, and the feelings that came along with them, were flooding back.

"You don't like applesauce?" Jan waved the spoon in a figure eight. "Not even flying applesauce?"

Lottie, sitting in the bouncy chair Harmony had sent along, looked as if she knew she'd been had, but she opened her mouth and let the spoon land on her tongue. She swallowed, but the moment the applesauce was gone, she put her hand over her mouth to seal out more.

"I guess you've really had enough, huh, sweetie?" Jan took a warm cloth and wiped Lottie's hands and face as the little girl tried to evade her. "Your mommy used to wait until I turned my head. Then she spit out half her dinner. I don't know where she kept it while she waited, but I hope you don't do that."

Lottie screwed up her face, and Jan lifted her out of the chair. She had been a young mother. Harmony *was* a young mother. Theoretically even though Jan was now a grandmother, she was still young enough to have more children of her own. So why did she feel like an old woman who had been dragged behind an ice-cream truck after three hours of her charming granddaughter's company?

"Let's go find Vanilla," she told Lottie. "Then we'll build another house out of blocks."

Lottie began to sniffle. The baby needed a nap — no mother ever forgot the signs. But so far she hadn't been interested in taking one, even after Jan had tried every trick to get her to sleep.

Just as Lottie began to rub her eyes, Taylor came into the living room to stand beside her. "I'll tell you what used to put Maddie to sleep. I would sing to her."

"I tried that."

"No, you don't understand. *I* would sing to her. I have such an awful voice poor Maddie fell asleep in self-defense. Her father sings like an angel, and he tells me that whenever he sang to her, she would stay awake for hours just listening — which we can take with a grain of salt since Jeremy's a bit of an egotist. But maybe I ought to give the next lullaby a try."

Jan held the baby tighter and began to sway as Lottie fidgeted in her arms. "If Harmony comes to get her and Lottie's fussing, she's going to think I'm not reliable."

"Are you kidding? She's still going to think she's the luckiest woman in the world. A mom right here in town who wants to help? It doesn't get better."

Jan had heard enough of Taylor's history to know that as Maddie was growing up Taylor's own mother hadn't been in the picture. "I hope she feels that way. I love being here for her. I just wish . . ."

"You could do it more often. I know. But two weeks ago would you have believed we could arrange this? And we'll arrange more, I promise."

In an odd way, that led into a subject Jan had been contemplating since meeting Adam Pryor. She knew from Taylor that Adam would be teaching a self-defense class at her studio, beginning next Thursday afternoon. Nobody, not Adam or Taylor, had suggested she pursue it, but the idea had grown on its own. She didn't need an invitation. She needed the courage to stand up for herself, and if she could walk into that classroom, wouldn't that be half the battle?

There was still no guarantee Rex wouldn't find her one day. And the one thing she did know was that she would never go back to Topeka or anywhere with her husband again.

"I want to take Mr. Pryor's class." She cleared her throat. "Adam. Adam's class. Self-defense."

Taylor just nodded. "That's a good idea. Why didn't I think of it?" Then she smiled. "Of course I thought of it, but it had to be up to you, right?"

"I'll probably suck."

Taylor laughed. "We'll all suck."

"You're taking it, too?"

"I really need to be sure what he's teaching fits with all the other classes on the schedule. Everything Adam says sounds great, but I'd be running in to check on him every chance I got, and that's disruptive. So I decided I ought to take the class myself. Not to mention it's never bad to be prepared, especially when you're thinking about getting back into the dating scene."

"Are you?" Jan realized she was prying. "I'm sorry. Don't answer that."

"Why not? I brought it up. And yes. I mean, I don't have to hover over Maddie every minute anymore. People keep offering to fix me up with guys they know. If I say yes, I could run into a bad situation. Adam's class might help me get out of one."

"He's a very attractive man."

"Do you think so?" Taylor shrugged, but the studied casualness said everything Jan needed to know.

"Of course, if *he* was your bad situation, he could anticipate every move you used to thwart him," Jan said.

"He's clearly not somebody you'd want to start a fight with, is he? But he's got a gentle side, too. Did you see him with Maddie? She thinks he's great."

Rex had pretended to be gentle, at least at first. Jan wondered if she would ever be able to tell the difference between pretense and reality, or if any woman could.

"I think she's asleep." Taylor pointed at Lottie.

As they'd talked Jan had continued swaying. She was glad to see it had finally worked. "I wonder if I can put her down yet."

"She looks like she's out for the count."

As much as she loved her granddaughter, Jan was delighted to hear it. Even a few minutes to regroup would be welcome.

Five minutes later she inched the door to her bedroom closed and came back into the living room, where Taylor was doing stretching exercises. "Success."

Taylor folded herself into something resembling a square knot and held the pose. "Sometimes I wonder about having more children. You know, if I find the right man while I still have working ovaries. Then I remember how exhausting those early years were."

"More for you than for most people, I think."

"Worth it once, but again?"

Jan couldn't speak to that. She was so glad she'd had Harmony, even though bringing another child into the hell of her marriage had been selfish, even cruel. By then she had known another child wouldn't change

Rex except to make him more demanding, more insistent on perfection. Yet Harmony had arrived anyway, and now, asleep in Jan's room, was the precious little baby girl who was a gift to all of them.

Somebody knocked at the door, and Jan got up to answer it since Taylor was unlikely to untie herself anytime soon. She wasn't surprised to see her daughter in the doorway, and she gave her a quick hug.

"*You* probably shouldn't have opened the door," Harmony said. "What if somebody was following me?"

"I honestly didn't think. I'm sure you were careful."

"I zipped along a few rural roads and doubled back once to make sure I wasn't being followed. It feels like a game, or something out of a movie. Not that much fun, though."

Harmony looked tired, and a little pale, not like somebody who'd just been on an enjoyable date, but more like somebody who was under too much stress.

"What's wrong?"

"Nothing. How did Lottie do? Where is she?"

"I just put her down for a nap. She absolutely refused to go in earlier. I did try."

"She was probably so fascinated to have

your attention she didn't want to give it up."

"Let me make you a cup of tea."

Taylor was off the floor now and searching for her purse. She stopped long enough to give Harmony a brief hug. "I'm going to run over to the studio. Maddie's going to be home in a little while. Will you be here to catch her?"

"Absolutely," Jan said. "You go. Maybe Harmony will keep me company until Lottie Lou wakes up."

Taylor left, and Jan put the kettle on while Harmony flopped down on the sofa.

"So, the date?" Jan asked when she joined her.

"He's a really nice guy. Cute. Polite. Thoughtful." She hesitated. "Perceptive."

"That sounds good."

"I ended up telling him about my childhood."

Jan thought that probably explained why her daughter looked so tired. "Oh."

"I went off on him about the family who was throwing the party, about how the mother clearly thought everything had to be perfect and how unhealthy that was."

"I see."

"Do you? I'm still not sure why everything hit me so hard. I thought I'd gotten good at pushing my life before Asheville into the background. I even got pretty good at not worrying about you all the time. Not perfect, but better."

"One of the last things I said to you before you left Kansas was not to worry about me."

"Did you stop worrying about *me*?"

Jan didn't know how to answer that, and one thing she had learned from her life with Rex was to say nothing unless she knew exactly the right thing to say. And even then, not to say it with conviction.

"I finally figured out there wasn't anything I could do from here," Harmony said after a moment. "I couldn't call the police and report my father for abuse, because even if they bothered to show up at your door you would have sent them away. If they guessed you were just afraid to talk to them, what could they do? And having them involved would have made your life so much worse."

Jan agreed silently.

"When I was a little girl, my secret wish was that my father would simply disappear one day. And now he has, and you're here and safe. If God is at all merciful, He will understand why I hope Dad never reappears. And maybe He'll see I'm trying hard not to feel any joy that something awful might have happened to him."

Jan swallowed, because her throat was as

dry and bitter as burnt toast. "You told your date all this?"

"He's just a random guy, but he's a good listener. It was like I was talking about people on Mars, though. He comes from this big happy family. You know how he tried to relate to what I was saying? He told me he used to be jealous of his younger brother who had asthma because he got out of every chore that involved dust or mold."

Jan knew they were perilously close to talking about Buddy. But before she could steer the conversation in a different direction, Harmony did it for her. "We're all under strain. I'm sorry."

Jan rested her hand on her daughter's knee. "Why should you be sorry? All this is part of who you are. And it's hard not knowing what's going on with everything. Wondering every time we see each other if somebody's watching. It's not exactly a happily ever after."

"Mom, it's a lot better than the alternative. Don't think it's not."

Jan thought maybe that phrase ought to be her motto. For decades she had told herself that living with an abusive husband was, under the circumstances, better than the alternative. But how right had she been?

She changed the subject because what else

could she say about that? "Let me tell you about your daughter's day."

By the time they finished their tea and caught up on their respective afternoons, the baby began to cry, and Harmony went into Jan's room to get her.

"I think we'd better scoot," she said when she came back with a fussing Lottie. "That was a nothing nap. I think she's teething. Maybe she'll sleep some more on the way home."

Jan gathered up the supplies that Harmony had brought with her, but Harmony asked her to hold Lottie instead so she could put everything in the car herself. Being seen outside together was still a bad idea.

While Harmony packed, Jan danced around the living room with the baby, then at last she reluctantly handed her to her mother.

"I forgot to tell you one thing," she told Harmony as they made the transfer. "I'm going to take a self-defense class at Taylor's studio. I start next week."

Harmony stopped fussing with Lottie's dress. "Self-defense?" She waited a heartbeat; then she shrugged. "Too bad you didn't get the nerve to do that years ago, huh?"

Jan realized that not knowing what to say

to her daughter was becoming a habit. Yet nothing occurred to her. Not explanations Harmony already knew. Not excuses. Not reminders that she'd had no way to take classes and a husband who would have punished her for trying.

Harmony looked stricken. "Mom, I'm sorry. I didn't mean . . ."

But what hadn't she meant? While Jan had protected her daughter whenever she could, Harmony's life had been blighted by confusion and fear. She still paid a heavy price for something she'd had no control over. Didn't it make sense she would be lashing out now?

"Nobody knows better than I do how hard those years were for you," Jan said.

"You and I need to get away from here and have some fun together." Harmony's eyes were moist, as if she was trying not to cry. "Do you know about the Goddess House?"

"Taylor mentioned it."

"It's up in the mountains. It's so beautiful up there, quiet in a good way. I need to help Cristy — she's the caretaker — take care of some of the garden produce. Let's go up together. Can you get away tomorrow? I'll see if that works for Cristy, and if one of the other goddesses wants to come. If so, she can pick you up. Taylor will probably be busy getting everything ready at the studio, but maybe Samantha. Or Georgia."

They would be surrounded by other women. Strangers who didn't know her. Jan suspected that was as much a part of her daughter's strategy as anything else. Fun. Relaxation.

No chance to talk.

Jan didn't know how to say no. They needed help, communication, closure so much more than they needed fresh country air, but how could she give her daughter those things?

She managed a smile. "Let's see if we can work it out."

Harmony shifted the baby to one hip. "Thank you so much for taking Lottie. It was wonderful to have you here to do it. Let's just remember the wonderful and forget everything else, okay?"

Jan hugged and kissed them both; then she stood back as Harmony opened the door one final time.

More than anything, just as Harmony had said, she wanted to forget everything else. Sadly, she was afraid that no matter how hard they both tried, that was going to be impossible.

CHAPTER 16

From the audio journal of a
forty-five-year-old woman, taped for the
files of Moving On, an underground
highway for abused women.

The Abuser had strong opinions on every
subject, including the care and feeding of
an infant. My son was a large baby, healthy
and continually hungry. The Abuser put a
stop to breast-feeding, convinced my milk
wasn't good enough, even though our
pediatrician was pleased at how quickly the
baby was growing.

The Abuser believed in schedules and
never coddling little boys. I held our son
too much. I paid too much attention to his
crying. It was my fault he didn't sleep
through the night immediately, and my fault
when the pediatrician discovered our son's
eyes were misaligned and he needed surgery.

At the same time the Abuser showed great

interest in our baby. I would find him in the nursery, telling our sleeping child about his job and the fools he worked with. While he never rocked or fed him, he paid close attention to everything I did to make sure it was correct. After football season arrived I was delighted one evening to find the baby propped beside his father watching Kansas and Kansas State compete for the Governor's Cup.

The kindness he had shown me faded away, but he was more careful not to injure me. I was his son's caretaker. Like any beast of burden I needed to be well taken care of so I could give my best. Busy with my son and exhausted at day's end when my husband demanded sex, I didn't discover a suspicious hole in my diaphragm until I was pregnant for the second time.

The day he learned our second child was going to be a girl, the Abuser shoved me to the floor and kicked me.

Today Jan was wearing shorts, and although they were perfectly modest — not a single revelation that was better left to the imagination — she felt self-conscious. She had worn shorts frequently right into her marriage, but to Rex shorts and even capris were immodest. Both had slowly disappeared from her dresser drawers, destined for some mysterious burial ground of provocative clothing, along with sundresses, halter tops and skirts with hems above the knee.

With her new shorts she wore an Evolution T-shirt that Taylor had given her, and her newly cut hair just skimmed the neckline. Taylor's stylist had angled it around her face and added wispy bangs, and the gray she had earned strand by strand was now disguised with henna. The young stylist had promised that the subtle red glow would flatter Jan's complexion, and while she had doubted it, now she was glad she hadn't argued. She looked like a different woman, one who thought she might deserve a place in the world, and that alone was worth the money.

Today both the shorts and the shorter hair were good ideas. Sunday had dawned bright and clear, as well as unseasonably hot. Before ascending the mountains to the Goddess House, Taylor had called Cristy Haviland to get a weather update. Cristy had advised shorts and bathing suits, and added that if they got too hot working in the garden, they might want to visit one of several swimming holes in the vicinity.

Despite Harmony's prediction, Taylor and

Maddie had been enthusiastic about making the trip. The Evolution Café wasn't ready and wouldn't be for two more weeks, but tomorrow the studio would open as planned with half a dozen core classes. More would be added as Taylor felt she had everything in place, but for now she thought she had done whatever was possible to prepare. She had welcomed a day of fun before the real work began.

Jan hoped the day would be fun, but the trip up the mountain on a narrow, winding road with nothing but a steep drop-off beside them hadn't been a good start. She had stayed absolutely still and silent as they climbed, to be certain Taylor wasn't distracted. Even now, when they had reached the top and the scenery was rural America at its most charming, she still didn't feel comfortable. They passed a modern general store, a lovely chapel beside a stream and farmhouses. The stretches of land between were much greater than in her former neighborhood in Topeka, but the isolation here felt all too familiar.

"I think I've become a city girl," she told Taylor, now that she felt free to talk again.

"Not a fan of open spaces?"

Jan didn't say the obvious, that there was safety in numbers, which was why Rex had settled her in the middle of nowhere. "I spent too many years managing acres of grass. Living in the country is a lot of work."

"Around here they call grass pasture or the hay field, and use it to feed their animals."

"A better approach."

"Cristy's not a country girl, but she's having a great time with the vegetable garden. It's got a long way to go, but I think it was therapy for her."

"Therapy?"

"She's had a hard time. She went to jail for a crime she didn't commit, and she came here afterward to heal and pull her life back together. As part of that she's just learning to read. Cristy's smart, but she's also dyslexic and she never got the help she needed in school. One of the goddesses, Georgia, has been working with her, and she's made amazing progress. She's not tackling *War and Peace* this week, but the last time I talked to her she was inching through *Little House on the Prairie*."

"And she likes being out here alone?"

"She's not as alone as it seems. She's made friends with the neighbors, and she cleans at a local B&B, plus the goddesses come up regularly. There's a guy in the picture, too, from her old hometown, so I

257

think her free time is happily spent."

By now they had turned off the main road and were taking a narrow gravel driveway that climbed a hill. "This isn't as bad as it sometimes is," Taylor said. "We had it graded in late spring and new gravel added. You just have to drive slowly and admire the view."

The view *was* admirable. Once they reached the clearing, Jan took her time getting out so she could enjoy it. Above the parking area a two-story log. house looked down with windows like eyes that had seen centuries of foolishness but still remained open to record the continuing story. Terraces had been cut in the hillside and secured with ancient boulders. She recognized peonies, lilacs and forsythia, although none were in bloom. The fall here, when the leaves began to turn in a few weeks, would be spectacular, and she hoped she could come back to see it.

"This is my family home, the Sawyer Farm," Taylor said as Maddie got out and sprinted up the path to the house, brown hair flying out behind her. "The farm came to my mother through her grandfather's family. She grew up here with her grandmother and her father, who wasn't good for much, apparently. They were dirt poor.

Mom couldn't wait to get away, so she left as soon as her grandmother died. At the end of her life she could finally see the house and the land with new eyes, and that's why she left it to our small group of women and asked us to use it to help others."

Jan had heard most of the story from Harmony, although she hadn't realized the house had belonged to Taylor's family. "The goddesses."

"We're multiplying. Cristy's joined us, and Rilla was a natural. 'Goddesses' is just something we call ourselves, a reminder we're supposed to practice mercy."

"You certainly have. With me."

Taylor looked surprised. "That's the crazy part of this goddess thing. I don't feel merciful, Jan. You've been such a huge help, and you'll be an even bigger help once I'm at the studio at crazy hours. I don't know what I did before you came to live with us."

Jan gave her a spontaneous hug, and they were still laughing and hugging when Harmony's car appeared. Jan broke away to wave at her daughter, then to help Taylor unload some things she had brought for the house: a new cutting board, half a dozen brightly colored dish towels and several sets of sheets.

Harmony parked beside them, and Jan

went to help with Lottie.

"Did you just get here?" Harmony asked, handing the baby to her mother before she started to sort through bags to get anything she would need for the morning.

"I'm surprised we didn't catch sight of you coming up the mountain behind us."

"Maybe you and Taylor were too busy chatting."

"Not coming up we weren't. I couldn't form a sentence. That road scared me to death."

"It's intimidating." Harmony sounded as if her mind was elsewhere, and when she went back to digging through bags, Jan and Lottie started up toward the house.

A lovely young woman with curly blond hair was on her way down to meet them with a multicolored mutt who looked large enough to consume a bag of dog food every day. Clearly this was Cristy and an unidentified companion, and when they met in the middle Cristy greeted Jan and Lottie with a smile.

"Got anything you need help with?" she asked.

"We've got it." Harmony came up behind Jan; then she leaned forward to kiss Cristy's cheek before she introduced her to her mother.

"And this is Beau," Cristy said. "Beau, show some manners."

Beau promptly sat on Cristy's foot and held out a paw to Jan.

Cristy yelped. "Shake fast before he breaks my toe."

Jan did as instructed. The dog jumped up and ran the rest of the way down the path to see if anything had been left behind.

"And how are you?" Cristy asked Lottie, taking the little girl's hand. "You look so happy in that dress. Did your mommy pick it out?"

Harmony answered for her daughter. "Her father has suddenly decided that all those Asheville children's boutiques meant for visiting grandmothers were really meant for him. But it *is* cute, isn't it?"

Jan had hardly paid attention to her granddaughter's dress, but now she looked down. It *was* cute, a bright sky-blue with applique ducklings on the pocket and yoke. "He has good taste."

"She's going to get dirty in the garden," Cristy warned.

"I brought play clothes. I just couldn't resist the dress for the trip. She'll outgrow it so soon."

They continued to chat as they climbed. The sun was warm on Jan's hair and bare arms. Now that the trip was behind her, she was beginning to relax. On the porch she was introduced to a tall, serious-looking young man.

"This is Deputy Jim Sullivan," Cristy said. "But nobody calls him anything except Sully. First time we met he arrested me. These days he just hangs around and hopes I'll make him dinner."

Sully smiled at the young woman, and Jan was pretty sure the deputy was hoping for more than dinner from Cristy.

Harmony held Jan back as the others went inside.

"Mom, I didn't get a good look at you when we were at the car. Your hair looks great. And you're wearing shorts. I've never seen you in shorts in my life."

"Taylor made the hair appointment. You really like it? I never expected to be a red-head."

"You look ten years younger. And relaxed. You look beautiful. I should have thought of the hair myself. I don't know why I didn't."

"Because we aren't together most of the time."

"And you and Taylor are." Harmony hesitated. "I'm glad she's there for you."

Jan wasn't quite sure whether Harmony really was glad or not from her tone.

"Thanks to you."

Lottie fussed to get down, and the two went inside where Jan could put her on the floor to play with her toys while everybody else planned the day.

The afternoon moved along at the same leisurely pace. The vegetable garden was expansive, but the kitchen not as much. To work productively they split into teams, some harvesting the last of the tomato crop, and some working in the kitchen to can the harvest using two water bath canners Cristy had borrowed.

Midway through the day they switched jobs. Jan didn't enjoy either, but she did enjoy working with the other women who told stories and laughed together. In the earliest years of her marriage, before she had realized the scope of her mistake, she had loved taking care of her house and yard. The first fall in her new home she had planted hundreds of daffodil bulbs in the woods in memory of her parents, and in the spring she had cut flowers every week to adorn the dining room and entryway tables. But fresh flowers couldn't change a home darkened by shadows to one bright with sunshine, and eventually she had left them to bloom alone in the woods.

By three they were all hot, tired and growing cranky, and Sully had gone back to Berle to get ready for his night shift. They cleaned the kitchen and left two dozen quart jars of tomatoes to finish sealing on the counter while everybody but Jan slipped into bathing suits. A waterfall-fed pool beckoned from the neighbors' property, and Cristy had called earlier to be sure it was all right if the women went there to swim. She warned Jan that "swim" was optimistic since the "hole" was only a rock-lined indentation less than ten yards across and four feet at the deepest end. But the water would be cold and refreshing after working in the sun or standing over a stove.

"I'm sure I can find you a suit," Taylor told Jan before they left the house. "There's a trunk of clothing in the attic, and not from my ancestors. It's stuff we've been accumulating in case anybody needs something they forgot to bring along."

"I'll just wade," Jan said, although she didn't really intend to do that, either. "I'll be the lifeguard."

"We would have to work really hard to drown in that swimming hole. You'll see."

Fifteen minutes later, after they had hiked along a path that was really nothing more than weeds trampled into submission, Jan did see. Maddie entertained Lottie by pretending she was trying to catch a monarch butterfly that lit on wildflowers along their path. The baby didn't care that Maddie, who had already lectured the women about the important migration of the monarchs, never even got close.

The swimming hole was exactly as Cristy had described it, and the waterfall was really little more than a trickle. But there were flat rocks rimming it that were perfect for sunbathing, and plenty of room to splash.

Outer clothes were shed to reveal bathing suits and, for Harmony, the tattoo of a fairy on her right shoulder. Everybody but Jan and Harmony waded in.

"I'll take the baby until you've cooled off," Jan said.

Harmony raised an eyebrow in question. "You're not coming in at all? It's shallow, Mom. You'll be fine."

Jan would rather not have made a point of this, but she shook her head. "I'm going to watch."

"Suit yourself." Harmony deposited Lottie in her mother's arms and waded into the pool until she was deep enough to sit and immerse herself.

"It's freezing," Maddie squealed. But if it was, she didn't seem to mind.

Jan sat on the edge of a rock where she

could dangle her toes in the water as the others splashed and floundered. She told herself that no one would pull them in, that she and Lottie couldn't fall in no matter how hard they tried and that even if she was wrong about both, they would only get wet to the waist.

Still, her hands were shaking when Harmony waded over to take Lottie and introduce her daughter to the water.

"It feels great," she told Jan. "You would cool off and feel a thousand times better."

"I'm fine."

"You can stand under the waterfall. If you stand way behind it you'll just get the spray. You can do that, can't you?"

Jan noticed that the others were listening. "I'm fine right here."

Harmony shrugged, and she and Lottie began to wade toward the middle. Jan told herself not to say anything. Nothing was called for, but she couldn't help herself.

"Hold on tight, okay? Slippery when wet."

"We're fine," Harmony said, as if she were placating an irrational child. "I haven't drowned her yet, Mom."

For a moment Jan couldn't breathe. The air around her seemed to sizzle with evil, and the bright skies were extinguished. She looked into the distance to shut out everything until the wave of dizziness that encompassed her began to ebb. Then she slowly got to her feet. The others hadn't noticed. They were playing at the other end, and Lottie was screeching with either delight or dismay as Harmony dipped her lower into the water.

Jan made herself speak. "I'm going back and lie down for a while. The sofa in the living room is calling my name."

Harmony looked up. "Wait, I'll come with you."

"No. Please. It's an easy walk back. I could find it in the dark. You stay and have fun."

"You're sure, Jan?" Taylor was frowning. "You look pale. You're sure you won't just feel better if you wade in and cool off?"

"I just have a little headache. A glass of water and a nap will make the difference."

"Just follow the path and you'll see the house after the garden," Cristy said.

By the time Jan got back to the house, she was no longer trembling, but she still felt nauseated, and her head was pounding. In the kitchen she took two aspirins and made herself drink a glass of cold water. Then she lay down on the comfortable living room couch, but she didn't close her eyes.

Because if she closed them, she knew exactly what she would see.

At some point her self-control must have faltered, because the next thing she knew she heard the other women climbing the steps to the porch. When they came inside she was sitting up, and she assured them she felt good enough to can another dozen quarts, which was met with groans. Still, she had broken the tension and changed the subject.

After Taylor changed back into her traveling clothes, she joined Jan in the kitchen as she tested the seals on the tomato jars. "Cristy and Harmony are talking about making dinner here, but I think I've stayed as long as I can. Do you mind missing that?" Taylor asked.

"Of course not."

"I'll order a pizza from a local place in Asheville, and we can pick it up on the way home. Okay?"

"Perfect."

"I'll tell Harmony."

Jan rested a hand on her arm. "I'll tell her. She'll understand. It was so good of you to bring me up here."

"I needed it, too. Otherwise I would have stewed all day."

Jan found Cristy before she found Harmony. They hadn't been alone yet, but Cristy had obviously been considering what to say. "Do you have a minute?"

Jan smiled politely. "I was just looking for Harmony to say goodbye."

"She's upstairs. I just wanted to say something. I know a little about what you've been through, Jan. Harmony filled me in. I wanted you to know I was abused, too. Not physically. In a different way, but by the same kind of man. It's an awful thing to be at the mercy of somebody you thought you loved, but the man who tormented me is out of my life for good now. I hope yours is, too, but if he's not, you can come here and stay with me. Or just come anytime and talk if you need to. I understand, at least a little. I want to help if I can."

For a moment Jan couldn't speak. Then she just reached out and hugged the other woman. Cristy hugged her back. Nothing else needed to be said.

Upstairs she found her daughter changing Lottie in one of the guest rooms. She stopped in the doorway. "Harmony, Taylor needs to get home, so we're going to leave now. I'm sorry I'll miss dinner, but it was wonderful to see you and Lottie today."

Harmony turned, and it was clear she had been crying. "I'm so sorry."

Jan didn't have to ask why; she just stepped inside and closed the door behind her. "I know."

"I've always known something must have happened to you when you were a little girl. I've always figured that's why you're so afraid of the water. I don't know why I tried to make you get in the swimming hole today." She paused. "No, I do know. I've been unhappy, maybe even angry. You and Taylor are so close. It's like she's your daughter, not me, and I know that's stupid and immature and —"

"And natural."

"Not for me."

"You're just human. I'd guess you're angry about a lot of things, sweetheart, and I can't blame you for any of them."

"I hate that you have to live with somebody else to protect us. This should be our time together." She managed a smile. "And at the same time, if you have to, I know how lucky I am it's Taylor. She's trying to do what I can't, the way I was able to do things for her mom. It's karma. You know about karma?"

"I'm well-read — if not too bright when it comes to men."

They looked at each other, and then they both began to laugh. Harmony grabbed

270

Lottie and together the two of them hugged Jan.

"I'm going to be a grown-up about this," Harmony said. "Please forgive me for lapsing now and then?"

"More than forgiven."

"I'm signing up for that self-defense class. I told Taylor at the swimming hole that I want to be in it."

Jan tried to read her daughter's expression. "You're going to be in the class, too? Not just because Taylor's in it, I hope?"

"No, because if my father shows up in Asheville, you and I are going to face him together. And I need to be strong and smart, just like you do."

Jan wanted to protest, yet wasn't Harmony right? And didn't every woman need to understand her strengths and limitations and work with both?

Still, she did have to ask. "Do you think it's a good idea? Both of us in the same place at the same time every week?"

"I'll be careful driving into town to be sure nobody's following me, and we'll be coming from different places. If you go a little early and I come right on time, that should help. There hasn't been a sign of anybody watching, though. I know it's too early to feel safe, but we'll take precautions."

271

"Good," Jan said, nodding. "It's a good idea."

Harmony looked relieved. "I'm glad you think so."

"We're going to come out of this on the other side. Together. Happy. Stronger."

"You used to tell me that when I was living at home, remember? I held on to it all those nights when Dad was screaming at you." Harmony looked sad. "I'm still waiting for that happy ending. But maybe it's closer?"

CHAPTER 17

On Thursday Adam arrived at seven for his
seven-thirty class. He had stopped by on
Tuesday to drop off equipment and take
another look at the upstairs room that faced
the river, as well as the sign-up sheet and
registration information. Eight women were
registered, and while he had hoped for a
few more, eight was good enough, particularly since Women's Self-Defense had been
a late addition to the Evolution schedule.

A harried Taylor had said she was pleased,
even though she and two of her friends
made up nearly half the students.

The "friends" had interested him most of
all, since one of them turned out to be Jan
Seaton and the other was Harmony Stoddard, a turn of events that had surprised
and delighted him, although he couldn't say
so, any more than he could announce that
he knew Harmony was Jan's daughter.

Tonight he wore sweatpants and a T-shirt,

and carried nothing with him. In the early weeks he had no plans to discuss weapons. He had seen stun gun cell phones, knives masquerading as lipstick cases, flashlights that fired a single shotgun cell and any number of other dangerous inventions that made the world a scarier place. He didn't plan to promote any of them. His plan was to teach awareness, strategy and basic skills, and for that he only needed the body shields he'd dropped off, plus his own good sense.

Before going upstairs he walked around the reception counter near the entryway and stopped in the doorway to Taylor's office. She was sitting at the pine table she used as a desk, talking on the telephone, but she held up a hand to keep him there as she finished what sounded like a routine call for information. When she hung up she smiled.

Taylor smiling was like splashes of sunlight at the end of a dark tunnel. Nothing was illuminated, and then suddenly everything was revealed. He wondered if she realized what a punch in the gut it could be to a man.

"We're up to ten." She raised a fist in the air and pumped it twice. "And we have another possibility, only she can't make it tonight."

He had to return the smile, because that

kind of enthusiasm was delightful in an adult woman. In a month or two a few extra registrations wouldn't get more than a quick nod, but now, at the beginning of what was clearly an ambitious project, she was probably seeing dollar signs, even respect, with every phone call.

"Your other classes go okay?" he asked, in no hurry to leave.

"Smaller than I like, but the classes themselves were good. Some of my former students have started to sign up here, even though I'm trying not to cannibalize other studios. I'm hoping word of mouth will spread to Asheville newbies, or people who've never studied yoga. The tai chi class has three students, but the first class went well. With luck they'll go home and tell their friends."

"It takes time."

"The renovation was such an undertaking. A real money hemorrhage. I need to stanch the flow."

Adam knew the value of walking through an open door. "Those business loans can be awful."

"It was family money, but that's just as bad."

He wanted to ask whose and why it was problematic, but he also knew the value of not walking too far inside when he hadn't been invited. "All those expectations."

"Just my own."

He waited, but she didn't go on. "Well, since we're talking money, how would you like to spend a little more?"

"Absolutely not. On what?"

"A punching bag."

"Really? Are we going to box?"

"Nope. But women are taught not to strike out, so a punching bag can be a good way to begin feeling comfortable as the aggressor."

"I didn't think you wanted your students to be aggressors."

"I want them to be comfortable taking the initiative if they have no other choice. A bag also helps with reflexes and stamina. All important."

"Are they expensive?"

"Depends. You could start smaller, maybe forty pounds, and cheaper to see how useful it is. You would probably want to invest in a freestanding bag and maybe begin with one you could store between classes, although that's not the best option." He could almost see her thinking. "And gloves, of course."

"Are you saying you have to have this?"

"No. I'm thinking longer term — if self-defense becomes a serious part of your schedule."

She looked interested but not convinced. "I'll file that away."

This evening Taylor was wearing shiny blue yoga pants and a T-shirt, oversize and bearing the Evolution logo, that had slipped down over one shoulder to reveal a thin purple strap. Adam didn't want to notice more than he absolutely had to, but he couldn't quite look away. He settled on an excuse. "I like the T-shirt. Did you design it yourself?"

"A friend. I should give you a T-shirt, too. They're a great advertisement. I'll bring it to class with me. Extra-large? Extra-extra?"

For a moment he couldn't help himself. He imagined inviting Taylor to measure his chest. He pictured her arms around him as she slid the tape into place.

Bad move.

"Maybe you should bring both and I'll check them out. I'll see you upstairs." He hesitated; then despite himself he added, "Want to come warm up with me? If you don't mind, I'll be asking your help tonight for demos until the other women are more confident."

"Warm up? You're kidding, right? I'm so

warmed up after teaching today I might ignite."

He didn't want to think about *that,* either. She smiled again, and the smile stayed with him as he climbed the stairs.

Harmony was impressed with Evolution. She had stopped by to register on Tuesday, and Taylor had given her the grand tour. Now, ten minutes before class was to begin, she arrived to find that Jan had gotten here ahead of her as planned and was settling Maddie in the café area with snacks and homework.

For a moment as she watched them together, Jan's dark hair swinging over her cheek as she bent over the table, Harmony was a child again back in Topeka, trying to keep a kitchen chair from scraping the wooden floor as she pulled it closer to the table so her mother could help with her homework. Scraping noises had been forbidden, as had talking in normal tones when her father and brother were watching television.

The vision evaporated as Jan straightened and saw her. "Just in time. How's your Spanish?"

Harmony joined them and looked down at the book on the table. "Nonexistent."

"You took Spanish in ninth grade."

"Do you know how many years ago that was?"

Jan looked sheepish. "A million? A minute? It seems like both."

"So, what do you need, Maddie?" Harmony asked the girl, who looked resigned, if not happy to be there. She was wearing an Evolution T-shirt, which seemed like a good sign.

Maddie pulled out two worksheets and laid them side by side. Worksheets had come a long way since Harmony's childhood. These were brightly colored and filled with silly cartoons featuring a variety of characters in motion. A man driving a car. A woman pushing a child on a swing. A dog jumping over a fallen tree. Maddie pulled out a list of words and laid it beside the illustrations. "I'm supposed to figure out which word belongs where."

"Did you learn the words in school?" Jan asked.

"Sorta."

"When I was in school, 'sorta' meant I was supposed to learn them and 'kinda' forgot," Harmony said.

"Sorta."

"Is this vocabulary in your Spanish book?" Jan asked.

Maddie giggled. "Kinda."

Harmony and Jan looked at each other. "Good luck," they said together.

"I have a lot of homework. And the answers are scattered all through the chapter." Maddie still looked hopeful.

"You have a lot of time."

"Not as much as you think. I also have to write an essay for English class about what I'm going to do on Halloween this year."

"That sounds like fun," Jan said. "What *are* you going to do?"

"Edna and I want to be the Three Bears and trick-or-treat for the food bank. You get, like, cans and stuff to give them, and maybe Lottie could be baby bear. Would you let her?" She addressed the last part to Harmony. "We could pull her in my old wagon."

"Bears, huh? That sounds like a nice warm costume."

"I don't know where we'll get costumes, but if Lottie can be the baby bear, we can try. And she's so cute we'll get more cans."

Harmony and Jan left Maddie to figure out the vocabulary words and the mystery of Halloween costumes on her own.

"She's growing up," Harmony said on the way upstairs to the classroom.

"I remember everything about you at that

age. She's older *and* younger than *you* were."

"A million years and a minute?"

"Exactly."

"For a moment when I came in, I flashed back to sitting at the kitchen table with you helping me every night. Buddy was always done before dinner."

"He was done because he just scribbled whatever he felt like on his papers, and he never let me check to see if he had done the work correctly."

"I remember the time you tried to make him."

Both of them fell silent. Rex had taken Buddy's side that long ago night, shouting that Buddy didn't need a woman telling him what to do or how to do it. Harmony remembered that something had miraculously intervened at that point, a phone call, the doorbell. Whatever the miracle, that night Rex's anger had been deflected before it turned to violence. But Jan had been careful never again to question her son about his homework in front of her husband.

"He came to me later that night, after his dad went to bed, and showed it to me," Jan said. The words were halting, as if forming them brought pain. "He was just a boy arguing with his mother, like boys all over the world. He knew something was wrong with what had happened, and he felt bad about it and wanted me to know he did."

Harmony couldn't squelch a response. "Or he wanted something from you."

"He never wanted anything from me other than what I gave him every day. My confidence he would straighten out and grow up to be a good man. My love."

Arguing about Buddy was useless. Talking about him at all was useless. Like their father, Harmony's brother had been a bully. In middle school and high school he had been suspended half a dozen times for fights — which were never his fault. At age twenty he had picked one fight too many in a crowded barroom where he never should have gone in the first place. When the fight was over Buddy was in the emergency room and his opponent was in jail. Buddy died and the other man went to prison. One life ended and one destroyed.

Score a big one for Rex Stoddard.

They reached the classroom, and Jan hesitated at the door.

"Don't be nervous," Harmony said.

"There's nothing I could learn here that would stop your father." Jan stared into the open doorway.

"What's the alternative? We could buy

guns and spend our evenings at the local firing range."

"Could you really pull the trigger?"

Harmony considered, although she thought her mother had meant it as a rhetorical question.

"I don't know," she said, cutting off an onslaught of images of her father, some threatening, some the everyday images most girls carried around of the man who had raised them. "If he ever comes after either of us, I may wish I had one."

Without another word they both went inside.

Adam sized up the women milling around the room taking off sweaters or changing into sneakers from the hard-soled shoes they had arrived in. The mixture was interesting. He was used to young women with buff, lean bodies, women who could march fifteen miles with eighty pounds on their backs. Those women had come to him for advanced training. By the end of the class they could flip or disable him while they chatted about where they hoped to go on their next assignment. These women were simply hoping to survive a hostile encounter long enough to seek help.

There were two students who were over

fifty, both average weight, and while one looked a little soft around the edges, the other obviously worked out, probably Zumba or Pilates. There were two, including Jan, in their forties. Jan, who had positioned herself on the far end, looked as if a strong wind might send her soaring to the closest mountain peak, but the other woman was short and bulldog-broad. She had perfected a glare that was so fierce it might keep her safe without any help. Everyone else, like Taylor — who hadn't yet joined them — was in her twenties or thirties, a range of body types and conditioning.

"It's time to start," he said, clapping his hands. "This class is about discipline, and that means we start and end on time. In between we work hard. But you wouldn't have signed up if you didn't agree with that philosophy, right?" He added a smile to soften his words just as Taylor slipped through the door and closed it behind her. He gave a brief nod before he asked the women to line up along the front.

He walked back and forth in front of them, meeting their eyes. "This is not an exercise class. And it's not a physical conditioning class. It's not karate or judo or anything close. You're here to learn how to protect yourself, and that's all. But let's be honest. The stronger and faster you are, and the more stamina you develop, the better your chances, right? Because no matter what I teach you, you won't be able to break free if somebody grabs you and you don't have any strength in your arms." He held up his own and made a fist to demonstrate what they might be up against.

"And you won't be able to get away if you can't run faster than your attacker for at least a block or two. And you'll need stamina for both those things and others, because a lot of the time, the first thing you try may not work, and you'll have to go from plan A to plan B. And you need stamina to keep trying."

He smiled again and waited a few seconds for them to think that over. "So we're going to warm up with some jumping jacks and crunches, plus a few other basics. It looks like some of you are no stranger to those, while some of you may not have done any recently. But this is your life on the line, so I don't need to remind you that pushing beyond your comfort zone is to your benefit. Just don't push yourself so hard we have to call the guys with the stretchers, okay?"

The next twenty minutes were painful to watch. Some of the women didn't even break a sweat. Some looked ready to quit after five repetitions. He varied the exercises, making certain to give them a little time in between to catch their breath.

He reminded them to breathe. He reminded them that no attacker waited for them to warm up and stretch, so they needed to stay in good condition. He demonstrated better posture or placement when it was needed and occasionally smiled encouragement. But mostly, he stayed alert.

Crunches were the final exercise for the night. He asked for fifty and laughed at the groans. Then he watched Jan struggle with what looked like a sit-up before he squatted down beside her. She immediately slid away to put distance between them. He considered that, then moved closer. She slid sideways again.

"You're going to hit the wall at that rate." This time he didn't move closer. Instead, he lay down on the floor in the space she had vacated. "Watch how I do it." He pulled up his knees and did a half curl toward them, then uncurled until his back was flat on the floor again.

"You were doing sit-ups," he explained, without looking at her. "You don't need to come all the way up. This is easier on the back, and the abdominal muscles get a full workout. If you continue all the way up, they just act as stabilizers, and your hip flexors finish for them. We want to strengthen the abdominals, because they protect so many organs."

He sat up and noted that Jan's daughter had gotten to her feet and was now standing over him, her freckled face twisted with some barely suppressed emotion. "I'll help her," she said.

He considered Harmony's expression for a moment and wondered exactly what to say. She was unhappy, but exactly why he wasn't sure. "No. You need to work on your own fitness. This is my job."

"I'm fine." Jan waved a hand as Harmony began to argue, as if to shoo her back to her spot in line. "And thank you for the demonstration," she told Adam. "I was doing them all wrong."

He noticed that the hand she waved was trembling. He smiled in reassurance. "Why do more than you need to, right? If half a sit-up is better than a whole?"

"I'll work on it."

He got up and stood over her. "Let me see you do one."

She looked as if she were considering flight, and then she seemed to realize how impossible it would be to get away. As if all

287

her options had ended, she lay down flat and pulled herself into a perfect crunch, held it a second and flattened against the floor again.

"Excellent. That's what we want. And don't worry about holding it." Adam moved off, pondering all the possible reasons why Jan had looked as if she'd expected him to kick her.

After crunch number fifty was completed, he gave them a breather and asked them to pull chairs into a circle while he talked about ways to protect themselves on the street.

He started by pulling out his cell phone and pretending to have a conversation while he strolled back and forth. Abruptly he stopped and pointed at one of the older women. "Want to tell me why this is a bad idea on the street?"

She considered a moment. "Your attention is on the call, not on your surroundings?"

"Very good. Let's break that down a bit. I'm distracted. What else?" When nobody volunteered, he gestured in Taylor's direction, because she was nodding.

"You can't hear someone coming up behind you?" she asked.

"Exactly. My hearing's impaired because

someone is chattering in my ear. One more thing. Anybody else?"

A young woman who looked just out of her teens answered, "I don't think you can use a cell phone as a weapon, so, like, your hands are already busy and you can't hit somebody who attacks you."

"I like the way you think." He smiled at her. "Staying safe means we have to stay alert to our surroundings. We have to listen and avoid distractions if we can. That also means no headphones, right? No matter how cute they look on television. No headphones on the street. We have to be ready to defend ourselves. But in real life sometimes you have distractions you can't control, and sometimes you have packages. You almost always have a handbag, right?"

Most of the women nodded. He explained the necessity of not carrying a handbag on the dominant shoulder and had one of the women demonstrate how difficult it was to strike out with her dominant hand if she was carrying a purse on that side or had one slung over that shoulder. He explained how important it was to only carry packages that would fit in one arm so the other remained free. He moved on to safety in elevators — although there were precious few to worry about in the area — and the importance of having keys in hand when walking from the car to the door instead of waiting to fish them out on the stoop. He had women role-play both scenarios and showed how easy it was to sneak up on them when they were pawing through their handbags.

He carefully stayed away from calling on Harmony or Jan.

"Before we move on to an important technique, let's talk about assessing our surroundings," he said. "How safe do you feel in your local parking garage? How about hiking alone?" They talked about trusting instinct, displaying confidence, having an escape plan.

Adam ended the discussion for the night, sure he would lose participants if all they had a chance to do in the first class were jumping jacks and lectures. They needed something fun to work on, something they could take home and practice.

"What's the first strategy to consider, no matter what the situation?" he asked.

"Screaming?" Harmony said.

"Okay. And what would you scream?"

"Help!"

"That seems logical, doesn't it? But what do you think of first when somebody yells help?" When nobody answered he answered for them. "You think, oh, gosh, a person in trouble needs me to do something, and I might not be able to do it without getting hurt myself. At best you might dial 911 or hope somebody else already has. But what if that person shouted *fire*?" He shouted the last word.

Everybody jumped.

"I'd get the heck out of there and see if the building was burning," one of the women said.

"Exactly. So shout fire whenever you need help. Chances that everybody will pour out to see what's going on are much better. Nobody thinks they'll be called on to be a hero. They'll think maybe they're running to safety."

"That's sneaky," Harmony said.

"Who cares?" He smiled at her, but she didn't smile back. He was getting a pretty strong vibe from Harmony Stoddard, and not a friendly one.

"The best response in any situation is to try to get away," he continued. "That should always be your first response. You don't stay to fight. If you can't get away, you scream. If that doesn't bring the results you want, you'll need to move on. Just to be clear, what we're learning next is not usually the *first* thing you try. But it might be part of what you'll need if nothing more peaceful works. Agreed?"

They were all on edge now. The aggressive part was about to begin. Some of them looked eager. Some looked nervous.

"Later we're going to practice breaking free from our attacker so we *can* run, but not tonight. The reason is that most of the time your attacker is holding on to you, a wrist, maybe, or worse. You've asked him to release you, and he's made it clear he's not going to. You have to get his attention because he's not listening. And that's what we'll start with tonight. We're going to practice horizontal elbow strikes, just one of the strikes you'll learn. I'm going to demonstrate, and I'm going to ask Taylor to help. Then, after she's had a chance to practice a little, we'll line up and each of you will have a chance to try it on one of us. Okay so far?"

He went to the closet where he'd stored his equipment and removed two body shields. "Nobody's going to get hurt," he said as he held one of the shields against his chest. "These are designed to take a lot of force. If you think you have a lot of power, get in *my* line. If you're not that secure, I think Taylor will take your blows just fine with protection. Taylor?"

"I'm game," she said.

"Game to let me use you in my demo, too?"

She rose in one graceful movement and joined him up front.

"Sometimes you need to break away when you're being held at close range," he said once she joined him. "There's no room to throw an effective punch or wind up for a good kick. We'll be practicing other possibilities, but to begin tonight let me introduce you to the power of your elbow, or more accurately your forearm just below it and the triceps area above it. But these two strikes are only powerful when you put your body weight behind them."

He moved over to stand right in front of Taylor. She gazed up at him. This close to her he noted how thick and long her eyelashes were and how her huge round eyes were tilted at the corner.

His attention was wandering, exactly what he warned his classes against, and he pulled himself back on task.

"An elbow strike won't work from a distance. It's too easy for your opponent to turn or step away before you connect. So to make sure you're in striking distance, you'll be using your opposite hand to grab any part of your opponent that you can. Hair,

293

clothing, flesh." His left hand came up, and he cupped the back of Taylor's head and wove fingers into her hair, bringing her closer.

"Now she's in striking range and it's not easy for her to move away fast enough to stop me." As he spoke he swung his torso to the left and brought up his right arm, moving forward to aim his elbow and forearm toward the side of her head, stopping inches away as she gasped in surprise. She tried to pull away, but he held her firmly for a few seconds.

"She wants to move away to avoid more, but she can't. Another good reason to grab her with the other arm first." He released her and stepped away.

From that point on he answered questions, demonstrated again, although now Taylor's eyes were narrowed in suspicion as she waited for the next surprise. He asked her to grab him from behind, which was much too enjoyable. He demonstrated how easy it was to swivel, bring up his forearm and disable her hold on him.

"We're just going to practice the strikes tonight," he said, after he thanked her. "You won't be grabbing anybody. Taylor, do you mind going first? Then, when you've practiced a bit, you can take a line."

He wasn't surprised to see how easily she had absorbed the lesson, despite being his guinea pig. She needed practice, of course, as everyone did at first, but she was a natural athlete, and yoga had taught her flexibility and balance. She was ready to hit him, too, having been the brunt of his demonstration. She smiled first, as if to say, *now it's my turn, buster;* then she swung her elbow into the padded shield he was holding.

He whooshed out loud, not because he'd really had any air knocked out of him, but to show how impressed he was. Everybody applauded and laughed. He told her to continue, and he coached a little, suggesting she twist farther and keep her arm level, but she needed little other than practice. At the end he stepped back and congratulated her. She wasn't even winded, and everybody clapped again.

"Now it's your turn," he told the class. "Form two lines." He watched as they eyed each other, then his line and Taylor's. Harmony took her mother's arm and moved her toward Taylor's.

He couldn't let Harmony continue to control the session or her mother's progress. "Jan, you'll be better over here."

"I don't think so," Harmony answered for her.

"I would appreciate it if you came over here, Jan," he said politely. "Taylor has enough people in her line."

Harmony looked as if she planned to argue, but Jan pulled away. In a moment she got into his line and a clearly unhappy Harmony went to the back of Taylor's.

"Five strikes each arm, then to the back of the line," he said. "I'll be watching both lines and coaching, and we'll repeat until I'm sure you're getting the idea. Once I'm confident, I'll have you stand with your backs to the shields, then twist to slam the target."

By the time Jan got to the front, she looked as if she wanted to crawl into a hole.

Adam knew fear when he saw it. He knew what it was like to be afraid himself. But if Jan wanted to protect herself, she had to develop confidence. And the only way to do that was to move through the fear to a better place.

"What's stopping you?" he asked for her ears only when she didn't raise her arm.

She gave one quick shake of her head.

"Let's just start by raising your arm until it's level. You don't have to hit the shield. Just twist in that direction and brush your arm against it. Can you do that?"

She was wide-eyed and breathing hard. He waited. She finally nodded. She stepped closer and raised her arm. Had her arm been weighed down by chains, it wouldn't have been harder to lift.

"I'm going to reach around the shield and help make your arm level," he warned. "Don't move."

She flinched, but she let him gently move her arm into position. Done, he held the shield with both hands again. "Now swing your arm and your body, and brush your arm against the shield. Can you do that?"

"Are you okay?" another voice said. He realized Harmony had broken from her line and was addressing Jan. "Do you need help?"

"I've got this," Adam said.

"But —"

"I've got this." Their eyes locked. Hers were stormy. "Are you planning to become her bodyguard, or are you going to let her do what she intended when she signed up? Learn to defend herself."

"You have no idea —"

"Harmony!" Jan spoke with more energy than she had shown since crossing the threshold. "Go practice with Taylor."

He wondered what life had been like for

these two back in Pawnee Parkland as Harmony was growing up. Had the two of them banded together over every little thing? Why had they needed to? And where had Rex Stoddard and the dead son, Rex Jr., better known as Buddy, fit in? The possibilities intrigued him.

"I don't see the point of this," Harmony said.

"I hope you'll stay after class for a few minutes." Adam nodded to emphasize his words. "We can work this out."

"That'll be the day," she mumbled, but she started back to her line.

"Jan, are you ready?" he asked.

She swung her arm, not hard, not powerfully, but she brushed it firmly against the shield.

"Good for you," he said. "Now let's try that again."

CHAPTER 18

Harmony knew she was a quivering mass of contradictions. One minute she was attacking her mother for no good reason; the next she was defending her whether she needed it or not. Her blighted childhood might be the root cause, but she was a grown-up now, a mother herself, and she should be able to control her tongue and actions, if not her emotions.

She promised herself she would do both when she finally got Adam Pryor alone. Her mother disappeared downstairs, and one by one the other women disappeared, too. Taylor had been the first to leave, probably to take care of paperwork in her office. Five minutes after the class ended, Harmony was finally alone with Adam.

"Thanks for staying," he said, while his back was still to her. He was putting the body shields on the shelf of the closet, and he didn't turn. "I was afraid you weren't going to."

"Well, I didn't want to."

He shut the door and faced her. "Want to tell me why?"

"Because I behaved like an idiot."

He smiled. "I feel better already."

"It's just that I know Jan, and I know she's a little timid. I was trying to help."

"Funny thing about helping. Sometimes the harder we try, the worse we make things."

"I guess."

"I can tell this class is going to be hard for her. I'm going to make it as easy as I can, but at a certain point, it can't be too easy or she won't learn a thing she needs to."

"I know. I'll try to step back."

"I'll go you one better." He assessed her, not the way a man assesses a woman he's attracted to, but the way a drill sergeant might assess a new recruit. "I want you to do something you don't want to do. I want you to drop out of this class and join my second one."

"Second class?" She realized she had been slumping. She pulled herself to her full height. "No way. You don't even have a second class."

"I do now. I've singled out three of the others who can move faster and asked them to change nights. Once I square it with Taylor we'll start training together on Wednesdays, same time, when I happen to know this room is vacant. I want you in that class, away from Jan."

She stared at him. "But I just said I'll back off."

"I'm sure you mean it. But you won't do it. I don't know what the deal is there, but she's your pet project. And you don't need a project. You need to focus on learning what I can teach you, and she needs to do the same. And while you're in the same room, that's not going to happen."

"And what if I say no?"

"Then I'll have to ask you to stop coming. Because I'm not going to teach you together, and she registered first."

Harmony couldn't believe this. She had looked forward to being in the class with her mother, to seeing her every week — even if it wasn't completely safe or advisable. Now Adam was wiping away that possibility.

She wanted to be angry, to be the injured party, to tell him what she thought of men in general, particularly those who tried to control women.

But in the end, she knew he was right.

She spoke the rest of her thoughts out

301

loud. "I registered mostly because she was in the class. If we aren't in it together, what's the point?"

"You want my opinion?"

She shrugged, the best she could do.

"I'm not a psychologist, okay? But I've worked with a lot of angry people in my time, so I recognize the signs. You're angry. I don't know why, and I don't know at whom, but you're angry, Harmony, and learning to defend yourself can help you get control. Because a lot of time we're angry at people who have used us badly, and knowing they can't do it anymore?" He smiled a little. "It's powerful."

She wanted to tell him she wasn't angry, but she knew the words would come out in a rush. An *angry* rush. Because Adam was right.

They stared at each other. He was willing to wait her out, something she wasn't used to. In the end she was the one who broke eye contact. In addition to everything else, she knew that being in the other class would be safer. She and Jan wouldn't be arriving at the same time on the same day. If anybody was trailing her to find her mother . . .

"Shall I just come next Wednesday instead? Or shall I wait for a phone call?"

"I'll only call if the time doesn't work out.

But if it doesn't, we'll find one that does. I promise."

"I don't know how my life came to this," she said before she'd even considered her words.

"You aren't the only one," he said cryptically.

She waited for an explanation, but none was forthcoming. She gave a final nod and left.

Taylor was smiling for no reason. She was aware of it and still helpless to stop. She was also humming, a monotonous, tuneless mixture of notes that didn't resemble any song she had ever heard, but humming happily, nonetheless.

Adam's class had gone well. He was a good teacher, with a good handle on classroom dynamics.

Adam himself? That was harder to think about. As were the moments when he'd held her against his body and looked deep into her eyes. Of course, a moment later he had slammed an elbow toward the side of her head, but still . . .

"What's so funny?"

She looked up and found the man in her thoughts standing in her doorway. She smiled at him. "I was just thinking that most of the men who try to hold me in their arms aren't planning to whack me in the head as part of the experience."

"You were absolutely safe."

"My head's still on my shoulders, it's true. I'm glad."

"You were a great partner. You didn't even squeal."

"It happened too fast."

"How about all those other men? You know, the ones who weren't planning to whack you?"

"I may have exaggerated their numbers."

"That would surprise me."

She knew it was time to change the subject. "So, are you satisfied?"

"Only partly. I want to split the class. How would you feel about giving me Wednesday night, too, same time and place?"

"You're kidding."

"Not. Jan and Harmony can't work together. You saw what happened. And the class is evenly divided between women who can move at a relatively fast pace and women who are going to require extra help. I've talked to most of them already and they're willing to change to Wednesdays."

"Without asking me?"

"I saw no point in asking you if they weren't willing. But they all know it's up to you. I told them it was just an idea, and the room might not be free."

She tried to think of all the reasons why this was a bad idea. "Does this mean you're teaching two classes?"

"You mean am I getting paid for the extra time? No. Same deal either way. Half the tuition. I have the time, so I don't mind extra hours. What else am I doing?"

She thought that was an interesting question, so she pursued it. "What else *are* you doing? Are you finding enough in town to keep you occupied?"

"Exploring. Sightseeing. Checking out the business scene, neighborhoods."

"Do you like what you see?"

He was looking at *her,* and he continued to, making it clear when he answered that he wasn't talking about Asheville. "Very much."

Taylor felt heat rising in her cheeks. "Glad to hear it."

He didn't pretend he'd meant anything else. "I realize that dating my boss is probably a bad idea. But considering how little you're paying me, I think I can take a pass on that. Would you consider going out with me? Or should we stop the flirtation right here and make this relationship strictly business?"

"Flirtation?"

"You're right. Not the best word. It's not that innocent, is it? It's more grown-up, more . . . interesting."

"You're pretty sure you're reading me correctly."

"I spent a lot of years learning to read people. I'm not always right, but I'm almost always close. And I've had a lot of training learning to read my own reactions."

"And you're reacting to me?"

"That's a fair assessment."

"Are you always this direct? Whatever happened to, 'Want to catch a movie on Friday?' "

"Is that how it's done?"

She had a strong sense he knew exactly how it was done. Adam was far too attractive not to have been through this moment multiple times. He was teasing her.

She stood and moved around the table to face him. "Let's say we *were* flirting. Where would we go?"

"Anywhere you wanted."

She folded her arms. "Do you like to hike?"

"I do if I'm not on a forced march."

"So if we were flirting and I said I'd like to hike, you might agree."

"I *would* agree."

"I'll have to remember that if we ever flirt again."

"Come hiking with me on Sunday. Can you spare the time away from the studio? If you can't, we could just grab dinner."

"Maybe we should maintain a moderate distance. I do employ you."

"Chicken feed."

"The terms were your idea."

"You can fire me if I get to be a problem."

She didn't think that was in the cards. "I'll think about it. But it'll be a short hike. Then you come to my house for dinner. Maddie likes you. I'll feed you eggplant and broccoli and see how you do. You're flirting with a vegetarian. Those are the ground rules."

"I think I'll sign on."

"We'll see. More grown-up, more . . . interesting?"

"A clever turn of phrase, wasn't it?"

"Did you practice that?"

"It came out of my mouth fully formed. So how about the Wednesday night class?"

"Will you do all the organizing and get the details set up?"

"Already there, if you'll give the permission."

"I'm the one getting the bargain, so sure."

"I liked demonstrating elbow strikes with you tonight."

She couldn't resist. "Just think twice about anything else you intend to demonstrate. I'm taking self-defense classes."

"Wednesday nights? That's going to be the fast class. And you're definitely a fast learner." He smiled before he disappeared back into the hallway.

CHAPTER 19

Jeremy was sitting on the front porch when Taylor, Jan and Maddie arrived home. Taylor watched as her daughter ran up the walkway and jumped into her father's arms. Jan smiled at him and let herself into the house to give the three of them privacy.

"Big surprise," Taylor said, in as friendly a tone as she could manage. Jeremy was given to whims, and apparently making the trip from Nashville to Asheville this evening without calling had been one of them. Had she known, she would have made arrangements for him to pick up their daughter at the studio.

"I know it's late, and I'm sorry," he said, setting Maddie on the ground but keeping an arm around her shoulders. "I expected to get here a lot earlier, but we had some car trouble. I thought I'd arrive before Maddie got home from school to surprise her.

Then I thought we might not get here at all."

Taylor liked Jeremy better than she used to. She had nearly forgiven him for impregnating her at sixteen and pretending — at least for a while — that he wasn't the culprit. Through the years Jeremy had stepped up to become a good father. She didn't forgive easily, though, and the faintest whiff of the past still lingered.

"Car fixed?" she asked when nothing better occurred to her.

"Everything's fine. Willow's at my parents' house. They just got back from a cruise, and we wanted to surprise them, too."

Taylor had known about the cruise. The senior Larsens were good people and, like her own father, often available as babysitters when they were in town in the summers and early fall. The rest of the year they lived in Florida, and Maddie was already looking forward to a trip to see them over spring break.

"What's the occasion?" she asked. "For the visit."

He gave a slight shake of his head, and she realized he wasn't ready to explain. "Do you mind if she spends the night with us? I know it's late and we won't have much time together tonight. But if you don't mind we'll pick her up from school tomorrow and keep her for the weekend."

Since Taylor and Jeremy had joint custody, even if she had objected, she would have needed a better reason than Jeremy's lack of planning. Instead, she flashed on her upcoming date with Adam. "Will you bring her back sometime after dinner Sunday?"

"You need child care?"

"It might be helpful."

"That'll work. Half-pint, think you can get all your stuff together lickety-split?" he asked.

"Can I!" Maddie disappeared into the house, leaving her parents to face each other.

"Willow's pregnant," he said softly. "I didn't want to blurt it out. We wanted some time alone to help her see it's going to be a good thing for her, too."

Taylor wasn't in love with Jeremy, although the women who saw him in concert with the Black Balsam Drifters would probably think she was crazy. He was tall and broad-shouldered, with sun-streaked brown hair and blue eyes against a golden tan. He'd been the class bad boy in high school, and today he continued that onstage by dressing in black and singing country songs he'd written filled with sly sexual innuendoes and invitations. In reality, though, he was levelheaded and responsible, and while sharing a child they'd created when they were children themselves was never easy, they had muddled through the bad times.

With all that in their past, she was still surprised that she felt a stab of pain at the news his new wife was giving him another child. Not because she wanted that honor. But because Jeremy had clearly moved on with his life, and she? Well, she had hardly even been on a date since Maddie's birth.

"Congratulations," she said, forcing warmth into her voice. "I know Maddie will be thrilled to have a baby brother or sister."

"I hope so. She'll always be first in my heart."

She was touched. "It took a while, though, didn't it?"

"Never as long as you wanted to believe." He smiled, as if he was so used to Taylor's zingers that he didn't even feel the sting. "But Willow and I are happier than I thought I could be. She keeps my feet on the ground and my head in the clouds so I can keep doing what I do best."

"You're really lucky."

"What about you, T? Don't tell me there's not a guy out there for you?"

Jeremy hadn't called her "T" since high

school. She was so taken aback that for a minute his question just faded into the background.

"I'd forgotten you used to call me that."

"You've forgotten a lot. Like how nuts I was about you."

"What?"

He shook his head. "For years you've told yourself we were just two kids in high school fooling around to get back at our parents. But it's not true. I was as in love with you as a seventeen-year-old guy can be. Which, granted isn't all that much."

"Jeremy Larsen! By the time I told you I was pregnant, you already had another girlfriend!"

"Because you dumped me. You don't remember that?" He lowered his voice. "We were both virgins. That first time wasn't very good for either of us, as I recall. You took off afterward and told me to get lost."

"That's not what happened." But even as she said the words, she wondered. The pregnancy loomed large in her memory, but the way she had gotten pregnant, and the events immediately afterward did not. They had been eclipsed.

"It *is* what happened. And I ended up with another girl to get even with you. Don't tell me you don't remember any of this?"

"You denied Maddie was yours."

"I was furious at you. And scared out of my mind."

She didn't know what to say.

"I *was* in love with you," he repeated. "Although not so much when I found out I was going to be a father. I was a kid. I blamed it on you."

She shook her head, not in denial, but in hopes that all the information in it would settle into the right spaces.

"Taylor, you were hot," he said, and he winked. "And forbidden, which didn't hurt."

"Well, if any of this is true, it's nice to know someone thought so once upon a time."

"Are you telling me that one bad relationship all those years ago has soured you on men?"

"Wow, the ego!"

He grinned at her, and Jeremy had a substantially powerful grin. "So there's a guy?"

Her view of the past was still jiggling around in her head. "It's just been me and Maddie for so long. I know the surgery helped. I know she's living a normal life now and that will probably continue. Her doctor's optimistic we can start weaning her off

her meds in another year. But I'm not sure
—"

"I think you've forgotten what it's like to have a normal life, too."

"Normal? I have the studio and all that work." She shrugged. "And what will Maddie think? A baby sister or brother, a step-mom, then me going off and finding some guy? It would be too much to cope with. It was just us before."

"It never was just *you*, Taylor. Come on. She had me, your dad, my parents and, for a little while, even your mom. But beyond that, how good is it for Maddie to think she's the center of your universe? Isn't that a pretty big strain for a kid entering adolescence? Doesn't she need to cut herself free to forge her own path? How easy will that be if she thinks she has to be front and center in your life?"

She hated to admit it, but Jeremy was making sense. And hadn't she told herself all the same things?

"There *is* a guy," he said. "I can tell."

"Just somebody who asked me out, that's all."

"Want me to check him out for you?"

She had to smile. For all Jeremy's bad-boy persona, Adam could probably wrestle him to the ground without breaking a sweat.

"Thanks, but I'll do the checking."

"Good luck. I want the best for you."

"Why? So I'll get off your case?"

"That's only part of it."

He grinned again, and without considering, she pushed herself to her tiptoes and kissed his cheek. "Thanks for telling me I was hot."

"Still are. I'm sure this guy has noticed, too."

Maddie chose that moment to come barreling outside with her overnight bag and her books. "Jan helped me put everything together!"

"She'll tell you all about Jan," Taylor said. "You two have a good time, and please tell Willow I missed seeing her. Next time, for sure."

They left in a flurry of goodbyes, and Taylor stood there well after Jeremy's car pulled away.

"Hot," she said finally, shaking her head before she reached for the doorknob. "Who knew?"

Jan was pouring water in the teapot when Taylor came in. She had made enough herbal tea for both of them, just in case.

"Maddie get off okay?" she asked.

"Jeremy wanted some time alone with her.

He and his wife are going to have a baby, and he wanted to tell her in person. That man's just full of surprises."

From her expression, Jan thought Taylor was fine with the news. "Maddie will be happy. She adores Lottie. In fact, she and Edna want to be the Three Bears for Halloween, with Lottie as Baby Bear."

"When did she tell you this?"

"When Harmony and I were getting her settled with her homework in the café." She went to get cups and saucers, the honey bear for sweetening the tea, spoons.

"I can't remember what I did without you. What *did* I do?" Taylor asked.

Jan just smiled. "I used to make Halloween costumes for my children every year. Once they were old enough for school, Rex didn't want them going through the neighborhood begging, as he called it, and by then we were going to a church that didn't believe in celebrating holidays, anyway. When they were little, though, I sewed a new costume every year and we took them to the mall to get treats. I kept them all, too, but they went up in smoke with everything else."

"I'm sorry. Do you remember what they were?"

"Harmony always wanted a long dress,

317

satin or velvet, something soft. So one year she was Sleeping Beauty, another Cinderella. A pink dress and a blue dress. Lots of froufrou, sequins, rhinestones, bows and ruffles, lace, the more the better. One year Buddy, my son, was Daniel Boone. I made him buckskin pants and a jacket out of suede. I even made a coonskin cap from fake fur."

Taylor whistled. "That's pretty elaborate."

Jan perched on the stool beside her as they waited for the tea to steep. "I made all Harmony's clothes when she was growing up. Rex was less likely to complain about the cost of fabric than buying off the rack."

"I can't sew two seams together, but Sam and Edna both love to sew. I just can't imagine Sam having enough time to make a bear costume, and Edna's good but she would need help. I'm going to strike a blow for something simple like ghosts or zombies. Aren't zombies big this year?"

"I could help them make the costumes. Do you have a sewing machine?"

"That would be a waste of good money."

"I can still help." Jan considered her next words carefully and decided they were true. "I'm pretty good."

Taylor had just lifted the top off the teapot to check the progress, but she put it back in place and faced the other woman. "I think that might be the first time I've heard you say something good about yourself. You must be fabulous if you feel comfortable saying it."

Jan realized what Taylor said was true. In recent memory, when had she praised herself? When had she admitted she could do something right, even well?

"Maybe it was the class tonight." She smiled as she thought about that. "I'm already brimming with courage."

"It wasn't easy for you, was it?"

Jan shook her head. Whether Taylor meant the class or the admission that she was a good seamstress didn't matter, because both had been difficult.

"Adam's splitting the class," Taylor said. "Those who are a little quicker will go on Wednesdays from this point, and those who need a bit more help will stay with Thursday."

"I'll be in one class, and you and Harmony will be in the other," Jan guessed out loud.

"You're okay with that?"

"He's a good teacher. I'll be fine."

"I don't know the story of every woman who was there tonight, but for somebody like me, the class is pretty straightforward. We practice defending ourselves against something that may never happen. It's good exercise. It's smart. But it doesn't feel urgent or even important. It must have felt different for you tonight."

Jan poured the tea before she spoke. "For me? For me, Taylor, it felt like the end of one world and the beginning of the next."

"For very different reasons it felt that way for me, too," Taylor said.

As if on cue, the two women held their teacups in the air and clinked in toast. "Here's to Adam Pryor," Taylor said, "and to taking back our lives."

"One day at a time."

They drank to that.

CHAPTER 20

Like many teenagers Taylor had rebelled against her mother's attempts to rule her life by following as few of her decrees as possible. This meant a messy room and a messy life. As a young unwed mother, though, she had quickly learned she couldn't parent a premature baby, with all Maddie's attendant needs, without cleaning up her own life first. So the disorganized teenager quickly turned into a young woman who believed there was a place for everything.

Which was why on Sunday afternoon, without even looking, she was able to thrust her hand into the correct section of her closet and know that any long-sleeved shirt she pulled out would be perfect for a hike with Adam. No fuss, no soul-searching. Just stick in her hand and . . .

Taylor looked at the shirt she'd snagged. Pea-green and possibly even a little short at the cuffs. A shirt she'd meant to give to charity in hopes that somebody who needed one had shorter arms and a complexion the color flattered. Because the shirt certainly didn't flatter her.

She realized this exercise could, in theory, go on all day. She would blindly thrust in her hand, grab a shirt and decide, for whatever reason, that it wasn't the right one. Despite a life that hadn't lent itself to attracting men, she was no different from any other woman. Today she wanted to look nice on her date with Adam, so she might as well admit it.

Five minutes later she settled on a cotton knit the color of amethysts, with lavender stitching and buttons that matched the lavender tank top she had slipped on beneath it. When she'd inherited her mother's jewelry, she set aside most of it for Maddie and passed a few pieces to Harmony, but she had kept the things she knew she might wear, including amethyst studs and a short silver chain with tiny amethysts strung along the length of it. She tried them both now, decided they were still simple enough for a hike and silently thanked her mother for her excellent taste, something she had never done when Charlotte was still alive.

She pulled on her most comfortable jeans

— which also happened to fit best — and dark blue hiking boots. The next part was hardest. Normally she wore little if any makeup. When was there time to apply it? Today there *was* time, but she was curiously reluctant to primp. What did that say about her interest in a man she hardly knew?

"Are we getting the anxiety out of the way before the man arrives?" she asked herself in the mirror. "Because you know, don't you, that this is really, really lame?"

She compromised by using a little blush, a little mascara, a little lip gloss. When she'd finished she looked nice but not substantially different, which was what she'd hoped for. Then she went to see what Jan was up to in the kitchen.

"You look so pretty," Jan said, followed closely by, "I won't be here for dinner." Vanilla, who wanted to catch a nap in the middle of the kitchen floor, flopped onto Jan's feet, and she leaned over to pet her.

Taylor wasn't sure she liked the sound of that, and she wasn't oblivious to the sudden absence of eye contact. Maddie gone. Now Jan. "Why? What's up?"

"Rilla has a friend who repairs and sells cars, so she's taking me to his house to look at a couple he's got. He insisted it had to be tonight."

Taylor thought the timing was a little strange. Sunday nights most parents were busy getting their kids set for the rest of the week. She had a feeling Rilla's timing might have more to do with Taylor's date with Adam than with the car guy's schedule. She imagined that Jan had enlisted her help.

"You're sure you're not coming back in time to eat?" she probed.

Jan shook the dog off her feet. "No, we're leaving just about dinnertime. Rilla says we'll grab something quick on the way."

Taylor was sure Rilla hadn't seen the inside of a fast food restaurant in two decades and wasn't about to start tonight, but she played along. "You'll miss my famous black bean burgers."

"I'll have to take a rain check."

Someone rang the front doorbell, and Taylor froze.

"Would you like me to get it?" Jan asked when Taylor didn't move.

"Whose idea was this?"

"Didn't you say it was Adam's?"

"But I said yes."

"Why wouldn't you?"

"You of all people know the answer. What if he's really a jerk?"

"Then you'll figure that out today and say no next time he asks. You'll be watching and listening, right? You won't make excuses for bad behavior."

"It's like I've been in a time warp. Most women my age have probably been on a thousand dates. Two thousand."

"You won't be going on this one if you don't hurry up."

The bell rang again. "This is stupid. I'm being stupid." Taylor lifted her chin and strode across the room to throw open the door.

"Hey, Adam," she said casually. "Right on time."

His eyes lit up at the sight of her, and the corners of his mouth turned up, as if he liked what he saw. "Why would I be late? I looked forward to this all morning."

She wondered what exactly he'd been looking forward to. Hiking? A home-cooked meal? Being with her? She remembered Jeremy's words, and she felt her cheeks heating. She, who never had time to blush.

"I've got a day pack with snacks," she said, turning away. "Do you have a water bottle?"

"On my belt."

She hadn't noticed because she hadn't let her eyes travel that low. But she *had* noticed he was wearing a blue V-neck knit shirt that matched *his* eyes. She wondered if he knew how perfect that was, or if he'd just grabbed the shirt on sale somewhere, the way her father would have. Jeremy would have chosen carefully. Adam? A mystery man.

He stepped inside and greeted Jan, and they exchanged a few pleasantries as Taylor got the pack.

"There's a nice hike not too far out of town," she said as she slipped the pack over her shirt.

"Where's Maddie?"

"Off with her dad for the weekend. He'll drop her off tonight."

"I thought he lived out of town."

"He's just here for a few days." Taylor straightened and realized she was ready. She hesitated.

"You two have fun," Jan said, as if she realized she needed to fill the gap. "Watch out for bears."

"Are you afraid of bears?" Taylor asked Adam.

"Anybody with good sense is afraid of bears."

She was glad he hadn't pretended he was so brave he didn't have to worry. He was sensible and honest. She liked that in a man.

"I would take Vanilla to scare them away, but she'd just try to make friends." The placid golden doodle wagged her tail, as if that was part of her job, and went back to sleep.

"That's a pet, not a guard dog."

Taylor joined him at the door. "She could probably use a few self-defense lessons."

"I bet you like her just the way she is."

"Sorry to say, but yes. She was the runt of the litter and my mother's favorite."

"Your mother raises dogs?"

"I'll tell you all about it."

She did tell him. Adam was surprisingly easy to talk to, and they chatted intermittently for the first hour. She told him about Charlotte, their estrangement after Maddie's birth, their reunion right before Charlotte died. She told him how Harmony and Charlotte had met, and how Charlotte had helped Harmony during her pregnancy. She didn't explain that part of the reason for inviting Jan into her home had been to offer the same kind of help to Harmony's mother. She didn't mention Jan at all, and Adam didn't bring up the subject.

He didn't talk much about himself, either.

The hike she'd chosen was steep, and they chatted less during the last half hour as they made their way up the steepest part of the mountain to the view she'd wanted to share.

"What do you think?" she asked, stopping

to perch on a rock thoughtfully placed by Mother Nature at the best spot to see the vista of mountains beyond them and the wisps of clouds that frosted them. Up this high the leaves were already touched with orange and yellow, and in a few weeks the mountain would be alive with hikers who wanted to be right in the heart of the fall colors. Today, though, they'd nearly had the path to themselves.

"I can see why you never moved away." He lowered himself to the rock beside her, their hips brushing.

"I tell myself that's very unadventurous, but my dad was here, and Jeremy's parents are here for the summers. I had a few good friends who could help, and I *needed* help with Maddie. I couldn't have managed everything alone."

"That's not unadventurous, that's smart."

"The thing is, even if I could move now, I wouldn't. This place is as much a part of me as the food I eat and the air I breathe. Actually it *is* those things, too. It's just who I am."

"And now you have your studio."

"I'll be here forever, I guess. Very different from your life. How many places have you lived?"

He took a moment to answer. "I've never

counted. A lot, though. Some here, some overseas. And it depends on what you mean by lived. When I was in training, I moved from base to base, some stays longer than others."

Taylor had read his résumé, so she knew that, like his own father, he had been in the air force until he was discharged last year. "What kind of training?"

"I started out in security forces and moved to combat rescue. I was in a number of different schools for that, on different bases. I'm not sure anyone would call what we did during training 'living.' "

"Are you allowed to talk about what you did?"

"Jumped out of planes, swam underwater until we almost blacked out, learned mountaineering and land navigation skills, did extra work in weaponry, escape, evasion." He glanced at her. "For starters."

"I like physical challenges, but that sounds extreme."

"It's an extreme profession. I was never sure whether it was a piece of good or bad luck that I didn't wash out right away. Or at least drown or break my neck trying not to."

She wasn't sure if he was kidding. "You don't mean that."

"Don't I?"

"That bad, huh?"

"Not bad. Tough. Vitally important, but tough. I did my part. Then I got out."

By his tone she knew Adam was finished discussing that part of his life. "You said your father was in the air force, too?"

"He suggested I do something else when I told him I'd been accepted to the academy."

"That must have been discouraging."

His expression warmed, and he smiled. "You're good at reflecting what I say, aren't you? You know how to keep a conversation going."

"You listened so well when I told you about my checkered past. I thought I would return the favor."

Their gazes locked. His thoughts were impossible to read. She wondered what part of that was his training, which must have included learning not to give away information if captured.

"Dad had complete faith in me," he said without breaking eye contact. "He just suggested I might want a real life. He said an intense man needed simpler days, that I would take becoming an officer to heart so completely I would live and breathe it 24/7. If I married, my wife would leave me inside of a year because she would quickly realize she wasn't even a close second."

"Harsh."

He gave just the slightest shake of his head. "Insightful."

"Did that happen? Did you marry and divorce in under a year?"

"I never got that far. I found women who were even more devoted than I was and wished them well when they took off for a new base or assignment."

"Is that why you left?"

"There were lots of reasons, none of them very interesting. But that was one. I needed to ratchet down and find out how normal people live."

"Any luck? I've wondered, too."

"At least I was getting combat pay." His gaze softened. "You weren't."

"Yeah, but I got Maddie."

"And now you have adolescence ahead of you."

"I'm practically an adolescent myself. I figure I'll know what she's thinking before she does."

They both laughed; then he turned away to look at the view again. "Looks like you have some good help. Jan's right there. You mentioned your dad and friends. . . ."

"Jan's a new addition, but I'm already wondering how I lived without her. Having somebody right in the house when I need her is so perfect."

"You were lucky to find her."

"She found me," Taylor said without thinking, then realized she had said too much, starting with "Jan's a new addition."

"What, she came to the door and asked for a job?"

"No, she —" She considered but knew she had to say something quickly. "She's the friend of a friend. She was starting over and needed a place to do it." This was too close to the truth, but it was the best she could do on the spur of the moment.

"Starting over is tough. At her age, I'm guessing a bad marriage."

"Bad," she repeated, since saying nothing would confirm his suspicions and deepen them.

He stood and stretched. "I never would have guessed she's not an old friend. I thought for sure she was, or maybe a relative. You get along so well."

"We certainly do." She stood, too. She'd just gotten a taste of what Jan and Harmony had to go through every day. Telling a version of the truth when possible, but never the whole truth. Pretending things were different than they were. And who knew if designing this spider's web that could catch and trap them someday was for any good reason? Who knew where Harmony's father was and if, indeed, he was even trying to find his wife or daughter?

"Ready to turn around?" he asked.

"We'd better if we want to get back before dark. I hope you're still staying for dinner."

"I'll be starving after this."

"Dinner will be one step above MREs, I'm sure, but maybe not what you're used to. Black bean burgers."

"This is probably the right moment to tell you I'm a vegetarian, too."

That surprised her. "Honestly?"

"Have been for a couple of years. Too much heart disease in my family to risk red meat, although I love a good steak. It's easier now that I'm a civilian. I eat seafood sometimes, but rarely."

"And never shrimp on grits."

He looked surprised. "You remember that?"

She wasn't going to tell him she remembered everything he had ever said. How revealing was that? She couldn't swear to the science, but she suspected a surge in hormones whenever she was with Adam did something to sharpen her memory.

"I'll race you to the bottom." She turned and started down, but at an amble, not a jog. The mountain path was nothing to fool with.

He was right behind her. "It's nice being with a woman who likes physical activity. What do you like to do besides yoga and hiking?"

There really *was* something wrong with her. The only physical activity that leaped to mind was one she wasn't about to discuss. "Just about everything," she said, for lack of a better answer.

"How are you on a bike?"

"I used to teach a spinning class at the gym."

"I mean a real bike. You know, fresh air, sunshine, real scenery?"

"A little rusty, but my bike's not. I ride with Maddie, but for obvious reasons not very fast or far."

"We could fix that next Sunday."

Another date. She might not span the thousand-date gap very soon, but she was making headway. "Do you know any good bike trails?"

"Want me to ask around?"

"Sounds good." And it did. Really good. Someone else in charge for a change. Somebody who liked to do the same things she did. Even somebody who ate the way she did.

She warned herself this was already too good to be true, but she couldn't make herself believe it.

Adam grilled the burgers in Taylor's backyard while she dressed a quinoa salad with the last of the summer's peaches and handfuls of basil from her garden. They ate outside, even though the temperature was falling and both of them had to don an extra layer.

He drank beer, and she drank wine. During the second generous glass she realized she hadn't thought of her daughter or her studio for more than an hour. Adam didn't tell jokes or funny stories, but he had a wry sense of humor that surfaced just often enough to put her at ease. She thought his father had been right. Adam *was* intense, although most of the time he hid what he was thinking or feeling. She hadn't gotten past the first layer, but she also thought there might be a slow unfolding as they grew to trust each other.

She was hopeful, because she thought she might like what she found.

Stars were visible in a dusky sky when they took everything inside. Jan would probably be home soon, and Maddie, too. Sunday night rituals would commence. Shampoo and the combing of tangles, which Maddie still liked her to do. Putting out clothes for the morning. Checking homework if Jeremy or his mother hadn't already done so.

Finding out how Maddie felt about becoming a big sister.

Life as they all knew it, yet as Taylor walked Adam to the door she thought life suddenly felt different. Not because of Jeremy's announcement about a baby. Not because Jan was living in the house now. Not even because Maddie was heading full throttle into adolescence.

Life was different because Adam was in it. For however long, at whatever pace, he had entered her life and changed it. She was no longer just someone's mother.

"I had a nice afternoon," he said at the threshold. "And dinner was great. Thank you for cooking for me."

"You did some of the cooking."

"I can flip burgers. I started my work life at McDonald's."

She wrinkled her nose. "I'm glad you went on to other things."

"Like war and misery?"

"I'll warn you, I march for peace whenever I think it's required."

"I fought for peace when it was required, or at least that was the hope."

"So maybe we're not that far apart?"

They weren't far apart, as a matter of fact. They were standing together in the doorway, not an easy feat considering Adam's size. She gazed up at him and wondered what would happen next.

He didn't keep her in suspense. He rested his hand on her shoulder, lightly for such a wide, strong hand, and then he bent and kissed her. She leaned forward as naturally as if she'd already been on those thousand dates, and the kiss went quickly from casual and gentle to something more heated.

He finally took a step backward. "Good night."

She smiled, although what she really wanted was to grab his soft blue shirt in her fist and kiss him again. "I'll see you on Wednesday night at the studio."

He smiled, too, and then he was gone.

She wondered what she would have done if he had asked for more than a simple — okay, not that simple — good-night kiss. Even as a teenager experimenting with sex, she had felt her brain fully engaged. She had known exactly what she was doing the night she and Jeremy made love, although she'd been woefully casual about potential consequences.

Now she was no teenager. She was a

grown woman, a mother. And the moment Adam kissed her, her brain had turned to jelly. And the rest of her?

Molten lava.

Was it Adam? Was it years of denial?

Did she care?

She decided she didn't. She went back into the house to wash dishes. Maybe, just maybe, she could become a totally devoted mother again before her daughter came home.

Or maybe not. And who knew which was better for both of them, anyway?

CHAPTER 21

From the audio journal of a
forty-five-year-old woman, taped for the
files of Moving On, an underground
highway for abused women.

I can't say I wasn't warned how dangerous
my situation was. At my next doctor's appointment, when I confided the way my
husband had reacted after the news from
the ultrasound she gave me the number of a
safe house. During my examination the
Abuser paced the waiting room with our
toddler son, unhappy they hadn't been allowed to stay with me. When I emerged, the
safe-house number committed to memory,
he questioned me closely. What had I told
the doctor about the fading bruise on my
hip? Had she explained that pregnant
women are often clumsy and that I should
be more careful where I set my feet?
By then the truth of my situation was too

hard to pretend away. Of course, he had been sorry after he kicked me. He hadn't intended to shove me; that was an unfortunate accident. His intention had been to grab and steady me because I had looked as if I might faint. But the kick? Did I really believe he would kick me on purpose? That was an accident, too. He had leaped to my side and simply misjudged, for which he apologized. Maybe pregnancy made men clumsy, too, he'd added, as if the whole episode was part of a stand-up comic's routine.

In my own defense, I wasn't fooled. Whenever the Abuser made what sounded like a sincere apology, I still remained absurdly hopeful. But each time he lied and expected me to believe his words, I grew more discouraged. How could a man change if he couldn't admit he needed to? If he couldn't see that hurting me was wrong, would he ever ask for help in controlling his temper?

The doctor had pointed out that men who abuse their wives are likely to abuse their children, too. Even if they don't, the child who observes abuse may learn to believe it's acceptable, even expected. Was that what I wanted for myself and my baby? Or how about the little boy in the waiting room who

Taylor was going to be a problem.

At six he got up, showered, shaved and dressed, and by six-thirty he was sitting at a small restaurant within walking distance of his apartment having pancakes and coffee. By eight he was back at his home after taking the longest route home through tree-shaded neighborhoods and streets that turned up little to interest him.

Settled in a corner armchair, he pulled out his cell phone and made the call he had contemplated since waking. He went through the usual procedures and personnel until the man who supervised him was on the phone.

"Got anything useful yet, Pryor?"

"I'd say the wife and daughter's locations were pretty useful."

"Right. I was looking for something new."

"They're both living simply. The daughter gets child support, and she works, but she shops at thrift stores and lives on the farm in an apartment above the garage. Her car is decent, but it appears the baby's father gave it to her. He bought it. He signed it over. I doubt money was exchanged."

"How about the wife?"

"Lives with another woman in a smallish house and provides child care when the woman is working. Doesn't have a car.

might grow up to identify with his abusive father?

That day the Abuser dropped us at home and went back to work, and I spent the rest of the afternoon silently repeating the doctor's question as I changed diapers and read storybooks to my sweet little boy. That evening when my husband came home, he had two bags filled with gifts for our baby. Pretty, frilly pink gifts. Yes, he admitted, he had wanted another son. But if our baby girl was anything like her mother, then he would love her as much as he loved me. What man wouldn't count himself lucky to have two beautiful females in his life?

Adam went to bed late and woke early. If the familiar nightmare had visited, he didn't remember, which was fine with him. He had fallen asleep thinking about Taylor, and after waking, he lay, arms folded under his head on the lumpy pillow that had seen one too many renters, thinking about his reasons for being in Asheville.

Danger came in many forms. He was familiar with most of them and eternally wary. So it was no surprise that all his senses were on alert. Physical security wasn't the issue. Nobody here wanted to hurt him; nobody was going to leap out from behind a bush and mow him down with an M-4 carbine. He was in Asheville to do a job, a job on which he had made significant progress.

Jan Seaton *was* Jan Stoddard, the mother of Harmony and wife of Rex. Tracking her hadn't been simple, but neither had it been particularly difficult. From the beginning he had figured the daughter was the key. After trying other tactics, he had gotten access to the Stoddards' phone records and combed through them carefully. In the past two years there had been several calls from Asheville, and the last one, about sixteen months ago, had been made from an Asheville café.

Suspicion aroused, he had called the number, identified himself as an old family friend and asked to speak to Harmony Stoddard. The manager, with no idea what she was revealing, told him Harmony no longer worked there, but as they continued to chat he'd learned that she was still in the area, working at a kennel. The kennel bred service dogs, and before they hung up the manager told him the general area where to find it. He had asked her not to tell Harmony about the call, since he was hoping to surprise her, and she had wished him well.

Finding the kennel had been as easy as finding the Capable Canines web Finding Harmony had required fashioned surveillance, which had t up a tall blonde woman who, when his distance photos were blown up, look be a slightly more mature version o Harmony Stoddard pictured in her school yearbook. A day later while he still watching the Reynolds house a debating what to do next, a bobtail tru had pulled up just beyond the road leadi to the farmhouse and a dark-haired woma had gotten out, a woman he recognize from a photo taken several years before at New Year's open house for Rex Stoddard's clients and staff.

Jan Stoddard.

Bingo.

Now that he'd located Mrs. Stoddard, Adam's job was to find out everything he could. That, too, hadn't been particularly difficult. He'd seen Taylor and her daughter arrive slightly after Jan, seen them leave with her not long after. He'd tailed them to Taylor's house, and the rest?

Now it wasn't simple at all. Because while this was a job that entailed no physical danger, the emotional fallout was going to be a problem. On more levels than he could count.

Dresses simply. Doesn't seem to have brought much with her. Got her hair cut and colored, but that's the only sign I've seen that she has money to spend."

"Still using an assumed name?"

Adam grunted in affirmation. "*I've* got questions for *you* now."

"I don't know why. You know what we know."

"Maybe you didn't think this was important. Do you have any reason to think that Stoddard abused his wife?"

"Abused?"

"Jan Stoddard is skittish, like she's used to having somebody come at her regularly. Sometimes she flinches when I get too close. She's in my self-defense class, but she's terrified to even pretend she's confronting an attacker. Half the time I can barely hear her when she speaks, like she's sure whatever she has to say will get her into serious trouble." He stopped. He could have gone on, but he figured he had made his point.

"Nothing like that's come up."

"Did you go deep enough that it would have?"

"When we decided to go deep we hired *you* to figure out what part the Stoddard women play in our little drama. But I can tell you this. I'm not a big fan of women who claim they're abused. It's not like they can't leave. I had a cousin who regularly got beat up by a boyfriend, and she never told anybody in the family, not for a year or even more. Then he went to jail for something else, and she finally told her mother. The family got her counseling, a new place to live, the whole nine yards to the tune of big bucks, but when he got out, she went right back to him."

Adam knew that arguing would be pointless. "You're saying that even if Rex Stoddard was regularly beating his wife, she's just waiting here for him to show up so they can be a happy little family again?"

"I'm saying these things are complicated and you don't have much to go on yet. If she *was* abused, that could give her the motive for a number of things, right? Including shooting the mister in the head with a gun from that arsenal they found traces of after the fire. I'm sure you've considered all the others?"

"There are a number of things to check."

"This whole thing is dragging on. You got a lot at first, but make sure that continues or we'll have to rethink what we're paying you."

"I can't just make things happen. They'll

happen when they do, *if* they do. And you're only paying when I'm working. I'm a cheap date."

"Because *you* don't want something full-time. You're a loner. Just remember what this is about. It's not social work, okay?"

Adam hung up and considered his next call; then he picked up his phone again. He was glad he had a long empty day ahead of him. He was going to need every minute.

Jan had a car. Her own car. On Monday afternoon, on the way to the studio to pick it up, Taylor listened patiently as an unusually vocal Jan explained why this car was so important to her.

The story clarified more about the years of abuse. The only time Jan had owned a car herself was when her parents died and she inherited their station wagon, and then only for a month before Rex sold it for her. He had patiently explained she didn't need a gas guzzler, and the value would go down every day that she hesitated. She could put the money away and buy something more appropriate once it was needed.

Of course, that day never arrived. At first solicitous Rex-the-boyfriend claimed he would be happy to drive her everywhere, or she could have use of *his* car whenever she needed it. In the first months of their marriage, whenever she suggested getting a car of her own Rex-the-husband made excuses. Eventually he hadn't bothered to respond. By then she had known what would happen if she pushed.

"Why do you think he didn't want you to drive? Was he afraid you would leave him?" Taylor asked when Jan finished.

"If I'd had my own car, I might have made friends, and maybe talked to them about what was going on at home. Without a car?" She shook her head. "Of course, we had a phone, but after a while who could I call?"

Taylor was afraid she might be pushing too hard, but she really couldn't stop herself from asking the next question. "Did you realize what was happening, and you just couldn't stop it?"

"It didn't happen overnight. It happened a little at a time. He had explanations, excuses. He bought me gifts and told me how badly he felt that he couldn't afford better for me yet. He made promises, gave me lavish compliments. The abuse came in spurts. In the early years, when he wasn't in a rage he was funny and kind, and so very sorry when he exploded. I was lulled into submission."

"You loved him?"

"I loved a man who never existed, but it took too long to see and believe it. I know it's hard to understand." Jan's voice caught. "What's the expression? You had to have been there?"

"Harmony *was* there, but I've never heard her say she loved her father."

"Like all little girls, she wanted her daddy's attention, but our son was the favorite. By the time Harmony was old enough to understand what was going on, there were few things to love about Rex."

"I'm just glad you're both away from him."

"I just wish I knew for sure."

As they pulled into the studio lot, the mood lightened again. Jan changed the subject and chatted about all the things she was looking forward to. She couldn't wait to study the manual so she would know everything the car could do. She was going to buy a car seat for Lottie so they could go for rides whenever she babysat. She even thought someday soon she might brave the drive up Doggett Mountain to the Goddess House to spend some time with Cristy.

"You'll meet *all* the goddesses next Sunday," Taylor said. "I just found out we're having a harvest celebration, and everybody's coming up to the house."

Jan's car was parked in the corner of the lot. They parked beside it. Jan couldn't stop smiling, and Jan smiling was a lovely sight.

"It's great," Taylor said as she got out and circled it. "And it only has thirty thousand miles?"

The perky little Honda seemed to preen in the sunlight, its sleek blue chassis soaking up the rays. Jan stroked the hood. "He was selling it for his cousin. It's cute, isn't it? He had several cars ready to go, but he said this was the best bet. He gave it a complete tune-up, replaced the brake pads and filters, and repaired a few dents. He said I can bring it back anytime in the next six months if anything develops, either to repair or get my money back, and Rilla says I can trust him."

"That *is* a good deal."

Yesterday Jan had given Rilla a check for the car from her personal bank account, which had then gone straight into Harmony's. This morning Harmony had written her own check and done all the paperwork for the title and insurance. Finally she and Rilla had dropped the car off and hidden the keys under the driver's seat.

Even the cloak-and-dagger nature of the transaction clearly hadn't spoiled it for Jan. Officially the car might belong to Harmony

Stoddard, but the car was her very own, bought and paid for with her own money, and she was delighted.

Taylor completed her circuit and came to stand beside her. "So, where are you going to go to celebrate?"

"I'm going to buy a sewing machine."

"Wow."

"I can't remember a day like this one. First the car, which I needed, and second a sewing machine, which I don't need but . . ."

Taylor could hear that this much freedom was heady, if also a little frightening. "To make the girls Halloween costumes?"

"Not just. I have a granddaughter, and while I can't compete with all those expensive frilly dresses her father's buying her, I can still sew for her. And for Maddie, if she'll let me. I just . . . well, I just want one."

Taylor realized the significance, and she moved closer and gave Jan a quick hug. "I think you should have anything you want, Jan. Anything at all. You sure deserve to be happy."

"I'm getting some practice. Waking up in your house every morning makes me happy, for starters."

Another car pulled into the lot, and Taylor saw who it belonged to. "Adam's here." She hadn't expected to see him. She did a quick mental assessment and wished she had washed her hair that morning instead of waiting until tomorrow.

"I'm going to take off," Jan said. "I can't wait to get behind the wheel and drive."

"You have fun. Will you be home for dinner?"

Jan looked surprised; then she smiled. "I could stay out, couldn't I? I don't want to, but I could."

"Of course. I can bring Maddie with me tonight. The last class ends in plenty of time to get her home and in bed."

"No, I'll be home to help you cook. It's just . . ." Jan's smile widened. "It's so nice to have a choice." She looked as if she had just seen the sun after years in solitary confinement.

Taylor realized that comparison was too close to the truth. Sometimes out of nowhere she would feel herself standing in the older woman's shoes and imagine, just for seconds, what it must have been like to have her world so curtailed, so subject to the whims of a psychopath. The false charm, the lies, the manipulation and, most of all, the abuse.

Years of living with that? For a moment she wasn't sure she could breathe.

Jan was oblivious. "So off I go just be-

352

cause, well, I can!" She went around the car and got into the driver's seat, then fished under it until she held up the keys for Taylor to see. She gave a quick wave, then backed out carefully, and in a moment she was gone.

Just as Adam got out of his SUV.

"Did I scare her away?" he asked, walking over to where Taylor was standing.

Mentally she shook her imagination back into place and took a deep breath. No one was abusing her. No one was stalking her. No one was lying to her. She was standing in the parking lot of her studio, and Jan herself was off to spend a happy day alone.

"She's not one bit scared. She's in heaven. That's a new car — new to her, at least. She's off for a drive. And she's going to buy a sewing machine, too. She's having quite the day."

He gave a soft whistle. "She must have a depleted bank account to show for it."

"Money well spent, all of it." Taylor cocked her head in question. "Isn't this Monday?"

"You probably want to know what I'm doing here."

"It crossed my mind."

"I'm dropping into your drop-in yoga class."

She was flattered and intrigued, while at the same time slivers of anxiety were working their way into place. Adam as her student? Adam in a class where she needed total concentration? "Yoga?"

"I'm not working out as much as I used to. I figure the stretches will be good to keep me limber."

"You want to see me in action, don't you? I've seen you teach. Now *you* want to see *me*."

"I want to see you, yes." He sent her the slight enigmatic smile she found so darned sexy. The same smile he had gifted her with yesterday, right before he kissed her.

She tried to ignore it. "Well, I guess I can put you through your paces."

"I just bet you could."

Her heart was fluttering like a moth hopelessly beating its wings against a windowpane. One moment she'd been so wrapped up in Jan's life she'd found it hard to breathe, and now here she was, for a completely different reason, struggling to breathe again.

In defense she changed the subject. "There's been a change of plans for Sunday."

He lifted one eyebrow and waited.

She explained quickly about the harvest

celebration. She felt odd explaining about the goddesses in a sentence or two, so she left that part out. "These are my best friends," she said instead. "I'd like you to meet them. Will you come with us? We can bring bikes and ride once we're up there. When we get to the top of the mountain, biking's easy enough, and the road isn't busy."

"Will I be the only guy?"

"Most likely my dad's going to be there, and some of the other women will probably bring guys. Harmony and Jan will be there, so you won't feel like a stranger."

"Sounds like fun, but maybe not as much fun as having you to myself."

Again she wondered how she was going to teach for an hour with Adam watching every move she made. She set the ground rules. "You have to behave in my class, you know."

"Behave?" That smile reappeared.

"No double entendres, no flirting."

"Are we flirting?"

"Adam, if I'm imagining that, then I really have been alone too long."

"I don't want to throw you off your stride."

"Even a big guy like you couldn't do that. I'm good, Adam. You'll see."

"I very much look forward to seeing how

good you are."

She threw up her hands in defeat, then started toward the front door. He gave a soft laugh before he followed her inside.

CHAPTER 22

Harmony had planned to drive to the Goddess House on Sunday with Rilla and her family. That was until Taylor suggested she invite Nate, since Adam was coming, too.

"I didn't even think about inviting him myself," Harmony told Rilla as they packed a cooler filled with food. "It just never entered my mind. What's wrong with me? I have a boyfriend, more or less, and I never think about him."

Rilla held up a finger as if to say, wait, left for the living room, where she prodded her sons to finish getting dressed for the trip, and came back as if there had been no interruption.

"Can you call the poor guy a boyfriend if you never think about him?"

Brad, Rilla's husband, wandered into the kitchen and deposited a box of canning jars he'd rescued from the basement just as a door in the next room slammed.

"Are these the ones you meant?"

Rilla checked to be sure. Then she kissed his cheek. "My arms and legs. Thank you."

"Cooper and Landon just went out the front door."

"Will you check to be sure they're actually dressed?"

"I'll wrestle them into the car if they are."

Brad left with the canning jars, the door slammed again as he went after his sons and Rilla closed the lid on the cooler. "If you take this, I'll get the bread and cookies I made."

Harmony was used to these kinds of distractions midconversation. The Reynolds home was a noisy, boisterous place where laughter was loud, arguments were expected, rules weren't always obeyed.

It couldn't be any more different than the house she had grown up in, which made it particularly endearing.

She lifted the cooler, which after carrying Lottie seemed almost light, and nudged the back door with her hip. "I call Nate a boyfriend because I'd like him to be one."

"Really? You could have fooled me."

"What do you mean?"

"You know what I mean."

Unfortunately Harmony did, but she defended herself. "He couldn't be nicer.

358

Really. He has nice all sewed up. You'll see today."

"I met a lot of nice guys in college. I didn't fall in love with any of them until I met Brad."

"You're lucky. I haven't met that many myself."

"The world's actually filled with them. You don't have to grab the first one you see."

"If more women used their heads instead of their hormones to choose a man, there'd be a lot more happy marriages."

"So you're using your head? Is that fair to him?"

Harmony didn't know. But so far she'd seen no billboards on the highway announcing that Nate was falling in love, either. Maybe when he looked at her, all he could think about was dirty diapers and spilled milk.

But if they could get past these minor hang-ups, theirs could be one of those rare, logical courtships where two people who liked each other added all the pluses and decided to come together for all the right reasons.

"Easy come, easy go," Rilla said, limping after her.

"What do you mean?"

"I mean if you just drift into something

because it seems like a good idea, it'll be a piece of cake to drift out of it again when it no longer does. Is that any way to make a commitment?"

"As long as he's not falling madly in love with me, too, what can it hurt?"

"But what if he is?"

Harmony didn't know. She and Nate had never talked about their relationship — if you could call it that. The guy was so perfect she couldn't believe they weren't already planning a wedding. No, she was afraid the problem wasn't Nate's.

"Maybe I'm only attracted to jerks." She was sorry she'd said that out loud, but it was the truth, and Rilla was listening.

"Like Davis?"

"What a good example. And in high school I was madly in love with a guy who dumped me fifteen minutes before final exams. There are plenty more war stories, but you get the picture. I worry I'm looking for somebody like my father."

Rilla didn't try to reassure her. "And that's why Nate is so appealing?"

"He's the polar opposite."

"Using your head before you fall in love is a good idea. But then the magic has to take over. If it doesn't? Do you want to nurse a guy with a man cold or the stomach flu if you don't have any magic to back you up?"

Harmony deposited the cooler in the Reynoldses' van, told everybody she would see them at the Goddess House and went back inside to wake Lottie, who was napping in the Pack 'n Play.

Half an hour later Nate arrived. He wore khaki pants with enough pockets to stow everything a man needed for fishing, as well as the fish itself, a blinding white preppie sweater and a black baseball cap without a logo.

She wondered if he was afraid he might offend somebody if he took a stand on a team. He was that thoughtful.

Lottie and Nate hadn't met, and she'd debated how to dress her daughter for the big reveal. But in the end she'd settled on practical. No frilly dresses today. Lottie wore a royal-blue track suit that had once belonged to Cooper. It was warm and soft from wear, and Harmony would never be accused of trying to win points for her daughter.

"Aren't you a cutey?" Nate took the baby out of Harmony's arms and bobbed her in the air. He was clearly at ease, and Lottie, who hadn't quite woken up, seemed to sense it. She giggled with delight, and he laughed right back at her.

"I love babies this age," he said when Harmony held out her arms to take her back. He turned her expertly to fit Harmony's grasp. "Sometimes they freak out with strangers, but when they don't, they're just so sweet."

On a scale of one to ten, this guy was an eleven. Harmony made a note to remind herself about that tonight after he was gone and again tomorrow morning.

And on the trip to the Goddess House.

"I have everything together," she said. "Are you sure you want to drive? We'll have to put the car seat in your car."

"No problem. I'm an old hand with car seats. My sister has a baby. I'm her sitter of choice."

Ten minutes later they were on the road in Nate's late-model Ford Focus, a predictable, sensible car that suited him. He'd brought Lottie a present, a plastic music box shaped like a caterpillar that played an array of classical tunes every time she hit the button in the middle. He had patiently shown her how to use it before they started off, and now Mozart rang merrily from the backseat.

"How are Karen and Jeff?" she asked.

"Jeff's got another surgery scheduled next month, but they tell him it might be the last.

362

It's supposed to relieve a lot of his pain. He can't wait."

She was glad and told him so. "I went to Karen's blog. It's not what I expected. She's funny and irreverent —"

"Like you."

She smiled, pleased with his assessment. "She has a whole section of mistakes she's made. It's hysterical. I sent her a photo of the poor tomato plants in Marilla's garden where I spread fresh horse manure instead of the stuff that had composted. Karen used it yesterday in her gardening section and labeled it 'a Boo-Boo with Poo-Poo.' "

Nate laughed. He had a nice profile, and she admired it, the way she might admire an actor in a G-rated movie. "I'm glad you're coming with me," she said. "You know Taylor, and I think you know Samantha Ferguson and her mother, Georgia?"

"Sam was a year or two ahead of me. Miss Georgia was the best headmistress Covenant Academy ever had."

"She's the principal of an alternative school now, and she's engaged to a great guy named Lucas Ramsey."

"The mystery author?"

Why was she surprised Nate would know that? He seemed to be on top of everything, alert, aware, interested in everything around him. She lectured her hormones and told them to gear up fast as she caught him up on Georgia's romance with Lucas.

"When Lottie gets tired of that toy, I know a dozen children's songs we can sing for her," Nate said after she finished.

Harmony settled in for the drive. She was surprised they weren't yet climbing Doggett Mountain. For some reason it seemed as if she had been in Nate's car for a month.

Adam knew how to get information. He knew what he was entitled to and what he had to ferret out of the shadows. He liked to stay inside the law, but sometimes the law was a little fuzzy, or so he liked to tell himself. Getting Jan Stoddard's medical records wasn't fuzzy at all. It was clearly illegal. Which was why he had resorted to a few shady websites, a few phone calls where he'd pretended to be someone other than who he was, a few compliments in the right places.

Now, after days of work, he knew a lot more about Jan Stoddard and her trips to the local emergency room. It seemed that she had grown increasingly clumsy through the years, or so she and Rex had told physicians and nurses. She had a habit of tumbling down steps or falling off ladders. While

364

most people never fell face-first onto a sidewalk, Jan had managed it twice.

Or perhaps her husband just forgot he'd already used that story when he told it again the second time.

The red flags were waving, and emergency personnel hadn't missed them. But Jan had insisted the fault was her own and she didn't need help or counseling. Her husband would take care of her, and she was just going to do a better job of watching where she was going.

The last time she'd been to the local E.R., a doctor, who'd probably hoped to give her time to reconsider without Rex's hovering, had attempted to hospitalize her overnight for tests. Maybe she had a neurological problem that was causing all the stumbling and falling, multiple sclerosis perhaps, or Parkinson's. He'd suggested an MRI and maybe a CAT scan and most of all a quiet hospital room, but she had refused and gone home.

If there were more visits, they'd been to a different hospital, but Adam had enough information without looking any further.

Police reports were a different matter. Try as he might, he hadn't found anything to indicate that the police had ever been called to the Stoddard house. Of course, the house had been so far out in the country that neighbors probably wouldn't have heard any commotion. Jan herself had never made a complaint, nor had her children. Posing as a journalist, he called all the residents of Pawnee Parkland in a one-mile radius, which weren't that many. He asked about the Stoddard family and wasn't surprised to learn that they knew very little. None of them could imagine what had happened in that house the night of the fire or where the owners had disappeared to, but wasn't the whole thing a mystery and a shame?

Rex's employees were a different matter. Agents he spoke with were trying to carry on as if their boss would be back momentarily, even though Rex's absence had triggered a police investigation, and the Kansas Insurance Department investigators were involved, as well. One agent — who used the newer term "producer" — praised everything from Rex's thoughtful offerings of Starbucks coffee at monthly staff meetings to the extra services he provided their clients. Another had asked him to wait, and Adam had heard an office door close before the man returned. Then he'd given Adam a phone number so he could speak to an ex-employee for a different view.

The former employee, who'd officially

quit to take a job with the telephone company, had not been Rex's fan. He told Adam that Rex was an adequate if not pleasant boss until he felt someone had crossed him. Then he was known to retaliate. The punishment might be light. Someone who didn't get a report in on time might find he or she had been assigned to monitor telephone messages for the next few weekends instead of being part of the usual rotation. Or the punishment might be considerably heavier. For that Adam was referred to yet another ex-employee.

On Sunday, before he went to meet Taylor, he was finally able to connect with that woman, posing as a journalist again, as he had done with the others. Tami Murgan, who lived in Chicago, would only agree to talk if he promised not to use what she told him in his article. She said that while working for Rex she had advised a trucker with several speeding tickets that a company Rex's agency didn't represent might have cheaper rates.

"I felt sorry for the guy," she told Adam. "He was just a hardworking Joe who got caught doing what a thousand other truckers do. You know how hard truckers are pushed to get wherever they're going fast. He had a wife in a wheelchair who couldn't work, and he was afraid he'd have to stop driving and go on welfare if he couldn't get insurance he could afford. The other company gave him a deal he could manage. When Rex found out what I'd done, he was furious. But cold furious, if you know what I mean? He told me I'd made a bad mistake."

"He fired you?" Adam asked.

"Worse. He took all my best accounts and reassigned them, people I'd brought in myself through my own efforts. He said he couldn't trust me to do right by them anymore. But that wasn't all. Things started happening."

"What things?"

"My husband and I had a little cabin on a lake near the city. The office staff had been there for a party, so Rex knew where it was. The next time we went out to spend the weekend, we found all the windows had been shot out. Rain had leaked inside and ruined the floors and walls. Almost worse, the carcass of a deer had been left to rot on our porch."

"You know it was him? Not a hunter who'd had too much to drink?"

"It wasn't hunting season. We went back to Topeka after we did what we could about the mess and found that in the two days we had been away someone had broken into our garage and slashed the tires of our second car. At the office the next week? Rex told me he'd heard I was having a little personal trouble, and he hoped things got better. The thing is, I hadn't told anybody at the office what had happened, so how did he know?"

"You talked to the police?"

"We did, but they never got any leads."

"And you told them about Rex?"

"How could I? I didn't have a bit of proof. Two weeks later my husband got a job offer in Chicago with something of a promotion, so I gave notice. We sold our house and eventually the cabin, and moved here. Topeka was our home, but nothing good was going to come from standing our ground. Maybe the harassment would have stopped, but maybe it would have gotten worse, too."

Adam finished the phone call and hung up. Not one thing he'd heard in the past week was conclusive by itself, but together a pattern was forming. He knew enough about abusive men to recognize the pathology. Rex Stoddard had an anger problem. He had to be in complete control at all times, and he retaliated if anyone went against him in even the smallest things.

Some people saw a thoughtful, conscientious man, but those who had stepped over Rex's imaginary line saw the real one, paranoid, narcissistic and violent.

That was the Rex who had abused Jan Stoddard, and likely their daughter, too.

Adam had spent a lot of hours investigating, some of which would be impossible to justify. But Jan Stoddard, the abused wife, lent a different character to the family's story. What would a woman like that do to protect herself?

That was the question he still had to answer.

Since the weather was cool, he changed into jeans and a quarter-zip sweater. He fastened the bike he had rented to a portable rack on the back of his SUV and threw a pair of sneakers onto the passenger's seat in case he and Taylor really did get out on the road together. Then he set off for the house located between the Madison County townships of Luck and Trust. Since she'd planned to get there early, he had decided to drive alone, but he did some of his best thinking behind a steering wheel, so the time might be helpful.

As he drove he thought about the hours ahead. He was looking forward to spending the day with Taylor, even if it meant he had to relate to all her friends, as well.

He wasn't looking forward to the day because he was lonely. He was happy with his own company, a gift he'd received during his many moves as a kid. He made friends quickly, enjoyed them, then moved on.

He wasn't looking forward to this day because he needed a woman. If it was just about need, he would have chosen more wisely. The list of reasons he shouldn't be romantically involved with Taylor Martin was long and complicated.

He wasn't looking forward to it because he might find out more about Jan, either. Rarely did somebody blurt out their life story at a picnic table in between the burgers and the homemade ice cream.

No, he was glad to be driving up a steep mountain road because he'd been instantly attracted to Taylor, and the attraction was growing at an alarming rate. He had reached the point where everything she did struck him as either sexy or intriguing, and he wasn't sure which was worse. This was the time to call a halt, yet being with her was part of his investigation, so that was impractical, even foolish. He could tell himself to see her only when necessary, to stop engaging in what she called flirtation.

The problem? He wasn't listening.

He was no closer to figuring out how to handle the problem after he turned into the gravel driveway that matched his directions, or a few minutes later when he parked at the end of a line of cars that told him he was undoubtedly in the right place.

Taylor herself was standing under a massive oak up the driveway talking to a dark-haired woman wearing leggings and a purple tunic that reminded him of something he had seen in Pakistan. When she saw him, she started in his direction.

It was the most natural thing in the world to kiss her hello when she reached him. He didn't even consider. One minute they were just a few feet apart; the next she was leaning toward him and he was gratefully accepting her invitation. The kiss lasted seconds longer than it reasonably should have. He could feel his body stir in familiar ways, and the desire for something more clawing inside him.

"Well," he said, after she stepped back. "That's a great start to my day."

"I'm glad you found us. How was the drive?"

He didn't tell her that thoughts of her had kept him company the whole way. "Do you climb this mountain often? That's some road."

"My mother was born here. When Mom died she left this house and the property to a group of us to use. I'll explain on the way up to the house."

He put his arm around her and they walked that way toward a log structure at the top of a series of stone steps. He listened as she told the story of the property and the women who now owned it, strong, powerful women who would rally to protect their own. By the time he reached the house, he knew he was in more trouble than he'd imagined. Not only was he fast becoming infatuated with Taylor Martin; now he knew that she, and the women around her who called themselves the goddesses anonymous, were going to be a force to reckon with as he continued to investigate the lives of Jan and Harmony Stoddard.

CHAPTER 23

From the audio journal of a
forty-five-year-old woman, taped for the
files of Moving On, an underground
highway for abused women.

I can't speak for the many other women who allowed or still allow men to beat them, scream at them or systematically destroy their confidence. But even as the Abuser steadily made certain I was completely dependent on him, there were still moments at the beginning when I could have escaped. While most of my friends from college had moved away or lost interest, I still knew people who might help me. I had the phone number of a safe house, a doctor who seemed willing to get involved, neighbors who were close enough to run to if I needed them.

So why didn't I ask for help right away?

Why didn't I take my newborn son and leave?

Here are some of my reasons.

I believed in the institution of marriage. I believed that good marriages required hard work and compromise as well as patience.

I believed that I was somehow at fault, and if I just tried to be a better wife, the Abuser would never get angry again.

I believed that the stability of a loving home would smooth away my husband's rough edges. On my most hopeful days, I believed that rough edges were actually the only problems I was dealing with.

I believed that the Abuser loved and needed me, that without me, he would never find happiness.

I believed his happiness mattered.

I believed when he told me how much I meant to him, when he brought me presents or showed me kindness, that we had suddenly, finally, found a new and happier path. Every single time.

I believed that when the violence recurred, it was only a temporary lapse, that Dr. Jekyll was the real man and Mr. Hyde an aberration who would eventually disappear for good.

The story only becomes sadder because eventually I began to believe other things.

I believed I really wouldn't be able to survive without him.

I believed I couldn't support myself or my son alone.

I believed that underneath the violence, he had my best welfare in mind.

I believed that the real problem in our marriage was my inability to turn my life over to him, that my lingering desire for independence and the right to make all my own decisions was making us both unhappy.

I believed our marriage was a test I was failing, and if I just studied harder, eventually I would pass.

After several years had gone by, I began to believe that my happiness really didn't matter at all.

By then the only thing that did matter was protecting my children.

As a girl and a young woman, Jan had never been afraid of anyone. Only well into her marriage to Rex had she learned real fear. On that day she had realized that her husband, the man in whom she had invested so much devotion and time, was capable of a rage so deep that the lives of those around him would forever be threatened.

And that had changed everything.

How did a woman go back in time to the

person she once had been, untouched by knowledge that people were not necessarily good, that some people liked to cause pain and despair, that sometimes those people could hide the blight that stained their souls for months, perhaps even forever?

She supposed a woman didn't. She just moved forward. The phrase "sadder and wiser" existed for a reason.

"We've been assigned to work on these together," Ethan Martin told Jan with a tentative smile as he placed a bushel basket between them on the metal glider that graced the Goddess House front porch. "What do you think, are we up to snapping a bushel of beans?"

She tried to smile but couldn't quite. "I'm game if you are."

"We could work in the kitchen if you'd rather, but it's sunny enough that it's not too cold out here. What do you think?"

It wasn't a simple question, not for her. She wasn't sure which would be more intimidating, facing a man across the long, narrow table that took up a wide swath of the Goddess House kitchen, or here, where she could look out at the terrace leading down to the parking lot or up to the simple family cemetery that sat on a ridge above.

She realized she hadn't answered, that

Ethan's question still hung in the air. "We'll be fine here," she said. "If we get cold we can move inside."

"I've always thought someday I'd like to come up here and sit on this porch for a week. Just sit here and stare out and think."

Earlier in the day Taylor had taken Jan to see her mother's grave in the cemetery, and she wondered now if part of Ethan's wish was to feel close to the woman he had loved. Or perhaps that hadn't even been part of their equation. She knew Taylor and her mother had been estranged until right before Charlotte's death. She also knew that Ethan and Charlotte had been divorced, but that they, too, had reconciled. She just didn't know details.

"It's a beautiful spot," she said for lack of anything better. She reached for a handful of green beans and saw that he'd included a couple of plastic bowls. "Are these for the ends or the beans?"

"I'll get newspaper for the ends and we can just toss them on the floor." He left and Jan started to snap, dropping the ends in her lap.

"It was a bumper year for pole beans," he said when he returned. "Cristy and Sam are going to blanch them and put them in freezer bags. I'm glad we bought the new freezer. It's nice to have things to eat right here if somebody comes up on a whim."

He was making conversation, simple conversation for Jan to take part in. Nothing threatening. Nothing profound. She was expected to participate, but for the life of her, she couldn't. She was bound by fear, by years of inexperience, by an ego that had been so degraded there had been mornings in Topeka when, on waking, she had been afraid she had disappeared completely overnight.

"We don't have to talk," he said at last. "It's enough that we're sitting here together. We don't need a sound track."

"I'm sorry." She felt her eyes begin to fill.

"Why? You don't have to get to know me better."

"It's just that . . ."

"That you haven't had much practice," he finished for her, although that wasn't precisely what she had planned to say. "Jan, I know what you've been through. Of course you're not sure about me, even if I am Taylor's father. When I divorced Charlotte, it took me forever to try conversation with another woman. I was so angry at her, and I was pretty sure every woman I met was exactly like her."

"But didn't you . . . ?"

When she didn't finish, he did. "Get back together? We did at the end of her life. She changed so much, or maybe she just finally got to be the person she'd always wanted to be and couldn't quite manage."

She surprised herself. "Rex will never change." She managed to glance at him, and Ethan was nodding, as if she had said something profound.

"No, he won't," he agreed. "Charlotte was driven by the past, but she was never a bad person. Just on the wrong path. From what I know of your husband . . ." Now *his* voice trailed off.

"Did she enjoy hurting people?"

"Never. Which didn't mean she *didn't* hurt them, but she never derived pleasure from it. She just thought she was doing what she needed to for everybody, that she had to forge ahead for the rest of us, and we would all be happier when we realized it."

"Everything Rex does is for Rex. Nobody else is real to him."

"I'm so sorry you've had to go through this. No one deserves what you've lived with."

"Rex thought I did." Then she surprised herself again, and most likely poor Ethan, by laughing softly. "But *I* don't think so anymore, at least not most of the time. And

380

I guess that means I won."

"Good for you."

"When did you get over being angry?" she asked, a question that seemed to come from nowhere and everywhere. "At Charlotte. After the divorce."

"That's a good question." Ethan snapped a handful of beans. She could hear them popping, and she glanced over to see if she had offended him. But he was staring into space, as if thinking about an answer.

"You don't have to tell me," she said. "I don't know why I asked such a personal question."

"I want to, only I can't pinpoint it. I let go of the worst anger a little at a time, I guess. I found another woman and I married her, but the relationship was doomed, because underneath it I was still in love with Charlotte. I didn't realize it. Judy did. That's hard to understand, isn't it?"

"Harder for her, I bet."

He smiled. "She's happily married now. We're friends of a sort."

"That's good."

"You married for love, didn't you?"

"It doesn't always work out."

"Do you remember when you realized it wouldn't?"

Turnabout was fair play. She had asked a

personal question; Ethan had the same right.

"I know the exact moment." She grabbed another handful of beans and snapped them with more strength than the job required.

He didn't push for details, as if he realized she wouldn't — couldn't — talk about whatever had pushed her over the edge. "I would guess that's when you began to make plans to get away for good."

"No. It was when I tried to get away and couldn't that I knew I had married a monster, not a man."

"Jan, I —"

She took a deep breath. "It's okay. I'm sorry I told you more than you wanted to hear."

"That's not true. I would be happy to hear every bit of it when you're ready. There's nobody here today who wouldn't do anything they could to make this nightmare recede for you."

"Is it ever going to?" She was looking straight at him now. He was still a handsome man, lean and trim, dark hair more than half-gray, warm golden-brown eyes like Taylor's.

"The fact that you can talk about it, even a little, tells me it will. But I hope . . ."

"What?"

"That you'll find somebody you can really share it with. Somebody who can help you through it."

"Your daughter's helping."

"I'm glad."

"I'm not ready to talk to anybody like a professional, if that's what you mean."

"Sometimes it helps."

"I know."

He smiled encouragement. "I believe you're going to be okay, Jan. I think you've already made amazing progress. It says a lot about the person you were before all this began and the person you continued to be throughout it. However you do it, you have my admiration."

"I wasn't sure I could have any kind of conversation . . ."

"With a man?"

She nodded.

"I bet you really didn't think we'd have this particular one, did you?"

They wouldn't have, except that he had managed, with just a few words, to make her see they had something in common. Ethan had a gift.

"Did Charlotte . . . ?" She paused, trying to figure out how to phrase what she wanted to ask. She shrugged. "Did she ever tell you how lucky she was to have had you in her life?"

His eyes softened. "More than once."

"I'm so glad."

Analiese Wagner was so different from any minister Harmony had ever known that sometimes she couldn't quite believe Analiese was real. She was, though. Real, not perfect, but warm and funny and accepting of human frailties. She understood that as a child Harmony had been disheartened, even frightened by, her Sunday-morning experiences and that the family's minister had once told Jan it was her job to be such a good wife that Rex no longer wanted to beat her.

Harmony still didn't attend services at the Church of the Covenant, even though Analiese was one of the goddesses. She thought it was likely she would never step foot in church again except for funerals and weddings, but she still liked being with Analiese. The other woman wasn't really old enough to be her mother, but Harmony liked to imagine she had grown up with someone like her, someone confident and kind, but still tough when she had to be. She couldn't imagine Analiese allowing anybody to lay a hand on her. She might forgive that man for his transgressions, but she wouldn't give him a chance to try again.

Not like Jan.

"So it's just you and me," Analiese told Harmony as they started down the path to Zettie and Bill Johnston's apple orchard next to the Goddess House. They had been assured the apples that hadn't been picked would welcome their intervention.

Harmony was glad to be outdoors. Lottie was napping upstairs with one of Rilla's boys, and Rilla had promised to listen out for both of them. Nate? Nate was enjoying the companionship of Lucas and Georgia, who were building more shelves in the root cellar, so they could store all the food they had harvested.

Nate had offered to come with her to the orchard, but why would a cabinet maker pick apples when his skills were more useful elsewhere? And did either of them mind the separation?

Harmony tried to find a comfortable way to carry the bushel basket she'd taken from the porch. She gave up and dropped it in the Radio Flyer wagon Analiese was hauling behind her. "I thought Edna and Samantha were going to help."

"They decided to work on the apples Cristy already harvested earlier in the week so there will be room for ours in the kitchen."

"Rilla's doing that, too. We'll have apple pies with dinner tonight."

"The Johnstons have a cider press. Next week whoever comes up can help them make cider out of leftovers. Zettie said we can have half if we do."

Harmony thought all this food preparation was a bit much. The canned and frozen food would be great for Cristy, who worked hard to make ends meet, but between the produce they'd managed to harvest this first summer from the Goddess House garden and the largesse of neighbors, there would be far too much for one young woman. Some of the surplus might be eaten by visitors and the other goddesses, but the real purpose of both the weekend and putting food by for the winter was to build their community. They didn't have long stretches of time to spend together. They needed to catch up, to plan for the future, to decide if they were living up to Charlotte's request that whenever possible they work together to reach out to women who needed them.

Women like her mother.

"I like your mother," Analiese said, as if she were privy to Harmony's thoughts. "You look so much like her, I would have known

386

her anywhere."

"I have my father's coloring and hopefully nothing else."

"It's hard to see redeeming qualities sometimes, isn't it?"

"Especially when they don't exist."

"I can't argue. I've met people who buried whatever was good about them so deep inside that no one ever saw it again."

"I think some people are just born bad and there's nothing to bury."

"Sociologists and theologians will argue that one into eternity, but I don't think we really know the answer. And even if it's true, how do we figure out who those people are, and who's just lashing out because they've been so badly hurt?"

"Did you ask to partner with me for this job?"

Analiese laughed. "I am so transparent, aren't I?"

"And quick. You got right to it, didn't you?"

"I'm good."

Analiese was a lovely woman, nearly black hair pinned on top of her head, the palest blue eyes, a well-proportioned figure she had to fight to maintain. She liked bright colors and exotic fashions, and today she was wearing a hip-length tunic she'd gotten on a trip to India over cropped leggings. The purple tunic was embroidered with spidery gold-and-silver thread, and Harmony didn't know another person who could get away with wearing it to do something as mundane as picking apples.

"What if I tell you I don't want to talk about my father?" Harmony cast her gaze on the path at her feet.

"Then we won't."

"I'm assuming you didn't intend to give me an 'honor your mother and father' lecture, right?"

"Of course not."

"I did try that already. Shouldn't the Ten Commandments have codicils, you know, like wills do? Honor thy father and mother unless they are completely dishonorable, then get the heck away from them?"

"We could try that, but it gets sticky. Thou shalt not covet thy neighbor's wife unless she happens to be smarter and prettier than yours? Thou shalt not steal unless your baby needs milk?"

"If I had no other alternative I would steal to feed Lottie. I wouldn't like it, but I would."

"That's why some people are only comfortable living by the letter of the law, while some are only comfortable reinterpreting it.

But in this case the whole commandment about mothers and fathers is really extraordinary. 'Honor thy father and mother that your days may be long in the land that the Lord your God gives you.' In an overwhelmingly patriarchal society, for once mothers didn't get short shrift."

Harmony was silent.

When she didn't answer, Analiese said, "Honor doesn't necessarily mean obey or even love. I think it means you do the best you can with what you're given. After all, there's also scripture that says 'Fathers, do not provoke your children to anger.' "

"Did you bone up on appropriate Bible verses before our walk?"

"No, they pay me the big bucks to stay current."

Harmony couldn't help laughing, and Analiese smiled at her. "I think this has to be a hard time for you, right? Your father's missing and might be stalking your mother or even you. Your mom's living across town after you've been apart for years, and you're probably ambivalent about her being so close."

"I'm not. I wish she could be right in my apartment with me."

Analiese didn't respond. Harmony defended herself. "My mother's the only

389

reason I'm more or less sane. She tried so hard to make things good for all of us. She was the rock I clung to. When my father wasn't home we had a normal life, and sometimes even when he was there, she managed to make it all feel normal."

"But it wasn't." It wasn't a question.

"That wasn't her fault."

"Then you never blamed her."

"Of course not."

"I think you're more magnanimous than I would be. Or even than I was. My father weighed more than three hundred pounds when he died, and even though he was the one who kept demanding more and more food, I still blame my mother for stuffing him until his heart finally stopped."

"That's different. Your parents were on the same team, more or less. My mother was just trying to keep my father happy so he wouldn't take out his anger on us."

"That's not the same team? The Keep-Daddy-Happy team? She put up with a lot, didn't she, to make sure he got everything he wanted?"

They had arrived at the apple orchard, but they stopped at the edge. Analiese faced Harmony. "As a kid sometimes I felt I was right in the middle at home. I was over-weight, too, but I slimmed down, one miserable ounce at a time. I couldn't figure out why my father couldn't at least try, or why my mother didn't help. I tried to make him see he needed to diet, but I was the only one who ever did."

"Nobody could make my father do anything." Harmony didn't want to think about this, but now she couldn't help herself. "He could be nice, kind even, but if he thought we crossed him in any way, he went into these rages. I remember . . ." She did remember, unfortunately, and she wished she didn't.

"Something you don't feel like talking about," Analiese said.

"I had a doll. My mother sewed clothes for her, a whole wardrobe. I called her Cissy, and she was like the sister I didn't have. One day I did something to make him mad. I can't even remember what, something silly, I'm sure. Too much noise, or not finishing all the vegetables on my plate, or fidgeting when he said grace. He always went on and on at the table pretending to pray, making notes about every little thing that had gone wrong, about the people who had treated him badly, about the things my brother and I had done that we shouldn't have. . . ."

She realized she was drifting. "Anyway, he

was so angry that evening. He went to my room and got Cissy and threw her in our fireplace. He made me light the match to start the fire. I was crying so hard I burned my fingers."

She looked up from the ground. "I was never allowed to have a pet, but I think that was my mother's doing. She knew he might do the same thing to an animal if we ever got attached to one."

Analiese looked more sad than ministerial. "I'm so sorry. I'm afraid I understand too well. I lived with a man who liked to get even, too. My husband."

"You were married? I forgot."

"I was young, he wasn't. He died just as I was getting ready to leave him. But I would have, no matter what he said or did. Nothing would have kept me there."

"My mother is different. She couldn't leave. I wanted her to."

"Why?"

"Why couldn't she leave?" Harmony shrugged. "She was afraid? He stole all her confidence, and he told her he would kill her. She believed him."

"Did *you* believe him?"

"I wanted her to go, anyway." Harmony swallowed because her throat felt as if it was closing. "I wanted her to go no matter what he said. I tried to get her to come with me when I left for Asheville. When I got here I tried to get her to join me. I told her we would find a way to stay safe. But she refused and refused. And now she's here, and I'm so glad she is, but I look at her and I think about all those wasted years and how miserable I was at home, and I wonder why she was so weak that she couldn't do it!"

Analiese didn't say anything.

Harmony didn't, either, not for a long time. From the apple trees she heard the squawking of crows, but it was the only noise in the orchard.

"Okay, you win. I'm angry," Harmony said at last.

"Why wouldn't you be?"

"I love her. I know what she went through."

"But you know what *you* went through, too."

"All I've wanted for years and years was for Mom to get away." Harmony felt the tears in her eyes, and she wiped them with the back of her hand, like a little girl.

"Now she has," Analiese said, "but your father is still controlling things. And you can't work through the hurt and the anger, because being with her is so dangerous right now. You're just hanging out and waiting for

393

him to do something, and trying to be mature while you do."

"I guess I'm not very good at it."

"I think you're splendid, but I think you're under fire, too."

"So what do I do?"

"We can talk anytime you need to. That might help for starters."

"I want to find out what happened to my father. I want to know where he is and what he's planning. Until I know that, nothing else is going to matter."

"Do you want me to see if I can set up something? I used to be an investigative journalist. I still know people."

"We're afraid making inquiries might alert somebody we're here."

"I can almost guarantee complete discretion."

Harmony considered. "I'll talk to Mom, but there's only one way he'll never be a danger to us again."

"I know."

But Harmony had to say it out loud anyway, because she knew Analiese would understand. She met her friend's eyes. "He won't be a danger if he's dead. And if he is, then I won't have to worry about honoring him, will I? And I won't have to be afraid or angry. I can just get on with my life, and so can my mother."

CHAPTER 24

Harmony was still attending the self-defense class at Evolution. In a month of classes she had learned a number of things she might need if she was grabbed on the street or if she ever dated a guy who didn't take no for an answer.

With Nate, of course, she didn't have to practice the word or the strategies. Nate kissed her good night. Sometimes he held her hand or draped an arm around her shoulders, the way he had at the goddesses' harvest campfire nearly two weeks before, but most of the time he was happy just to chat, the way a best friend would. There was little chance that some evening he would start making demands she didn't want to meet. She was afraid if he did, she would simply dissolve into laughter, and after a second, he would probably join her.

She had even wondered if Nate might be gay, but since she was as unenthusiastic about moving forward sexually as he seemed to be, maybe he was wondering the same thing about her.

She knew her mother was making some headway in class, too. On one of their phone calls Jan had said that Adam had praised her for her ability to get out of a wrist grab. Since breaking free usually began with some form of strike, that really was progress.

Harmony might not be as good as Taylor, whose reflexes were so sharp she only needed one demonstration to understand what was required, but she was physically active and strong, and she was holding her own.

Tonight, though, there was a new member of the class. A sleek red and still somehow menacing punching bag.

"I know from experience it's hard to strike a real person, even one who's as well protected as I am when we work together. It's a lot easier to put your full strength into a strike or kick if you're aiming at a punching bag. So that's why Taylor has graciously purchased our friend here." Adam gestured to the heavy bag behind him, suspended from the ceiling in the corner. "Tonight you're going to practice with B.G. here, wearing gloves made for the purpose. B.G. stands for Bad Guy, by the way."

Adam stuck his cap on the top of the bag and turned it with the bill to the back. Then he waited for the polite ripple of laughter to subside. "The gloves will protect your knuckles and wrists when you go after B.G., but they have to be used correctly."

As he launched into the rules, Harmony listened. Keep your wrists straight. Stay balanced. Hit, don't push, the bag. Her mind wandered as he continued the lecture. She imagined landing a solid punch and what it would feel like. Adam was right. She didn't want to hurt him or anybody else. Although her mother had often managed to intercede and turn the tide of her father's rage she still knew what it felt like to be struck and struck repeatedly, and she didn't want to inflict pain.

But a punching bag?

They lined up, and Adam passed out gloves and showed each woman how to adjust them. He checked hers when he got to the back of the line.

"Tighten the wrist guard just a little," he said, and watched her do it. "And the padding should fit over your knuckles." He took one hand, then the other, and felt to be sure. "You're good to go."

"What are the chances we'll be wearing

boxing gloves if somebody jumps us on the street?"

He flashed a quick smile. "What are the chances that at that point you'll be so worried about your knuckles you won't try to use what we've learned here, anyway?"

She liked Adam well enough. She still harbored a grudge because he had separated her from her mother, but she knew both of them were probably progressing faster. He was definitely an attractive man, as different from Nate as a bear from a border collie, but she was also aware that he and Taylor were working their way toward some kind of relationship. Taylor hadn't said they were a couple, but Adam had shown up at the Goddess House for the harvest celebration, and the two of them had taken a long bike ride together just before evening fell. They had been late returning for the campfire, and neither had seemed sorry.

"This is going to be good for you," he said, before he headed back to the head of the line.

"Why?"

"Because you've been holding back. You won't have to now."

"Doesn't everybody hold back?"

"Not the way you do."

She wondered about that as he demonstrated what he wanted them to do. They were going to practice jabbing the punching bag to get a feel for the way it reacted; then they would graduate to trying some of their strikes. This would help them develop confidence and translate what they knew in their heads into muscle memory.

She watched as Taylor began. Adam coached her, reminding her not to twist her body, to avoid winding up for a strike like a pitcher at the mound. She landed several good jabs, and finally he sent her to stand behind Harmony.

"How did that feel?" Harmony asked as Adam began to work with the next student.

"Strange, like a lifetime of training to be a good girl was for nothing."

She'd had plenty of that training herself. Her father had always begun whatever punishment he planned to mete out with the phrase "You were not a good girl today." It had meant anything from "You forgot to turn the knife blades toward the plates when you set the table" to "Buddy says you made a face at him on the school bus."

She was still thinking about that when she got to the head of the line. Adam showed her what he wanted her to do. Keep her wrist straight; keep her body aligned; follow through on her punches.

She let him finish, and then she struck the punching bag with what she thought was plenty of force. It barely moved.

"Okay," he said, "let's try it again." He moved around her, and with his hands on her shoulders, he repositioned her. "The most powerful part of a strike comes near the end. You want to contact the bag when your arm is almost extended. You don't want to push the bag, you want to smack it. Try it from there."

She did, and she was surprised how much better the strike felt. She heard a pop, which signaled she had made a connection with some actual power. She was encouraged.

Adam worked with her a bit more, and then they all tried it again. "You want to get this right," he said as the women each moved forward to take a turn. "You want your muscles to remember how this feels when you do it correctly, not when you're making mistakes. Breathe out when you hit the bag. Don't hold your breath. Get used to that, too."

She was ready when it was her turn. She practiced all the things he had told her, positioned herself just the way he had and she punched with some actual force this time.

"Good," he said. "You've improved a

hundred percent already."

The third time up she was even better, stronger, more confident. Then Adam changed the routine.

"Okay, you're starting to get the feel of it," he said. "So now we're going to do a couple of combinations at the bag. We're going to practice the strikes you've already learned. I'll demonstrate."

They all stepped back. He executed a short series of movements. He began with a cupped hand to the side of the bag, approximating the location of an attacker's ear, which could cause disorientation as well as pain. He followed with a hammer fist to B.G.'s nose — or what passed for one in their imaginations. The third strike was to the groin, and the reason for that was clear to everybody.

"For that one you can use a fist, an open hand or a knee," he said. "Whatever seems most possible. So try them all. You need force and accuracy, not fancy footwork. That's three strikes in a row. Taylor, want to start? We'll walk through them slowly until it feels right, and then you can take off."

Harmony was fascinated. This was more like real defense, not just disjointed individual strikes that seemed to have little application. A woman who needed to defend herself would need more than one blow to persuade her attacker she was serious. She would need an arsenal, as many strikes as it took to get him to back off or roll over or whatever he had to do to get away from her.

Then she could run away, which was the purpose of everything they had learned.

Taylor managed the three required strikes using the fluid, connected movements of a dance sequence. A bummed-out Harmony knew she would never manage that perfect choreography, but as it turned out, Adam wasn't impressed. He told Taylor she wasn't putting enough strength into the movements, that her attacker might be intrigued by how lovely she was as she performed, but he certainly wasn't going to be thinking about his injuries, because he wouldn't have any.

She tried again, with more force, and he told her she needed practice. The next woman tried her version, and he coached her while Taylor got in line behind Harmony.

"I thought you looked great," Harmony said.

"That's my plan. Bad Guy will be wowed by my yogilike calm and grace, and he'll let me go because I need to share it with the world."

"Works for me."

When it was her turn Harmony got into position and focused as if her life or at least her safety depended on it. Then she performed the sequence, putting every bit of energy in her body behind each strike.

"Excellent," Adam said. "But you're separating the strikes by seconds. B.G. here has plenty of time to recuperate and block the next one well before you wind up to try it. Can you move faster?"

She thought he was being unfair. There had been nothing more than a hiccup between strikes. But she tried again, moving faster this time.

"Better," he said. "But you're telegraphing what you're about to do. Take him by surprise."

She focused harder and ran through the sequence with the most speed yet, sparer movements, maximum strength.

"Again," Adam said.

She went through it again.

"Again!"

Frustrated, she slammed her palm against B.G.'s ear, brought her fist down on the region of his nose and this time used her knee in the punching bag's groin area, nearly stumbling backward when the bag swung away from her.

"Again!"

She turned, furious he was keeping after her the way her father always had no matter how well she performed at anything. She had never been good enough for Rex Stoddard, and now apparently she wasn't good enough for Adam Pryor, either.

She would never be good enough for anybody.

She lunged for Adam's ear with an open palm. He jumped aside so she didn't even graze his cheek, but by then she was already aiming for his nose with her fist. Knowing what was coming, he blocked that easily, too, but by then her knee was lifting to slam between his legs.

He danced away just in time.

She heard a horrified gasp behind her, and somehow that, not the surprise on Adam's face, brought her back to reality.

"Oh God . . ." She stepped back and put her face in her hands.

"Take five," Adam told the class.

Harmony could hear the other students moving back and away. She was too humiliated to look up and see. She was too humiliated to ever lift her head again.

She felt hands against hers, pulling *her* hands apart. And she was forced to look up.

"Well, you got the sequence down," he said.

"I'm . . ." She swallowed.

"You're living somewhere else," he said. "I've been there, so I know. Nobody understands better. Sometimes the past slips into the present. But you're okay. You're here, and we're all friends in this room."

She tried to nod and couldn't.

"Who are you angry with?" he asked gently.

And because above all she owed him an explanation, she had to answer. "My father."

"I get it."

"No, you don't."

"I think maybe you fought back tonight the way you couldn't when you were growing up."

She had revealed too much and she tried to retreat. "I never needed to fight back. Nobody ever hurt me." She finally looked into his eyes and saw he didn't believe her.

"The past is nothing to be ashamed of. You felt cornered again, and you fought back. You defended yourself. That's part of what this class is about. Now you have to channel the anger and deal with old feelings in a new and better way. You have to gain control."

"I'll drop out."

"Not an option. You're going to finish. Then I'm going to find a good martial arts program for you, and we're going to get you enrolled for the next session. You have enormous ability, Harmony, but you need discipline and training, and you need to deal with your past. They'll help you."

"It's nothing I can't manage on my own."

He smiled sadly. "Sure it is."

She closed her eyes.

"Don't let this defeat you," Adam said. "You struck a blow to liberate yourself tonight. Now you just need to remember who the enemy is."

"I *know* who the enemy is."

She felt a hand on her shoulder. "Of course you do," he said. "And now you're going to learn how to stay safe from him and the damage he did. Forever."

CHAPTER 25

Rain sluiced from the eaves of Taylor's house to the walkway and flower beds below, glistening silver sheets and symphonic splashes. Maddie and Edna sat on the sofa with their chins resting in their hands, staring out at the wind-whipped landscape.

"I am so, so sick of rain," Maddie said.

Taylor had heard that sentence countless times in the past week. At least half-a-dozen repetitions ago she'd given up answering or encouraging her daughter to be positive, and now she clamped her lips and continued to chop vegetables for soup. They had received an uncharacteristic amount of rain for autumn, enough that low-lying creeks had flooded and leaves had been knocked to the ground before they'd had time to make the leap on their own. The studio was high enough to avoid flooding, but much of the River Arts District was holding its breath. She was hopeful the rain would end soon and they would get back to a normal fall.

Edna, usually upbeat, looked no happier. She was a lovely girl, just a year older than Maddie, with her mother Samantha's wild curly hair and latte-colored skin. Samantha was of Korean, African and European heritage, but nobody except Samantha knew what Edna's father had added to the ethnic feast. Samantha was noticeably silent about him, and as close as she and Taylor were, that subject had always been off-limits.

Taylor turned her attention back to the carrots and listened to the girls chat.

"We could carry umbrellas." That solution came from Maddie.

"They'll turn inside out in this wind."

"We can't *not* go, Edna. Our costumes are too amazing. And we're getting old! Next year we probably won't even want to trick-or-treat." Maddie lowered her voice just a little, although Taylor could still hear over the thunk of knife against cutting board. "Boys will think we're silly."

"Who cares?"

Taylor tried not to smile. Edna probably *didn't* care. She had been born with a unique confidence that set her apart from Maddie's other friends. At twelve going on forty, she was thoughtful, whip-smart and absolutely capable of making everybody see things her way, including the aforementioned boys. Taylor's mom had predicted that Edna might well be the first female President of the United States.

"Well, what do you think we ought to do?" Maddie got up and pressed her nose to the windowpane. "We'll be warm in the bear costumes, but we won't stay dry."

"We could have a Halloween party inside."

In the kitchen Taylor rolled her eyes.

"Nobody's going to come," Maddie said. "It's too late."

"Maybe it's not. I mean, if they're like us, they don't have anything else to do tonight."

"We don't have food, games, a place to have it. . . ."

"I bet your mom would let us have it here. Or maybe in your grandfather's workshop?"

Taylor was feeling more and more like a fly on the wall, a particularly hideous, menacing fly since it was Halloween. She waited to see what else the girls' fantasy might require of her. Run out in the storm to buy cider, popcorn and pumpkins? Magically clear Ethan's workshop of dangerous tools and towering stacks of lumber?

"You're right," Edna said, after she'd apparently run through all the pros and cons.

"Dumb idea. And besides, we're supposed to be getting cans for the food bank."

Which was why, Taylor decided, her own mother had seen political success in Edna's future. The girl could compromise, and she could organize. Tonight a whole group of kids in her class were supposed to ask for food bank donations instead of candy, thanks to Edna.

Of course, if anybody wanted to give them both . . .

The front door opened and Jan blew in. "It is *miserable* out there," she said, but not as if she was reporting something they didn't already know.

Taylor dumped veggies into the broth and began to clean up. "I was beginning to think you'd washed away."

"You girls still want to go trick-or-treating, don't you?" she asked the duo on the sofa.

"Our costumes will get ruined."

"They're just costumes, but I've got the perfect solution." Jan pulled a big sheet of yellow vinyl out of a shopping bag. "Rain slickers!"

"No way!" Edna jumped up to join Jan by the door. "You can make slickers?"

"More like ponchos, I guess, but we'll fix them up so they're maximum protection, minimum disguise, so your costumes will

411

show. I've got enough of this for Lottie, too, but I'll need help to get them done in time."

"You bet!" Edna threw her arms around Jan. Maddie had joined them by then, and for a moment the three were a joyous tangle of arms and legs.

"Jan, you are brilliant," Taylor said, drying her hands on a towel as she went to see the new purchase. "You know how to do this?"

"I'll figure it out. I bought plenty of this stuff, and it was on sale. I wouldn't trust it to last for years, but it will last a night. And they'll be warm enough wrapped in fake fur that nobody's going to come home sick, unless they eat too much candy."

"You already did so much."

"I have absolutely loved every minute of it."

Since that was obvious, Taylor said no more. "So you want me to call Harmony and ask her to bring Lottie like she planned?"

"What are the Three Bears without Baby Bear?"

In a flurry of conversation, the girls and Jan disappeared into her bedroom, where she had set up her new sewing machine, complete with sewing table. Taylor didn't know much about these things, but from what she could tell the machine could make a baby's layette, change its diapers and rock it to sleep while it sewed new crib sheets and matching quilts. Jan had assured her the machine wasn't even top-of-the-line, and Taylor thought that was a good thing. Anything more high-tech might redecorate her house with flowery pillows and polka-dot curtains while everyone was sleeping.

While she pulled a can of tomatoes out of the pantry, she dialed Harmony's cell phone. Harmony answered right away.

For obvious reasons Taylor never mentioned Jan's name over the phone. Her grasp of surveillance practices was limited, but why take chances? "The resident seamstress is making yellow slickers to go over the bear costumes. Are you game?"

"They're going to look like Paddington Bear in triplicate."

"That's too subtle to matter. Say you'll come."

"Nate wants to come, too. Is that okay?"

"Why wouldn't it be?"

"He loves Halloween. Knowing Nate, he'll probably dress up."

"The girls will love him." Taylor waited, because this was the perfect moment for Harmony to say she was falling in love with Nate, too, but the silence extended.

"If you don't want him to come, tell him I

said no," Taylor said at last.

"No, we'll have fun, and he'll help carry Baby Bear. He saw Lottie's costume and thought it was amazing."

All three of the costumes were. Edna, as Papa Bear, was clothed in coal-black fur adorned with a shiny top hat, a satin vest with a striped tie, tuxedo pants held up by wide suspenders and a stumpy little tail that wagged when she pulled a string at the waistband of her pants.

Maddie, Mama Bear, had soft brown grizzly fur topped by a short yellow polka-dot housedress and a white eyelet apron, an Orphan Annie wig and feet showcasing patent leather Mary Janes with big yellow bows.

Lottie, Baby Bear, was a polar bear cub, with bright pink overalls edged in ruffles, and lacy lavender bows for the neckline and the top of her head.

Neither Jan nor the girls had been overly concerned with genetics when designing the bear family.

"I'm making a huge pot of soup for everybody, so please plan to eat here. Maddie and Edna made corn muffins to go with it." After Harmony promised to arrive by six Taylor hung up.

Nate and Harmony. She had been so

certain they were perfect for each other. Which just proved that logic had very little to do with choosing a mate or even a lover.

Which made her think of Adam.

Of course.

The Wednesday self-defense class had been postponed because of the holiday, so both classes would meet tomorrow. And this meant he was free tonight.

Before she could talk herself out of it, she picked up the phone again and dialed Adam's cell. When he answered she leaned against the stove and imagined him in the black T-shirt he'd been wearing the last time they were together. Or possibly just coming out of the shower.

For a moment she couldn't speak.

"Taylor?"

No surprise he had caller ID. She stood a little straighter. "Sorry. Look, we're having something of a Halloween get-together over here. Just veggie soup and kids coming and going. I'm staying home to give out treats if any ghosts and goblins are brave enough to go out tonight, and I could use some company."

"What about Jan?"

"Male company."

He gave a low laugh, which seemed to be directly connected to her spinal cord.

"Someday we'll need to spend time together without an audience."

"Really? Why?"

He laughed again.

"Come about six?" she said.

"I wouldn't miss it."

She hung up and imagined spending time with Adam that didn't include the goddesses or her daughter or Jan. Or bikes. Or hikes.

She smiled and left the kitchen to see whether she needed to wash the new shirt she had just decided to wear tonight.

When the plan to include Lottie in trick-or-treating was hatched, Jan had assumed she and Harmony wouldn't be in the same place at the same time on Halloween night. Then Taylor had pointed out it was perfectly logical for Harmony to come to her house since they had been friends for some time, and who would question one friend visiting another? As long as Jan didn't announce her presence by answering the door for trick-or-treaters or someone scarier — or accompany her adorable granddaughter along the route with Harmony beside her, all seemed safe.

"I can't believe what you did." Taylor was examining the hastily designed and crafted ponchos that would — if the rain didn't let up — top the bear costumes. "They're so cute."

"Maybe they won't have to use them. It seems to be clearing."

Taylor wrinkled her nose. "I'll believe it when I see it. But it's only drizzling right now. Maybe we'll luck out."

Jan took bowls from the island and set the table as Taylor added seasoning to her soup. Adam was coming, Harmony, Nate. Altogether she counted seven, although they might eat in shifts. She hadn't celebrated Halloween in so long she was almost as excited as Maddie and Edna. She was also smart. Once the three bears left, she would disappear into her room to let Adam and Taylor have privacy. She had a distant view of the street, and she planned to hem a dress she had made for Lottie while she sat near the window and watched the parade of costumes go by.

The Stoddards had never had trick-or-treaters in Topeka. They had lived too far from other houses, and Rex always turned off the outside lights to be sure any brave souls knew they weren't welcome. In later years he had banned Halloween decorations, too, calling the holiday the work of the devil.

She wondered if he had sensed his own evil nature and hadn't wanted the competition. Or perhaps, more charitably, he just hadn't wanted reminders of the person he was becoming.

Or always had been.

If she ever learned she was completely safe from Rex Stoddard, would he still occupy so much of her mind? Or could she then finally put the Abuser and her past behind her? Taylor had given her an older-model computer she no longer needed, and Jan had spent hours on the internet reading about abuse and recovery.

There were proven ways to relegate trauma to the past. Of course, one of them was talk therapy, and while someday she probably would find a counselor or join a support group, she wasn't yet ready. First she wanted to finish telling her story. Afraid that sharing it with a counselor would make recording it feel less important, she wanted to finish the tapes first.

She was intrigued by Taylor's suggestion that she turn them into podcasts to help other women entrapped in volatile relationships. Believing she might make a difference made it easier to put one foot in front of the other every day. And if Rex did reenter her life, she wanted her version of their time together made public so the world would know what kind of man he really was. Because when he found her, and when she refused to return to Kansas with him, she wouldn't live to tell the story.

She realized where her thoughts had taken her, a familiar and well-trodden path. She reminded herself that today she was safe, and so were Harmony and Lottie. Today was about celebration, because today she was with people she loved, and despite the rain, this was going to be a perfect Halloween.

The doorbell rang and she disappeared into the kitchen as Maddie came running from the back of the house to answer. Adam came in, stomping his boots on the inside doormat that Taylor had installed when the rain just wouldn't quit. Maddie took his rain jacket to hang it in the hall closet.

Balancing easily on one leg he removed first one boot, then the other, and stood them in the plastic tray beside the door. "Something smells good."

Taylor left the stove to welcome him. "Because we know the girls won't have enough sweet things to eat today, I decided to finish the meal with chocolate cupcakes."

"As long as you're the one staying up all night with them, I think it's a great idea."

As Maddie skipped back to her bedroom Jan watched Taylor and Adam together. The casual greeting should be over, but they looked in no hurry to part, standing as close as they could get without pressing their bodies together. They lowered their voices as they chatted, and she fiddled with glasses from the cupboards, putting ice in them, unnecessarily setting them on a tray, adding napkins, a sugar bowl, lemons, until they finally joined her.

She greeted Adam, then added, "I don't know who will want tea, but we're all ready if they do."

He took the tray from her hands to carry it to the table. "I hear you made some great costumes."

She followed with the pitcher. "I had fun doing it."

"Are you going trick-or-treating with the girls?"

"No, Harmony and her friend Nate can take care of things."

"Then you'll help us give out candy?"

She had prepared. "I'm pretty tired. I think I'm going to head to my room after dinner and watch something spooky on television while I do a little sewing. I'll let you and Taylor do the honors out here."

"It's a strange holiday, isn't it? Strangers

come to your home in disguise and make demands. I wonder who came up with that."

"It must have been a simpler time when people didn't worry so much about strangers."

"I don't know. Sometimes it's the people we know best who cause the most trouble," Adam said.

She couldn't argue with that, nor could she agree and invite more questions. The doorbell rang before she could respond anyway, and she headed back to the kitchen to hide herself again.

Harmony came in with Lottie in her arms, followed by Nate and a stranger. Taylor went to take Lottie and balanced the baby on one hip.

"Jan," Harmony called, "come meet Fletcher Bailey."

Jan was startled, first as she always was when her daughter called her by her name, second because she had been singled out to appear front and center when there was a male stranger in the house. She took her time going into the living room, struggling to compose herself for the introduction.

Fletcher Bailey was tall, as tall as Nate, slender but broad-shouldered. His hair was nearly gray, but his face was youthful, dark eyebrows, gray eyes with laugh lines engraved around them. She judged him to be close to her own age, with barely repressed energy. He stuck out his hand when Harmony introduced her as Jan Seaton, and she, having no choice except to make a fool of herself, tentatively took it.

His palm was neither rough nor smooth, and his grip was strong but not so strong she felt captured. He held her hand just long enough to make sure she knew he had.

"I know I'm interrupting dinner," he said in explanation, "and I promise I'm leaving. But Nate and I have been friends a long time, and he told me about the costumes you made, and he wanted me to see them. I couldn't say no."

Jan tried to make sense of a grown man interested in Halloween costumes. "Really? They're nothing special."

"Are you kidding?" Nate said. "Harmony showed me Lottie's. It's the cutest thing I ever saw, and she said the others were just as great."

"I'll see if the girls will let me show you," Harmony said, disappearing down the hall to Maddie's room.

"Fletcher's both managing and artistic director at On Stage," Nate said.

"That's one of Asheville's community theaters." Fletcher smiled. "The best one.

Nate helps build sets in his free time."

Jan still wasn't making sense of this. She knew something was required. "That sounds like fun," she said, and knew she sounded silly.

"Fun is the perfect start."

Before she could ask what he meant, the girls came in carrying their costumes. "Harmony said you want to see these. We have to wait until after dinner to change." Maddie glared at her mother, who had obviously given that order.

Fletcher gave a low whistle and took Maddie's costume to examine it. "Jan, you did all this?"

"I assembled it from bits and pieces. I got a dress at the Salvation Army and remade it. Same thing with Papa Bear's pants."

He looked at Edna's costume, too. "You girls will be the hit of trick or treat," he said. "These are amazing."

The girls left, costumes in hand, Nate and Harmony disappeared into the kitchen with Taylor, and Jan was left there to make conversation with a stranger, the last place she wanted to be.

"You're really gifted," he said. "Did you study costume design?"

That struck her as funny, and despite her discomfort she laughed. "Only if you count

423

watching television and trying to figure out how the actors' clothes were made. I was bored a lot. Sewing was my outlet."

"You're not from here?"

She didn't want to say too much, not sure what he knew about Harmony. "The Midwest."

"So you're new? Nobody else has had time to snap you up?"

"For what?"

"I very badly need a new costume manager. Mine just moved to Alaska."

"Could she have gone much farther?" she asked without thinking. Fletcher's enthusiasm was contagious. "Did you scare her away?"

"Him, and no, I didn't, but not for lack of trying. He wasn't very good, but I couldn't very well fire him, because you don't fire volunteers. You just find better things for them to do with their time and hope they agree."

"You sound like a taskmaster."

He smiled again, and she didn't feel threatened. His gaze was warm and focused but not intrusive. She didn't know how he managed that, but it interested her.

"Would you consider finding out?" he asked. "I'm told I'm easy to work with, and we do have fun, although it can get crazy right before we launch a show."

She still wasn't clear. "Find out what?"

"If I'm a taskmaster. Will you come and work on costumes for our next show? We're doing *Camelot,* and we need somebody with talent and vision to dress our knights and ladies."

She took a step back. "Oh, you don't need me. I would have no idea in the world what to do."

"It's new, but that doesn't mean you wouldn't know what to do. You'd be working with a team, and most of them are experienced, although not a one of them wants to take any responsibility. They'll bring you up to speed pretty fast. It's fast-paced, but it's also great fun. I promise you'll enjoy yourself."

She couldn't let him get away with that. "That's a pretty big promise. You don't know me even a little."

He smiled again, and his gaze warmed even more. "We can change that, if you say the word."

CHAPTER 26

Taylor was glad that when she first began looking for studio space, her father had talked her out of a building closer to the river. The district owed much of its charm to the French Broad River, which flowed nearby, but the river was also easily enraged and prone to spilling over its banks. That morning, as she'd driven in circles to find a new way to reach the studio, she had glimpsed the building she hadn't bought. She'd hoped the owners, stained-glass artists whose magnificent windows had recently been featured in *Southern Living* magazine, had moved all their work to the second floor — along with their tools, display cases, furniture — before the water moved in.

Now it was afternoon, and while the rain had stopped at least temporarily, the river was still creeping higher.

"I think we ought to sponsor a free evening

at the café for all the artists and shop owners who've been flooded this week," she told
Dante, the café's thirtysomething hipster
chef. "Maybe next Friday night. Wine, heavy
hors d'oeuvre, desserts. A little live jazz.
Something to help people feel better. Maybe
give them a chance to vent. You know." She
could only imagine how everyone who had
been affected by the rising water was feeling
today.

Dante, whose thrift-store clothing, long
side-swept bangs and thickly rimmed glasses
disguised an easily discouraged man, was
making copious notes on the smart phone
that was never far from his reach. He looked
up. "You're saying I'll really get to cook for
a change?"

She rested her hand on his buffalo-plaid
shoulder. "I'm sorry things aren't happening here as fast as we want. And these
detours don't help."

"I'm losing my enthusiasm."

"I've scheduled a bigger ad in the *Mountain
Xpress* next week, and if we get the word
out and get the locals in next Friday, maybe
that will drum up new business. But the
classes are filling up, and pretty soon the
café will. Just as soon as people see how
good your food is."

He looked somewhat mollified. "How

much do you want to spend?"

"How much should I?"

"I'll work out some figures and get back to you."

"Meanwhile don't go overboard on lunches for the next week or so. Maybe one soup, one sandwich special? Enrollment is up but attendance is down. People aren't sure how to get here anymore. I'm calling students and giving directions and updates, but as soon as I tell them to get here by one route, the police close another road."

"I got here. You got here. What's wrong with these people?" He headed for the kitchen, and Taylor envisioned him pulling out every pot and pan to decide how each would best serve the menu he was already planning in his head.

Dante was a find, and she didn't want to lose him, which was at least part of the reason for the party. Cooking at Evolution was a part-time affair, and the rest of the day he created ironic sculptures out of scrap metal, so ironic that when she had toured his garage-studio she had been at a complete loss how to respond, in case she had entirely missed the point.

Adam had been with her for the tour. Sensing her dismay, he had asked Dante questions about what motivated him, what he hoped people took away from his work, and by the end of the tour the sculptor-chef had been beaming.

For an enigmatic guy, Adam was good at getting others to fill the void.

Adam, who had said something about stopping by this afternoon, but so far had not done so.

Taylor was reminded of high school. She really didn't want to sink back through time to braces, calculus and rejection, so she headed for her office.

Adam was lounging in her doorway, waiting. Her heart thumped a little harder, but she only acknowledged his presence with a smile and nod, like a perky bobblehead doll. "I bet you're here to tell me I need a trampoline for the studio, right? Or a trapeze? That's why you finally showed up."

"In case one of my students is waylaid by a circus performer?"

"To what do we really owe the honor?"

"Your delightful personality and kick-ass body?"

She considered. "I think we have to reserve 'kick-ass' for you. I'm not there yet, although I've heard my elbow strikes are feared in every corner of Buncombe County."

"A woman no intelligent man would fool

around with."

"What's your IQ?"

"Not that high when you're on the scene."

She melted. At least that was how it felt. Everything inside her was suddenly warm and gooey, and heat was pooling in parts of her body that seemed to have been reserved just for this moment.

"What's the plan?" she asked, and she was surprised how husky her voice sounded.

"Dinner? Anywhere you want to go."

"We could try something in West Asheville. Near your apartment."

His dark eyes flashed, as if she'd ignited something inside him. "You want to see my apartment? It's not much to look at."

"Unless you have a better place to sight-see?"

His hand shot out, and he pulled her against him — of course, she went willingly. "You know all this teasing? You're playing with fire."

"I hope so." She raised her face to his, and they kissed, nothing gentle or sweet, but filled with enormous promise.

"There's always takeout," he said after he moved away.

She was out of breath, and her cheeks felt hot. "I'll be done here about five. Jan's dropping off some papers after she picks up

Maddie from school. I'll see if she can watch her tonight."

"You do that. I'm going to hang around and hope you can get away earlier. I'll find a place to work out."

She couldn't help herself. "Don't work off all your stamina."

"I think you'll be grateful if I work off some of it." He left before she could respond, which was a good thing, since she was suddenly strangely tongue-tied.

What was she doing? She'd practically tossed the guy on his back and stripped him naked. She, whose sex life heretofore had included a fling on Jeremy's rec room sofa, which hadn't produced anything like pleasure — although it had produced a baby.

She was a dozen years older now, and she certainly wasn't trying to prove anything to her parents. In the intervening years she'd been either uninterested in the men she met or so suspicious of even a flicker of attraction she'd squashed it like an annoying insect. She had been focused on caring for Maddie. But now?

Apparently now her firmly restrained libido was, like the river below them, spilling over its banks to seek a new level.

Of course, it was also quite possible that if Adam had shown up any time in the past decade, she might not have been quite so restrained.

She wondered about that. She could pretend this was all about sex, but she was smart enough to know it might be something more, as well. He fascinated her. For a powerful man he was gentle and insightful about the feelings of those around him. She had been deeply moved by the way he dealt with Harmony's surprising explosion in class. He seemed to sense Jan's hesitation to rejoin the human race, and he respected her fears, moving slowly, carefully, so as not to scare her away.

It was too soon in their relationship to think about love, but she did think maybe it wasn't completely out of the question.

She realized she was smiling, and she was still smiling when Harmony walked through Evolution's front door with Lottie balanced on one hip. Taylor went to take the baby before she gave her friend a one-armed hug.

"What's up? I don't usually see you here this time of day."

"Lottie had a doctor's appointment, and it took him forever to see us. I skipped lunch thinking I would eat afterward, and now I'm starving."

"You're here because you know the café's not doing well, aren't you?"

Harmony tried to look repentant. "Does that mean you won't feed me?"

"You're such a pal. Dante will be delighted to feed you. You can tell him it's on me."

"You're kidding, right? Of course I'll pay. I'm here so you won't go broke."

Taylor smoothed the baby's hair away from her face. "Lottie's okay?"

"She's been tugging at her earlobe, but the doc thinks it's probably just a new tooth coming in."

Taylor started toward the café. "Did you have any trouble getting here?"

"Not after I made the third detour. There's water everywhere. I thought we'd walk down after I eat and get a closer look."

Taylor lowered her voice. "Your mom's going to be here in a little while. She's dropping off some papers I left at home after she picks Maddie up from school. Just so you know."

"Do you get the feeling all this cloak-and-dagger stuff is unnecessary? My father's vanished. For all I know, maybe after all those years he decided to run away from Mom. Nobody in Kansas has traced her here. It's like nothing there changed one bit after she left. It makes you wonder if she'd left a long time ago, would anybody have noticed?"

"Do you really think so?"

"I've been away from home so long it gets foggy for me sometimes. My father's a violent, hateful man — that part's not foggy. He made lots of threats, sure, and I remember them. But I wonder if she'd just taken Buddy and me and walked out when we were little, if good old Rex would just have moved on with his life."

"I've gotten to know your mom pretty well, and it's hard to imagine she was wrong about something so important. She's so relieved to be away from him. It's like she's just been released from prison, and I can't believe she was a willing prisoner."

"All I've wanted since the moment I left home is to know she escaped and know she was finally safe. That's it. All these years in Asheville, that's all I wanted, and now it's come true. So why do I suddenly have all these doubts about what was really going on at home?"

"Because it didn't matter before. You loved her, and her welfare was uppermost in your mind. Now she's here and safe, and you can finally think about more than that."

"Adam says I'm angry."

Taylor thought Adam was right, and while she understood completely, she wished it weren't so. Jan had a hard enough road

434

ahead of her, and she needed her daughter. Of course she, of all people, could see this, since she, like Harmony, had allowed anger to color her own relationship with her mother right up until the very end of Charlotte's life.

And that, more than anything, forced her to speak.

"I hope you can work through this. You're entitled to your feelings, but . . ." She floundered for the right words.

"I know. She needs my support. I love her so much it should be easy."

"Nothing about mothers and daughters is easy. And speak of the devil?" Taylor pointed out the window that looked over the parking lot. "Your mom, my daughter. Generations in turmoil."

Harmony reached for Lottie. "What can I do to avoid this with Lottie, do you think?"

"I don't know. Stop caring? That might stem the tide."

"Not possible."

Taylor shrugged. "Then your guess is as good as mine."

CHAPTER 27

From the audio journal of a
forty-five-year-old woman, taped for the
files of Moving On, an underground
highway for abused women.

I have debated whether to record this. But
who am I trying to protect? The Abuser,
who taught me to put his ego and needs
above everyone, and whose shadow still
hovers over me? The son who left this world
too soon? The daughter who never saw her
father at his most demonic? For her sake
should I preserve a hint of false decency for
the man whose genes she carries? Or will
knowing the truth help her understand and
accept her childhood, and the chain that
kept me bound to my husband and home?

The story is best told quickly. During my
second pregnancy, after I realized that the
man I had married would never change
except to grow more cruel and violent, I

began making plans to leave and take my son and unborn daughter with me. As careful as I was, the Abuser learned my intentions.

I remember that the particular summer afternoon when my life changed forever was a sunny one, and the Abuser was particularly kind and solicitous. It was a Wednesday, when he was normally at the office, but he had taken the day off. He thought I might enjoy a picnic with our little boy before our daughter came into the world, and he had chosen a spot for us beside a gentle creek. The picnic area was remote and rarely used, and since it was a weekday the area was deserted. I laid out our lunch, and because it was hot, I took our son by his tiny hand to wade. His father took the other, the trusting, soft hand of the little boy who adored him.

Then, where the water deepened, my husband took my beloved child in his arms, lowered him into the water and held him under the surface while he told me that he knew I planned to run away, and that our son would be better off dead if he couldn't be with the father who loved him.

I screamed and fought and tried to free my baby, but only when I promised I would never, never leave him did he lift our little

437

boy, who was no longer breathing, out of the water. The Abuser carried him to the shore, and with little emotion he cleared our son's airways and breathed life back into him.

Then he ate his lunch and lounged in the sun to enjoy the rest of our day together.

Why didn't I report this to the authorities?

What proof did I have that it had ever happened? The Abuser was a successful businessman and church leader, and sadly, as he had told so many, I was "too easily overwrought" to be out in public very often.

The only proof was engraved forever in my heart and soul.

I was married to a man who would do anything to get what he wanted. If I'd had any doubts in the past, now I had seen the ultimate demonstration. If the Abuser loved anyone, it was his son. And I know on that day he would have drowned him like an unwanted kitten if I hadn't come to heel.

Later, of course, he explained his actions. As always, I had driven him to it. The thought of losing me and his children had overwhelmed him, and as I must know, he had been temporarily insane. Of course, he would have come to his senses in time to keep our son from dying. How could I ever think otherwise? But a man in turmoil was a man who might do anything before he regained self-control.

He hoped I had learned never to force him over the edge again.

Maddie was on a roll. Jan remembered Harmony at the same age. While pouting and complaining had never been an option when Rex was at home, alone with her mother she had indulged in both. Preadolescence was a fearsome thing. One slight, one snide comment, one raised eyebrow, and the whole day took a downward slide into a pool of despair.

"So then she told me my homework was late and she was going to lower my grade. Even though I told her yesterday that I hadn't understood the assignment and needed an extra day to do it again and get it right."

Jan parked and turned off the engine, opening her door before she answered. "It sounds like you thought she wouldn't care if it was late."

"Who cares if it's late? Late's not as bad as wrong."

Jan refrained from pointing out that on time and right would have been even better.

"It must have been a complicated assignment."

Maddie opened her door, then tugged Vanilla out of the backseat of the car, which was one of only three parked in the Evolution lot. "It wasn't complicated. Not exactly."

"But easy to misunderstand."

They were halfway up the sidewalk to the patio before Maddie answered, "Well, I was kind of not paying attention when she told us what to do. But I did do it right at the end, and that ought to count most of all. It's supposed to be about learning, right?"

Vanilla stopped to sniff one of the planters on the patio, and Jan turned to look at the river below them. She loved everything about Taylor's studio except the proximity to the French Broad. She couldn't be around any body of water without remembering the day Rex had nearly killed their son. The two would always merge. Bright sunlight, the water pooling around her knees, her baby son's hand in hers.

Today, even from this distance, the rushing water made her dizzy, and abruptly she turned away.

"Have you ever seen the river this high?" she asked Maddie, hoping to change the topic.

"No. One of my friends said she went tubing before it got so fast."

"That's a terrible idea."

"I don't know why. She said it was fun."

"Only if it's shallow and slow. The river's dangerous now."

"Well, I want to see it up closer. I'm going to ask my mom if I can walk down nearer the edge."

Jan forced herself to breathe. She suspected Taylor wouldn't let Maddie go unless she was accompanied all the way. And the girl was rebellious, but only a little. She was also too smart to purposely put herself in harm's way.

"I don't know how long we can stay. Your mom might be in the middle of something. I think we're supposed to drop off the papers and run."

"I want to spend the night with Edna. She asked at school. I have to ask Mom, so she'd better not be too busy."

Jan wished she could alert Taylor that letting Maddie spend the night elsewhere was the best possible solution to her daughter's mood and the best hope for a peaceful evening.

Vanilla finished sniffing, and Maddie opened the back door into Evolution. The dog and girl went in search of Taylor. Jan followed at a slower pace, and when she turned the corner she found her own daughter and Lottie in the hallway.

"I didn't know you would be here," she said, before she could think better of it.

Harmony didn't hug her, as if to point out they were supposed to be strangers. "We were both at Taylor's for Halloween. The sky didn't fall in. But I'm sorry. If I'd known you were coming, I would have stayed away."

"I'm sure it's okay." Although she wasn't sure at all.

"I was starving, so I stopped for a wrap." Harmony held up a paper bag. "I'll eat it on the way home."

Jan leaned over to give her granddaughter a quick kiss. "You're leaving because I showed up, aren't you?"

"You say that's important. Nothing's changed, has it?"

Jan heard the "you say" and tensed. "Of course, you'll be the first to know."

Taylor and Maddie and the dog came out of the office, and Maddie's pout looked deeply and permanently engraved into her face. "I want to see the river up close. I'm not stupid. I won't get too close and fall in or anything."

Taylor turned to Jan and ignored her

daughter. "Maddie wants to spend the night with Edna. Did she tell you? Would you mind very much helping her pack and get over there?"

"Like I can't put pajamas and a tooth-brush in a backpack?" Maddie said.

Taylor put her hand on Maddie's shoulder, and not to comfort her. "Maddie, I bet if you work harder you can be polite. And this would be the moment to start. Nobody's going to do you any favors if you're rude."

"Nobody's doing any —" Maddie stopped herself, as if she'd realized that one more salvo in her personal war against authority would ruin all her plans for the evening.

"I'll be happy to get Maddie to Edna's," Jan said quickly, in case Maddie decided to go for broke. "Then I have a meeting." She glanced at her daughter. "The costume department at On Stage meets tonight, and I thought I might go see what it's all about."

"Cool." Harmony sounded as though she meant it, and Jan relaxed an inch.

"I still don't see why I can't walk down to the river," Maddie said, in a politer tone. "I promise not to get too close."

Harmony shifted Lottie to the other hip. "I was going to take a look myself. I'm go-ing to leave my wrap in the car and walk

443

down. Maddie can come with me if you're willing." She addressed the last to Taylor. "I'll make sure she gets back to the studio."

Taylor considered. "Okay, but leave Vanilla with Jan and me. You don't need another distraction."

Jan wasn't surprised Harmony hadn't invited her, nor was she unhappy. What she was? Worried. Fear of water would be Rex's permanent legacy, even though there was no logical reason to feel anxious because her daughter was taking Lottie and Maddie to the riverbank. She would be careful, and Maddie, despite the bravado, wasn't prone to taking risks. Still, her own legs were threatening collapse.

Harmony nodded toward the door. "Come on, Maddie. Let's boogie."

As the trio disappeared down the hall to the back door Taylor held Vanilla by the collar. There was a path of sorts down the hill from Evolution's patio, then a flat stretch with railroad tracks cutting across it, and finally the river, which today was closer to the tracks than Jan had ever imagined it.

Taylor told Vanilla to sit, and the dog obliged, but it was clear she didn't like being left out of the fun. Taylor continued to hold her collar. "So who invited you to the meeting tonight?"

"Fletcher called this morning."

"He seems like a great guy. Nate's been building sets for On Stage ever since he got out of the army, and he says everybody loves Fletcher, even when the chips are down."

"It's so easy to get what you want by being nice, isn't it?"

"Only if what you want falls within the parameters of human decency." Taylor hesitated. "Speaking of which, I may not get home until very late tonight. If at all."

Jan didn't have to ask why. She had seen Adam and Taylor together often enough to know what was happening. "I won't wait up."

"You'll be okay in the house by yourself? You'll turn on the security system?"

Jan wasn't worried about tonight; she was worried about now. She wasn't okay, not even close. Inside she was screaming.

She faked a smile, something she'd had a lot of practice doing through the years. "I'll be fine. I think I'm going to go out on the patio and watch what's happening below."

"Why don't you join them? It's not a steep climb."

Even though Taylor was beginning to feel like a second daughter, there were some things Jan didn't want to share. "I might."

"Vanilla and I are going to finish my

paperwork. Come on, Nilla."

Jan headed down the hall the way the others had gone and peered out through a window looking over the patio. She couldn't see Harmony or the girls, and she knew she had to walk outside to watch their progress. She took a deep breath and opened the door, walking to the edge and peering down while trying to avoid looking at the river. The trio wasn't at the water's edge, or even quite to the railroad track, but they were getting close.

Maddie was walking right beside Harmony, which helped calm Jan's churning stomach. She didn't have to watch; she knew that. She could escape back inside, maybe have a cup of tea in the café. Or she could start down the hill herself so she was closer.

Just in case.

The first made sense; the second didn't. She stepped off the patio and took the steps to the ground below, anyway. Then she started down the hillside path. She wasn't sure why she was following the others. Perhaps to surprise her daughter, who believed her fear of water was a childhood leftover and could be overcome. Perhaps to assure herself that nothing happened. Perhaps to prove to herself that Rex was no

446

longer controlling every move she made. The river was still far away, and she knew she could stop before she neared it.

The ground had leveled, and she was nearing the railroad tracks when she heard something behind her. The air seemed to vibrate, and a blur shot past on her right. A moment passed before she realized the blur was Vanilla.

"Vanilla!" She stepped up her speed and shouted again, but the dog, who was well ahead of her now, didn't hesitate. She continued running, barking with excitement. Jan began to run, although she knew that catching the dog before it caught up to Maddie was impossible.

She ran anyway, as if pursued, not even sure why until she realized the dog was giving Maddie and the others a wide berth and heading straight for the water.

"Nilla!"

Now she wasn't the only one shouting. She could hear Harmony calling the dog, and Maddie, too. But Vanilla had other plans.

Jan ran faster. Her stamina had increased from Adam's class, and so had her strength. But fear propelled her steps. The dog was headed straight for the river.

And so was Maddie.

"No, Maddie!" she shouted, but the girl ignored her. Harmony was running, too, but she was hindered by the child in her arms, and Jan sped past her and headed straight for Maddie.

"Maddie, don't get near the water!"

By that point Vanilla was wading, and then, as if the golden doodle had dropped beyond the overflow to the deeper waters of the river itself, she was swimming.

"No, Maddie!"

But Maddie was too far ahead to catch, and she was determined to rescue her beloved dog. She floundered along the edge of the water, then into it, and before Jan could reach her, she was swept by the current downstream.

Jan could hear Harmony running behind her, but it would still be seconds before she reached the bank and she had Lottie. Jan kicked off her shoes and was in the water before Harmony could reach her.

The water was icy, and for a moment it snatched the breath from her lungs. She had learned to swim and swim well as a child, but she knew immediately there was no hope of swimming in this. The current was swift and strong, and it swept her faster and faster. The best she could do was keep her head up to search for Maddie and save what strength she had to combat the current until she neared the girl. She was rewarded almost a minute later when she saw her not far away, driven directly toward a fallen tree that lay across the riverbank, its limbs clawing the water like skeletal fingers.

With all the strength she could summon, she aimed for the tree, as well, fighting the current and the cold that numbed her arms and legs. She knew if she passed the tree, she had no hope of rescuing the girl, and perhaps no hope of getting out herself. She put everything she had into each exhausted stroke, but in the end it was just enough. As she was about to drift past the tree, she grabbed the limb extending farthest into the river and held on tight.

She hadn't accounted for the pressure of the water flowing beneath her. Her legs were pinned under and against the limb, and for a moment she thought she wouldn't be able to move again. But little by little she inched toward the spot where she thought Maddie had landed. She was moving so slowly, and fear clutched at her. While the tree had seemed a haven, in reality it was a prison. Maddie was too small, too light, to fight her way to safety. Jan couldn't even see her now, and she imagined the child being knocked unconscious by the force of the water and the unforgiving bulk of the tree.

Struggling and clawing, she moved along the branch to the trunk, searching for Maddie.

She saw her at last, three feet away. As she had feared, Maddie was pinned against the trunk, her face in the water. With everything she had left, she reached the girl and, holding the trunk with one arm, managed to cup her body around Maddie's and then lift her face out of the water by her hair, just high enough that she could breathe.

The girl gasped, then began to panic and fight uselessly.

"Don't fight, Maddie! Hold on to the tree!" Jan shouted. "Grab anything you can and don't let go."

Maddie continued to flounder, and Jan knew she wasn't going to be able to keep her from going under again.

"Stop!" she shouted. "Find something and hold on. I'm going to lose my grip!"

She heard a splash from the riverbank, and she saw someone moving along the tree toward them.

"Just another few seconds!" a man shouted, and she realized it was Adam. "Hang on to her, Jan!"

Jan could feel her own grip on the tree slipping away, but she struggled to keep

Maddie's face out of the water. Then, just as she was sure she couldn't hold on to either the girl or the tree a moment longer, Adam was turning Maddie onto her back and dragging her to the bank.

"Hang on to the tree. I'm coming back."

She wrapped both arms around the trunk, or at least she thought she did. Everything was hazy now, and her arms were so cold she couldn't feel them. Her legs floated under the trunk, and the force of the water pinned her there.

If she let go . . . If she let go . . .

She felt strong arms reaching for her, one wrapping around her waist. "I've got you now," Adam said. "Help if you can. Hang on where you're able, but we're going to move toward the bank. I'll keep you afloat."

The trip seemed to take hours. She thought she grabbed for handholds. She thought she kicked to break the inexorable grip of the water. She thought she felt ground under her feet.

Then she was on the bank.

"Maddie?" She was on her back on the ground, and she tried to sit up but couldn't.

"I want you to turn to your side. I'll help," Adam said. He knelt beside her and helped her before he answered. "Maddie's going to be okay. You saved her life. Taylor's got her."

Tears ran down her cheeks; at least she thought they were tears. She coughed, and water flew from her lungs. For long moments she couldn't speak again. When she was breathing easier she tried. "I think she . . . hit her head. I don't think she was conscious when I . . ." She couldn't form the words.

"We're going to get you both to the emergency room. Harmony ran back for my car."

She managed to sit up and put her head in her hands. "Take care of Maddie."

He squatted down beside her. "You did a good thing, a great thing. Don't ever underestimate yourself again."

She gazed up at him. "The dog . . ." She shook her head.

"She got out just beyond the tree where the river curves. She was washed right up to the bank. She's with Maddie."

Jan began to cry in earnest. Not because Vanilla had survived. Not even because Maddie had. Because she herself had survived, and the little boy she had rescued all those years ago by her terrible promise to his father had not.

CHAPTER 28

Adam was tired to the marrow of his bones. The rescue, the race to the hospital with Maddie, Taylor and Jan in his SUV. Then hitching a ride back to the studio with Dante, after both he and Jan had been checked over and released. Retrieving Taylor's car and parking it in the hospital garage, and finally waiting in the emergency room until he was sure Maddie was going to be okay. Maddie was a cute kid, and he'd been worried about that bump on the head and the time she'd spent in the water, which had been cold enough to suck the heat from her slender body while her heart rate and blood pressure soared.

He hadn't been surprised the doctor had decided to keep her overnight. Not that long ago the girl had endured brain surgery to ward off epileptic seizures. But the staff who had examined her had been confident she was going to be okay. And while Adam was no particular fan of doctors, after getting to know far too many at the end of his military career, this one had seemed to know his stuff.

Once he was home he had time to put things in better perspective. This evening was supposed to have been very different, but maybe it was better that he wasn't giving Taylor a tour of his apartment — or more accurately his bed — right now. As upsetting as the day had been, maybe one good thing had come from it, because Taylor had become an incredible complication. Adam needed to do his job and leave town. It was that simple and suddenly that complicated. He had made a commitment to see the Rex Stoddard case through to its conclusion. Nothing he had done here in Asheville was wrong by those standards. His job required secrecy, sometimes even lies, but it was a job that had to be finished.

He could still give notice, admit his real reason for being here and ask Taylor for forgiveness. She might have trouble understanding his role in the Stoddard drama, but in the long run he was afraid she might have *more* trouble understanding why he had turned over the case to someone without the time or inclination to give Jan Stoddard the benefit of the doubt.

Everything he had seen today was more evidence that Jan was a person of high standards coupled with regrettably low self-esteem. Both were compatible with his theory that Rex Stoddard had married a woman far above himself on the evolutionary chain and then worked off his daily frustrations by punishing her for her superiority.

Nobody risked her life in a mountain river in November just to prove a point. Jan had gone in after Maddie because she was a person who would put a child's safety before her own.

As he stood and stretched, his stomach rumbled. Somebody on the floor below was frying chicken, a smell he recognized all too well from a summer job when he'd served up buckets of the Colonel's finest. After that experience he hadn't particularly liked anything deep-fried, but now, even though it had been a long time since he'd tasted meat, his stomach growled once more in response. Lunch had been hours ago, and he couldn't even remember what he'd eaten.

He was rummaging through his fridge for leftovers when his cell phone rang. He fished it from his pocket and put it to his ear.

"Adam Pryor."

"I got your message, but I was swamped. Couldn't this wait until Monday?"

Adam's gaze flicked to the clock display on his stove. It was seven on a Friday evening, but it wasn't unusual for Philip Salter, the head of the special investigation unit of the Midwest Modern Insurance Company, to still be at his desk and cranky.

"There was a major incident here." Adam described Maddie's near drowning and Jan's rescue, leaving out most of the details about his own part in it.

"Unless Rex Stoddard suddenly appeared to help you get the kid out of the water, I'm not sure why you're calling."

"I'm calling because Janine Stoddard risked her life today. It was a close call for both of them. This is a good woman. I think we're looking for Rex Stoddard in the wrong place."

"Maybe you *are* in the wrong place. That remains to be seen. But we're looking for Stoddard everywhere we can, and so are the police. Maybe his wife saves little kids with one hand and helps her old man embezzle money with the other. Or maybe she's just keeping busy while she waits for him to show up."

"I'm more and more convinced she's glad to be rid of this guy. There's no doubt in my mind he was abusing her. And any woman who can leap into icy floodwaters isn't one who would wait for her husband to show up and abuse her some more."

"People are funny. You know that. They get used to things, make excuses, even hope their lives stay the same because they don't know anything else or they're scared of change. Maybe he did knock her around, but maybe that's what she knows, what she feels comfortable with."

"No."

There was silence for a moment as Philip absorbed that. "Then how about this? Mrs. Stoddard looks for a way to get back at Mr. Stoddard after years of mistreatment. She's no dummy, right?"

"Right."

"Maybe she sees that the best way to get back at him is to file claims that don't exist from his very own agency. Then, when the bogus claims are finally discovered, make it look like he's the one who did it. She gets back at him *and* she gets out with a tidy little nest egg. She leaves town, maybe burns down the house he paid for on the way out, reunites with her long-lost daughter and has the last laugh."

"That's a nice bedtime story, but I haven't seen any evidence to support it. How would she make those claims? Nobody ever saw her at his office. Nobody ever saw her *anywhere* except the annual holiday open house. It's not like she was sneaking in at lunchtime to use the computers or file bogus paperwork."

"She probably had access to his keys. Maybe he was a sound sleeper."

"They lived almost forty-five minutes from his office."

"He was on a bowling league. Maybe that's what she did on league night. She played a con game instead."

Insurance fraud investigation was filled with twists and turns. Adam got that. In the air force he had investigated airmen who'd tried to cover murder with a friendly slap on the back, rape with a flashy alibi, theft with convoluted fantasies, so he never took anything he saw or heard at face value. When he'd been ready to work again, his training and inclination to question everything had made him a natural for this job.

But he was still capable, for all that cynicism, of recognizing good people when he found them. And Jan was one of the good ones.

"It's unlikely she was in this with him or without him," he said. "Frankly I still think it's unlikely *he* was involved, either. Stoddard might be a first-degree asshat, but everybody who knew the guy says he counted pens and legal pads at the end of the workweek to make sure nobody was taking them home. And he went a lot crazy if he thought anybody who worked for him was being disloyal to the agency or dishonorable."

"Did anybody you interviewed say he abused his wife? That's a big surprise, too, isn't it? Maybe he was the master of disguises."

"Rigid perfectionism goes hand in hand with the abuse scenario. In Stoddard's warped mind, beating his wife was probably meant to make her a better person. But stealing? Being dishonest and disloyal to the agency he'd built from the ground up? My money's still on somebody else."

"He disappeared right before the fraud was discovered, Adam. So did Mrs. Stoddard. And you still think that's a coincidence?"

"I think his disappearance is connected in a way we haven't determined. I think she just jumped ship when the opportunity arose."

"And one or both of them burned down the house."

"There were no propellants, no signs of arson."

Philip didn't sound convinced. "Wonderful. When you see her, tell her to be sure she makes a claim on her homeowner's insurance. I'm glad the Stoddard house wasn't on *our* bill."

Adam knew his boss was being sarcastic, so he didn't bother to point out that Jan had no interest in anything except lying low. Like a woman who was terribly afraid of something or somebody.

"I'm glad Jan Stoddard saved the little girl," Philip said, "but you still need to watch her and see if the husband shows up or if she's suddenly living the high life. Unless you think this assignment's getting too personal? We can take you on as a full-time investigator next month here in Chicago, or maybe just put you on another freelance case someplace where you're not emotionally involved."

That was too close to home.

"I'll let you know if anything else comes up," Adam said, "but if nothing does, don't say I didn't warn you."

He hung up and went back to rummaging for leftovers. After he threw out everything that was no longer edible, he salvaged half a tub of hummus, one slightly-wilted stalk of celery and a stale bagel.

He dipped the celery in the hummus and realized the hummus was moldy.

This was what his life would consist of if he stayed on his present course. Moving from place to place. Peering through a long-distance lens at the lives of others. A third-rate apartment, a rental car, pathetic left-overs.

And nightmares.

He tossed the bagel back in the refrigerator, the hummus in the garbage and opened a can of beer instead.

Taylor hadn't been surprised when Maddie told her to go home and sleep in her own bed instead of spending the night on the fold-out sleeper in her hospital room. Another girl her age had settled in, and the two had hit it off. Maddie's roommate had been in a car accident, and like Maddie, she was being monitored through the night in case she had suffered something more than cuts and bruises.

Taylor had quickly made her exit. If Maddie changed her mind the hospital had her cell number. And if she stayed, she might keep hammering home how serious this whole event had been. Maddie already understood that, and Taylor didn't want to frighten her even more.

Now, as she stood at Adam's door and considered her next move, the smell of the food cradled in her arms was more powerful than the temptation to turn around before he learned she had been here. Even more powerful? The need for human warmth.

She needed Adam.

She lifted her fist and knocked. If he wasn't at home, she might sink to the floor, open the bag with its environmentally unfriendly containers and eat everything she'd bought all by herself. If the restaurant had forgotten to add plastic cutlery, she was hungry enough to eat with her fingers.

The door opened and Adam appeared on the threshold. "Wow."

"Tell me you haven't eaten."

"So far the closest I've come is inhaling the chicken grease from downstairs. How did you get in? The door downstairs is always locked."

"One of your neighbors was going out." She held up the bag. "Rigatoni melanzane, and in case you don't like eggplant — because not everybody does —" she knew she was babbling, but she couldn't stop "— I also got fettuccine Alfredo. They make it

462

with peas and mushrooms, and it's so good."

He took the bag out of her arms; then with his free hand he scooped her inside and closed the door, then set the bag on the floor and kissed her.

She was dizzy from hunger, desire, the need to remember the world was turning as it should again, and for a second she wasn't sure which was more powerful.

Then he pinned her against the door with his body and let his hands travel to her waist, let his fingertips wander inside the waistband of her jeans. The snap gave way. The contest ended abruptly.

"Maddie?" he whispered.

"She's fine. I was afraid I might smother her if I stayed. She didn't need me."

"That's good, because I do."

They probably should talk first. She knew that. Say a few things about relationships and expectations and sex in general, but she had no more words. The day had sharpened everything inside her. Loss, fear, gratitude. She was a quivering mass of emotions ready to erupt. And this time when he kissed her, she released them to flourish on their own.

But she couldn't release need. It flourished inside her.

They undressed each other like clumsy

teenagers. Arms in the way, buttons snagged in buttonholes that had been wide enough that morning. She kicked off one shoe and the other refused to follow. Adam's shirt caught at his shoulders, and she had to tug so hard she was afraid she might hurt him.

His bed took up most of the shabby room, which under the circumstances was a good thing. The trip there was blessedly short, although long enough for her to send the second shoe flying just before she fell to the sheet.

"You're so beautiful," he said, "and I promise I'm going to take a long look and say all the right things. Later."

He was beautiful, too, muscular arms and chest, long powerful legs. They were fleeting images. The rest she drank in with her hands, the length of her body against his, the drugged pleasure of hurried kisses in intimate places.

She didn't warn him how long it had been for her, or how little she remembered. She didn't care. She didn't need experience to know this was special. Adam was special. He wouldn't be gentle, but he would be controlled.

Foreplay was a word best explored another time. Or maybe that was what the weeks leading up to this explosion had been.

Whatever the answer, she wrapped her legs around him and gave herself without reserve.

"I'm having that long look I promised," he said later, propped on one elbow and gazing down at her.

She smiled up at him. "Anything new?"

"You're amazing. Perfect. All those hours of yoga. You could probably tie yourself into knots."

"Didn't we just do that to each other?"

"I think we *untied* a few." He traced a finger down her cheek, around her lips, down her neck to her breast, where it made slow circles around her nipple. "Taylor, I didn't use a condom. Everything just fell to pieces. I lost track of reality."

"I'm healthy. You're healthy?"

He nodded. "Certifiably, if that helps. I'm just thinking you might not want another unplanned pregnancy."

"Once a decade, that's my motto." She lifted to kiss him. "Actually I'm on the pill. Have been for a couple of years. I was having life-altering PMS, and it helped."

"Good. I hope I never do anything to hurt you."

"You didn't. You haven't." She looked into his eyes. "But somebody hurt you." She let

465

her hand travel to his chest, where a long scar streaked across it. She had expected tattoos, perhaps, but not this.

"That's what happens when you're in a war zone."

She waited for him to go on, but she saw that he wasn't going to.

She didn't push. "Dinner's cold."

"I don't care, do you?"

"I'm starving."

"I have two plates, and they both happen to be clean. How's that for planning?"

"Plates but no condoms?"

He bent down and let his lips follow the path of his finger. "I didn't say I didn't have condoms. I said I didn't use one. You bewitched me."

"It's always the woman's fault."

"I'll rephrase. I *let* you bewitch me."

"We're never going to eat, are we?"

"What do you think?"

They did eat eventually. He had two forks, too, and a tiny microwave. By the time they got to it, the food tasted as if it had come from one of Asheville's finest restaurants instead of a pizzeria with pretensions. They shared each dish, fed each other bites, laughed, scooped up the remaining sauce with their fingers and fed that to each other, too.

"You're not going back to the hospital?" he asked when the dishes were finally in the sink and they were back in bed.

"Maddie doesn't want me there. She's turning into me at that age. She's struggling so hard to break free, and I'm her jailer. She may need rescuing a time or two more before she's eighteen." She leaned over and kissed him. "You know I'll never be able to thank you enough for going into the river after her."

"You made a good start tonight."

She laughed. "Of course, tonight is *all* about gratitude."

"I'm glad I was watching from the window. I just had a bad feeling when I saw Vanilla racing down the hill. Jan must have, too."

"I called Maddie's father and told him what happened. Once she got to her room Jeremy talked to her on my cell phone and gave her a stern lecture, or as stern as he gets. He's a marshmallow."

"I hope he didn't blame you."

"He was a rebel, too. He said that kind of behavior is inevitable for a kid with our genes."

"She learn anything?"

"She was pretty clingy in the emergency room. She must have said she was sorry twenty times. So maybe she is, and she'll listen better next time. But I don't think she was trying to prove I was wrong about the river. She was just trying to save Vanilla. The instinct was good, the reality pretty disastrous. If it weren't for Jan and you, she probably would have died. And I was the one who let that idiot dog out of my office."

"You would have gone into the river if I hadn't. I just got there faster than you did."

"You're stronger. It took a lot to get to her and haul her out with the water pushing against the tree like that. We were so lucky to have you there. And so lucky to have Jan."

"I hope you'll always feel lucky."

She kissed him again, then sat up. "Maybe I ought to go home? It's getting late."

"Stay."

She cocked her head and searched his face. "You're sure?"

"My bed's big enough for two. Get some sleep before you have to head back in the morning."

She was surprised. Sex was one thing, a pressing, volcanic need that had eclipsed everything else. But sleeping together? That was intimacy. By now she knew him well enough to realize that asking her to stay was the larger commitment.

"I have an extra toothbrush," he said.

"Can I sleep in your T-shirt?"

"Why don't we both sleep in the same thing?"

"What's that?"

"Nothing."

The dream began as it always did. He was flying above the clouds. The freedom was heady, but even as Adam soared higher and higher, he knew the breeze that buoyed and supported him would soon disappear, and he would begin the terrifying free fall that would end where even now smoke and flames were shattering what had been a peaceful landscape below.

He could hear screaming, adult and children's voices, women wailing, men screaming prayers that no higher power heeded, because the wailing continued, the flames shot higher and he plummeted toward them.

Moving was essential. Somehow he knew he had to move. That he had to struggle against the fall. That he had to . . .

"Adam!"

The voice had no meaning for him, but the name? The name was familiar.

"Adam, wake up."

His eyelids flew open. He was sitting up

in a room that wasn't strange but wasn't home, although he couldn't picture anything that went with that word. The room was dark, but light trickled through a door cracked open beyond him. He concentrated on the light, and the woman's voice. The light was steady, not the flickering of a spreading fire. The woman was not screaming.

"You're okay," she said, just loudly enough for him to hear. "You're in your own bed, in Asheville, with me. Taylor. It's only ten o'clock."

Long moments passed as sleep faded away, inch by inch, and the nightmare crawled back into whatever hole it lived in when he was awake. He forced himself to breathe slowly. A distant memory, another woman's voice, a much older one, teaching him how to bring himself slowly back to reality.

Finally he lay back down and stared up at the thin slice of light streaking across his ceiling.

"A nightmare?" Taylor asked.

"Yeah."

"A really bad one." It wasn't a question.

"Yeah."

"Maddie was born so early they didn't know if she would live. For years afterward

470

I had dreams she was flying away from me, like a baby bird with tiny feathered wings, and I couldn't catch her. Somehow I knew if I didn't, I would wake up and find she had really flown away forever." She paused. "With adolescence approaching I may start having that dream again."

"In my dream I'm the bird." He'd spoken without thinking. The coincidence — birds, death — had seemed worthy of comment, and he was in no mood to go back to sleep.

"And you're back in Iraq or Afghanistan." Again, no question.

"Here's the funny part. You name anything dangerous, and I'd probably done it in the three years before I almost died. I thought I was hot stuff, you know, invulnerable. After all, I'd made it through combat rescue training, and if I could survive that . . ."

She touched him for the first time since the nightmare, just took his hand and wove her fingers through his without saying a word.

He squeezed, surprised at how good the connection felt, unexpected and welcome solace. "I volunteered for missions where only half of us returned uninjured or alive. But I don't dream about that. I dream about the day I was asked to accompany a humanitarian assistance convoy carrying necessities

471

to an outlying village near Bagram Air Force Base."

He turned so he could see the outline of her profile. "I wasn't happy in my job. The thing is, I'd left security forces for combat rescue, but a month before that mission I'd been moved back to security. My commanding officer thought I needed a break, that I was getting cocky, taking risks that put others in danger."

"Were you?"

"I took a lot of risks, but we all did. That was our job, but he said he saw something that worried him. He said sometimes an airman who's had good luck forgets bad luck is always right behind him, and I needed time away from what I'd been doing."

"I'm guessing that's when you had bad luck."

"In a war zone any time you go outside the wire it's dangerous. But the trip had been largely uneventful. We made it to the edge of the village. There was a bazaar where whatever goods the local merchants could scrape together were on display. Villagers, mothers with their children, old men and women. They were all coming to the bazaar to watch our convoy arrive. By then I was feeling better about my job. The villagers had so little. The convoy was there to help. There was nothing in it for us except goodwill."

He turned away to look back at the ceiling. "Then the whole place exploded. A suicide bomber had been hiding in one of the booths undetected. I remember the screaming. I smelled smoke and felt the heat of flames. I remember thinking it was all so ironic, that I was supposed to be one of the guys who rescued people like me, and then I remember floating above it all looking down and seeing the bodies of children."

"Oh, Adam." Taylor squeezed his hand.

"I was clinically dead before they finally got me stabilized. You can see the scar on my chest. You can't see the injury to my brain. That and post-traumatic stress were the bonuses that finally earned me an honorable discharge and disability compensation."

"Are you back at the bazaar in your nightmare?"

"I'm looking down on the scene. It's always the same."

"Are the dreams getting further apart?"

"That's only the second time I've had one in this apartment. I saw a V.A. psychologist for months. She taught me to cope, but the techniques don't always work."

"Does anything special set it off?"

473

Change set it off. He knew that from his sessions with the psychologist. A new town, a new bed, a new assignment, the feeling that until he settled in again and knew his way around, he wasn't in control, that anything could happen.

Change like falling in love.

How much more out of control could a man be? Especially when he was lying to the woman about his reasons for being in town?

"They seem to be random," he said, which was another lie.

"Do you think I triggered it somehow? I mean sleeping here beside you? Or Maddie's experience today?"

"Maybe the thing with Maddie. I wasn't able to save those kids at the bazaar. I just lay there and quietly died."

"The suicide bomber killed them, Adam. You were trying to save lives."

He pulled her close and settled her against him. "I don't usually talk about this."

"I know. I think there are a lot of things you don't talk about."

"You should run screaming."

"I don't think so. You're one of the good guys."

As her breathing slowed and she fell asleep

pillowed on his arm, he wondered how long she would think so.

CHAPTER 29

From the audio journal of a
forty-five-year-old woman, taped for the
files of Moving On, an underground
highway for abused women.

Despite everything, why would I allow children to live in a marriage like mine? Of course, by the time my daughter was born my mistake horrified me, but by then I was in so deep I couldn't find my way out. Keeping up with two small children, a large house that had to be spotlessly clean and three meals a day exhausted me. There was no respite, no friends to spend time with or talk to, no dinners away from my family. Except for the grocery store and Sunday mornings at the church the Abuser had chosen for us, I was a prisoner in my own home, at his mercy for whatever punishment he chose to administer.

It's also important to note that not every

moment was grim. When the Abuser was feeling happy and charitable, life in our house could be pleasant. He was a good provider and the master of thoughtful gifts. When I ran the house and cared for the children to his exact specifications, he let me know how grateful he was. Most Friday nights he rented movies and ordered pizza. After church services we always went out for fast food and ice cream. There was laughter, too, but only when I was certain laughing was safe. The Abuser had no sense of humor about himself or any action he had taken.

Sometimes weeks would go by without retaliation for any real or perceived misjudgment on my part, but by then I had lost hope the good times meant anything. I was simply grateful for the calm and tried my best to drag it out while I prepared for the inevitable storm brewing just over the horizon.

My son quickly learned that the best way to please his father was to copy everything he did. My daughter learned that the best way to please her father was to stay out of his way. Both children avoided the worst of his wrath by treading their chosen paths, but when even that didn't work, I learned to deflect his anger so more often than not he aimed it at me.

There are millions of women worldwide who time and time again step between their abusers and their children. We do it for two reasons. We love our children and want to protect them.

And far less virtuous? Each of us knows we deserve to pay a terrible price for marrying men who thrive by destroying innocence.

By eleven Jan finally felt warm enough to shed her fleece blanket and just snuggle in the flannel robe she had bought because it was a lovely rusty red, and red was a color Rex had associated with fallen women. She had showered twice, the second time draining the hot water heater, and now she was on her second and final cup of hot chocolate. She still doubted she would sleep. The house was quiet, but her thoughts were not. She was sorry to be alone with them.

Early in the evening Taylor had called to say she was staying at the hospital with Maddie. Even river-rat Vanilla had gone straight to Harmony's, so that Rilla, the skilled dog breeder, could check the dog to be sure she was really okay.

Reading hadn't helped Jan fall asleep. Television hadn't helped. No matter what she did, the whole nightmarish afternoon continued to play in her head. Blaming herself for everything was a legacy Rex had bequeathed her. Convinced she should have found a way to stop the events before they began, she had tried repeatedly to figure out where she had gone wrong.

Could she have pleaded with Harmony not to take the girls so close to the water? Could she have asked Taylor not to let Maddie go with them? Of course, but when had she been given the right to control the lives of others, particularly when old fears were making the decisions?

In the end, even if the decision to follow the others downhill had sprung from her personal nightmare, it had been the right one. She would never know what might have happened if she hadn't reached Maddie so quickly. If Adam had located the girl immediately, he might have been able to reach her in time. But those extra minutes facedown in the water might also have been fatal.

Just before another try at sleep, somebody tapped on the front door. She froze, wondering who would be knocking this time of evening.

Before she could run through a list of frightening possibilities, she heard her

479

daughter's voice. "Mom?"

She crossed the room and flung the door open to let Harmony in. They embraced and held each other for a long moment. At the riverside Harmony had known her presence wouldn't be needed at the hospital, and she had taken Lottie and Vanilla home so they wouldn't be in the way. And of course, once they had been seen by a doctor, Taylor had called Harmony to report that the waterlogged trio was going to be fine.

"What's wrong?" Jan asked, holding her daughter away at last. "Have you heard something?" She left the question open, because so many things were up in the air.

"No. No! I was just worried about you. I couldn't get Lottie to sleep for the longest time. She knew something was wrong. She's little, but she knows."

Jan was afraid that was true. Children knew, and children remembered. She had always been sure that on some level Buddy had remembered that day at the creek.

"She's with Rilla?"

"She doesn't mind. Once Lottie's asleep she'll be out for the night."

"Hot chocolate?"

"That's always been your cure for everything."

"It was one of the few I could administer without being questioned." Jan went into the kitchen, with Harmony following, and poured milk into a mug and set it in the microwave to warm. "Vanilla's okay?"

"Rilla gave her a hot bath and dried her with a blow–dryer. Then we covered her in blankets. Tonight we put her in bed with the boys. She's fine. She's acting like she's just gotten back from a day at the spa. Stupid dog."

"Maddie went after her without thinking. I doubt she realized the water got deep so quickly, and when she lost her footing, she just got swept away."

"You saved her life."

Since it might be true, Jan simply shook her head. "We'll never know."

"You went into that water like you'd been doing it every day of your life. I've never seen you swim."

"It's like riding a bicycle. You never forget."

"You do if it scares you to death."

"Watching Maddie drown scared me more."

"I would have gone in after her. I was going to give Lottie to you."

"Watching you rescue Maddie would have scared me the most."

Harmony's eyes filled, and Jan turned to take the milk out of the microwave. She replaced it when she saw it wasn't steaming and added more time.

"I . . ." Harmony rubbed her nose on the sleeve of her Radiohead sweatshirt. "You know what they say about your life flashing in front of your eyes when you die?"

"Mine didn't, don't worry." Jan struggled for humor. "That *would* have been scary."

"Well, mine did. I remembered all the times you threw yourself in front of me when I was growing up to keep me safe. When Dad looked for an excuse to hit me, you were right there making yourself the target. When he came home in a bad mood, you made sure I went to my bedroom or outside so you could calm him down or offer yourself as a sacrifice."

"Whatever I could do to protect you was never good enough."

They were silent until the microwave dinged. Jan took the milk out and carried it to the counter to mix in the powdered chocolate. Then she carried it to the table and Harmony joined her.

"Do you want something to eat with this?" Jan asked.

Harmony sat, but she didn't pick up the mug. "If you knew nothing you could do was good enough, Mom, if you knew Dad was never going to change, why didn't you just leave Buddy with him, take me and get out? Didn't you see if you left Buddy behind, Dad might have left us alone? He might have let us have a life outside that hellhole?"

"We can't know that."

"We can. He almost never hit Buddy. Buddy was his treasure, his stupid legacy to the world. And Buddy didn't need you. He always took Dad's side. He was Dad's eyes and ears in the house. Almost every time I got in trouble, Buddy was behind it. It was like I was his guinea pig. He wanted to be like Dad, and he practiced on me." She began to cry.

Jan rested her hand on Harmony's arm, and her heart squeezed painfully. "You never knew your brother the way I did. He was confused and unhappy, and your father tormented him, too, only in a very different way."

"He was never cruel to him!"

"Crueler than he ever was to you."

Harmony reached for a napkin and wiped her nose. "How can you say that?"

"Because I was there."

"Buddy used to set traps for me, and if I took the bait, he would run to Dad and tell him what I'd done. Once he found the key to the gun cabinet and left one of Dad's guns on a table, do you remember? I picked it up thinking I would take it to you so we could figure out what to do with it, and then Dad came in and saw me. Buddy told him I'd opened the gun cabinet and taken it myself."

Jan remembered the unfortunate aftermath. "As hard as this is to understand, Buddy didn't hate you. He was just fascinated with guns, like boys often are. And he didn't want his father to see him doing something he wasn't supposed to. So he lied. But he didn't set out to hurt you."

"How do you know that?"

"Because he talked to me. Sometimes on the nights when your father was gone Buddy would open up. He wasn't bad — he was confused. He saw the way his father treated us, but he couldn't believe his own father was bad, because what would that do to his world? He had to choose, but it was never easy. He wanted to do the right thing, but as he got older that became increasingly less clear. Your father praised him for all the wrong things. When I could I tried to counteract that, to make him think about other people's feelings, to assure him that his own mattered, his real ones, not the ones his father told him he was allowed to have."

"You're saying you had an influence on him?" Harmony shook her head. "We're talking about the same person, right? The one who picked on anybody he didn't like? The one who got kicked off the football team for slamming another player's head against the goalpost? The same guy who started one too many fights at the local bar where he was too young to be and died because of it?"

Silence fell, and Jan felt the weight of it smothering her.

"Are you saying that you stayed with my father all those years, that you subjected yourself and sometimes me to his violence, just because you thought that Buddy needed you?"

Jan knew she had to be honest, that it was past time for her daughter to understand. But she struggled for a way to make things clear without revealing every detail.

"He did need me," she said at last. "He needed somebody who loved him and believed in him."

"Dad believed —"

Jan held up her hand to stop her. "Let me say this my way. Your father *never* believed in your brother. He only believed in himself. Something terrible happened to Buddy

485

before you were born. He was a wonderful little boy, my sweet baby, but by then I had realized he wouldn't stay that way if we remained with your dad, so I tried to leave. Secretly and carefully, but in the end without success. That day I saw the full extent of your father's cruelty and need for revenge."

"What —"

Jan held up her hand again. "I'm not going into it. Afterward I realized the only thing I could do was try to help Buddy be the person he was meant to be. Again, secretly and carefully. I had to be the push to your father's pull. The only choice left was to keep my little boy in touch with his humanity. And so I tried. I believed it was a better choice than sacrificing both your lives. Because I believed then — and I still do — that your father would rather have killed us than let us go free. And nothing the law could do for us would have stopped him."

"It didn't work. Buddy lived and died a bully."

"No, he took his own life."

"No, he was killed in a bar fight."

"One of many he started, yes. Buddy was tempting fate and hoping, I think, that he would lose. And he finally found peace."

Harmony stared at the table.

"He used to bring me flowers," Jan said softly. "When nobody else was home he would pick them, dandelions or the daffodils from our woods. And sometimes we would sit together and talk about the conflicts raging inside him. Of course, he didn't know what to call his feelings, and he didn't see clearly what had happened to him. By then he was so much more your father's son than mine, but I believed . . ." She swallowed hard. "I believed that once he left home, all the seeds I planted would grow. That he would see his father for the man he is . . . or was. In the end, maybe that's why he died. Because he was torn inside. All the time. And he just wanted it to end."

"Why didn't you take another chance and leave sooner? You helped me leave and nothing happened. Dad never found me. He never came after me. How do you know he would have come after you, or *us,* all those years ago?"

"After you left, not a day passed when your father didn't remind me that he could find you if he wanted to. He said he had a good idea where you were, and if I tried to leave, he would find us both."

Harmony looked stricken. "But, Mom, you *did* leave, and he didn't find us."

"And I'm still not sure I did the right thing."

"But you finally got out of there. You found help and you left."

"In the months right before I ran, something changed in your father's life. I don't know what, but I do know *he* was different. He watched me, as always, but he didn't seem to care as much. It was like he'd moved on to something else in his mind, that he had something new to be angry about or absorbed in that had nothing to do with our home or me. I realized if ever there was a time to go, it had arrived."

"And that's really why you've stayed here and haven't moved on? Because you think he lost interest?"

Jan hesitated, but this, too, she thought Harmony should know. "No, I've only stayed in Asheville, sweetheart, because more and more I think he'll never find either of us."

"Because Moving On was so careful? Because *you've* been so careful?"

Jan covered her daughter's hand and squeezed. "No, Harmony, because I think your father must be dead. That's the only answer that makes sense."

CHAPTER 30

On Sunday morning Davis turned into the driveway exactly when he'd told Harmony he would. He had given twenty-four hours' notice, and explained he and a date were taking Lottie to the Biltmore Estate for the first day of the annual Christmas celebration. In a gesture of goodwill she'd promised to have the baby's stroller ready, and he'd told her not to bother. He'd bought one to keep in the car, along with a crib to put in the extra bedroom of his house.

The same house he'd bought to convince Harmony she should marry him. Okay, she was a little bitter. No surprise there.

"I hope this date actually likes kids," she'd said sweetly, right before he hung up.

When he pulled up she was pushing Lottie in the baby swing dangling from the limb of a century-old maple.

Leaves were falling steadily now, flaunting their extravagant colors like exotic carpets on the farmyard floor. The trunk of the maple sported a heart: "B.R. loves M.R." Harmony had never asked Rilla when she and Brad had taken the notion to carve something so flagrantly romantic into the old tree. But Harmony wondered if she would ever find a man whose initials she wanted to share with the world.

Davis stepped out, and a young woman in a flowered skirt and lavender sweater joined him. She had shoulder-length dark hair and long, elegant legs and she smiled almost shyly at Harmony before she came to watch the baby in the swing.

"Oh, she's adorable."

Harmony stopped pushing the baby and turned to the woman, who was extending her hand.

"I'm Fiona. And you must be Harmony."

Harmony took the hand that was not, as she had expected, pampered and mani-cured, but had short unpolished nails and a rough palm. She murmured a polite re-sponse.

"Fiona's a geologist," Davis said. "With the state."

"What does a geologist do in Asheville?" Harmony asked.

"I investigate requests for mining per-mits."

"Really? Don't you think they're already leveling too many mountaintops?"

Fiona smiled, not offended. "I can find ways to deny permits you wouldn't believe. You and I probably see eye to eye about that."

"Lottie's all set?" Davis already had his daughter out of the swing, and the baby was squealing with joy as he lifted her into the air. She recognized her father and was delighted to see him again.

"She slept later than usual, so she's in a good mood," Harmony said.

Fiona was beaming at Davis and his daughter. "I have six nieces and nephews under the age of four. Good moods are always appreciated, aren't they?"

Harmony couldn't help herself. She liked this woman, and she wanted to take her aside and tell her to run for the hills while she could. Davis Austin was not the guy for her.

Yet just beyond Fiona stood the man Harmony thought she knew so well, the suck-up accountant and son of prissy Gloria Austin, and this Davis was clearly smitten with his baby daughter, making certain he took part in her life whenever he could, even setting up his household so she could eventually be an overnight guest.

"I hope the three of you have a great time," Harmony said. And while some part of her didn't want Lottie to have fun with anybody except her, a more substantial part was being truthful.

Someday Lottie would have a stepmother. If she was lucky it would be somebody like Fiona, and when that event happened, Harmony wanted her daughter to be happy about it. Because if necessary, Harmony could be a grown-up.

"We were hoping to be at the estate until midafternoon," Davis said. "She'll be okay if you don't feed her until then?"

"She's getting most of her calories from other places now, and she likes milk from her sippy cup. She'll be fine. I packed everything you'll need."

Fiona told Harmony how nice it had been to meet her; Davis put the baby and the backpack with supplies in the car, and the three drove off together.

She stood beside the swing for a long moment, watching the car disappear down the driveway as maple leaves swirled around her ankles.

She had hours of baby-free time ahead, and she felt oddly disoriented. On Sunday projects came to a halt at the Reynolds Farm, and only the most necessary chores were done. Rilla had a mom-to-be in the kennel about to whelp a litter of golden doodle puppies, all of whom would hopefully be smarter than Vanilla and more suitable to become service dogs. But Harmony had already checked on the mom and brought her up to the house where Rilla could keep a closer eye on her. And while Harmony often ate meals with the family and helped with preparations, on Sundays she and Lottie ate all their meals in their garage apartment to give the Reynoldses time alone. So there was no bread to knead, no vegetables to clean. She had leftovers for her own dinner, and Lottie's would be simple to prepare.

She was contemplating how to fill the hours until Lottie came home when her cell phone rang. She answered without looking at the screen.

"This Harmony?"

The voice was unfamiliar, and she was immediately suspicious. "Who's this?"

"My name's Bea. I'm a friend of Jan's."

Harmony had heard all about the lady trucker who had helped her mother escape from Topeka. She leaned against the tree and closed her eyes. "Did my . . . Jan give you my number?"

"For emergencies."

Harmony thought maybe her mother had told her that, although their conversations were usually so quick and quietly spoken she wasn't surprised she'd forgotten.

The word *emergency* registered. "Tell me, what's wrong?"

"Honey, I don't know how you feel about everything that's happened in your family. I'd really rather talk to your mom."

"You called her?"

"She's not answering."

"Sometimes coverage is spotty because of the mountains." She tried to remember if her mother had mentioned going anywhere today. Jan had said she wanted to go up to the Goddess House to spend time with Cristy. Maybe she had.

Or maybe . . .

Harmony imagined her father finally showing up in Asheville. She imagined him finding her mother.

Jan wasn't picking up phone calls.

Emergency wasn't nearly a strong enough word.

"I don't know where she is or why she's not answering," she said, "but I'll find her and give her your message right away. You just have to tell me what it is. If my father's on his way here or worse —"

"That's not it."

"You're sure?"

There was a pause, a rather long pause; then Bea said, "Yeah, I am."

"Is it *about* him?"

Another long pause ensued, and she thought Bea had covered the receiver and was speaking to someone else. Then she came back.

"I didn't want to do it this way. We didn't. I don't know how you really feel about your dad, honey."

Harmony realized where this was leading. One moment she'd been blind to it, and the next she understood with absolute clarity.

"He's dead, isn't he?" she asked.

"They found his body last night."

Harmony could almost feel herself moving away from the tree to stand apart from her body, to turn and watch the tall blonde holding the telephone. That woman's father was dead, and Harmony knew she must be suffused with relief. Just relief. Not joy, not sorrow.

Blessed relief.

She closed her eyes and waited a moment. Reality shifted, and when she opened her eyes again, she was the woman leaning against the maple.

"How did he die?" Her voice was calm, although inside she felt something unidentifiable, something waiting to erupt.

"Can't we leave that part for Jan?"

"No, we can't."

"We think he was shot, but we can't say anything for sure yet. We have a friend in the sheriff's department, and she'll have more for us later. Whoever did it buried your dad in a shallow grave not far from your old house, on a tract where they've been doing some construction. Maybe whoever did it thought that part wasn't going to be developed. It was wooded, but you know how they take trees down these days."

Harmony realized she was nodding. Nodding and nodding, and exactly why and at what, she wasn't sure. "When? Do you know?"

"A while ago. Not recent."

Her father had been dead, and none of them had known it. All their elaborate precautions to keep Jan safe had been for nothing. Rex Stoddard had been in Topeka when he died, not on the road looking for his wife and daughter.

Then she realized what that could mean.

"How long is *a while*?"

"I guess they'll do an autopsy, and we'll know the answer then."

"But you have some idea, don't you?"

"I don't like talking to you about this."

"Two months? Could it be that long?"

"Might be," Bea said, as if the words were being dragged from her throat.

"He didn't come home the night Mom escaped. Was he already dead?"

"We don't know."

Harmony thought out loud. "Somebody kills my father about the time my mother disappears. Nobody's going to think that's a coincidence. They're going to be looking for her now, aren't they?"

"I guess you need to hear all this so you can pass it on to Jan. Seems like there's more to this than just murder."

"*Just* murder?"

"Right, like that's not bad enough. Seems like somebody's been making off with money from your father's agency, making bogus claims and raking in the checks. Could have been your dad. At least that's what they thought before they found his body."

"You knew about this? About the money? And you didn't tell Mom?"

"No, it's been hush-hush. We're just truckers, hon, with some connections. That's not something we'd be privy to. But it's not so hush-hush now that his body's been found. See, they've been trying to find him, quiet-like. Probably hoping they could sneak up on him before he squirreled away whatever he'd snatched for good. But now I'm afraid you're right, and they've got to be wondering where your mom fits into this picture."

"Do they think she killed him?"

"I don't know what they think. This is all new."

"Do you want her to leave here? Go somewhere safer like you planned at the beginning? Where she won't be found? Do you want her to get ready?"

"We can't do that. Whatever we think, it's not about rescuing your mom from your father anymore. It's about murder."

Of course, Moving On couldn't be involved in a murder investigation. Harmony realized she wasn't thinking straight.

Her father was dead.

Someone had stolen money from the agency he had started himself.

About the time her father died her mother had fled into the night, leaving a burning house behind her and no forwarding address. A burning house with an arsenal of guns her father had liked to fondle and sometimes point at his wife.

She couldn't think about that now. "I've got to get to Mom."

"We can still tell you whatever we learn. There's no law against that."

Harmony had the presence of mind to say thank you. She hung up, thumbed through the numbers in her contact list, stabbed the one for Taylor's cell phone and waited, praying Taylor would answer.

She did. Harmony wasted no time on an explanation.

"Taylor, are you home? Is Mom there?"

"No, I'm in my car, and Jan left the house a little while ago."

"Where'd she go?"

"She was heading up the mountain to see Cristy. Jan wants to make her a dress for the sheriff's Christmas ball in Berle. It's a big deal for Cristy, going back on Sully's arm, considering that it's the same sheriff's department that put her in jail."

Harmony was only half listening. "When did she leave?"

"A while ago. Maybe forty minutes?"

The Reynolds Farm was closer to the Goddess House than Taylor was. Harmony figured that meant her mother might only be twenty minutes ahead of her on the road up Doggett Mountain.

She owed Taylor an explanation, but first she had to talk to her mother. "I'll see if I can catch her."

"It's a lovely morning to be up there."

Harmony didn't tell her it was no longer a

lovely morning. Today the police might suspect her mother of murder. She had to find Jan, and they had to make a plan.

Jan had debated how smart it was to drive up Doggett Mountain alone. The road was narrow and treacherous, and while traveling the snaking turns should be frightening, she had been certain the trip wouldn't be nearly as bad if she was the one in the driver's seat.

Now that she was ascending the mountain she wasn't worried about the road itself. She was worried about being nudged off it to tumble to her death in a fiery explosion, a scenario that hadn't occurred to her until it was too late to change plans. It would be an unexpected and dramatic finale to a life in which she had largely cowered in the shadows at the mercy of the man she had chosen to love, honor and obey.

Until death did them part.

So far she had only spotted two cars. One heading down the mountain, another behind her filled with teenagers who had picked up speed when she pulled over at an overlook to let them pass. She hoped she didn't find their car belly-up on the road ahead, wheels spinning, smoke rising.

She hoped she didn't see Rex in her rearview mirror.

Today's trip was a bold subtitle in her imaginary autobiography. In the two months since she had come to Asheville, she had moved from fear of nearly everything to shy curiosity. She would forever be affected by her past. She would cringe at loud voices, avoid arguments, struggle to please, take blame where she deserved none. She would probably never be completely comfortable around men. She couldn't imagine herself in a relationship again. And yet . . . In two months so much had changed. In two more? In two years? Ten?

By the time the ground began to level and the scenery settled into rolling farmland, she was triumphant at her new achievement. And triumph? Well, triumph was a triumph all its own, because Rex had never allowed it.

And there he was again. Rex, who either hadn't found her or was toying with her, or was — as she had warned her daughter — dead.

What did it say that the last was the possibility she most hoped for?

She found the turnoff without incident and crept up the length of the gravel driveway. When she reached the parking area she got out to gaze up at the log house. No smoke spiraled from the chimney, and the porch was empty. Most significantly Cristy's canine companion, Beau, wasn't on his way down to greet her.

Cristy's car wasn't parked in her usual spot. In last night's phone call the young woman had warned she would probably have to start the morning at the local B and B. Leaf-peepers had come out in full force, and she had said she might need to strip beds and do laundry. Jan was supposed to make herself at home. The young woman had promised to leave magazine photos of dresses she liked, as well as a length of periwinkle-blue fabric she had found on a clearance table in Asheville, so Jan could think about what to do.

On the way up to the house Jan heard another car come up the drive and she turned, expecting Cristy. She saw, perplexed, that it was Harmony instead.

She walked back down the series of terraces and waited for her daughter to emerge.

"This is such a nice surprise. Did you know I would be here?" she asked as Harmony got out.

She realized then that it wasn't a nice surprise for her daughter. Harmony's eyes were red-rimmed, and her pale skin was flushed. She shoved the door closed behind her, then hurried to her mother and threw her arms around her.

"Sweetheart, what on earth?" Jan stroked her hair.

"Bea called." The tears were still in Harmony's voice.

The morning turned dark. Just that quickly. The triumph, the joy at a new accomplishment, vanished, and old friend fear came calling.

"Your father's found us?" she asked.

"He's dead."

For a moment Jan couldn't make sense of that. She had told Harmony Rex's death was a possibility. On the way up the mountain she had admitted to herself how much she hoped for it. But now the reality?

The reality was something very different.

Jan held Harmony away and searched her face. "They're sure?"

"They found his body in a shallow grave not far from our house, Mom. They think he was shot."

"Shot?" Jan heard the word, but it held no meaning.

"They don't know much, but Bea promised they'll keep us up to date when they hear anything else."

Jan had always known that one day Rex, in a fit of rage, might pull one of his cherished guns from the locked case, not to take his usual potshots at small animals, but to murder the wife who never reached his standards of perfection. She had never expected *him* to die that way instead.

Harmony's words were going round and round in her head. "When? Do they know when?"

"A while. That's all she said. Maybe as long as you've been here."

Jan understood the real reason behind her daughter's serpentine journey up Doggett Mountain, why she had sobbed as she'd driven. Why she still looked distraught.

Not because she was devastated that her father had been killed. Because she was afraid her mother might be charged with the crime.

And why wouldn't she be?

"They'll think I killed him." Jan acknowledged it out loud.

"I know you didn't."

The mere fact that Harmony had to reassure her tied the knots in Jan's stomach that much tighter. "Of course you know I didn't. But for the record? Your father didn't come home the night I left Topeka, but that wasn't the first time. I assumed either he had gone out of town without warning me, as he liked to do, or he was testing me. Only when he fell off everybody's radar did I wonder if he was dead. He didn't show up here. He didn't show up at work. . . ."

"I thought he was out there somewhere stalking you . . . us . . . and he'd sacrificed the agency and gone into hiding until he found you. It was like him, wasn't it? To favor revenge over everything else?"

Revenge. Rex had proved he would calmly drown his own son because Jan had planned to escape. Abandoning a well-run agency that could get along without him had seemed insignificant in comparison. Until the weeks had dragged on.

She had known. Deep inside she had known he was dead. But murder?

"No one else will believe this," Jan said. "They'll question why I didn't step forward and tell my story."

"You were terrified he'd find you."

"If he died the night I left Topeka . . ."

"Mom, they can't pinpoint it that closely. Forensics aren't exact."

Jan began to think out loud. "Even that's not in my favor. If he died sometime after, but they can't determine when? If there's even a chance he died that night, they'll have a scenario all ready. Your father came home and we fought. Somehow I killed and buried him. We had a house filled with guns — I'm sure they found traces after the explosion. Besides, Rex used to brag about his collection, so others knew. Why would the authorities believe me if I tell them I never had access? It only takes one gun, one night."

"But how could they prove that?"

"It's all about reasonable doubt, isn't it? I left town about the time of the murder and hid for two months. And before I left I set fire to the house to destroy evidence and confuse the authorities."

"But we can prove abuse, Mom. I saw him beat you."

"You're my daughter. Of course you want to protect me."

"There must be doctor's records. Hospital records. Too many injuries."

"It won't help. The police will need a motive. They'll say I killed him because he hit me one time too many and I snapped."

When Harmony didn't reply, Jan saw there was more she hadn't yet revealed.

"What else did Bea say?"

Harmony chewed her lip.

"What?" Jan asked again.

"The police have been searching for Dad since the fire."

"Of course they searched. They searched for me, too, I'm sure. Although apparently not hard."

"No, they were looking for *him* because there was money missing."

Jan listened as Harmony explained what Bea had told her, then both of them fell silent.

Jan was the one to break it. "I've been living in Asheville without a job. I bought a car with cash. By now they've checked our bank accounts, and they'll see I didn't withdraw anything before I left. So I must have gotten the money somewhere else."

"You can prove you had a separate account even Dad didn't know about. You have all the paperwork."

Jan knew she was frightening her daughter. She didn't point out that when the police looked closely, they would find she had paved a trail to freedom with carefully planted lies for weeks before she disappeared.

Just as a murderer might have done.

She pulled herself together, or tried to. No matter what, she was still Harmony's mother. "This isn't the right moment to assume anything. Rex was your father. He's gone. You must be feeling something other than concern for me."

"Relief. I'm a good person, and the fact I don't feel joy? I'm sorry, but that's the best person I can be right now."

"The way you feel might change. We're both in shock."

"I just want to leave him and everything he did to us behind. Maybe someday I won't hate him anymore. I don't want him to have power over me ever again."

Jan thought that was probably a form of forgiveness. Letting go of the nightmare. Moving forward. No longer keeping Rex Stoddard at the center of their lives. It was a whole new way to live. It would take time. More than time.

Help.

"We both need to talk to someone," she said. "Now we can, without worrying it will bring him to our front door. And I have to talk to the police. I have to go to them before they come to me."

"They'll want to talk to me, too."

"We'll go together."

"When?"

Jan put her arm around her daughter's shoulders. "Let's go up to the house and make a cup of tea so we can figure this out."

"It seems bigger than a cup of tea, Mom. Even bigger than a pitcher of hot chocolate."

Jan didn't know what to say. In the weeks to come, she was certain that was going to be true over and over again.

CHAPTER 31

Taylor was taking the day off from work. With a deep sense of gratitude for her daughter's survival, she had shepherded Maddie to church that morning, a destination nearly as foreign as Outer Mongolia and as high on her bucket list of must-see places. The last time she had been to Church of the Covenant was to attend a formal memorial service for her mother.

She admired, even loved, the Reverend Analiese Wagner, so it was no surprise that Analiese's sermon about the Bible's fallen women kept her rapt attention, and the music performed by a church choir from Raleigh had her on her feet clapping along with the rest of the congregation.

Everything had changed since Taylor had been forced to attend the obligatory Friday chapels of Covenant Academy, the private school that was still associated with the church. In those days she had been labeled by teachers as a rebel and an outcast, and she had been sure that the Friday sermons, preached by a minister with no sense of humor, were aimed straight at her. Today's message of love, hope and strong women was a relief.

Rather than go to a class with her contemporaries, a still chastened Maddie had stayed for the service, but afterward she announced she hadn't been too bored. Taylor thought that was high praise. Then when some of Maddie's school friends detailed the plans their religious education class was making for a Christmas party, Taylor suspected she and her daughter might no longer be strangers here.

In this, as in so many corners of her life, she knew she needed to move on. The prodigal daughter might find her way home.

"Edna would like it here," Maddie said on the way to the car.

"We'll bring her next time when we don't have plans for after the service."

"Do I have to go to lunch with you and Adam?"

Maddie liked Adam, so Taylor probed. "Where would you like to go instead?"

"The mall."

Taylor could see the battle lines forming. She wasn't ready to have a teenager, or for mall roaming and bare midriffs and piercings. A decade ago she had been a teenager herself.

"And what would you do?" she asked.

"Go to Build-A-Bear. Edna and I want to make bears that look like our Halloween costumes. So we can remember how cool they were. I still have money Daddy gave me when I was in Nashville."

Relief became a laugh. "You'll need a grown-up."

"Miss Georgia said she would take us."

Taylor was fairly sure that "Miss Georgia" would soon become "Mrs. Georgia," since she and Lucas Ramsey were already making plans to build a house together and Georgia was sporting a very lovely ring.

"I don't see any reason you can't go," she told Maddie. "Are you supposed to meet them there?"

"Can you drop me at Edna's?"

"Do you have your money?"

"Can I borrow some until I get home? I have to dig it up."

"I'm sorry?"

Maddie looked a little sheepish. "I kind of buried it behind Papa's workshop. In a plastic bag. You know, in case Jan's mean husband came looking for her and tried to take our money, too."

Taylor hadn't realized that the tension around Rex Stoddard had infected her daughter. Maddie had bravely kept that to herself.

"I don't think you need to worry about your money, sweetheart, or about Jan's mean husband. He seems to have disappeared."

"He could still be looking for her."

Taylor thought that was more and more unlikely, and told Maddie so. She also pulled out her wallet and gave her daughter most of what she had. She thought maybe this bear would be on her, a gift to the child who had silently lived with fears of "Jan's mean husband" and never hinted she was afraid. A bear who would quite likely be the last stuffed animal her daughter bought for herself. Because before too long boys would begin presenting them as gifts.

A bear because her daughter was alive and well and still, thankfully, a child.

She put her arm around Maddie and squeezed. Maddie didn't even pull away.

Taylor dropped her at Sam's, chatted a moment with her friend, then headed downtown to the restaurant where she was meeting Adam. He liked Indian food, she liked Indian food — the destination had been a natural.

She managed to find a parking place on the next block, no easy feat on a pretty Sunday afternoon near the inevitable end of pleasant weather. Adam was waiting outside when she arrived. He raised an eyebrow when he saw she was alone; then he swept her close and kissed her on the sidewalk.

"Maddie still okay?" he asked when he released her.

She took a moment just to admire how nice he looked in a dark dress shirt and faded jeans. "She sends her regrets. She's off with Edna and Georgia."

"The restaurant's crowded. I put my name in, but there's a thirty-minute wait."

"We could stroll around Asheville and look in windows." She paused. "Or we could go to your place and come back later."

"Much later?"

"I had a big breakfast."

They took his car, which was parked closer than hers. The drive was short. He told her how pretty she looked in one of the few dresses she owned, and she told him about the church service. His phone rang as she was describing Analiese's sermon, and he turned it off without even checking to see who it was.

In his apartment they shed their clothes right along with their inhibitions and fell into bed together.

Today they took their time, not rushing to conclusion, but letting the inevitability sustain them. He touched her with his wrists, his fingers, his palms, caressed her with his lips and tongue, made the simplest movements breathtakingly erotic. She forgot to wonder what would please him and simply tried, gauging his reaction and gathering information along with pleasure. If Friday night had been like the outline of a story, this afternoon was about expanding the plot, understanding the nuances, the unexpected twists and, most of all, the characters.

Adam, who always weighed his words, was surprisingly communicative in bed. He asked if something pleased her, made adjustments, asked again, just enough to let her know her satisfaction was important. At the same time he let her know what mattered most to him, what excited him and what excited him too much.

Patience was eventually eclipsed by need.

Afterward, lying in the crook of his arm, one finger tracing the scar on his chest, Taylor wondered out loud, "Does this ever get old, do you think?"

"You're asking me?"

"Well, if it does, maybe I ought to prepare.

You know, lower my expectations."

"You have high expectations?"

"I guess I think it changes, but gets old? I just can't see it, though I could be wrong."

"From what you told me it got old for you right after you tried it the first time."

She laughed. "But not for you?"

"I've been pretty happy moving on afterward."

She knew enough about him to realize how true that must be. Adam had never settled anywhere. Of course, men and women in the military had spouses and families, but nobody would ever claim it was easy to nurture intimacy while serving on foreign shores.

"You never thought about settling down?" she asked.

"Not much."

"We're so different. You've been everywhere. I've been nowhere."

"Everywhere's not all it's cracked up to be." He stroked her hair. "Everywhere is just what I was used to."

"Maybe we should trade places. I should wander, and you should stay in Asheville and find out what it's like to see the same people, shop at the same stores, eat at the same restaurants."

"From what I can tell, in this town they

open a new restaurant twice a week."

"I think I would go to Paris first. Maybe hang out on the Left Bank with the students. Isn't that where they hang out?"

"I was never there."

"Next I'd go to Sydney. I've always wanted to go to Australia."

"Practically next door to the Eiffel Tower."

"You haven't been in Sydney, either?"

"Have. My dad was stationed at Nurrungar in South Australia. We went to Sydney on holiday."

"You're like a geography lesson."

"New places get old after a while. You find yourself looking around for somebody to talk to about what you see, and there's nobody who knows you or cares. You make friends, sure, but they move on, and you lose touch before the plane door closes. When I was wounded I must have gotten a hundred cards from people who knew me, men I'd served with —"

"Women you'd slept with," she finished.

"You may be blowing the number out of proportion."

She smiled, but she sobered quickly. "And there was nobody hanging out at your side? Nobody to help?"

"Professionals. My mother called a lot, but she has arthritis and traveling is brutal for her. I was used to being alone, but I can't say that's what I needed."

She wanted to tell him she was sorry, but she knew he would be embarrassed. "It would be different here. You would be bombarded by people wanting to help. When Maddie was born, there were people everywhere. Friends of my father's, Jeremy's parents and some of their friends. Girls I'd gone to school with, even teachers. My mother wasn't there, though. We fought about the pregnancy. She told me if I went through with it and didn't give the baby up, I would learn how much fun it was to raise a child on my own."

His arm tightened around her, pulling her a little closer.

"She and my father fought over that," Taylor went on, "and *she* left instead. It was years before I spoke to her again. She tried to fix things, to say she was sorry, but I wouldn't let her. I was so angry, and I just let it eat me up. Right before she died I finally let her back into my life, but I'll never forgive myself for waiting so long."

"Did she forgive you?"

"Absolutely. She understood. That's the funny part. Because forgiveness wasn't Mom's strong suit, either, but by the end she'd gotten really good at it." Tears filled her eyes, and she blinked them away. "I miss her, and I miss all those years we wasted."

"There are lots of ways to keep yourself apart from people. Moving's not the only one."

"Maybe it's a talent we share."

"Maybe not. Maybe we've both figured out it's not a good thing."

She liked the sound of that. Adam wasn't making commitments, and she hadn't asked for any, but maybe he wasn't going to move on right away.

Maybe he had found something here in Asheville that had convinced him a few roots might not be a bad thing.

Her stomach rumbled at that moment, and he rubbed it before he sat up. "There's a little place just a few blocks away with decent takeout. They make a good pumpkin curry. Why don't I run over and pick up whatever they have ready? You can take a nap."

"You don't want me to come?"

"I like the idea of walking into my place and finding you waiting."

"I like the idea of a nap. Somebody wore me out."

"Somebody tried." He kissed her, then sat up and began to pull his clothes on. She admired the view until he was clothed again.

"Anything you don't eat other than meat?" he asked at the door.

"Beets."

"I'll go easy on the borscht." He smiled before he closed the door behind him.

She snuggled deeper into the mattress and closed her eyes, relaxing into sleep almost as soon as she heard his car leave the parking area.

She didn't know how long the nap lasted, but not more than minutes. On the floor below somebody slammed a door. She jerked awake, and that was that. No matter how badly she wanted to fall asleep again, a longer nap was out of the question.

She tried anyway, then gave up and lay with arms under her head and stared at the ceiling. When she considered her life to this point, this relationship was a major detour. From the moment she had found she was pregnant, her life had centered on her daughter.

And now there was Adam.

Strangest of all was how little she really knew him. Adam was a man a woman could live with for years and still not know completely. He wasn't used to sharing. He wasn't used to staying around long enough to try. He hadn't asked her for anything except sexual satisfaction. Yet this was the same man who had risked his own life to save her daughter. A man a woman could trust with her life and maybe even someday with her heart.

She realized where her thoughts were heading, and she sat up, not willing to go there. If Adam had asked little from her, she had asked just as little from him. They had been — and were still — wildly attracted to each other. They enjoyed each other's company, liked many of the same activities and, as far as she knew, shared common values. But if this could be called a relationship, she was sure the rest had to grow slowly. She wasn't going to make demands or ask for promises. This was a one-day-at-a-time proposition, and over-thinking could mean the end.

And the end? That was the one thing she knew she didn't want.

Since the nap had ended, a shower sounded like a plan. She was sure Adam wouldn't mind if she used his shower stall and a towel. Once they ate, she needed to head home. She might invite him to come and watch a DVD that evening, maybe serve dessert instead of dinner since they were eating a large meal now. She wasn't ready to say goodbye.

She straightened the bed and retrieved her

clothes off the floor. In the bathroom she smiled at how neatly Adam kept his things, the toothbrush hanging in a holder, his razor on a folded washcloth on the edge of the sink. Granted there wasn't much room for a mess, but his military background was obvious. Everything had a place. She wondered how he would like living with a child who had to be reminded daily not to throw her belongings every which way.

Adam's towel was hanging neatly from the lone towel rack, but replacements were out of sight. There was a corner storage unit, and she opened it hoping there would be a fresh towel on one of the shelves. She was rewarded by a short stack, neatly folded, but when she removed one from the top and the others slid forward with it, a manila envelope fluttered to the floor. She bent to pick it up and photos slid out.

With more time to think, she would have wondered why Adam kept photographs under folded towels. But there was no time. Because staring back at her was her own likeness, a shot taken from some distance, judging by the fuzzy print quality, a shot of herself with Jan, talking in the front yard of Taylor's house.

The photo wasn't recent. She saw that immediately. Jan's hair was still long. She was wearing one of the few outfits she'd brought from Kansas. Maddie was lounging in the doorway.

Maddie, her *daughter.* In a photograph taken with a long-distance lens.

With trembling hands she shuffled through the small collection. She and Maddie only appeared in the first. But either Harmony or Jan was in every photo, and each shot had been taken from a distance. No one had given this photographer permission. He hadn't been close enough to ask.

Adam was working for Rex Stoddard. Taylor could think of no other explanation. The self-defense class? A useful ploy to get close to Jan, whom he'd traced to Taylor's, and maybe even close to Harmony.

She couldn't imagine the reason. If Harmony's father knew where his wife and daughter were, why hadn't he shown up to reclaim them? From everything she knew, he was the kind of man who would think that way. His wife and daughter belonged to him, the way his car or lawn mower did. If they'd refused to go back with him, and of course, they would have, he probably would have employed desperate measures to get his way.

If not his first choice? Something far worse.

Adam was obviously being paid to work undercover. Most probably he was a private investigator whose responsibility began and ended with a paycheck. He had been paid to locate the Stoddard women, and now he was finished.

Only he *wasn't* finished. Adam was still here in Asheville. He was still teaching in her studio. He was even having sex with her. And why? What did he hope to find out now? Was he watching Jan and Harmony to be sure they didn't move on before the man who had hired him could get to town? Two months had gone by. Unless Rex Stoddard was in jail or a hospital recovering from a terrible illness, he'd had plenty of time to arrive. He could have walked from Kansas by now.

She didn't have all the pieces. She needed more.

First she needed to leave.

A shower was out of the question. While she considered what to do with the photos, she tugged on her clothes. Taking them home made sense. When Jan returned she could show the photos to her, and they could decide what to do together. She remembered that Harmony had been looking for her mom. Taylor would call Cristy and see if Jan and possibly Harmony were at the Goddess House. Together they could decide on their next steps.

She was forced to sit on the bed to pull her shoes on. It was that or a beat-up rocker, since the room was noticeably light on furniture, and the rocker was neatly piled with books. Her stomach clenched when she thought about what else she had done on this bed. She had been used, and she knew that once Adam had gotten everything he wanted — whatever that was — she would have been just as easily discarded.

Clearly she was a walking target, a woman without a scrap of judgment. She was no smarter now than she'd been at sixteen when she'd had sex with Jeremy on his rec room sofa.

Ready to go, she paused. Adam would return, wonder where she had gone, even wonder *how* she'd gone, considering that they had driven here in his SUV. Fortunately she could walk downtown to retrieve her car. It might take thirty minutes, but by the time she got there, maybe she would have some idea what to do next.

She burned to leave him some hint, or better yet an unmistakable sign that she was onto him. He hadn't gotten away with this. She had discovered the truth.

In the end she left the photo of herself

with Jan and Maddie on the bed. Just that one photo, right in the middle.

As far as she was concerned, that said it all.

CHAPTER 32

When he saw all the takeout possibilities, Adam considered calling Taylor. The restaurant had half-a-dozen specials, all of which looked promising, but since he'd told her to take a nap, he didn't want to be the one to wake her. Instead, he ordered too much food, just to be sure she was happy. At least this week he would have decent leftovers to keep the stale bagel company.

People streamed in and out as he waited, the usual Asheville mixture who frequented vegetarian restaurants. Retirees or tourists in casual resort wear, some in suits after morning services at their church of choice. Hipsters who had assembled outfits from the Salvation Army or eBay and finished them with neon high-tops. Hippies with their finery imported from Third World countries and an assortment of dreadlocks, piercings and tattoos. Harmony would blend right into this crowd, even though her style was a little more upscale. And oddly so did he in his dress shirt, short hair and jeans.

At first he hadn't been much of a fan of the city. Asheville had felt disorganized, as if its residents couldn't make up their minds who they were, so they had landed here temporarily while they figured it out. Everybody fit in and nobody did. The most average middle-aged, middle-class man or woman might mention that he or she had been Napoleon or Marie Antoinette in a past life. Once a man in a conservative gray suit had approached him on the street to say he could see Adam's aura, and he was afraid Adam was seriously screwed.

Which was an insight that had hit too close to home.

Of course, while all observations held some truth, they were also exaggerations, and eventually he had begun to relax and figure that out. People here were freer with their idiosyncrasies, but they also seemed to suffer less from them. They were generous, funny, friendly, worth getting to know.

Like Taylor.

When his number was finally called he picked up his order and walked home, since parking would have been more of an issue than a three-block stroll. He wondered if

527

Taylor would be awake or if he would have a chance to kiss his Sleeping Beauty.

That, of course, could be dangerous.

At the house he unlocked the door and climbed the stairs, nodding to a second-floor neighbor who passed him going down. On the third floor he set the take-out bag on the floor and opened his door. His apartment was empty. Assuming Taylor was in the bathroom, he crossed to the counter to set down the bag. Only as he went back to close and lock the door did he notice the photograph on his neatly straightened bed.

For a moment he didn't understand. He moved closer and skimmed it off the covers to take a closer look. He stared at the familiar faces and replayed the circumstances that had probably led to finding it here.

Then he sank to the bed and closed his eyes.

"You sound upset," Samantha told Taylor after they'd chatted a moment about Maddie staying at her house for dinner. Sam had promised to drop Maddie at home by eight, since tomorrow was a school day.

Taylor didn't know what to say. Until she could talk to Jan and Harmony, she wasn't sure what she could reveal. Of course, this was Sam, who was completely trustworthy, but they were also talking on the telephone.

"I might need to reserve a shoulder to cry on," she said.

"You always have one. But I'm thinking man trouble."

"You're smarter than I am. You must have figured out a long time ago that men are *always* trouble."

Sam, who had plenty of men to go out with but none to love, made a noise low in her throat that could have meant anything.

"I'll tell you about it when I can," Taylor said.

"I'll be here."

They hung up, and Taylor stared at the wall wondering how she could bear to tell Jan and Harmony they had been discovered.

A car door slammed near the front of the house, and she guessed she was about to find out. Then somebody pounded on the door, and she realized who, in all likelihood, was standing on her doorstep instead.

This confrontation was inevitable. As she expected, when she opened the door, Adam was on the porch.

"Adam Pryor, minus his long-distance lens." She didn't step aside to let him in.

"You need to hear directly from me what this is about."

"Really? You mean rather than continue to make educated guesses?"

"I think you'll need a lot more education to get this right."

"I was thinking along these lines, Adam. You're working for Rex Stoddard, and you've ingratiated yourself with me so you can spy on his family. Now good old Rex can come to Asheville with his arms open wide and tell Jan and Harmony how sorry he is that he ever developed that nasty little habit of beating the crap out of them."

"I'm not working for Stoddard. I'm trying to find him."

She sucked in her bottom lip as she rolled his words around in her head. "Have any luck?" she asked at last. "Because you've been here long enough to search every house in Asheville."

"I want to explain everything."

"I love explanations. It's just that I like them *before* I sleep with a man, or hire him to work in my studio, or introduce him to my family and closest friends. So you're a little late."

His expression didn't change. "I've never spoken to Rex Stoddard or even been on the same street with the man. I work for an insurance company that did business with his agency. Disastrous business, as a matter of fact. Somebody there made off with a boatload of money."

Of all the excuses Taylor had expected, insurance fraud hadn't been on the list. She tried to decide whether she should close the door in his face or hear whatever tale he had to tell.

In the end she stepped back to let him inside. Whatever Jan and Harmony were facing, they needed to know what Adam had to say. Whether it was a pack of lies or the absolute truth, they needed to know.

Reluctantly she flipped a hand toward the sofa, then chose a chair where she could watch him.

"Was anything you told me true?" she asked. "Clearly you weren't in Asheville because you were looking for a place to settle and you liked the mountains."

"I do like the mountains."

"Don't play games, okay? Or this will be finished really fast."

"I tracked Jan here using phone records. Somebody had called her from a café in town some time ago, and I made an accurate guess it was Harmony. Finding her was easy from there. I was here waiting and watching by the time Jan arrived."

Taylor knew a chunk of time had passed from the night Jan left Topeka to the evening she'd arrived at the Reynolds Farm. To confuse the trail she had ridden with several truckers going in different directions before she'd finally made the journey to Asheville with Bea. So this much could be true.

"Then I assume you followed her here, to my house," she said.

He took over again. "Here's all I knew at the time, Taylor. It looked like a substantial sum of money had been embezzled from Midwest Modern Insurance Company —"

"They employ you?"

"I'm freelance. They're not the only company I work with, but that's how I make a living."

"So when you said you had other income, at least that part of your story was true."

"Everything I told you was true. I just didn't tell you everything."

"Interesting omissions."

He seemed to choose his words. "Mostly they use me for jobs like this one, where I settle in for a while, watch and wait. It's cheaper to pay me by the hour for surveillance than to use somebody on staff. And I like moving around and working part-time."

She didn't care. "Why don't you get to the good stuff?"

"Somebody was making what looked like legitimate claims against policies from

Midwest Modern sold by Stoddard Insurance Agency. All the paperwork was in order, and there was a lot of paperwork. An independent adjuster in Topeka verified the claims. The money was paid. Only somebody in our fraud division noticed anomalies in the data. There were more claims coming via that route than statistics would dictate. These weren't huge claims, not each by itself. Nobody needed to replace a whole rig, for instance, which would have sent up a red flag. But sometimes the damages were heavy enough that payments were substantial. And when our folks started going over the claims again, there were other signs, like possibly inflated bills. It's harder to get away with this kind of thing now."

"So? How could this have anything to do with Jan?"

"Once Midwest had enough evidence to suspect fraud, Stoddard was asked if they could examine his records and interview his agents. Midwest told him it was routine, but of course, he did everything he could to delay things, because that's the kind of jerk he is. Midwest lost patience and told him they would pull the plug on his appointment if he didn't cooperate. That would mean his agency wouldn't be approved to sell their policies, and they were one of the bigger companies he was affiliated with. So he doled out a little of this and that, and from his attitude and the little they were able to see, they began to suspect the fraud was even more widespread, and Stoddard seemed to be the one who had signed off on a lot of it."

"And they suspected Jan, as well? She was hardly even allowed out of the house."

"At that point they were just getting access to the records so they could figure out who was doing what. They decided to keep the investigation in-house until they had enough proof to make a thorough report to the Kansas Insurance Department, so the department could prosecute. They figured the fraud was a coordinated effort, but in theory Stoddard himself was right at the top."

"So when did you get involved?"

"The adjuster who'd verified all the suspect claims vanished before we could get to him, and nobody was able to locate him, so they hired me to look. I still haven't been able to trace the guy. In the meantime we learned that the so-called policyholders who received payment weren't at the addresses where the checks had been sent and nobody remembered them. They probably never existed, and somebody just waited and snatched the checks out of mailboxes. Police reports on the accidents went missing or had never existed in the first place. Anyway, the whole thing was simultaneously sophisticated and unsophisticated. Whoever was in charge varied everything, which made it harder to spot theft, but at the same time he didn't realize how much can be tracked and flagged at top levels today, and how carefully records can be analyzed."

She was tired of Insurance Fraud 101. "Jan. This is supposed to be about *Jan.*"

"You have to understand, everything I've detailed took place over a fairly short period of time. Then Stoddard disappeared the same day his house exploded. So if there were records in his home office, they're gone forever, which seems convenient. About the same time Stoddard's wife escaped to Asheville, a trip we've since learned she preplanned very carefully, even to the point of laying a false trail so she would be harder to track. She has no visible source of income, yet she's living pretty well and not looking for a job. She has a new car, a new sewing machine." He shrugged.

"And you think what?" Taylor wanted to be sure she understood. "Because I happen to know Jan had some money of her own that her husband never knew about."

"It's not what I think that's important. It's what the police think, what Midwest Modern thinks."

"The police?"

"It's what the police *will* think. Jan hasn't been charged with a crime, so even though I tracked her here, Midwest didn't have to notify them right away. A decision was made to keep an eye on her ourselves and see if her husband showed up, or if I saw any proof she was in on the whole thing. We didn't want more eyes than we needed, because we didn't want either of the Stoddards to get suspicious or scared away."

"You think the Stoddards coordinated their escapes? You think they've hidden the money somewhere, and when things simmer down they can reunite and take a lifetime Caribbean vacation under assumed identities?"

"No."

"Then what?"

He leaned forward, but whatever he intended to say was lost when the front door opened, and Jan and Harmony walked in.

Taylor got to her feet and crossed the room. "Listen, before you say a word in front of Adam, a lot has happened that —"

Harmony interrupted. "We know, Taylor. My father's dead."

Surprised, Taylor stopped. "What?"

Harmony looked confused. "That's not what you were going to say?" Her gaze zipped to Adam.

Taylor turned and saw that he'd pulled his cell phone from his pocket and was reading something on the screen. "Adam, I want you to leave. You can do whatever you're going to do on that phone somewhere else."

He finished reading what was most likely a text before he stood. "I didn't get a chance to say what I most needed to. You need me, even if you haven't figured it out yet."

For a moment Taylor thought he meant she needed him in her life, in her bed. She started to protest, but he held up his hand.

"The smartest thing I could have done was to let somebody else take over here, but I didn't, because I became convinced Jan was the victim, not the criminal. I wanted to get to the bottom of this myself because I knew I might be the only one who cared."

"What is he talking about?" Harmony asked Taylor.

"Taylor will fill you in." Adam walked past them to the door. Then he turned. "This is going to get worse before it gets better, Taylor. Don't shut me out. I may be able to help."

She went to close the door behind him.

"How can you possibly believe we could ever trust you again?"

"Because even if you don't like the way I've been forced to do it, my job requires me to use every skill I have to get answers. And I think Jan and Harmony deserve answers."

He was gone before Jan spoke. "Please tell us what's going on."

Taylor saw that both women looked stricken. She ushered them to the sofa and left to put the teakettle on. Harmony had her arm around her mother when she returned.

"Your father's dead?" She listened as Harmony described what they had learned from Bea.

Jan finished the story. "I'll be the most likely suspect. I had the best reason to kill Rex. About the time he died I burned our house down and kept right on going. They'll think I had access to his guns, that it was easy to shoot him."

"What was Adam talking about?" Harmony asked. "Why does he know anything about us? Did you tell him why Mom is here?"

"He figured it out, because that's what they pay him to do." She started at the beginning, took a break to pour the boiling water over teabags in the kitchen and came back to finish her explanation.

There was a silence after she was done, as if the truth about Adam's job was taking time to sink in. Jan spoke after Taylor came back with a tray holding three cups of tea and set it on the coffee table.

"All this time he knew Harmony was my daughter?" Jan wasn't really asking; she was thinking out loud. "He tracked me here? He even got here before I did and waited?"

"Apparently Adam's good at what he does." Taylor felt a lump forming in her throat. She wasn't sure if she was furious or devastated. Right now it didn't even matter, because most of all she had to stay calm so she could help figure out what to do next.

"My father didn't steal that money," Harmony said. "I would never defend him if I didn't have to, but that agency was his pride. Truckers from all over the Midwest and beyond came to his agents for the best deals. He loved being able to tell people he was Rex Stoddard of Stoddard Insurance. The way he looked in the community and industry was more important than anything to him. I think that's half the reason he didn't want Mom to leave. He was afraid she might tell somebody what kind of man he really was, and even people who didn't believe her might look at him differently."

Taylor was trying to put the puzzle together. "Could there have been some reason he needed money? Something more important than his reputation or his agency?"

Jan slowly shook her head, but Harmony glanced at her mother. "You said in the months before you left he started to act differently. Remember? Like he had something on his mind?"

Jan looked the way she had in her first weeks here, cheeks pale, shoulders hunched. "He was at the office longer hours. When he was home he seemed preoccupied. That was one of the reasons I decided to leave when I did. He was every bit as critical, but he wasn't concentrating on me in the same fanatical way. I thought maybe I'd just managed to fade into the background so much he was finally beginning to lose interest in tormenting me."

Taylor poured milk and sugar into Jan's cup and held it out to her. "Drink this."

"I can't absorb it all." Jan took the cup and obediently raised it to her lips, but the movement was robotic.

"On the way back we talked this over," Harmony said, "and Mom thinks she needs to go to the local police and tell them who she is and what she knows. If she doesn't tell somebody, she's going to look guilty. Now that Dad's dead, she doesn't have a reason to hide."

"If Adam found me, the Shawnee County sheriff will find me." Jan set down the cup, and her hands weren't quite steady. "It seems even more necessary to go to the police and let them know my side of the story before anybody else comes looking."

"First, shouldn't we check with somebody who knows about these things?" Taylor mentally paged through friends and acquaintances to find a lawyer or a connection to law enforcement, but the only person she could come up with was Sully, and while he might give Jan advice, this problem was way out of his jurisdiction.

"Brad's a lawyer," Harmony said. "Rilla's Brad. He'll help."

"No, I don't want a delay." Jan got to her feet. "I know you're both trying to help, but I've spent most of my life letting somebody else tell me what to do. This time I have to decide. I'll talk to Brad after I go to the police, but right now I'm sure this is what I need to do next."

Taylor suspected the local authorities would be bored by Jan's story, since what happened in Kansas was no concern of theirs. They would probably send her statement on to their counterparts in Topeka and wash their hands of it, but Jan was right, at least she would be on record as having stepped forward. No one could accuse her of hiding now.

Harmony got to her feet, too. "I can't believe all this time Adam was watching us and waiting for my father to show up."

"He was doing his job," Jan said.

"He was lying through his teeth." Taylor heard the bitterness in her voice, but she didn't care.

"He said he wants to help," Jan said. "I'll need to think about that."

Taylor didn't have time to form a response before somebody knocked on the front door. She realized it was the first time since Jan had moved into her house that she'd heard a knock and not thought immediately that it might be Rex Stoddard.

"When this is all cleared up, your life is going to be better," she told Jan as she got up to answer it. "You can really move on without being afraid."

Jan just closed her eyes.

CHAPTER 33

Adam leaned back in the driver's seat, still parked in the same spot where he had often done surveillance, and stared out the windshield. The morning's weather had held such promise, but now the afternoon sky was stormy, which seemed fitting.

"Yeah, well, nobody regrets not picking up your call more than I do, Philip," he said into his cell phone.

Philip Salter sounded harried. Sunday should be a day of rest, but apparently this one didn't qualify, not for either of them. "I got the call about Stoddard last night. I called you right away. I called you this afternoon. You don't check your messages?"

Adam had spent yesterday hiking in the mountains and considering his life. The fact that he had forgotten to check for messages when he got home, that he had even turned off his phone today when Taylor was telling him about her morning, said everything about where his head was.

"I check my messages," he said. "It's the weekend. I wasn't expecting to hear from you. Let's move on."

"They found the body just before dark, or I should say a front loader moving logs uncovered it. He wasn't buried very far in, like it was done by somebody in a hurry, or somebody without much oomph. Maybe a woman."

"That's a lame assumption."

"I'm just telling you what they told me, okay? The grave was about a mile and a half from what used to be the Stoddards' home. And they don't know when he died, but it was some time ago, for sure."

"How did they identify the body?"

"Wallet. Business cards. A photo of Stoddard carrying a bowling ball and wearing the Stoddard Agency team shirt. And no, the ID won't be conclusive until they do an autopsy, but the man's been missing long enough for them to make a pretty fair guess."

"Why did they call you?"

"We've been checking in regularly with the detective who had Stoddard's disappearance and the agency stuff on his plate. Now Homicide's got the case. The new guy called to see what we knew that they didn't, if anything."

"And you told them where they could find Janine Stoddard." Adam had expected that. This was no longer just about insurance fraud. Wait-and-watch was no longer an option. "Did they say what they'll do?"

"No surprise, but they don't really share their strategies with outsiders."

"If they have the budget, they'll send somebody here to convince her to go home with them."

"They sounded awfully pleased I'd told them where to find her."

Adam wondered how long the Shawnee County Sheriff's Office would wait. In their position, he would have hopped a plane the moment he learned Jan's whereabouts. Waiting longer could mean another disappearance. And convincing the local cops to intervene might be tough, since there was no real evidence to charge her with a crime.

Not that they would need much with all the circumstantial evidence that pointed her way.

"It's out of our hands now," Philip said. "Time for you to write up a report. A couple of new things have come up, and you might like one of them."

"You don't want me here when they interview her? You don't want me looking around the agency in Topeka to find a more likely suspect? I'm still looking for the adjuster."

"I don't think you'll be impartial."

Adam knew he was right, but did he care?

"Here's something to think about," he said. "Rex Stoddard is dead and Janine Stoddard is his next of kin. Consult a lawyer, but I bet that means she can give permission for us to search everything and anything so we don't have to waste time on legalities. And she will, because I'll tell her it's the best way to find out who stole the money, as well as who probably killed her husband."

"You'll tell her?"

"I'll tell her it will be in her best interest *if* I'm right there to make sure nothing's missed."

"This is beginning to sound like blackmail. Why do you care so much?"

"I think this woman went through hell at the hands of the man she was married to. For whatever reason she wasn't able to get out until a couple of months ago. I'm not excited about seeing her go to a different sort of prison for something she didn't do."

"If she didn't do anything, she won't have to worry."

"You know better than that."

"What if you find she *is* the guilty party on one or both counts?"

"I'll help her find a good lawyer, but I won't cover anything up."

Adam could almost hear Philip debating with himself. When he spoke he didn't sound happy. "No, you're off this case, Adam. We'll go through the courts to get the records if we need to. I don't want any appearance we're working with or for Mrs. Stoddard."

"I won't turn my phone off again, and I'll be in touch."

"Be in touch soon, and only to see if there's another job for you. Don't go out on your own, or you'll be going out on a limb."

Adam disconnected.

He considered what to do next. He had to talk to Jan, but doing it with Taylor in the room wasn't the best idea. She was hurt and angry. Understandably angry.

What had he hoped? That he could go to her with proof he had tried to help Jan? That he could explain that while he had hated not being honest from the beginning, he had been certain she would see how important it had been for him to stay undercover? That she would understand and be so grateful he had proved Jan's innocence that she would forgive this minor glitch on the trust continuum?

Taylor had a history of not forgiving easily, something she freely admitted. Her own mother had nearly died without forgiveness. Knowing all this, he had still become involved with her, as if a few words of explanation would fix everything.

They were never going to be all right again. And he felt hollow inside knowing it was true. She was different from the other women he'd had relationships with. And he had been different when he was with her.

He was still trying to figure out how best to talk to Jan and convince her he was on her side when a car pulled into a space in front of Taylor's house. It was a nondescript, midsize American sedan, this year's model or last, with New York plates. No bumper stickers, nothing showing through the windows. A rental, he guessed, and probably from a counter at the Charlotte Airport. A man in a navy sport coat got out and consulted something in his hand, looking up at Taylor's house before he slipped whatever it was in his pocket. Then he started toward the door.

Adam waited until the man lifted his hand to ring Taylor's bell before he got out, too.

"Detective Sergeant Rafferty, from the

Shawnee County Sheriff's Department. I'm here to see Janine Stoddard. Is she home?"

Taylor considered closing the door in the man's face. His nose, flat and broad, looked as if it might already have had a few brushes with a door. He was late middle-aged, with a full head of silvering hair and the wind-roughened complexion of an outdoorsman. He looked like somebody who would be more at home in jeans and a flannel shirt splitting logs.

"Why do you want to see her?" she asked.

"That's between me and her, ma'am."

"Really? I could swear this is my house. Which makes your presence on my doorstep my business."

"I can see her outside, if that's a problem. But I do need to see her."

"I'm going to close the door now," Taylor said. "I may or may not open it again. If I don't, I would suggest you get a warrant if you want to talk to anybody here."

"I'm not conducting a search, ma'am, so I won't need a warrant. I just want to talk to Mrs. Stoddard. We don't have to talk here. Let's let her decide, okay?" Taylor closed the door, almost surprised she had been allowed to.

Jan, who had clearly heard, was already on her feet, and Harmony with her.

"Well, that was quick," Taylor said, trying to sound calm. "Jan, I know you want to tell somebody your side, but I really advise you to let Harmony call Brad Reynolds before you say a word. I don't know what kind of law Brad practices, but he'll know somebody who can help. Talking to him first is just a step between talking and not talking to the authorities, and now there's no chance you can give a statement without being asked for one."

"I don't have anything to hide."

"People go to jail even when they aren't guilty. Cristy did. She's told you her story, right? She was set up. And even if somebody's not trying to set you up, you might look guilty enough to get convicted, even though you didn't do anything."

The doorbell rang again. Detective Sergeant Rafferty was getting impatient.

"Let me tell him you're going to talk to your lawyer, so right now you have nothing to say."

"I'll look guilty." Jan sounded as if she were thinking out loud.

"Who cares what one detective thinks?"

"She's right, Mom," Harmony said. "If there was ever anything to gain from going to the police and announcing who you are, it's too late now. They know who you are.

They know *where* you are. You need to talk to Brad before you do another thing."

The doorbell rang again, and before Taylor could do anything the door swung open. There were two men on the porch now, and Adam was the one who had pushed open the door, judging by his still-extended arm.

"Jan is under no obligation to talk to this man," Adam said without preamble.

As she went to the door again Taylor felt anger thread through every cell. "I asked you to leave."

He looked past her. "Jan, it's in your best interest not to talk to the detective here, and certainly not to go back to Kansas, even if he insists it's the only way you can clear your name. His job is to get enough evidence to arrest you. Why make it easier?"

Jan moved up to stand beside Taylor. She trained her gaze on the detective, not on Adam. "Do I have to talk to you?"

"No, ma'am, but if you do maybe we can get this all straightened out this afternoon. You want to get on with your life, don't you? I mean, I know you must be grieving the loss of your husband —"

Taylor would never forget the sound Jan made. It wasn't a laugh; it wasn't a sob. It was something unholy and still, considering everything Taylor knew, completely appropriate.

"Thank you, Detective," Jan said after she took a deep, unsteady breath. "But you obviously don't know anything about me or my husband, and for today, at least, you're not going to learn more. I'm not going with you. I'm not speaking to you. And for the record, I'm not running away. I'll be right here if you ever get enough evidence to arrest me. But unless that's your intention, the owner of this house has asked you to leave. I suggest you do."

Taylor wanted to applaud. Jan was still pale, but she stood straight and tall, and her gaze didn't waver.

Rafferty shook his head. "You're getting some bad advice here."

"You've been told to leave," Adam said, turning to the man at his side. "You need to go."

Taylor watched the two men stare at each other like wolves preparing for a battle to the death. When Rafferty finally nodded to the two women in the doorway before starting down the sidewalk, she didn't think he was giving up as much as regrouping for another attack.

Adam didn't waste time. "Jan, I'm the one who traced you here, so in a way it's my fault Rafferty found you, too, but at the time

I was looking for your husband, and I thought you might lead us to him. Taylor's told you who I am and why I'm in Asheville?"

"She has."

"It's never been my intention to hurt anybody." Adam's gaze flicked to Taylor, then away. "But fraud was committed, and I was being paid to get to the bottom of it. I've told my superiors I think you're a victim, not an embezzler. Will you help me prove I'm right?"

Taylor knew she had to stay silent. No matter what she thought of Adam Pryor — if that was even his name — this was Jan's decision.

Harmony spoke. "How can we trust you after you lied to everybody?"

"I know it's going to be tough. But I believed in what I was doing. Insurance fraud isn't a victimless crime. It's right between income tax fraud and identity theft in importance, and billions of dollars are lost each year. Every time somebody gets away with the kind of money we're talking about here, everybody's premiums go up. Then people who really need it can't afford insurance anymore. Everybody suffers."

"How are you going to help me?" Jan asked. "What can *you* do?"

"I can find who did this. I'm going back to Kansas, and I'm not going to stop until I figure out how this whole thing came down. If you let me interview you and dig for anything you might know, then we have a chance of putting this to rest."

Taylor couldn't keep silent any longer. "That sounds like what Rafferty just told her."

Adam angled his body so they were eye to eye. "No, it's different. Rafferty thinks he knows who killed Rex Stoddard. I don't. Not yet. But I'm going to find out."

"Here's what *I* think. I think there's nothing you won't do to get what you want. Just a theory . . ." She turned to the woman beside her. "Jan?"

"You've been good to my daughter and me," Jan told Adam. "Was that part of your —" she searched for the right word "— cover, too?"

His tone softened. "No. Never. I figured out pretty fast that both of you deserved to have people be good to you. Especially men."

"You're right about that." She was silent a moment. "Taylor, may Adam and I talk here, or would you prefer we do it somewhere else?"

Taylor didn't know what to say. She was

sure Jan was making a mistake, yet could she tell her so, as if Jan wasn't an adult who understood everything she was risking?

"I have some grocery shopping." Taylor made a show of looking at the wall clock behind her. "I'll be back in about an hour."

"We'll be finished," Adam said.

"I'll get my keys. Jan, I'll bring dinner home. Harmony, you're welcome to stay. We'll eat early. I missed lunch."

She went to get her purse and her keys, and left the house by the back door to avoid facing Adam again.

CHAPTER 34

After Taylor left, Adam went out to his car to get a tape recorder and a notepad, and Harmony and Jan were alone.

"I can't stay," Harmony said. "I have to be at home when Davis drops off Lottie. I could ask him to bring her here, but she's going to need dinner and maybe a nap. She'll be a mess if she doesn't get both right away." She searched her mother's face, as if she expected to see it crumbling feature by feature.

Jan took her hand and squeezed it. "I'm going to be fine. You don't have to worry. Talk to Rilla when you get home and see if she thinks Brad should be the one to handle the legal end. If I have to talk to the police, I'll want a lawyer with me."

"Do you realize that now you can just drive out and visit anytime you want? You could move in with me, Mom. We don't have to live apart anymore."

Jan didn't point out the obvious. If things didn't go well and she was convicted of Rex's murder, they would be living apart for a very long time. "It's too crazy right now to be thinking about a change, but you're right, we can stop playing hide-and-seek. We can see each other whenever we want."

"Who killed him?"

Jan slowly shook her head. "It just seems obvious it had to do with whatever was going on at the agency. But I don't know anybody I can talk to there. Your father told everyone on his staff I was mentally unstable and couldn't be trusted." She grimaced. "I'm sure they pictured Mrs. Rochester in *Jane Eyre.* The maniacal wife locked away in the attic, only in my case, it was Pawnee Parkland."

"At the end didn't Mrs. Rochester burn down the house?"

Jan and Harmony stared at each other; then Jan began to laugh. She couldn't help herself, but she knew she was dangerously close to hysteria. "Truth's stranger than fiction," she said after a few deep gulps of air and a huge effort of will. "I'm sorry, honey. You probably think I'm mentally unstable, too."

"I think there was one dangerously unstable person in our home, and it wasn't you."

Adam came back inside, and Harmony kissed her mother's cheek. "Don't tell him anything you don't want to, and call my cell if you need me. Nap or not, I'll bring Lottie, and we'll come over."

"I trust Adam."

Harmony looked less sure, but she held one finger in the air and wagged it at him, as if beginning a lecture. "I have to leave, so you can't interview us together. But go easy on my mother."

"Interviewing people together doesn't work, too easy to get sidetracked. Right now I need everything your mom remembers. You've been away from home so long I'm anticipating you won't have much to add."

"If I think of anything, I'll call you."

He took out his wallet and handed her a card. "Call my cell phone. Anytime."

Harmony glanced down and read out loud, "Licensed private investigator. You know, if you'd just handed out these cards at the beginning, Taylor wouldn't be furious with you now."

"If I had, your mother would have taken off, and I wouldn't have put two and two together about the kind of man your father was."

558

"She's innocent."

"Let me get busy proving it."

Jan watched the byplay. She had protected Harmony to the best of her ability throughout her childhood, and now Harmony was trying to protect her. Would there ever come a time when both of them could think about ordinary things?

"Give Lottie a kiss for me," she said.

"We'll just be a phone call away."

Jan waited until Harmony had closed the door; then she settled herself on the sofa. "We should get moving. You told Taylor you wouldn't be here when she gets home."

Adam rarely showed emotion, but she saw something flicker in his eyes. Dealing with the aftermath of his deception was going to be challenging. She wasn't sure he would ever earn back Taylor's trust, and she wasn't sure he would try. Lost causes would not appeal to him.

"When this is over," she said, "I hope you'll try to fix things. She's worth it."

He didn't pretend not to understand. "Right now I'm not sure *I* am."

She knew then that she had been right to trust this man. "Of course you are."

"Will she think so?"

She leaned forward and put her hand on his. Just for a moment. "She would be a fool to turn away a man whose worst fault is trying too hard to do what's right and suffering too much every time he fails."

Adam set up his tape recorder and got Jan's name and permission on tape to interview her. Then he took out the legal pad he'd brought from the car and a new pen just to jot down reminders of anything significant.

"I'm going to start with the zinger," he said. "Jan, did you murder Rex Stoddard?"

She looked surprisingly composed, but then it took a tough lady to survive everything she had. "No."

"Did you set up false accounts at Stoddard Insurance Agency? Or file false reports? Or in any way try to take money out of the agency by illegal means?"

"I didn't even take money out of the agency *legally.* I had nothing to do with the agency, and about the only time I had contact with the staff was at the annual New Year's open house. Even there Rex made it difficult for me to hold a conversation with anyone."

"Did you want your husband dead?"

Jan drew her lips into a tight line, half concentration, half disgust, he thought. "I wanted him out of my life," she said. "And God help me, as the years went by I realized

560

that, most likely, the only way that would happen was if Rex died first. So yes, I suppose in that way I did want him dead."

"Did you ever do anything to hasten his death?"

"No."

He went on in the same vein for a while. He didn't expect anyone else would ever hear this tape, but he wanted confirmation of the abuse. He was glad Jan didn't try to play down her feelings about it or about Rex himself.

"I'm sorry to ask this, but can you tell me the worst example of your husband's brutality? Just a few sentences?"

Her breath caught, and for a moment he thought she wouldn't answer. Then she spoke softly, and related a story about her son and a near drowning that made him want to rest his head in his hands.

"God . . ." Adam thought he had seen everything, but he hadn't expected anything that horrifying. For just a moment he wished he had been the one to put Stoddard in his grave.

"My daughter doesn't know," Jan said. "She probably will someday, but I haven't told her yet. Of course, Rex excused himself and said he'd been temporarily out of his mind, but he wasn't. He was calm, so calm and so calculating. If I hadn't promised I would never leave, he wouldn't have pulled Buddy out of the water and somehow he would have blamed it on me. I knew then that I could never run, not because I had promised but because a man who would do that . . ."

Adam knew that kind of evil existed. The suicide bomber in Afghanistan who had carefully planned to kill anybody, women, children, the elderly, who happened to be at the bazaar had probably been a man like Rex Stoddard. Adam would never believe that kind of careless violence was simply about ideology, and certainly it was never about love. It was about power, revenge, control.

"I'm sorry," he said, and he heard the emotion in his own voice.

"Does that help you see why I had to stay?"

"It helps me see why somebody murdered him."

"Adam, maybe it was somebody who saw that part of Rex. But most people never did. All those years I thought it was just us."

"That's not true." He debated whether to go on, but he chanced it. "Do you remember one of your husband's employees, a woman named Tami Murgan? She was one of his agents."

"He talked about a Tami, although I don't think I met her. He was furious at her." She paused. "Those were bad weeks for me. When something went wrong at work, home was the place where Rex erupted. I tried to stay away from him as much as I could."

"Did he say *why* he was furious?"

She closed her eyes, as if she was trying to bring it back. "He was angry so often, Adam. Let me see if I can remember."

He didn't care how long it took to get the information he needed, but while he waited he thought about another place to finish the interview if Taylor came back. The hurt in her eyes had been easy to understand. So had the anger. She wouldn't want to find him here when she returned.

"I just can't remember specifics," she said after a few moments. "I tried to tune him out whenever I could, but Rex was no fan of strong women. Which is why he married me."

"I don't think that's true. In your case he saw your strengths and set about defeating them. Men like your husband do that routinely. If you hadn't been strong to start with, subduing you wouldn't have had any appeal."

"I was young when we married. My parents had just died. Rex stepped in to help settle everything. He was there to do anything I needed. I leaned on him. I was weak."

"A very natural reaction, but it doesn't mean you were weak. He knew how to manipulate you when you needed somebody to help and comfort, but I bet even then you weren't a pushover, were you?"

She looked reluctant to be that kind to herself. "When the violence began I made excuses for him. In between those episodes I believed he was a good husband. Until I finally faced how much he controlled my life and how nothing I was doing to fix our marriage was working."

They were off the subject, and Adam knew it. At the same time he wondered if this glimpse into the Stoddards' home life might prove valuable.

"When was he angriest at you? What were most of the episodes about?"

"Early on I learned not to argue with him or try to convince him I was right about something, because that always ended badly. Even if I didn't argue, if I stepped over any of the lines he had drawn in the sand, it was nearly as bad. Even silly things were a test of his authority. Once I bought a blouse because it was on sale. Rex watched every penny I spent, so I thought he would be pleased I'd gotten a bargain. Instead, he blew up because at some time in the past he had told me I didn't look good in green. I hadn't remembered, and I couldn't return it because the sale was final."

"So there were rules."

"Ever-changing and inventive."

"So you couldn't keep up with them."

"They were just excuses to attack."

Adam was impressed that despite everything, Jan had managed to keep perspective. "When you were out with him did he behave this way toward strangers?"

"He was never physically abusive to anybody in my presence. He never got in a fistfight, although he encouraged our son to — as he called it — stand up for himself." She looked away.

"That was hard for you."

"Of course." She sighed. "Rex would bully waiters and salesclerks, always with the excuse he was just trying to help them do their jobs. He could be so cold people always knew if he was displeased. He didn't have real friends, not even the people on the agency bowling team. They never came to our house, and he made a point of not joining them afterward at a bar."

"He didn't drink?"

"Never in my presence."

"Why did he sponsor a team?"

"He said it was important for office morale."

Adam tried to imagine how much office morale had been boosted by bowling weekly with a surly, judgmental boss. "Did you watch them play?"

"No."

"Was that part of his wanting to isolate you?"

"Of course." She frowned, as something else occurred to her. "But that wasn't the only reason. He was unhappy that his office manager was on the team. He thought she was an affront to womanhood and a bad model for me."

"What?"

"I know how ridiculous that sounds, believe me. I guess my brainwashing didn't take, not completely."

"What was her problem?"

"The same problem he had with women in general who didn't stay home and clean house, raise children and follow orders."

He thought back to Tami. "Tami thinks your husband tried to get even because she told a client to look elsewhere for a cheaper policy. She thinks Rex vandalized her house, and maybe her car, although she has no proof."

"It wouldn't surprise me. He would be careful not to get caught, but it's not hard to imagine him getting even. That was a regular event at our house."

"But Tami did something your husband perceived as bad for his business. . . ." He let the sentence hang without finishing it.

"That would infuriate him."

"And that's the kind of thing you meant when you said he had problems with women in general."

"Not really. I was talking about more subtle things. Women with loud voices and loud laughs. Too much makeup. Tight jeans. Short skirts. Shirts that exposed their midriffs. He practically foamed at the mouth. Poor Harmony had to pass inspection every morning before she left for school."

Now Adam understood the piercings, the tattoos and the freewheeling fashion sense of Jan's daughter a little better.

Jan continued. "Even at church, where he was a deacon, people kept a respectful distance. I guess the best way to say it? Rex simmered, and if you looked closely enough, you could see the steam rising."

"Can you remember any other reasons he

got angry with people at work? Particularly recently?"

"You're focusing on work."

"I think that's where we'll find our answers."

"I wish I could help, but he stopped talking about work."

Adam sat a little straighter. "Did he?"

"As part of getting ready to escape I was trying to sink into the background, become part of the scenery. Droop."

"Droop?"

"Like a wilting flower. I wanted him to think he'd drained all the spirit that was left in me after the children . . ." She swallowed and took a moment to compose herself. "After Harmony left. Some of it was real. I was so depressed for a while I didn't care about anything. Then I started to realize that maybe I could finally get out. He warned me he knew where she was, but I suspected he was on the wrong track. I thought maybe he'd be less vigilant about watching me if I just continued to wilt."

"You think that's why he stopped talking about work?"

"I was trying hard to be somebody who wasn't worth talking to. I thought I was being successful. Don't tell me I failed there, too?"

He smiled, because she was smiling a little to light the way. "You were probably very good at it. But I suspect he stopped talking about work for another reason."

"He didn't want me to know about something that was going on?"

Adam tried to put together a time line. Stoddard had been alerted to problems when Midwest began asking questions, but it was also possible he'd begun to have suspicions of his own before that. The timing would be a good thing to know.

Adam scribbled a reminder to find out exactly when Midwest had approached Rex. Then he looked up. "It would be helpful to know when you think you saw a change."

"What kind of change? You mean just not talking about work?"

He almost nodded. Then he realized how important her question itself might be. "What changes did you *see*?"

"This probably sounds silly, but he bought a new suit. He'd never worn cheap suits, but this one looked to be twice as expensive, although I never saw our bills."

"But you know fabric."

"Cut and style, too, and this wasn't his usual. He'd lost a little weight, and the suit was tailored to fit."

"Okay. What else?"

"He changed the way he wore his hair. He'd always gone to the local barber, but somebody new started cutting it, or else his old barber got some training."

The expensive suit and more expensive haircut could be signs that Stoddard had a sudden influx of cash, but Adam wondered.

"Any signs he was buying himself expensive toys to go along with the suit and haircut?"

"No, he didn't spend money on himself, unless you count his gun collection. And he never stinted on that."

"Was he buying new guns about the same time?"

She shook her head. "No, and he would have shown them to me. He knew I was afraid of what they could do, and he liked to show off."

"No other purchases? Land, car, things for your house?"

"No. In fact, he decided to refinish our stairs just a few weeks before all this happened, and he did the work himself to save money."

"Was that unusual?"

"Maybe a little. He seemed obsessed with it. And it was hard work. He did it all by hand."

"Was that how he relieved stress?"

"His second favorite way. The first was to catch me in some mistake and make me pay for it."

She said that so matter-of-factly that Adam winced. "Was he growing more abusive?"

She studied the question. He could almost see her turning it over in her mind. "He was more abusive when he remembered to be."

"Remembered to be?"

"Like my mistakes were no longer uppermost in his mind. Again, I thought I was just fading away and he'd stopped noticing me so much."

"What else changed?"

"Rex always liked to keep me on my toes. One of his rules was that I had to have dinner ready and waiting whenever he got home. He didn't vary the time by much, just enough to keep me scurrying around. I had to keep things warm or start something new if the old meal dried out."

Adam knew better than to comment. "That changed?"

"He started coming home later. A couple of times he came home and told me he'd already eaten. But even when he hadn't, he didn't seem to care if he had to wait for his dinner to be warmed up again. He didn't seem to notice it wasn't fresh and piping hot."

"So he was preoccupied, stressed, less apt to go after you because his mind was elsewhere. But at the same time he was paying more attention to his appearance."

"I might be making too much out of it."

"Can you remember when this started? Think hard. When did you start noticing things were a little different?"

"When we didn't take a vacation," she said without hesitation.

"What happened?"

"Every June we rented a little cabin near Council Grove Lake. We'd done it for years. Rex liked the fishing. I liked being close enough to other cabins that he couldn't risk somebody hearing screams, his or mine. But this year we didn't go. He said he was too busy."

"That was all he said?"

"I knew better than to ask."

"When did you usually go?"

"The first week. We had a standing reservation. Right before we were set to leave, he told me we weren't going. I'd already started packing food and supplies to take with us."

"What did you think?"

"Since it had never happened before, I

thought it was strange. Then on Friday night of the week we were supposed to be there, he didn't come home. He came home late on Sunday."

"You must have wondered about that."

"If Rex had to be out of town, he rarely told me ahead of time. That way I couldn't make plans, because I didn't know where he was or when he was coming back. Sometimes I think he was out there watching the house to see what I would do. Keeping me off-balance was a favorite pastime."

"And you worried about that the night you left for good?"

"Of course."

"So you set the fire to cover your tracks?"

"No. I didn't set the fire." She was emphatic, and she told him in detail how it had happened. At the end she spread her hands in illustration as she explained how quickly the fire must have caught. "I barely got out in time."

"Okay." He mulled over everything she had told him. Nothing stood out by itself, but all together he was beginning to think he might have a lead.

"Let me just ask something right now, Jan. This is a tough one, so don't reject it out of hand, okay? Just think it over."

He leaned forward so he could look

straight into her eyes. "Is it possible your husband was having an affair?"

CHAPTER 35

Jan had forgotten so much, or perhaps she had never known it in the first place. During the final six months of her marriage — a way of dating events that she would now have to become accustomed to — she had been solely focused on disappearing into the background or, when she hadn't been able to, convincing her husband that she lived only to serve him.

On the occasions he hadn't returned home at his usual times or even at all, she had been grateful, too grateful that he was still absent to spend much time wondering why. Rex had always done as he pleased. By the end of their marriage she hadn't expected or even wanted to know details. The less he had talked to her the better.

"An affair." She said the words out loud as she had several times already on the trip to Harmony's little apartment at the Reynolds Farm. The idea of her husband seducing or being seduced by another woman was so incongruous that even the words sounded foreign when she spoke them.

Her GPS reminded her to turn left, and she did so at the next road, marked by a barn with diagonal siding. She memorized the barn and the pond across the street for the next time.

The next time.

She couldn't believe she had only been to her daughter's home once. She remembered so little from that first night. She had been terrified Rex would find them both, unsure whether to stay in Asheville or disappear to New England.

And all along Rex had been dead.

Of course, she didn't really know if that was true. It just seemed clear to her that Rex must have died the night his home exploded in a fiery ball and lit the sky for miles around, or he would have surfaced immediately. Was he still alive when it happened? Had he seen the explosion and wondered? Or by that time was he already dead?

The new road was gravel, so she took her time. She had no deadline, because she hadn't called Harmony to tell her she was coming. If her daughter wasn't home, she could return again whenever she wanted to.

The world was a different place than it had been that morning.

At least for a while.

She followed directions, and after a few minutes she pulled into the Reynoldses' farmyard. The scene was familiar enough that she knew to park beside the garage before she turned off the engine.

There were lights in the apartment, and even with Harmony's windows closed she heard Lottie screeching.

It had been a long day for the little girl, and for her mother, as well.

Her grandmother knew exactly how they felt.

She got out, and in a minute she was knocking on Harmony's door. Her daughter opened it, bouncing the unhappy baby on her hip, and Jan held out her arms. Harmony made the transfer and shook out her own arms as if they had fallen asleep while trying to quiet her daughter.

Jan smiled. "I heard her all the way from Taylor's, so I thought I'd better drive out and see if I could help."

Harmony burst into tears.

Jan stepped inside and swung the door closed behind her. "Who should I take care of first?"

Harmony disappeared into the bathroom,

and Jan danced around the room with Lottie, singing softly as they waltzed together. Quick fix it wasn't, but the baby did begin to relax against her once she started "The Tennessee Waltz."

A song about infidelity was an odd choice, she realized, for a woman who'd just discovered her husband might have been having an affair.

Harmony returned, face still damp from a date with a washcloth, and held out her arms tentatively, as if to say she would take Lottie if absolutely required. Jan shook her head and continued their dance. Harmony sighed gratefully and headed into her tiny kitchen, returning with a sandwich leaking alfalfa sprouts and missing one sad little bite.

"Can I make you something?" she asked.

"I'm not hungry," Jan sang.

Lottie's eyes were closing. By the time Jan started "Fifty Ways to Leave Your Lover," she was asleep. Jan finished the song; then she pointed to her granddaughter, and Harmony led her to Lottie's crib in a room that was just large enough for that and a tiny dresser with a changing pad on top.

" 'Fifty Ways to Leave Your Lover'?" Harmony asked after they had closed the door and were back in the living room.

"I always thought of that as my personal theme song. Wishful thinking, I guess."

Harmony sniffed twice and left for the bathroom again.

Jan apologized after her daughter returned to flop down beside her on the sofa, but Harmony shook her head. "You could read me the cash register receipts in your purse and I would cry tonight."

Jan put her arm around her shoulders. "It's been that kind of day."

"Lottie had a great time with Davis and his new girlfriend. She was all smiles until they left. Then she fell apart."

"Too many new things to absorb."

"She was absorbing my anger and my stress and my anger. . . ."

"There was a double dose of anger there."

"He was dead all that time while we were sneaking around trying to hide from him. All that time! And it was just like him to do it on the sly so we would have to keep working around him."

"I think this is one time we can't blame your father. I doubt he had much choice in the matter."

"What did Adam say?"

Jan knew there was no hope of hiding anything from Harmony, and no reason. She had despised her father for almost as long as Jan could remember. At first Jan had tried to prevent it, but at a certain point she had realized that defending a sociopath was the same as excusing his actions.

She condensed the hour with Adam into a few points. "He asked good questions. For obvious reasons he thinks somebody who works in the office was the embezzler, or at least a partner with somebody on the outside. Among other things there were settlements for accidents that never happened. The adjuster who was assigned to those cases can't be located. Adam's going to see what more he can discover about the man's personal life, who his connections in the office might be."

"Were you able to help?"

"There's kind of a strange twist."

"What could be stranger than everything we already found out today?"

"Adam thinks your father might have been having an affair."

Harmony was silent so long Jan was afraid she was going to cry again.

"Honey?"

Harmony wasn't crying. Her voice dripped disdain. "I'm just imagining the other woman. What was wrong with her?"

"Your father could be unbelievably charming."

"Like a cobra."

"When I first met him I didn't see anything except his kindness. He was devoted to me and determined to make my life easier. He was handsome and polished and smart. I thought he was the answer to all life's problems."

"You got that wrong. He was their cause."

"I don't think he was responsible for global warming."

"What makes Adam think he was . . . you know?"

"Well, he asked a lot of questions." She didn't share the ones Adam had asked after he dropped the affair-bomb, questions about changes in their sex life or Rex's sexual appetites, but she told Harmony the others.

"I had forgotten a lot of things, but Adam teased out the answers. The final picture was of a man who was sprucing himself up and disappearing for long hours without explanation, a man who'd been focused on everything I did and was suddenly not nearly as interested."

"Dad having an affair." Harmony said the words slowly, as if she was searching for the punch line.

"Adam concentrated on women at the office. He asked me to remember who your father talked about most often."

"Did he ever say good things about any of them? I never heard him say anything good about women ever."

"Not *good* things, just how often Rex talked about anybody and what he said."

"Did you remember anyone in particular?"

"I remember that Liz Major, the office manager, was the subject of a lot of conversations."

"The same Liz on his bowling team?"

Jan was surprised. "You remember, too?"

"Of course. Even back then he went on and on about the way she dressed, describing it in detail, and the way she acted like she was the equal of every man there. I used to hate dinners when he got started on all the awful things poor Liz had done that day. I never figured out why he didn't fire her and hire a man."

"She could have sued for discrimination, and he would have hated a public lawsuit. That's the only reason he even hired women in the first place."

Harmony mulled that over. "Why would he start an affair now?"

Adam had come up with a theory, which he had shared with Jan to get her input. "Remember I told you I was trying to make your father think I had given up on life? So I began behaving like the puppet he'd been struggling to create all those years. Maybe he thought he'd finally won. With nothing else to accomplish at home, Adam thinks maybe he decided to find another woman he could humiliate and manipulate."

"He was a sick man."

Jan could tell that Adam's theory was, in fact, plausible to her daughter. "He's going back to Topeka tomorrow or the next day. But he's not going to be able to investigate for the insurance company. He said that wasn't an option anymore."

"Did they fire him?"

"I think maybe they did, or at least took him off this case. I think he's just helping now because he believes in me."

Harmony reached for a tissue. "This has just been such an awful day. If they don't find out who really killed Dad . . . If they try to pin this on you . . ."

"They'll find the real killer. But right now let's talk about you. You must be feeling a million things."

"I don't want to talk about me."

"I know there's a lot you can't understand or forgive," Jan said carefully, "but please listen to me. I know your childhood was light-years from perfect. I wish it had been different. More than anything I wish it, and I always will. I lost so many things when I married your dad, but I struggled to raise you to be independent and compassionate and not fall into the patterns you were forced to witness. Now I watch you with Lottie and I know I succeeded at that much. You're a wonderful mother and a wonderful person, and somehow you still came through everything at home with so much to give."

"I'm not compassionate. I will never forgive him. I'm so angry at everything he put us through. I don't think I'll ever stop being angry, even though he's dead."

"You're going to be okay, just not right away. Don't expect more of yourself than any truthful person could give."

"If we forgive him, isn't that like saying he didn't have choices? That we're excusing the awful things he did?"

Jan knew that both of them would wrestle with this for a long time, but she tried to put her growing insight into words. "It's not about making excuses for your dad. I think forgiveness is just letting go of the hatred and not letting it have power over us any-more. Maybe it's shutting that door once and for all and not holding on to him and the world he tried to create. If we don't move on, your father will win."

Harmony was crying now. "I don't know another woman, not a one, who could have guided me safely through my childhood with all its obstacles, Mom. Since you came to Asheville I've been angry at everybody, but I've never really been angry with you. I've just been wishing so hard that things had been different, that somehow you could have waved a magic wand and changed it all. But I know, better than anybody, what you faced. I know you triumphed, even if nobody else ever understands how much."

Jan swallowed the lump in her throat. "That means everything."

That sat in silence for a long time, Harmony's head on Jan's shoulder, Jan stroking her daughter's hair, until Harmony finally spoke again.

"Does Adam think you'll have to go back to Topeka?"

"I won't go back until I have no choice."

"Rilla called Brad. He wants to talk to you."

"Tomorrow."

"What will they do with Dad's body?"

No matter how Harmony felt about Rex, he was still her father. But Jan knew that the responsibility for final rites was hers alone.

"Your father would expect a funeral in our

church with eulogies about how much good work he had done and how beloved he was to his family. He bought a plot beside Buddy where he wanted to be buried."

Harmony sat up straighter and turned to her mother. "Please tell me you're not considering that. Is his death going to be a lie just like his whole life? Are we going to keep pretending?"

Relieved, Jan put her hand over her daughter's. "No, I've spent too much of my life doing what your father demanded. So if you agree, I'm going to have him cremated, and I'm going to ask that his ashes be quietly disposed of in whatever way is legal. But no matter what, he won't rest next to my son, and *nobody* will stand up in church on my watch and tell lies about him."

Harmony squeezed her mother's hand and they sat that way for a moment. "Whether you plan a memorial service or not, the church might have one, anyway. If they do, I'm going to go, and I'm going to speak. I'm going to tell everybody who Rex Stoddard really was. Maybe knowing there are men like him will help another woman in the same situation."

For a moment Jan pictured that scene. She realized how much their lives had already changed. "Let it go, sweetheart. Just let it go. I don't think we'll need to make airline reservations. If Adam's right about your father, the story will get out. If he really was an adulterer, and he was killed because of it, then his church won't have a thing to do with him. It's funny, isn't it?"

"Is it?"

"After a lifetime of trying to control everybody around him, at the end your father couldn't even control himself."

CHAPTER 36

Taylor wasn't surprised that at the end of her Monday morning class one of her beginning yoga students had pulled her aside and asked if she was feeling okay.

She *wasn't* okay, and she had been preoccupied from the moment the class had begun to warm up. She hadn't moved things along quickly enough, and she hadn't paid enough attention to each student's performance or given more than a few seconds of individual instruction.

She was glad the hot yoga studio was still on hold. She couldn't imagine how those students would have fared today.

Now, sitting at her desk, she had to face exactly how exhausted and discouraged she felt. Last night sleep had eluded her. Every time she closed her eyes she had thought about Adam and a new surge of anger had filled her. She wasn't sure exactly where the anger was directed, either. She was furious at him, furious at herself. She had emerged from sexual and emotional hibernation to find that the man she'd trusted had lied about who he was. What did it say about her that she had chosen so poorly?

She didn't even want to consider what it said about Adam.

On top of everything else, in four nights she was giving a party for all the local artists and businesses who had suffered in the flood. She had invited the goddesses, too, and nearly a dozen other friends. Dante was doing most of the work, but under the circumstances, the party felt like a lead weight she was carrying everywhere she went.

Worse, right now she had to figure out what to do about Adam's class. She had to either cancel it or find another instructor, but who could she find at this late date? She could call the karate studios in town and ask if they had somebody qualified to take over. There were five more sessions in the term, exactly the number Adam had already taught. She was sure her students wouldn't be happy at the switch, but they would probably continue to attend if the new instructor was acceptable.

If she couldn't find another instructor, then she could refund half their tuition, or even all of it if necessary, since they hadn't gotten exactly what they'd paid for. But first she needed to make those calls.

Using the internet as a resource, she tried three different karate studios and left detailed messages on three different voice mail systems. When she looked up from the last one, Adam was standing in her doorway. She set down the telephone and cocked an eyebrow in question.

"I came to clear out the equipment closet. It won't take long."

"I'm sure if I'm lucky enough to find somebody to take over the class, they'll have their own equipment."

"You've made some calls." It wasn't a question, and she supposed he had heard the last message she'd left.

She closed her laptop. "I think it's unlikely I'll find anybody."

"If you don't, will you refund the tuition?"

"Why, do you still expect your share?" He had agreed to take his cut after classes ended, which, she supposed, should have been a warning sign.

"No, I was asking because if that's your plan I want to write you a check to cover whatever you have to refund. You took me on in good faith, and it's not your fault things happened the way they did."

" 'Happened the way they did.' " She chewed her lip. "That's an interesting phrase. You must have known right from the beginning you wouldn't be here to finish the class. It was inevitable. I mean, who needs ten weeks to follow one abused woman and figure out if she's a criminal or a victim? Things were bound to 'happen.' " She made quotation marks around the last word with her fingers.

"When I took on the class, I intended to stay the ten weeks. I wasn't in a hurry to move on to another investigation. Even if I figured out what Jan and her husband were up to fairly quickly, I planned to finish the class for you."

"That was considerate." Sarcasm tasted like acid on her tongue.

"I think we need to talk, and this doesn't seem like the best place. Let's take a walk down to the river and see the aftermath of the flood."

She wondered if he had chosen that particular route to remind her that her own daughter had nearly died in the river, and he had been the one to get her safely to shore.

For a moment she considered refusing. Saying no would feel good, like punishment, only she doubted she meant enough to

Adam that he would feel slighted. And didn't she need a chance to tell him what she thought of him? Maybe then she could actually sleep tonight.

She got to her feet. "I don't have a lot of time."

"Thank you for letting me take some of it, then."

She grabbed her water bottle from the edge of the desk and clipped it to her belt loop. Then she preceded him out the door.

They didn't talk again until they were walking down the path to the flatter area below. The last time she had taken this route she had been terrified her daughter was going to drown.

Adam was the first to break the silence. They were walking single file since the path was steep and narrow, and he was behind her. "I don't even know where to start. I guess I'll just say I never wanted to hurt you, and I didn't enjoy lying to you."

"That's small comfort."

"I know, but I have to start with something. And sleeping with you? Taylor, that was never about my job. I knew from the get-go that eventually I would have to be completely honest about why I was here, and you would never understand. But somehow I pushed all that away."

She was glad she was ahead of him so he couldn't see how much he had hurt her. "We can definitely say that. Especially the part about me *never* being able to understand."

"When I realized I wasn't making any headway toward keeping our relationship casual, I thought about leaving town. Or getting somebody else to investigate Jan's part in —"

Anger licked at her. "Jan's part? You mean you still thought Jan had something to do with the money that disappeared?"

"Along the way I thought a lot of things. At first I thought maybe she and her husband had collaborated, that she was in Asheville waiting for him to appear so they could head into the sunset together. Then when I began to suspect Stoddard had used her as a punching bag, I wondered if she was so terrified of the guy she had to do whatever he demanded or face terrible consequences. By then I just didn't see her as having an active part in what had happened. I saw her as a victim, and I wanted to keep her from getting in deeper."

"How about now? What's the theory of the day?"

"The minute a body was found, this case ramped up a thousand percent. You do get that, right? Money's one thing. Since we know she had nothing to do with what happened at her husband's agency, we also know it's unlikely anybody can make an embezzling charge stick. There's not a shred of evidence. But murder? She had a rock-solid, unassailable motive. She had the means to kill him, a cabinet filled with guns —"

"Which she had no access to."

"Her word only. Harmony wasn't there the night her father died, hadn't been there for years, so even if she insists he never let her mother touch the guns, she can't prove that the day he died Jan didn't get hold of one anyhow. And she was married to the guy, living in the same house with him, so God knows she had plenty of opportunity to kill him."

"She didn't."

"She set the house on fire, even if she didn't do it on purpose. For days the authorities thought they were going to find both her body and her husband's because they both disappeared. A great way to cover an escape, wouldn't you say?"

"If she'd wanted to cover up a murder, wouldn't she have left her dead husband inside before she set the house on fire? Instead of burying him down the road?"

"Another reason she's such a good suspect. That grave right down the road. But in answer? Not if she was smart, and of course, she is. Because had she done it that way, she wouldn't have been able to count on the propane tank exploding, and she'd have no guarantee what shape his body would be in once the fire was extinguished. A bullet hole — in this case in his skull — would almost surely be detected."

She faced him, arms folded over her chest. "You think she did it, don't you?"

He shook his head, his expression inscrutable. "You asked me for the theory of the day. I'm just telling you what the cops will think. Because I've watched Jan and waited to see what happens next, I believe she's innocent. I'm almost certain the theft came from inside the agency, but I'm not convinced Stoddard himself had anything to do with it. And now that he's dead and forensic accountants can get hold of the agency records and comb through them, I think the money part will get resolved. It's the murder we need answers to."

"I don't know why you're telling me all this. So you've had theories and now you have new ones. You've said you intend to help her, and that's a good thing. If you can prove Jan's innocent, then more power to you. But how can any of this excuse using all of us the way you did?"

"You most of all?"

He said it so gently tears sprang to her eyes, and that infuriated her. She turned and finished descending the hillside until they were both on the flat area just before the railroad tracks.

He held her back when she started to cross the field. "Taylor, I don't know if ends ever justify means. I get less and less sure of everything as I get older. But once I began to believe Jan was innocent, I couldn't quit. I could have turned this over to somebody else, but I knew they wouldn't be half as convinced as I was that she was a victim. And you can't look for answers if you don't know the right questions. I thought I owed it to everybody to stay and see this through, and hopefully fix things. And I hoped . . ."

"What, Adam?" She shook off his hand. "You hoped maybe we would just overlook the fact that you'd lied about who you were? Or maybe I would overlook the way you insinuated yourself into my life so you could stay close to everybody involved?"

"I never felt good about it. I wanted to tell you, all of you, especially you. But I had a responsibility to the company and all the people they represent. These were serious offenses. I had to stay as impartial as I could, and I had to stay undercover."

She started toward the river, more for something to do than from any real desire to see how much the water had receded. He caught up and walked beside her until they were close to the bank.

The water level had gone down substantially. She knew that the studios that had been badly damaged were in the midst of removing what couldn't be saved and beginning repairs. The torrent that had carried Maddie to the fallen tree, visible from this spot, was now simply a river flowing as it should, soon to be joined by other rivers on their way north to Tennessee.

"Did you have sex with me as a way to ingratiate yourself and get more information?" she asked after they had stood silently together for a long moment.

"No. Sex made things harder, exactly the way I knew it would. And now everything I do is filtered through that. I don't want to hurt you anymore. If anything, that means I'll err on the side of overlooking anything that could."

"Then why, Adam? I was just so fatally attractive you couldn't help yourself?"

He was silent so long she was sure he wasn't going to answer; then he turned so he was looking at her profile. She didn't face him. She couldn't.

"You *are* attractive, very much so. But it wasn't only that. When I was with you, I felt like I was part of something. For the first time since I came home from that last mission in Afghanistan, I felt like I was connected to the human race again. And I just couldn't make myself leave that behind."

For a moment she was touched, deep inside her where anger had kept her from sleeping. Deep inside where she badly needed to be touched and hadn't allowed it. Not until Adam walked into her life and heart.

Then she remembered everything he had done. The intimacies, the lies, the stories she had believed. She faced him. "You weren't part of anything. Everything that happened between us was built on deception."

"I'm sorry."

As angry as she was, she knew this man didn't apologize easily. The words meant something, but she still felt too betrayed to accept them.

"I don't want your money," she said, turning to the river again so he wouldn't see the tears clouding her eyes. "Please clear out your things before I get back."

He didn't say goodbye. In a moment he was no longer there. She could feel his absence and the hollow place inside her he would never fill again. She stood staring at the water for a long time before she turned and began to trudge back up to the studio.

Adam had so little to pack for his flight to Kansas City, the closest large airport to Topeka, that he had his carry-on ready in fifteen minutes. He planned to drop off his rental at the Charlotte Airport, but he would come back to Asheville when his investigation was completed, to move out of this apartment and see Jan one more time to tell her everything he'd found. Then he would probably head to Chicago, where he kept a one-room apartment as his base camp, and start a new life.

Somewhere.

Since his encounter with Taylor, he had forced himself to think about Rex Stoddard's death and nothing else. So when somebody knocked on his door and he opened it to find Jan on the threshold, he wasn't even surprised.

"I brought you these," she said, holding out a stack of paper.

"You had time to think this over?" He stepped aside to let her in.

"I spent hours on it."

Adam had typed up their interview, then made a copy that he'd given her yesterday over coffee and a final round of questions at Waking Life Espresso. He had asked her to carefully go over his notes and make sure she agreed with everything he'd written. He'd hoped that looking at the interview again might trigger additional memories.

He shuffled through the papers. "Did anything new occur to you?"

"I scribbled some comments on the backs of a couple of pages. But I don't think any of it will be that helpful."

"You never know. Thanks for bringing this by."

"You're flying out this evening?"

"I'm going to leave for the airport in a little while. I just finished packing."

"Detective Sergeant Rafferty came to see me again around lunchtime."

He had expected Rafferty to be back in Topeka by now. His continued presence didn't seem like a good sign. "What did you tell him?"

"I saw Brad Reynolds at his office this morning, and he turned me over to one of his partners who has more experience in criminal law. So I told Detective Rafferty to talk to him."

"Good. I won't be surprised if he's on my plane. Right now there's not much he can do in Asheville except enjoy the mountain views."

"Adam, please don't feel bad about anything that happened. After I found out Rex was dead, I would have alerted the authorities and told them where I was if you hadn't already done it. They got here a little faster because of your involvement, that's all, but it doesn't make a difference. I just want you to know how much I appreciate you helping me now."

"You're comforting *me?"*

"I just wanted you to know I'm not angry. I understand why you were undercover."

"You're facing a lot. You know that, don't you? But you're standing here trying to make me feel better. I wish I could do the same."

She dredged up a smile. "I've been thinking this over since I saw my new lawyer. All those years with Rex I managed to keep a part of myself safe. As badly as he wanted to, he never controlled my heart or my mind. No matter what the future holds, that's going to continue. As terrible as it sounds, even if I go to prison, it won't be as bad as living with him. And there will always be a chance the real murderer will turn up.

In the meantime I'll have more freedom than I ever had at home."

She was trying to be brave, *was* incredibly brave to come to him this way, but he could hardly bear listening. "None of that is going to happen."

"You should still know that what I just said is true."

"Here's what I know. You're innocent, and I'm not going to quit looking for your husband's murderer until he or she is behind bars. Believe me, okay?"

Before he could consider, he put his arms around her for a long hug. Almost more miraculous than the things she'd said was the fact that she hugged him back and did not pull away.

CHAPTER 37

The last thing Harmony felt like doing tonight was chatting with strangers at a party, even if she *had* found the perfect black dress for practically nothing at a local thrift shop. She knew she could beg off, that Taylor would understand why she needed space and quiet. But her mother would be there, and Harmony couldn't imagine leaving Jan alone to face the first party in decades where she could mix and chat like a normal woman. Jan had promised she would be fine, but Harmony planned to be there anyway to lend moral support.

Rilla and Brad were going, too, and they had hired a teenager to babysit their sons. While they'd offered to add Lottie to the deal, Harmony had declined. Cooper and Landon were a handful on their own, so she had asked Davis, fully expecting him to say he was too busy. Instead, he had quickly agreed. In fact, he had offered to pick her up on the way to Fiona's condo, where they planned to watch Lottie together.

"You'll have a good time with your daddy," she promised Lottie, who was dressed in another of Davis's fabulous finds. Settling the baby on one hip and the diaper bag on the opposite shoulder, she carefully made her way down the steps. Tonight she didn't even have to provide a car seat. Davis had bought a brand-new one for his car and installed it. In fact, he had asked Harmony if she wanted one just like it for her own car. Harmony's car seat, while perfectly adequate, had belonged to Landon and showed it.

Mesmerized, she'd agreed, and Davis had dropped it off a few days ago, chatting happily as he did about crash tests and safety ratings. She was still fantasizing about brain transplants, transformative psychiatric drugs, even plain old mind-control techniques, as possible reasons for the changes in her former boyfriend.

Dusk had descended, and the lights around the farmyard were already glowing softly, even though it was only six. She had invited Nate to meet her at Evolution, but not until six-thirty, so she still had time. She set Lottie on her feet and took her hand. With help her daughter was beginning to walk now. The little girl toddled slowly through the grass, giggling as she went and stooping from time to time to examine clods of dirt or feathery weeds at her feet.

Harmony had been enchanted with her daughter from the moment of Lottie's birth. Sadly now she wondered if Lottie would be the only child she ever had. So far her own choices in the man department hadn't panned out. She had been wildly attracted to Davis, at least partly because he had been so sure of what he wanted. Luckily for her that romance hadn't lasted, but she had learned she wanted a man who loved her the way she was, one who was capable of putting her needs first when it really mattered.

Then, of course, there was Nate. He was the adorable boy-next-door, but not the one to steal her heart the way he might in a classic movie. Now she knew she would never fall in love with Nate. She hoped they would meet for coffee now and then to catch up on their lives, but he wasn't going to be the one she wanted to *make* coffee for every morning of her life.

Or, in Nate's case, enjoy the coffee he made for her.

She really didn't have a lot of hope that

with everything she had seen and lived through, she would ever find a man she could marry.

Headlights lit the farmyard. She scooped Lottie into her arms and went to meet Davis. The baby was so interested in the approaching car she forgot to protest.

When he got out he came over to take Lottie and dance her around as she laughed with delight. Then, holding her against his chest, he grinned as Lottie played with the buttons on his collar.

"She's wearing the dress I gave her."

"One of the million, you mean?" Harmony felt compelled to say something nice because, after all, Davis was doing her a favor. "You have good taste. I'll give you that."

"Grudging much? I'll take it, anyway."

"No, it's actually very nice of you to pick out things for her."

"She's my daughter." He smiled down at the baby. "I love her."

Harmony went completely still. Davis loved Lottie. She half expected to see the heavens open and a kindly bearded man on a throne smiling down at them. Because she knew a miracle when she saw one.

"Don't tell me that surprises you?" he said, noting her expression.

"To be honest, yes!"

"You didn't think I had it in me?"

"I didn't, no."

He pondered that for a moment, his heavy eyebrows drawn together. "I can see that. You have cause."

This time she really did flick her gaze to the heavens, just in case she'd been right.

"Look," he went on, "I'm not perfect. I know it, you know it. I screwed up with you not once but twice. But I'm not going to screw up with Lottie. You and I are going to raise her, and we're both going to be good to her. That's a fact and a promise. She's going to be happy and well-adjusted, even if you and I aren't married and never will be."

"I just have to ask —" The words were out before she could stop them. "I mean, how did all this happen? Because if you remember, you weren't all that glad I got pregnant."

"Were *you*?"

He was right. She had considered all her options before she'd settled into having Lottie and raising her alone.

"I wasn't glad at first," she said.

"Look, Harmony, you and I have something in common, only we never looked at it that way. You were raised in a bad situation. My situation certainly wasn't *as* bad, since nobody was bouncing my head against

607

the dinner table."

She had forgotten that she had shared that story with Davis. Rex had been upset at her table manners.

"In my house," Davis said, "my sister and I were just ignored. It was as cold as the Arctic Circle, especially if we demanded attention. I'd kind of buried all that until Lottie was born. But when I saw the way my parents treated her . . ." His eyebrows knit again, only this time in anger. "My father won't even come to meet her. And my mother?" He gave a humorless laugh. "Well, you saw that yourself. So I remembered. Everything."

"I'm sorry," she said, and meant it.

"You don't have to be. I needed the reminder."

She thought she knew where he was going. "And you don't want to be the same kind of father?"

"I won't be. So no, I wasn't ready when you told me she was on the way, and I wasn't happy, and I tried to manipulate the situation, just the way you said I did. But one day I saw this little girl and realized she was mine, and I still had a chance to be the kind of dad she needs, not the kind you and I have, but a real dad."

"Had. My father's dead."

"I'm sorry." But he cocked his head and made it a question, as if he was willing to listen if she needed to talk.

Unexpectedly she had to blink back tears. She took a deep breath. "You know the hardest part? The biggest thing I felt when I heard he was gone was relief, because now he can't hurt my mother or me. But I can't mourn him, and that's the only part that makes me sad. Just that. I never had a father I could mourn. What does that say about me, do you think?"

"Probably that you're honest with yourself, and you were way short-changed as a kid. It doesn't say you're a bad person, just one who went through a lot and came out okay, anyway."

Once she had thought she loved Davis, but she wasn't sure she had ever actually admired him. Now, reluctantly, she had to admit she kind of did.

She accepted his kindness with a nod. "I guess you're saying we don't have to let our childhoods control us."

"You're not letting yours. You're a great mom, even if you didn't have a great upbringing."

"No, but I did have a great mom as a role model. She did everything she could to neutralize the toxic waste my father brought into the house every time he stepped over the threshold."

"Yeah? Then in that way you were lucky."

"So, how do we pick the people we want to spend our lives with?" she asked without thinking. "I don't seem to be having much luck."

"You're asking me?"

"I like Fiona. She might be a keeper."

He smiled a little. "Could be."

"And you found her how?"

"You know what you *don't* want, right? Well, so do I. If you know that, you know the flip side. So you trust your instincts. You'll figure it out when it happens."

She couldn't believe she and Davis were talking about relationships, or that she had actually asked him for advice.

But as advice went, his wasn't that bad.

"I'm not planning to stay out late," she said. "I'll call you before I come to get her."

"You don't need to hurry. You look nice in that dress, so go have fun." Davis held out his hand for the diaper bag; then he went to put Lottie in the car seat. She watched as he chatted with the baby as he strapped her in, and she found herself smiling.

Taylor had to admit that Dante had outdone himself. Pepped up by this new opportunity to exercise his creativity, he had put together an awesome menu of finger food, dips and fresh vegetables, as well as fruit piled in two separate watermelons — one carved to look like a shark, the other a basket. A dessert table was piled with a variety of confections in fluted cupcake liners, and he had set up urns of coffee and hot water for assorted teas, as well as sparkling water, wine and beer.

Taylor figured if the studio managed to stay open another decade, she might earn back the cost of the party. She didn't care. The jazz trio playing in the lobby as people walked in and the abundance of food were calculated to raise spirits. While publicity for Evolution hadn't been the purpose, she knew the party wasn't going to hurt the studio's standing in the community, either.

Some of the goddesses had already arrived. Samantha had, as always, attracted the attention of a couple of men, and she was chatting in a corner to both as she balanced a plate of food and a bottle of water. Rilla and Brad were talking to Jan beside the watermelons. Jan looked wonderful in a dark red blouse and silky black pants, and she looked comfortable with the Reynoldses, even though Taylor suspected the subject might be the Shawnee County

Sheriff's Office.

Taylor was introducing herself to everybody who walked through the door. She already knew a number of the artists, and after greeting them, she listened to their tales of woe or triumph and sympathized. While she hadn't lost any property, she had nearly lost her daughter, which was common knowledge. More than one person asked about the man who'd rescued Maddie. Taylor smiled grimly and explained that he had moved away.

After the first half hour her father and Analiese came in together, which didn't surprise her. As Taylor's mother was dying, the two had become friends, and the friendship had continued. Ethan claimed that he attended Church of the Covenant irregularly, but the second time Taylor and Maddie had gone to Sunday services, he had joined them in the pew.

She hugged them both and thanked them for coming.

"I heard rumors my granddaughter was going to be here," Ethan said.

"She and Edna are running around upstairs. I think they want to see what they can do with the punching bag."

And, of course, that made her think of Adam.

"Want me to check on them?" Ethan asked.

"Maddie will want to see you."

He excused himself and left Taylor with Analiese. They strolled over to one of the serving tables to get Analiese a glass of wine and a plate of food. She chose the lowest-calorie options and only a few of those. While she claimed to have a problem with weight, Taylor had never noticed her gaining as much as an ounce.

"It's a beautiful night," Analiese said. "But the temperature's dropping, so I guess a quiet corner of your patio is out of the question."

"Trying to escape your congregation?"

"If any arrive. It's just been a long day. I don't think I'll last until the party ends."

Taylor led her into the next room, which was less crowded. "I can't imagine doing your job. You work all the time, and in between you have to practice what you preach. It exhausts me just thinking about it."

"Me, too. But you haven't chosen an easy job, either."

"It certainly hasn't been easy lately."

"I know about Maddie, and of course, Jan's story. On the way over, your father filled me in on the latest. That must be particularly hard. I know you've grown close to her, and you're probably worried."

"She didn't kill her husband."

"I'm sure of it. I'm going to see if I can get her alone for a chat in a little while."

"Do you think right always triumphs?"

"No." Analiese shook her head. "And sometimes when it does, it needs a lot of help."

Taylor felt a flare of anger. "You're nothing if not honest, are you?"

Analiese didn't answer; she sipped her wine and watched Taylor's face.

"Honesty's a lot better than the alternative, I guess," Taylor said after a deep breath. "I'm sorry I snapped at you. I just don't want things to go badly for her."

"I get that, but do you want to tell me what else is going on?" Analiese speared a piece of pineapple and popped it into her mouth.

Taylor knew she should go back into the other room and resume her duties as hostess, but she found herself telling Analiese about Adam and everything that had transpired between them. She doubted any of this was news to Analiese, since the goddesses often spent time with each other, but it felt good to unburden herself.

"If I'm really hearing what you're saying,

it sounds like the worst part of this for you personally is that Adam lied about who he was."

"Personally? Yes. I trusted him."

"And you don't trust easily."

Taylor shrugged.

"So while I'm hitting you with this, I'll add that you don't forgive easily, either."

Taylor could hardly protest. Analiese knew every detail of the last weeks of her mother's life. "Could *you* forgive Adam? We were . . . intimate. He never made any promises, and I didn't ask for any, but I thought at the very least I could trust him not to lie to me."

"The world would be so much easier to live in if it was black-and-white, wouldn't it? If we could just pretend there was only one way to act, one thing to say?"

"The truth would be the thing to say."

"Most of the time I think you're right, although you saw tonight how annoying it can be."

"I prefer to be annoyed."

"Prefer that over hurt?"

"Over hurt."

"I'm sorry you were hurt. And I guess he didn't try to explain."

Taylor knew Analiese well enough to see what she was doing. "Yes, he explained, and he apologized. Does that make up for what he did?"

"Not if you think this kind of thing would be a chronic failure on his part. If he seems like the kind of man who just explains and apologizes his way through life."

"No, he's not like that."

"Okay."

"Are you trying to tell me in your subtle way that I'm in the wrong here?"

"Is there a wrong place to be? Is it a destination?" Analiese held up her plate. "Right." She held up her glass. "Wrong?"

"He was wrong."

"Okay. Given everything you know, you still think so. But I wonder . . ."

Taylor didn't want to ask what she wondered, but in the end she had to. "What do you wonder?"

"If you're really happier because you're the one who's right?"

Taylor couldn't answer.

Analiese looked over Taylor's shoulder. "There's Harmony. I'm going to say hello to her before I look for Jan." She leaned closer. "It's a wonderful party and a great thing to do for all these people. You have such a good heart. I just hope nobody here ever makes a mistake and disappoints you."

Taylor stared after her. She knew she had been chastised, that Analiese was using stern measures to get her to think. They were friends, and friends sometimes had the right to do that. But she was so angry she couldn't force herself to walk back into the main room and resume hostessing.

She was still standing in the same place when her father found her. "It's a wonderful party," he said. "You outdid yourself." He read her expression and frowned. "So what's wrong?"

"Tell me, was I wrong to tell Adam to get out of my life?" She felt fairly sure her father knew the story of Adam's deception, which was becoming common knowledge among everyone who knew Jan and Harmony.

"I guess it depends on why you did it."

"I don't know how you forgive somebody who hurts you that way."

"I can relate to that. I was sure I could never forgive your mother. I seem to remember you were sure, too, and upset when I did."

"It's not the same thing."

"No, as I understand it Adam was doing his job, which requires some acting and a fair amount of deception. I can see why you're hurt, but right now isn't he in Kansas using both skills to make sure Jan doesn't go to jail? There seems to be some speculation he may have lost his job because he's pursuing this."

Taylor hadn't known the last, and for a moment it stopped her. Either Adam was lying again or he really did intend to make things right.

Then she realized where her thoughts had led her. "So that makes it okay that he lied to me and let our relationship progress to a point where honesty is everything?"

"I can't answer that, but I can see you're hurt. Now you have to decide the best way to put it behind you. I was never able to let go of the hurt until I forgave your mother and we moved on together. I almost missed the chance."

"It's not the same thing," she repeated.

"So you said." Ethan kissed her cheek. "Harmony and your friend Nate look good together, don't they? I'm going to say hello."

Taylor knew she couldn't stand there all night processing advice she hadn't wanted to hear. She straightened her shoulders and went to greet more partygoers.

Harmony's dress was more or less a sweater, three-quarter sleeves, vaguely scooped neck, a flirty little flounce at the bottom, and it emphasized every curve the designer had intended. She had dressed carefully. French braids wove back from the top and sides of her hair, while the rest hung loose, and rhinestones wrapped tightly around her neck. She knew she looked good. If even *Davis* had noticed, then she might need a photograph so she could remember how well she cleaned up.

Nate had told her she looked nice, too, but if she had shown up in torn overalls and an Asheville Tourists cap, he would have said the same thing.

Tonight he looked as attractive and approachable as always in a soft camel-colored sweater. She wondered if he had ever, in his entire life, worn a pair of pants that weren't perfectly creased.

"Nate, we need to have a conversation," she said, after she had made sure her mother seemed happily occupied. "Let's try the patio for a few minutes."

He filled a plate with desserts for both of them, and she took their wineglasses. They threaded through the hall, squeezing their way past other partyers. Outside, stars twinkled above them, but the air was definitely turning colder. They were dressed warmly enough for now, but in a few minutes they would need to go back inside.

The temperature and a stiff breeze made it easier to get right to the point, as did the fact that nobody else had been brave enough to come outside, so they were alone.

"You're a great guy," she said, launching in after a mocha truffle. "I can hardly believe I'm saying this, but I think we need to stop seeing each other."

He smiled, unperturbed. "You mean the romance is over? This is our Dear John conversation?"

She hadn't quite expected that. "Sort of. Yeah."

"Harmony, our romance never got off the ground. I know it, too, so don't worry. What's the expression? We're just not into each other?"

Relief filled her. Then as his words sank in she narrowed her eyes. "You're not into me, either?"

"Come on, you don't really want me to be."

She studied him a moment. "I mean, what's wrong with both of us? I'm beginning to think I'll never find a guy I can both like *and* hook up with. What's your story?"

"I've met somebody else."

"Oh. . . ." She realized she wasn't surprised. Nate was the catch of the century, and it seemed sad she hadn't had the desire to reel him in herself.

"I went to her condo to measure for new cabinets, and I got blindsided. She teaches first grade. Turns out we go to the same church, have a lot of the same friends. Her brother was in the armed services, too."

Now she had to smile. "Wasn't that what you wanted? Somebody you clicked with on every level?"

"I don't know. A lot of my friends have made mistakes. I wasn't in any hurry to make one, too."

"That's why you liked hanging with me. You knew this wasn't going to happen."

"Knew it right away. So did you."

"I thought, well, you know, I could *make* it happen."

"For the record, I like everything about you."

"Likewise." They both laughed. Then she sobered. "Is that why you came tonight? You were going to break this off?"

"No, I came because I want to introduce you to somebody. I'm not sure, but I think he'll be coming."

"You know, that's how *this* happened, don't you? Taylor set us up."

"And it's been fun, hasn't it? I've got a new friend for life. Nothing ventured . . ." He gestured and nearly spilled his wine.

"Who am I supposed to meet?"

He put his glass down on a table and held out his hand. "Let's see if he's here."

She took his hand and squeezed in thanks, although she wasn't looking forward to meeting anybody new. She still had too much to figure out, and besides, she had just failed at another relationship.

Inside they were met with a wall of heat. She didn't know how many people Taylor had invited, but the buzz of conversation and laughter was louder than the trio in the lobby. Evolution was rocking.

"Come on." Nate searched the room, then pulled her through the crowd into the lobby, toward the front door.

He stopped. "Timing is everything. Hey, Kieran." He didn't shout, but a man who was just coming in stopped in place. Then he saw Nate and ambled toward them. He wore faded jeans, a T-shirt with paint smears, a gold hoop in one ear and a three-day growth of beard. His hair was nearly black, wildly curling to his collar, and he smiled at Harmony before he flicked his gaze to Nate.

"Hey, bro."

The two men hugged quickly, then stepped back. "When I mentioned this party you didn't tell me you were coming," Kieran told Nate.

"Harmony's a friend of Taylor's." Nate turned to introduce her. "She invited me yesterday, so I stopped by to see what the fuss was about."

"Taylor and I were friends at the academy," Kieran told Harmony. "I haven't seen her since I came home from California. Nice place she's got."

Harmony was still processing the word *bro*. "Tell me about *bro*," she said. "Bro as in, we're homies, or bro as in, brother."

"Real as it gets," Kieran said. "Next brother down in the Winchester lineup."

"Kieran's been studying in San Francisco, but he's about to open a studio on Depot," Nate said. "His place missed the flood, so he's an imposter here." He looked at his watch. "Gotta run. Great seeing you both. Harmony, give me a call someday, and we'll have lunch." He lifted a hand in farewell and strode out the door.

"Have *lunch*?" Kieran asked.

She wondered how Nate could have made the nature of their relationship clearer. She smiled in appreciation and maybe in gratitude. Then suddenly she was smiling at Kieran, and he was smiling back, his dark eyes dancing. She felt that slightly wicked curve of his lips all the way to her toenails.

"A studio, huh? What kind of art?" she asked.

"Eclectic. Lots of mosaics. Right now I'm

making shrines out of found objects. Whatever inspires me at the moment."

"Cool. I'd like to see it sometime."

"It looks pretty crowded in here. Would you like to take a walk over there now?"

She did not want another disappointment. Not this time, and not with this man. "Just so you know. I'm a single mom, and I work on a farm. My daughter's not even a year old."

"I'm a struggling artist who happens to like kids." He held out his hand to draw her outside, and she took it. This time the evening breeze felt exactly right against her skin.

CHAPTER 38

What little was left of the Stoddard house had been roped off and ringed with yellow police tape. The site itself looked like the set of a low-budget apocalyptic film. Five days after leaving North Carolina, Adam stood silently and imagined a dystopian nightmare in which life had nearly come to an end and a pitiful handful of survivors were wandering the world to find each other and restart the human race.

Of course, if they did connect, no one would be interested in starting *anything* here. Even the trees at the far edge of the explosion site were charred skeletons, and debris that hadn't been burned to ash had melted into twisted, panicked shapes.

He knew how different everything must have looked before fire had obliterated Rex Stoddard's world. Jan had said Stoddard always kept a photo of the house on his desk at work, one without human beings inside the silver frame. Clearly the house had been a symbol of success to him, and he'd kept the sentimental family photos at home to taunt his wife.

"That last part didn't work out too well, did it, Rex?" He said the words out loud, although nobody was there to hear him.

Adam didn't believe that Jan had killed her husband. But the more he learned about the man, the more surprised he was that somewhere along the way she hadn't poisoned his meat loaf or dropped her hair dryer into the tub when Rex was having a relaxing bath.

His cell phone rang, and he pulled it out of his pocket and read the number on the screen before he answered.

"Jan?"

"I got your message. Is everything all right?"

"I'm standing here staring at what's left of your house."

"Not something I ever hope to see."

"You plan to sell it?"

"When everything's straightened out."

"Do you have anybody who can clear the remains after your insurance company completes its findings? There's no point in digging through what little is left. Nothing can be salvaged. Everything just needs to be hauled to a landfill. I can make the arrangements while I'm here, if you like. If somebody takes care of that much this winter, you can have fill brought in and the ground seeded in spring. Nobody's going to buy the property and rebuild the way it is."

"That sounds like the thing to do. I guess the house will be mine to deal with?"

From the conversations he'd had since his arrival, Adam knew that despite extensive testing and examination, none of the investigators had found any reason to believe the fire and resulting explosion had been the outcome of arson. As much as the insurance company had hoped to prove it, they hadn't been able to. At this point closing the investigation was a formality.

"I've looked into it a little," Adam told her. "Your husband never made a will, but your name is on the deed to the property, so you'll get everything connected to it outright, as well as life insurance, if you're the beneficiary. But you and Harmony will probably share everything else."

"And if I'm found guilty of murder?"

"That would change things."

Her sigh was loud enough to be audible. "My attorney is getting a lot of pressure from Shawnee County. The sheriff's department told him if we don't cooperate, I'll probably be arrested."

"Just hang in there, okay? Right now I've got a couple of questions."

"Go ahead."

"Did your husband keep a journal or make notes in an appointment book? Is there any place you can think of where he might have left evidence he was meeting another woman?"

For a moment all he could hear was the faint hum of their connection as she tried to remember. He knew how badly she wanted to help.

"I'm afraid not," she said. "He kept a calendar on his computer, but he was paranoid about the internet, so he was careful not to put information online if he didn't have to."

"Which was probably a good call, but I'm almost sure whoever pulled off the fraud had access to his computer. I'm sure the auditors are going over it with a fine-tooth comb."

"For years he used my name and our wedding date as his password, and our wedding photo was the first thing he saw whenever he turned it on. He used to open his computer and show me so I'd be properly grateful he loved me so much."

"Names and dates are the first things I

would try if I wanted to break into a computer."

"I doubt that's the password Rex was using at the end. He hadn't said anything about it for a long time."

Adam's mind was drifting as she spoke. Then it hit shore with a thud. Jan had made a point of saying she'd only rarely been to Rex's office. "Jan, you said open his computer. Are you talking about his computer at work? Or a personal laptop?"

"His laptop."

"Where did he keep it?"

"With him. Always. It was like an arm or a leg. He carried it back and forth to work."

"So it probably wasn't destroyed in the fire?"

"He never left it at home when he wasn't there."

Adam was thinking out loud. "And he didn't come home the night you escaped."

She completed the thought. "So he probably had it with him."

"Let's say he was meeting somebody that night. He's in his car, and he has the laptop." Adam was searching for a mental picture. "Where would he keep it? On the seat beside him? In the trunk? Under a seat?"

"No, he used to go on and on about fools

who made it easy to steal things from their cars, then expected to get reimbursed for their stupidity."

"You listened to a lot of rants, didn't you?"

"This one got him moving. He had a special locker installed under the backseat of his car, where nobody would detect it. He said he needed complete security when he was transporting his guns. A guy he met at a gun show made a new one every time Rex traded up. He used it for anything he wanted to keep safe, including his laptop. That way if he stopped for coffee or anything else on the way into work, nobody who broke into his car would find anything valuable."

"This locker, it needed a key?"

"No, the mechanism to open it was wired into the electrical system, so even if somebody stole the car *and* his keys they still wouldn't be able to get into it. He had to complete a sequence of moves before the seat popped up. Hit the door locks twice, hit the power windows, hit the door locks twice. Something like that. He was so proud of himself he used to show me how clever he was. He would pop the seat before he got out of the car, walk around to the rear door and get whatever he needed, then push it down again."

Adam thought this might be extraordinarily helpful if Stoddard's Toyota Camry ever surfaced. The car had disappeared along with the man, but finding Rex's body hadn't led the police any closer to finding his car.

And what else had he stowed in that convenient secret compartment?

"I've got another reason for calling," he said. "Do you remember that lake vacation Rex canceled at the last minute?"

She was already ahead of him. "He took somebody else, didn't he? I started thinking about everything you'd said, and the fact that he was gone most of that weekend."

"When this is all behind you, we'll go into business together."

She gave a small laugh, which reassured him she wasn't going to be upset at what he'd found.

"I got photos of all the women working at the agency in the past five years, and I took them with me to talk to the rental agent this morning. I asked if she remembered your husband, and she did. Then I asked if she remembered the woman who was with him. Turns out she's the same agent who'd checked you in the past four or five years —"

"Daisy."

"Exactly. So when she saw a different

woman with your husband, she was disgusted enough that she paid close attention. She was able to identify her from my photographs. It *was* Liz Major, who has been conveniently out of the office for several days and never at home when I try to speak to her."

Jan didn't respond. He waited a moment. "I'm sorry. Does this upset you?"

"No, but I'm picking myself up off the floor. I told you how much Rex despised her. He wanted to fire her, but he said she was the kind of woman who would take him to court and scream about her civil rights."

"Didn't Shakespeare say something about protesting too much?"

"This is good news, right? You have proof now that he was having an affair."

He wished it were that easy, but all he really had so far was proof of an additional link between Rex and Liz. Unfortunately the affair might actually hurt Jan, who could be portrayed as a jealous wife who had taken matters into her own hands.

"I've learned a lot about Liz Major," he said. "I don't have access to Midwest Modern's database since I'm no longer on their payroll, but the internet turned up plenty of useful information. She was born here, went to school here, and that means she potentially has hundreds of good contacts in the area. She's in several organizations, although she doesn't appear to take leadership roles. She was married and divorced after about five years and hasn't married again in the subsequent fifteen. I have several reports on people she may be associated with, and I've started following up on them."

"You can find all that on the internet?"

"It's the modern-day equivalent of hanging your underwear on the clothesline. Only the neighborhood is the world."

"Does any of it look useful?"

Adam didn't want to get her hopes up. He'd learned a lot, and not much of it was going to matter to Jan or this case. But he had one potentially promising lead.

He played it down. "Her former brother-in-law lives about five miles down the road from here. He's single, no kids, and he's still one of Liz's Facebook friends. I thought I would check around his place."

"Because Rex was buried nearby?"

"Exactly. If she friended him on Facebook, it's possible they still spend time together. Who knows what else they do?"

"He doesn't work in insurance, does he?"

"He's the assistant manager at a hardware store down the road from the little hobby farm where he lives."

"Nobody ever found the missing ad-juster?"

"Apparently he's a pro at disappearing."

"Do you think Liz has disappeared, too?"

"She claims she's having car problems, but she's been calling in every morning."

"I know you're doing this because you feel it's important, but please know I intend to pay you for all your time and expenses."

"This one's on me."

She didn't argue, as if she knew how futile it would be. "I wish you luck, Adam."

He knew she did. Lots and lots of luck. It wasn't just a turn of phrase.

He ended the conversation and decisively slid the phone into his pocket before he slipped up and asked about Taylor. Then, on second thought, he took it out again and went to his map application to pinpoint the location of Gary Major's little farm.

Liz's brother-in-law lived on what was probably a dirt road, and Adam zoomed in on the immediate area looking for a back way to his property. He was in luck. The acreage bordered a small farm road that looked passable and was at the opposite end of the property from a house that looked just big enough for a couple. There was a sizable pond, along with several structures, a barn that was at least twice the size of the house, something that looked like a shed and another shed close to the house but near enough to a creek that Adam thought it might be a springhouse.

Lots to see, but no guarantee any of it would be useful.

There was nothing else to do here, and he wanted to get to the Major Farm before Gary arrived home from work. The hardware store closed in about three hours, and thanks to Gary's Facebook photo and a quick stop to buy nails, Adam also knew that Gary was working today.

He had rented another SUV in Kansas City because he hadn't been sure what kind of roads he would face. Half an hour later he was parked behind the barn on Gary Major's property. He was pleased to see that the only animals in sight were half a dozen goats, penned in a smallish field and eating everything in sight.

The goats were far enough behind him that he suspected their nighttime shelter was the shed he had passed on the way to the barn. Now he wondered what the barn was used for. Before he explored he sat quietly and listened. There was noise from the paved road. The occasional car was just audible. Goats bleating. Crows in a cornfield that now held stalks bleached and withered by the sun.

Satisfied, he got out, but he didn't close his door all the way. He went to the side of the barn and cautiously peered around it. He waited long minutes, watching, but nothing moved except the goats in the field beyond. There was very little foliage here, two clusters of young trees, a row of lilacs that looked as if they had once flanked a building that hadn't lasted as long as the shrubs. Nothing surrounded the barn. He stayed close to the side and edged around the building. He paused at the corner nearest the house but still a hundred yards away, and waited.

Again, no movement and no new noises.

This time he didn't move slowly. As quickly as he could without making noise he strode toward the barn doors in the front, noted the smaller one to one side that probably led into an equipment room and stopped to try it. It was locked, and the glass panels were so scratched and dirty he couldn't see inside.

The larger double doors were fastened in place with a padlock, as well. Adam wondered if theft was really a problem in a place like this. Or was there something else in the barn that Gary Major was trying to protect?

He hurried around the other side and saw a window, placed there for light and not viewing, because it was just high enough that he couldn't see inside. Hay bales were stacked not far away, rectangular ones, about fifteen inches high, maybe twenty inches wide. He dragged two closer and piled them under the window so he could climb on top. This window, too, was scratched and filthy, and one pane was badly cracked.

He whistled softly. "A little gust of wind and . . ." He pushed. Hard. The pane fell into the barn in several pieces, and Adam's view was no longer obstructed.

It took a long moment for his eyes to adjust. The sun was bright above him, and the barn was twilight-dark.

Not dark enough, though, that he couldn't make out the shape of a car parked about fifteen feet away. A car that somebody had been repainting.

A car that looked, not surprisingly, like a Toyota Camry, a green one, like the one that had belonged to Rex Stoddard, that was well on its way to becoming a nice midnight-blue.

He had already made a call to the sheriff's office, already moved the hay bales back into place, when a woman in jeans came around the barn and stopped, her hand covering her mouth when she saw him.

He knew who she was, of course. Early that morning he had shown another woman her photograph.

"The sheriff is on his way," Adam told Liz Major, "so it won't do you any good to run or try to shoot me the way you shot Rex Stoddard. Besides, if you try, you're going to end up on the ground in cuffs." He watched to see her reaction and wondered if she would accuse Gary instead.

"I don't know what you mean." But of course, she did, and already her shoulders were drooping and her eyes filling with tears.

Adam smiled a little. "You know, we have time before the sheriff gets here, and I'm a good listener. Why don't you just start at the beginning?"

CHAPTER 39

In the interest of trying to keep Jan's mind off Adam's imminent arrival, Harmony was sharing the latest in her personal life.

"And Kieran's genuinely interested in other people, which is at least half of what I like about him. He banded together with other local artists, and they're all making space to sell work from their Latin American counterparts in their studios. All fair-trade stuff. They take turns going down to work with the artists there, to learn from each other, and then they bring back whatever they think they can sell here. He was in the peace corps in Nicaragua right after college, so he speaks fluent Spanish."

Jan put her hand on Harmony's knee. "What's the other half?"

Harmony looked confused.

"You said that was half of what you liked about him."

"You don't want to know the other half."

"You're probably right." Jan managed a smile, even though her future seemed to hang in the balance until Adam arrived. "I'm just glad you've met somebody you really like."

"Adam should be here by now."

"It's not a short drive from Charlotte."

Rilla passed by the doorway, then turned and came back. "Lottie's asleep. Landon told her a bedtime story about robots and marshmallows. Pretty hard to follow, but it put her right out."

"Thanks for letting us camp out in your living room," Jan said.

"You're kidding, right? This way I'll get to hear the good news quicker."

Jan hoped it would be news worth sharing. When he'd called in the late afternoon, Adam had apologized for not being able to tell her more, but he had just snagged the last seat on a flight to Charlotte and he'd been told to turn off his phone. He had promised he would call on the drive to Asheville, but she had asked him to tell her in person so Harmony could be with her to hear the news, too. He *had* managed to tell her she and Harmony would be happy, and she was holding on to that.

"Please stay when he gets here," she told Rilla.

"Oh, I don't think so. I'll let you two absorb it first."

Jan was grateful Rilla had offered her house, but she was sorry the meeting wasn't taking place at Taylor's. She hadn't asked, but she was certain Taylor wouldn't have stayed to hear what Adam had to say.

Rilla went to find her sons, and Harmony got up to peer out the window, as she had done half a dozen times. This time after a minute she whirled. "Headlights. I bet that's him."

Jan struggled to look calm, a skill in which she should be an expert after years of trying not to show her feelings. "Let's just remember to let him talk before we barrage him with questions."

Harmony left to open the front door, and in a minute she was back, ushering Adam into the living room. He hadn't shaved that day, and his clothes were wrinkled, but he was smiling.

"You must be beat," Jan said. "Was your flight okay?"

"You're worried about me? When are you going to start taking care of yourself?"

"If I'm lucky, you've been doing that for me."

He flopped into a comfortable easy chair — nothing in the Reynolds house was for show. "I promised you would be happy, but when I said it even I didn't have the best news. Liz Major is in custody of the sheriff, and right after I got off the plane I got a message saying she's made a full confession to the fraud and your husband's murder. All they had to do was show her your husband's laptop and the files he had been carrying around in that hidden locker. Then they told her things would go easier if she confessed. The story takes a while to tell. Do you want to hear the basics or the details?"

"Details, even if we have to wring them out of you," Harmony said, but her voice wasn't quite steady.

"I don't suppose there's a cup of coffee in the house somewhere?"

Harmony left for the kitchen, and Adam sat forward. "I don't think there's anything you'll have to go back to Topeka to take care of, Jan. You should be able to handle everything from here, but if I'm wrong, you can go without worrying. It's over. The whole thing's over."

She couldn't speak through the lump in her throat. Sometimes life changed in the blink of an eye, but it took longer to believe it.

Harmony brought coffee for all of them

and handed Jan and Adam theirs. Then she sat beside her mother and waited until Adam had a few sips.

He began. "About two years ago Liz met a guy named Ray Seagrave who worked as an independent adjuster. Seagrave handled claims for a couple of different firms, so he and Liz worked together. She says they fell in love. Anyway, by then she was sick of working at Stoddard Insurance, and especially sick of —"

As he took another sip of coffee, his eyes flicked to Harmony.

"You don't have to whitewash my father," she said.

"Fair enough. She really didn't like working with your husband," he continued, directing his words at Jan. "And eventually she decided she deserved to get even with him for the way she'd been treated through the years. She and Seagrave worked out a plan, and as these things usually go, it was a pretty good one. Policies for rigs that didn't exist. Damage from accidents that never occurred. Payments sent to empty houses in the country where mailboxes could be easily accessed. Liz and Seagrave were smart enough not to collect huge amounts, and to vary what they did and the companies they got payments from. But eventually, as you

643

already know, Midwest Modern got suspicious."

"She was in love with this Seagrave person, but she was having an affair with my father?" Harmony sounded as though that was the hardest thing to believe.

"As part of their strategy she made a point of being nicer to your father, so he wouldn't be as determined to look over her shoulder. She started making coffee in the mornings, asking his advice, just small things, but about six months into their plan, Liz realized your father was treating her differently." He paused. "Jan, I think that might have been about the time you started acting more depressed at home, in preparation to leave him."

"Interesting that maybe I influenced this." Jan wasn't sure how to feel about that, but she *was* sure she didn't feel guilty.

"Rex began taking Liz out to lunch to discuss agency business. On her birthday he sent her flowers. At first she thought maybe he was trying to disarm her, that maybe he'd begun to figure out something was up. But eventually she realized he was flirting. And Liz, not being the most moral kid on the block, decided to use it to her advantage. She figured that the closer they got, the less likely Rex would be to pay attention to what she was doing."

He paused for a couple more sips; then he set the cup on a side table. "So the affair began, and she was right. Rex treated her like a fragile blossom, the way he treated you at the beginning of your relationship, and Liz played along. Then, after a while, things began to go sour, and this will be familiar, too. He started trying to control where she went, what she did, how she looked. He got physical, too. Grabbed her by the wrist and left bruises when she disagreed with him or didn't consult him. By then she realized she'd unleashed something scary, but she and Seagrave were hoping for a bigger nest egg before they vanished, and they thought she could control the situation until they got everything they wanted."

"Seagrave knew about the affair?" That surprised Jan most of all.

"Apparently he thought it was a necessary inconvenience. Then Midwest Modern contacted Rex and told him they would like to send in an investigator. They played it down, but your husband realized immediately that the request was a big deal."

"So he started looking into things himself," Jan said, knowing that was what would have happened next. "It would have infuriated him that something might have been going on under his nose. And some of those nights when he didn't come home until after midnight, he was probably at the office going over files."

"I haven't seen the written confession, so I just have the basics. But apparently your husband finally realized he'd been played for a fool. So he arranged to meet Liz one evening after work at a motor inn south of the city. He had a gun, and once they were in the room he began knocking her around and threatening her, insisting that she confess what she'd been doing and return all the money or he'd kill her. She got the gun away from him and they struggled. She says the shot that killed him was accidental, but then, of course she *would* say that. Apparently nobody heard it, because nobody came to check. In a panic she called Seagrave, and he told her to stay put until he got there."

"Wow." Harmony turned to her mother. Jan patted her hand, because what could be said? Her daughter's face was pale. No matter how either of them had felt about Rex, this wasn't easy to hear.

Adam waited a moment for them to absorb it before he went on. "It's pretty clear that right after her call Seagrave panicked, took what money they'd already collected and disappeared, because he never showed up at the motor inn. It's also clear he had a working game plan and just exercised it a little earlier, because he still hasn't been found."

"They're still looking?" Jan asked.

"It's possible something Liz can tell the authorities will help, and she'll be happy to share the blame, I'm sure."

"I'm sorry, go ahead and finish."

"When she couldn't get hold of Seagrave again, Liz called her former brother-in-law, a guy named Gary. She says he always had a crush on her and she knew he would help. He arrived sometime after midnight, and they rolled Rex's body into an old rug Gary had brought with him and got it in the trunk of Liz's car. Then she drove Rex's car and followed Gary, who was driving hers. They went to his house first, and they stored Rex's car in his barn and got shovels. Then they took Rex's body to a wooded site down the road and buried it. It was close to dawn, and Liz said they didn't bury him as deep as they should have, but they still had to pick up Gary's car back at the motor inn and wanted to do that before anybody got suspicious. So they did their best. They thought it was good enough."

"And the fact that it wasn't far from our house had nothing to do with anything," Jan said.

"Except to confuse things and make you look guilty if the body ever turned up." Adam paused. "Although I'm just guessing about that."

"Then what? She simply went back to the office the next day and pretended she had no idea what had happened to Rex?"

"The fire bought her time. For a while people thought your husband had died inside your house. That gave Liz a chance to make plans. Gary told her if the cops ever started to suspect her of murder, a forensics team would go over her car, especially the trunk. I guess he watches a lot of cop shows. Anyway, Liz's car is now underwater in the middle of Gary's pond, and I guess they were hoping Topeka wouldn't have another drought anytime soon. In the meantime she was driving an old junker of his that ran about as often as it didn't. I'm not sure it occurred to either of them that the sheriff would wonder where her car had disappeared to and why she had no record of a sale."

Harmony asked the question that perplexed Jan, too. "Why didn't she just disappear like she'd planned?"

"Because Seagrave, who seems to have had all the brains, also had all their money, so she didn't have the resources to do it right. She was afraid if she tried to leave town she would look so guilty the authorities would find her immediately."

"But she stayed, even though she knew the fraud had been detected?"

"She certainly knew Rex had discovered problems, but apparently he never told her Midwest Modern had been the one to spot them first."

"He wouldn't have," Jan said. "He would have taken credit for figuring it out on his own. Even in a situation like that."

"So she didn't know Midwest Modern was already suspicious, and I'm guessing she probably believed she could get away with what she had done and maybe more. Since she was in charge of the office while everybody was searching for Rex, she figured she could sell a few policies and keep the premiums for herself, grab that money, then make her escape. Even after the auditors arrived, she figured she had a little time before anybody figured out what she'd been up to. There's a lot of paperwork, and bureaucrats move slowly. Gary started painting Rex's car in his free time so she would have wheels. Anything to help Liz."

"Then they found my father's body," Harmony said.

"At that point she realized she had to get out fast. She called off work to make whatever preparations she could, and Gary worked late into the night to finish painting the car. He'd already replaced the VIN on the dashboard with a different one, probably from a similar model at the local junkyard. He was almost there."

"Then you showed up."

"I did." Adam smiled a little.

"If you hadn't?" Harmony said.

"I hope the sheriff would have followed up once Liz disappeared."

Jan got up from the sofa and went to Adam's chair. She didn't have to bend over to hug him. He understood and was already on his feet. He held her and rested his cheek on her hair.

"Where would I be if . . . ?" She couldn't finish her sentence.

"We weren't going to let anything happen to you," he said.

She began to cry. A stranger had stepped forward and gone the extra mile to help her. Strangers. Because it wasn't only Adam who had stretched out his hand and led her to safety. The women of Moving On had helped. The goddesses had helped, especially Taylor.

And her beloved daughter who, despite her own difficult past, had put everything behind her to welcome her mother to her new home.

"You're going to be okay," Adam said. "Rex can't hurt you anymore, Jan, and now the law has no reason to try. You're safe. You're home. You're free."

CHAPTER 40

If Adam hadn't wanted to tell Jan and Harmony the results of his trip in person, he could easily have driven straight to Chicago and told his Asheville landlord to toss out whatever he hadn't taken with him. After all, he had paid a large security deposit, and the old guy was going to make out just fine.

Finishing what he'd started had been important, though. And watching the two women he'd grown so fond of absorb the fact that for the first time in decades they had nothing to fear from Rex Stoddard, or even the law, had been worth the expense, time and trouble.

Now after a final dinner at his favorite West Asheville restaurant, a shower and a catnap, he finished what packing there was, bundling everything else into trash bags to take outside tomorrow on his way to the airport. This time he would fly right to

Chicago, where he could figure out the next stage of his life.

His cell phone rang, and he grimaced when he saw the number, but with his future in mind, he answered.

"Yeah, I went out on that limb in Topeka that you told me not to," he said instead of "hello." "And I'm not sorry. The right person has been arrested for Rex Stoddard's murder, and Janine Stoddard is off the hook. But I hope I didn't cause you any trouble. I'm sure you know I resigned from my job before I went. You can show that to anybody who questions you."

Philip Salter grunted in response. "Nobody's questioning anybody. I got a call from the sheriff's office, not exactly thanking me, but telling me there are no hard feelings."

"There's still a mess to straighten out there, but if necessary Jan, as Rex Stoddard's widow, will do whatever she can to help expedite things."

"She told you that?"

"Yeah."

"You think she's planning to run the agency herself?"

"I think she's planning to sell it to anybody who wants it."

"Are you going to do this routinely? Get

involved with the people we're investigating and set yourself up as their savior?"

Adam had to smile. "I'm nobody's savior. I just knew she was getting a bum deal, and I thought I could fix it."

"If you work for us again, we'll be watching you a little closer."

"Did I say I wanted to work for you?"

"Door's cracked." Philip wished him well and hung up.

Adam took the final beer out of his refrigerator and flipped on the television. On the other side of Asheville he was sure Taylor was celebrating with Jan and Harmony. He imagined an impromptu, low-key gathering, because even though Jan was now officially off the hook, a man had died and another woman was in jail. But the women who called themselves the Goddesses Anonymous would probably arrive to tell Jan how glad they were that her nightmare had ended.

He was glad there was something to celebrate, but he shut off those mental pictures and found ESPN. He had a feeling this was going to be a long night.

Taylor sat outside in her car looking up at Adam's apartment. The irony wasn't lost on her. Adam had sat just this way on her street, watching the lights go on and off in her house, making note of cars that stopped, people who came in and out. His surveillance had been an invasion of her privacy. And in the end, in the strangest of ways, everything he had learned from watching her house had helped him track down a murderer and save a friend.

She'd done nothing but think in the days since the party and her conversations with Analiese and her father. Finally setting aside her own hurt, she'd found she could believe what Adam had told her, that their relationship and lovemaking hadn't been a way to get closer just so he could learn more. That his kindness to Harmony and Jan, his patience at the studio, his rescue of Maddie . . .

She was tired of thinking. She got out of the car and slammed the door. Last night she had dreamed about her mother. Charlotte had been standing by a window gazing outside. The room itself was unfamiliar, dark, almost dreary, but the view was extraordinary, a colorful flash of Munchkinland from *The Wizard of Oz.* Sunshine poured over the landscape, spreading caramel warmth everywhere it touched. Lollipop flowers bloomed under willows and oaks, and the songs of birds flooded the room, even with the window closed. Taylor crossed to stand beside her mother and gaze outside, too. Charlotte had taken her hand and asked gently if watching was going to be enough.

Then the dream had ended.

Life wasn't a trip to Oz. Too much of the time it wasn't caramel sunshine and rainbow-hued flowers. Days passed without birdsong symphonies, even weeks. Yet when she woke up this morning, Taylor had known that venturing outside for those moments of joy was the way she needed to live. Even before she had learned that Jan was finally free, she had been sure that finding Adam again and telling him she was sorry for the things she had said would be a step into the sunshine.

She took a deep breath and walked across the lawn to the door that led up to Adam's apartment. She tried the knob, although she expected to have to wait until a resident came or went. The door wasn't locked, which surprised her, since Adam was such a stickler for security. She climbed to the third floor and raised her hand to knock, then thought better of it. On a whim she turned that knob, too, and his door opened.

He was sitting on his bed watching the ancient television that had come with the apartment. He turned his head, but he didn't greet her.

"You're really something," she said. "You *knew* I was going to show up, didn't you?"

"I thought there was one chance in ten million."

"But you left the door unlocked, anyway?"

"You were worth the risk."

She moved to the bed and sat down on the edge, swiveling to face him. "I'm sorry, Adam. I really am. I . . . I don't get over things easily. It's my fatal flaw. But you hurt me."

He rested his palm against hers, not quite holding her hand, not quite ignoring it. "Do you want me to apologize again?"

"No."

"Just tell me I haven't lost you."

Tears blurred her vision, and she cleared her throat. "You never told me you'd found me."

"I could apologize for *that*."

She scooted over so that they were sitting side by side. He draped his arm over her shoulder and nudged her closer.

She rested her head against him. "Are you going to leave town?"

"I planned to."

"I would really rather you didn't."

"Did you give my class away?"

"I . . . Well, I didn't, for some reason. I told your students you'd been called away and I would get back in touch when I knew more."

"Creative."

"We could throw in an extra class for their inconvenience."

"You have good managerial instincts."

"I know teaching one class for me isn't really enough income to keep you here."

"Asheville's growing. I've been toying with the idea of opening my own business. Security consultant, or maybe a martial arts studio. I might like to work for myself for a change."

She examined his profile. He looked tired, exhausted even, and possibly just a tiny bit apprehensive. That gave her courage. "Will you stay?"

He shifted so he could look at her. "Neither of us is simple, Taylor, so this won't be easy. We're complicated and cautious and quick to judge. Both of us. You've noticed?"

"Isn't it good we understand each other so well?"

His gaze softened. For a moment she thought he was going to kiss her. But he didn't. "One day at a time," he said. "Let's see where they take us, okay?"

He was right, but she had a feeling she

knew their eventual destination. All they had to do was step outside together.

She slipped both arms around his neck. "I'm glad you found me, Adam. I'm glad I found you. If you kiss me, can that be part of this particular day?"

"It would be the best part," he said, right before he proved it.

CHAPTER 41

From the audio journal of a
forty-five-year-old woman, taped for the
files of Moving On, an underground
highway for abused women.

Recovery from abuse stretches over a lifetime. Even though the Abuser is dead, as I face each day I'll need to remind myself not to expect miracles. I can never regain the life he stole from me, the life of a young woman filled with friends and accomplishments and future plans. That life vanished years ago, but the one that stretches in front of me is now mine to create without his interference.

Sadly I know memories of abuse *will* interfere. I'll blame myself for never finding a way to leave him and save my children. Forever after I'll find myself wondering if I had tried another escape, would the Abuser have found us? I'll replay chapters of our lives, wondering — if I had changed this event or that one — if we might have found a way to be free.

And forever after I'll need to remind myself that the fault for the things that happened was never mine.

Healing takes time. If I expect the pain from abuse to heal quickly, I will always be disappointed. If I expect it to heal slowly, sometimes with setbacks, I will be happy at my progress.

Just as I did what I had to during the bad years, now I have to do whatever I can to move forward. The more I reach out, the better my chances of touching people. The more I reach for happiness, the more I'll begin to believe I deserve it.

The road to recovery could be a lonely one, but I've been so lucky to find friends to help. I'm grateful for everything they've done and given me, but I know I'll need more help along the way. My daughter will, too. We are so lucky there are people who can help us discover the things we need to put this behind us. We'll be able to find somebody who has been trained to understand our struggles, and I think, at last, we are both ready to look.

After a long, satisfying and most likely final

conversation with Bea, Jan put the cell phone Moving On had given her into the top drawer of her dresser. Even though Bea had told her to keep it, she planned to send it back, along with a sizable check. There were other women, far too many, who needed the help Moving On could give. She could never be grateful enough.

From the same drawer she took out a plastic bag of microcassettes. After a little research and with some new audio recording software, she had been able to make digital copies of all the tapes she'd recorded for Moving On. She lifted her purse off the bed and checked her hair and makeup. She was ready.

Soft music played in the living room: Nora Jones, she guessed, one of Taylor's favorites. Laughter accompanied the lyrics, Maddie's high-pitched squeals and Adam's lower rumble.

Life could change so quickly. This was a change Jan hadn't dared hope for. Yet Adam was here tonight, as he had been earlier in the week, helping Maddie make a salad while Taylor stood at the stove creating a stir-fry to go with it.

Adam smiled when Jan walked into the living room and gave a low whistle. "Hey, you look great."

She was still getting used to compliments, but she was making progress. She no longer expected each one to end with a lecture on how she could improve.

She smiled her thanks. "Harmony picked out the dress."

"Taylor tells me you're going to be her new assistant manager."

That was one of those landmarks along the road that Jan hadn't expected. Classes for the winter term at Evolution were filling up fast, and Taylor had finally realized she couldn't manage the studio administration by herself. Starting on Monday Jan would go in on weekday mornings to answer the telephones, take registrations and do office chores. The people contact would be good for her, and she was looking forward to gaining computer skills.

"I told her I would move out if she didn't let me pay rent," she told Adam. "This is our compromise."

Taylor looked up from her wok. "We couldn't manage without Jan around here."

"Do you have a minute?" Jan asked Adam. "I have something for you."

He wiped his hands on a dish towel and came around the counter. "What's up?"

She held out the bag of tapes until he took them. In the kitchen Taylor and Maddie began chatting about what to put in the stir-fry, but Jan kept her voice low, anyway. "I've been documenting my life with Rex. It's all on these tapes. I've been thinking about Liz Major. It might help if her attorney could prove Rex really was abusive. The jury might be more inclined to believe she shot him during a struggle."

"*You* want to help Liz?"

"I just want to be sure the jury understands what kind of man he really was. They need to know she wasn't the first woman he threatened with a gun."

"They might ask you to testify."

She had considered that. "I might welcome the opportunity."

"You're something, Jan."

"Just a work in progress."

"So much more than that." Adam tucked the tapes into a pocket. "I'll be sure they get where they need to go. You have copies?"

"Digital copies. I'm going to publish them as podcasts. Maybe they'll help somebody besides Liz."

The doorbell rang, and she straightened her skirt. "Well, here I go."

"You tell this guy you have to be home by curfew," Adam said. "I'll talk to him for you, if you want me to." His dark eyes sparkled.

"Oh, I think I'll be okay. I've done a little checking. Everybody loves him." She gave him a quick hug.

Fletcher Bailey had a great smile, and he used it to his best advantage when she opened the door. "I'm so glad we can finally get together for dinner."

"Me, too, but I just remember, I still haven't promised I'll help with costumes for Camelot."

"After I've wined and dined you, you won't be able to say no."

"I think you might be surprised. Saying no is my new hobby." She smiled to soften her words. "But I promise I'll hear what you have to say first."

"I love a woman who stands up for herself."

"Funny you should say that," she said. "Me, too."

He offered his arm and waited. The road to recovery might be a long one, but as she rested her hand on Fletcher's arm, Jan knew she might just be ready for the journey.

ACKNOWLEDGMENTS

Many thanks to my brainstorming friends, Connie, Serena and Shelley, who helped me while I was plotting this novel and whose fertile imaginations helped me create the women of Moving On.

I would also like to thank the very kind official in Topeka who was so helpful in my understanding of insurance fraud investigation and how investigations are conducted in that state. Of course, any mistakes are mine alone.

Even more than usual, my thanks to Michael McGee, who, during a year filled with moves and renovations, assumed control of our daily lives to free me to write this book. Thanks, too, for braving the first snow in western New York so I could finish the manuscript before we moved south for the winter. Your sacrifice was duly and lovingly noted.

QUESTIONS FOR DISCUSSION

1. Three different women in *No River Too Wide* experience very different relationships with the men in their lives: Jan, who is escaping a long-term abusive marriage. Taylor, who is finally able to think about having a man in her life. Harmony, who is trying to fall in love with the perfect guy. Did their struggles remind you of relationships or situations that you or friends have experienced?

2. Taylor, who was a major character in *One Mountain Away,* the first Goddesses Anonymous book, has a problem trusting and forgiving. Knowing this, and being confronted about this problem by people she respects, leads her to make a difficult choice at the novel's end. Do you think she took a big personal step? Under these

circumstances, could you have taken the same one?

3. Harmony, who has hoped for nothing more than to see her mother freed from her abusive marriage, discovers that now that her mother appears safe, her resentment toward Jan for not leaving sooner begins to surface. Was it realistic to you that her own feelings about her childhood would appear and need to be dealt with?

4. Before reading *No River Too Wide*, were you aware that 1.3 million women are physically assaulted by their domestic partners every year? Although this was only one aspect of the novel, are you more aware of the scope of the problem now and more aware of what signs to watch out for in new relationships?

5. Were Jan's podcasts helpful in understanding the way Rex slowly and carefully entrapped her in their marriage? At what point would an older, more experienced woman have begun to suspect Rex might become an abusive spouse?

6. Domestic abuse is one of the most chronically underreported crimes. Women

who have not personally experienced this sometimes find it difficult to understand why women stay with men who abuse them. Was Jan's predicament realistic? Were her reasons for being trapped in a marriage to Rex believable enough that you could understand them?

7. The women who call themselves Goddesses Anonymous try to reach out in whatever way is needed to women who need them. In what ways did they reach out to Jan? How helpful were they?

8. The female truckers in the novel who call themselves Moving On are fictional, but there are many women who reach out to help others affected by domestic violence. Throughout the world women have created shelters and help lines, as well as given legal and financial assistance. Do you know women who help in this way? Is there a program to help in your own community?

9. Rivers run through many of our lives, not just geographic rivers, but rivers of feeling. Did the metaphor of the river and what it represented to Jan remind you of

personal rivers you've had to cross or dive into?

10. How likely is it that Jan will recover from two decades of an abusive marriage and go on to live a satisfying life? Do you think she's taken the first steps by the time the book ends?